# Worlds of If

### Edited by

## Frederik Pohl,
## Martin Harry Greenberg,
## and Joseph D. Olander

# Bluejay Books Anthologies

*All Bluejay Books Anthologies are covered by
the Bluejay Guarantee*

*Forthcoming

# Worlds of If

Edited by

## Frederik Pohl, Martin Harry Greenberg, and Joseph D. Olander

BLUEJAY BOOKS INC.

*This book is dedicated
to all those
who live in
worlds of if.*

A Bluejay Book, published by arrangement with the editors.
Copyright © 1986 by Frederik Pohl, Martin Harry Greenberg, and Joseph D.
Olander
Cover/jacket art by Alan Gutierrez

Book design by TPM, Inc.

Artwork for Harlan Ellison Memoir by Dennis Smith

Manufactured in the United States of America

First Bluejay Printing: September 1986

ISBN: 0-312-94471-3 (paperback)
        0-312-94472-1 (hardcover)

This book is printed on acid-free paper. The paper in this book meets
the guidelines for permanence and durability of the Committee on
Production Guidelines for Book Longevity of the Council on Library
Resources.

# CONTENTS

# INTRODUCTION
# FREDERIK POHL

In the late 1950s Horace Gold's *Galaxy* group acquired another member by buying the limping competitor *If* from James Quinn.

It was a testament of faith in the old adage that two can live as cheaply as one. It seemed to make sense. Adding another science-fiction magazine to the group would not mean adding a whole new infrastructure. No extra body would come onto the payroll. There would be no need to buy an extra desk, typewriter, or wastebasket. The more paper and press time you bought, the cheaper your per-copy rate became—in those ancient days, it was still possible to find some meaning to the word "cheap" as touching on printing. Even the stories need not cost very much. Certainly not as much as those *Galaxy* bought. *Galaxy* was top rate in the field, paying three and four cents a word for what it bought. Horace Gold and Bob Guinn, the *Galaxy* publisher, calculated that out of the vast flood of "almost" submissions that came in every month there were surely three or four that could reasonably be published—and that could be bought for a penny a word.

And so it was. *If* became *Galaxy's* remainder outlet. Or, to put it in a more affirmative way, it became a place where newcomers could get an off-Broadway kind of start to their writing careers, and even solid professionals could find homes for their less successful ventures.

So Horace was given a budget of something like five hundred dollars per issue for the new magazine, and informed that the budget was ironclad. No overruns permitted. Not one extra penny.

That was not entirely realistic. Stories don't come in interchangeable uniform units of size. Authors make mistakes in counting words—sometimes, perhaps, they are not entirely mistakes. So do editors. Even if you count every word, the "set" varies. Some manuscripts are open and others very dense and tight. Five hundred words of straight exposition may not fill a page, while

1

five hundred words of chatter may run over to a second page.
Horace, smart and experienced, instantly realized all this and was
aware he faced potential trouble. It was not going to be possible
to tailor every issue to a fixed number of dollars and a rubber
yardstick of words. He found an ingenious solution. He called me
on the telephone. "Fred," he said, "here's what we're going to
do. You're going to get a check for a hundred and fifty dollars
every issue of *If*. In return for that, you're going to give me
whatever number of words I need to fill the blank pages. It will
probably average ten thousand words or so."

"Horace, old friend," I said, moving the ashtray closer as I
settled in for a normal Gold telephone marathon, "when I write a
ten-thousand-word story for you, you don't give me a hundred
and fifty dollars. You give me four hundred. That's my rate."

"Who said stories?" he demanded. "I'm talking nonfiction.
Other things entirely. Articles. Features. Fillers. You can do a
book-review column if you want to. Then you get free books,
too."

I bargained. "Can I review interesting new books on science as
well as SF?" I was busy educating myself on what all this nuclear
physics and cosmology stuff was about, and highly receptive to
anything that would build up my reference library.

He said, "You can review laundry lists if you want to, just so
you do it to please the readers. Besides, I'll make you officially a
contributing editor."

So I joined the *If* masthead, and stayed there, in one capacity
or another, for some fifteen years—rather a long time, actually; a
little more than half of *If*'s life span.

Now, it might seem to you that that is not a very promising
beginning for a venture. You're right. It seems that way. A
decade later *If* was voted the best magazine in the science-fiction
field—not once, but three years running—and you might wonder
how that came about, too.

Well, I'm not sure I really know why, but at least I have a
theory to offer:

*If* was fun.

By that I mean primarily that it was fun for me, as editor. You
see, the stakes were low. An editor could experiment quite freely
with *If*—as he could not, or at least not quite as impulsively, with
a magazine like *Galaxy*, say, or *Analog*. There was not much to
lose. Not in reputation, because although *If* had shown both

promise and even flashes of inspiration from time to time, it had never attracted a solid following of its own. At *If*'s skinflint rates, there was not much to lose in money, either. So when I officially became *If*'s editor in 1961 I played.

How do you "play" with a magazine? Well, you do things that you could never justify to an editorial board, or even a corporate executive vice-president. You follow impulse. I put together special issues as opportunity allowed. Discovering I had bought stories by Cordwainer Smith, Edward Elmer Smith, Ph.D., George O. Smith, and one or two less celebrated writers of the same last name, I published an All-Smith issue. When at last we reached the big time with a clean sweep of all the Hugo awards in 1967—Best Magazine, Best Novel, Best Novelette, Best Short Story, and even Best Artist—I celebrated with an All Hugo Winners issue. I observed that a lot of people writing in to *If*'s letter column were expressing curiosity about science-fiction conventions, so I began to publish a calendar of forthcoming cons in each issue. (I don't know what it did for the magazine—you never know any of those facts reliably—but it did triple the attendance at many cons in a matter of months.) As time went by I managed to get regular increases in the budget, but *If* was still relatively low pay. So I made a virtue of our poverty. The cheapest writers to buy were the newest ones. I began publishing a "First" story in every issue, and kept it up for several years, until I left the magazines. (Some of those "Firsts" went on to glory in SF—like Larry Niven—and some to other glories, like Jim Henson, whom you now see in all those credit-card TV commercials as creator of the Muppets.)

Play is fun. Evidently, what was fun for the editor was fun for the readers, too. *If* prospered.

When I talk about *If* I know I speak of it as a loved child. It is. But the child was a wanderer, with almost a dozen foster parents over the years: Larry Shaw, Paul Fairman, James Quinn, and Damon Knight before me (not to mention Horace Gold), and Ejler Jakobsson and Jim Baen after. Every one of them had his own (or her own) *If*. To most readers, editors are faceless people. They are thought of only as one thinks of, say, the mailman or the checker at the supermarket—as interchangeable cogs; as jobs, rather than persons—when they are thought of at all. (Who remembers the name of *Dune*'s editor? Or of Tolkien's?) But editors do make a difference. To the connoisseur the differences between, say, Damon Knight's *If* and Ejler Jakobsson's are as clear as the difference between sherry and Chianti. Each *If* is different. Each editor gave it some flavor of himself. But it is still all one magazine . . . and, sadly, one that is no longer with us, through little fault of its own or of its editors.

I've told you one of my theories about editing; now let me tell you another:

Nobody should stay in the same editorial job for much more than five years—certainly not for as many as ten.

The fun goes away. Staleness sets in. After a decade of editing *If* (and *Galaxy* and the others) I could feel it happening to me. And so, when I came back from a short trip to Rio de Janeiro in the spring of 1969 to find that Arnie Abramson, another publisher, was in the process of buying the magazines from Bob Guinn, I was glad (if nervous) of the excuse to leave off editing and go back to full-time writing.

But *If* really was fun to edit, and I hope these stories will be fun to read. They don't usually take themselves very seriously. But neither, usually, did *If*.

Of course, not everything about it was fun.

From where a writer sits, an editor on his golden throne looks mighty. He can decide, after all, whether the writer goes home that afternoon with a check for his next mortgage payment in his pocket. Or not. The editor, however, knows where his majesty stops. It stops where he has to deal with a Higher Power still, and His name is The Publisher.

My publisher for *If* was Bob Guinn, whom I liked and worked well with—mostly. We did have our differences. One of them had to do with how often *If* should be published. It is quite a long story (and I've told it already a number of times, notably in *The Way the Future Was*), but the way it came out was that, to humor me, Bob promised to make *If* monthly; and when he decided to reverse himself on that, he undertook to make it up to me by bringing about a new magazine, *Worlds of Tomorrow*, which would in fact come out every month; and when he actually was faced with making up schedules and print orders he backed away again, and *Worlds of Tomorrow*, too, came out every other month instead of what I deemed right and proper, monthly.

I don't tell this story to make fun of Bob Guinn, but to illustrate the thesis that publishers do things in strange ways, and for strange reasons; and to prove the point there is the sad story of the death of *If*.

By then Arnie Abramson was the publisher. *If* had not set any worlds afire lately, but it was actually in quite healthy shape; a mail campaign had brought in really an immense number of subscriptions, and so *If* was easily outselling its sister, *Galaxy*. The problem was, it appeared that, in the evolving world of science-fiction magazine publishing, the old adages no longer applied. Two could not live quite as cheaply as one. It made economic sense, or anyway it seemed to Arnie Abramson that it did, to bring out only one magazine instead of two. So there was *If*, selling marvelously well, and there was *Galaxy*, still fondly regarded but visibly dwindling. One of them had to die. So The Publisher made a publishing decision, and slew *If*.

Rest in peace, dear dead magazine. You gave a lot of us a lot of joy.

# AS IF WAS IN THE BEGINNING

## LARRY T. SHAW

I drove to Kingston from New York on Sunday night, through a blinding blizzard. I say "blinding" advisedly, because the snow and wind were as fierce as I've ever seen them, and the 1937 Chevrolet I had bought from Judy Merrill had no glass in the window on the driver's side. It was a couple of years before the New York State Thruway opened, and I had to inch my way along the parkway, stopping occasionally at a diner for coffee and to find out where I was. Although the distance is only about ninety miles, it took me all night.

When I arrived, cold and tired, at the offices of Quinn Publishing Co., James L. Quinn bared his teeth in a characteristic smile and asked why I hadn't been there earlier. It was his way of welcoming me to my new job as editor—or associate editor, to be accurate about it—of *If, Worlds of Science Fiction*.

Of course I could have left New York earlier, or taken the train or bus, and found a place to stay in Kingston Sunday night. I'm sure my reason for not doing so was enormously important at the time. The point is that Quinn got off to the earliest possible start in cooling my natural enthusiasm for the job, and remained expert at it throughout our association.

I have no record of the exact date, but it must have been in March 1953. Neither am I sure, now, exactly how I heard about the opening in the first place. Noreen says I once told her that Quinn ran a help-wanted ad in *The New York Times*. It seems improbable on the face of it that anyone would advertise for a science-fiction editor in *The New York Times*, but Quinn was improbable to begin with, and one of his most improbable facets was publishing a science-fiction magazine in the first place, so the possibility can't be ruled out. I have a couple of reasons for thinking otherwise, however.

I had gotten my very first magazine job of any kind at all through an ad in *The New York Times;* when I learned that the magazine in question was a trade journal called *Hat Life* I shrewdly bought a hat before I went to be interviewed. I don't think I got *two* jobs through *The New York Times*. And naturally I had been aware of the existence of *If* from the beginning, and naturally would have noticed when Paul Fairman, the original editor, departed. So my feeling is that I called Quinn and asked him if he needed a replacement.

I do remember our first meeting, during which he took me to lunch and told me how much he loved lobster while we ate chicken salad sandwiches or something similar. At any rate, it's clear that he hired me. But . . .

I assumed he was hiring me as editor, so the second small shock after the coolth of his greeting was his announcement that he planned to list me on the masthead as associate editor "for a while." Then I learned that he had already listed me as such on the contents page of the May 1953 issue, which was supposed to please me. The trouble there was that he had printed my name as Lawrence T., which I dislike rather intensely.

I had done considerable work on that issue before settling in Kingston, making the final selection of stories from a stack of about twice as many manuscripts that Quinn had weeded out, writing some of the blurbs, et cetera. Quinn accepted my story choices with no major arguments, but seemed puzzled over one of those I rejected. It was a harmless little thing called "I'll Kill You Tomorrow" by one Helen Huber, which Quinn eventually printed. I had yet to learn that he had a thing about female writers.

Such minor disagreements occurred almost every other day. There was a much more important question on my mind at the very outset, however. I had already formed an estimate of Quinn which turned out to be largely accurate, and, this being so, I wasn't sure whether he was going to let me publish the kind of stories I wanted. I knew I would find out immediately when I arrived with the manuscript of "A Case of Conscience" by James Blish in my luggage, determined to publish it. I had told Jim I wanted it, and a refusal from Quinn would have been an enormous disappointment and setback. I was prepared to fight.

If it was improbable for Quinn to be a science-fiction publisher, it wasn't particularly improbable for him to be a publisher at all. He was a typical small-town businessman, ultraconservative in politics and old-fashioned in habits. He was a glad-hander and a booster, and one of his favorite subjects was Kingston itself, a city of slightly under thirty thousand population with lots of old houses, historic atmosphere, and genuine charm.

I had often heard it from his own lips, so I wasn't surprised to read it in his editorial in the November 1954 issue, months after I had left: "Personally, I prefer a small city like this one on the banks of the Hudson. You get to know most of the folks and they get to know you. It's kinda good to have someone yell across the street 'Hi, Jim!' Or to stop and gab in the middle of the street until a car honks you on your way."

Personally, I never got to know most of the folks, in spite of the favor Quinn did me by getting me invited to a luncheon meeting of the Lions Club (or Rotary or whatever). I never called him Jim, either.

Quinn was more than a little anti-intellectual, and science baffled him, although he occasionally pretended to admire its accomplishments. His idea of a "real" science-fiction story was "The Rotifers" by Robert Abernathy (March 1953), a pleasant-enough triviality about a boy who discovered and eventually communicated with strange creatures under his microscope. In essence, it was actually a weird horror story, but the boy and his microscope spelled science for Quinn.

I've had many publishers say to me something like, "Larry, I want you to edit the best science-fiction [or custom car, or squirrel fancier] magazine in the field for me, but don't spend any money to start with." Quinn didn't mind spending money if he thought it was a good investment. His budget of a basic two cents a word was not bad at the time. He used wraparound cover art fairly liberally, and didn't accept paid advertising for several years.

What he did say to me, although not in so many words, was more like, "Larry, I want you to edit the best science-fiction magazine in the field for me—but don't put any science in it."

To his credit, he did agree to publish "A Case of Conscience." He obviously didn't understand it, but he didn't pretend to, either. He took particular pains to get an outstanding cover for it, let me blurb it extravagantly in advance, and even came up with his own capper of a cover line: "The most fascinating science fiction theme of 1953!"

It was a major victory for me, but there were many minor defeats to come. Much more typical was the time Quinn blew up because a writer had casually mentioned light-years in the course of a short story. He wanted one scientist to stop in the middle of the action to explain to another scientist what light-years were. Further, he wanted it spelled out on the page with the precise number of zeros it would be in miles.

I pointed out, perhaps not too calmly, that: the term had been used in hundreds of science-fiction stories, including several already published in *If*, and most readers would understand it with no difficulty; the two scientists involved would use it all the time, and certainly wouldn't stop to define it in the middle of a plot crisis; translating it into an equivalent number of miles would necessitate printing about a quarter of a page of zeros. Seething slightly, Quinn admitted that I was right on all counts; *but*, stubbornly, he insisted that there had to be some sort of explanation. I worked out a compromise in which one character said something like, "Yes, it certainly is a big hunk of distance." (I wish I could quote it exactly, but I haven't been able to locate the story as it was printed.)

Quinn also saw fit to warn me to avoid being "friendly" with the writers. I told him that most of the people he was talking about were already my friends, and I couldn't very well start being unfriendly to them just because I had a new job. Besides, one reason they were my friends was that they were good writers to begin with, and wasn't that one reason he had hired me? He subsided, but I don't think anybody won that round.

Paul Fairman and I were to become close friends a few years later. At the time he edited *If*, I knew him only by reputation, and his reputation was that of a Ray Palmer hack. What he turned out was a Palmer-style magazine, somewhat more dignified in appearance than a genuine Palmer product, but relying heavily on space opera; blood, thunder, and a little sadism; a touch of mysticism; a fannish feature or two; and a general air of chattiness between editor and reader. It was well done of its type, but its type was basically juvenile. The second (May 1952) issue featured a "novel" by Milton Lesser and a short story by his alter ego, Stephen Marlowe.

Like RAP's, Paul's editorials were largely anecdotal. He called the department "A Chat with the Editor," a title which hung on for years, and typically started off talking about himself, inserting plugs for the magazine here and there as he went along. In the second issue, he said that 624 letters and postcards had been received about the first issue in the week it had been on sale.

Again, RAP himself had frequently been caught in similar exaggerations. To cap this, Paul wrote an article about Palmer for the "Personalities in Science Fiction" department in the same issue, in which he said that Ray had spent eight years as a sheet metal worker, ten years as a bookkeeper, and four years as an estimator in the building trades before becoming editor of *Amazing Stories*—at the age of twenty-eight.

By Volume II, Number 1, May 1953, Paul was gone, and Quinn was listing himself as the editor. I believe that Paul quit, but we never discussed Quinn in any great detail. In any event, Paul lasted less than a year. I did the same, and so did Damon Knight later. At least I was not unique.

A minor point, probably of interest only to the technically minded, is that by its first birthday the magazine had dropped physically from 160 to 120 pages. Interesting, because most rotary presses print signatures of 16 or 32 pages; thus, pulps and digests with 160, 144, or 128 pages were the norm, but an exact 120 pages was distinctly unusual. It happened that J. A. Clement, the Buffalo, New York, printer Quinn used, had presses that produced signatures of 40 pages, and there was nothing in between 120 and 160. To the best of my knowledge, no reader ever commented on this.

Something else that disappeared early was *If*'s original companion magazine, *Strange, The Magazine of True Mystery*. Started at the same time as *If*, and edited by Quinn himself, this featured articles about the occult and supernatural. It was similar to *Fate*, but stuffier, and obviously did not find an audience.

There were also a couple of crossword-puzzle magazines (which still existed up until a couple of years ago, last time I looked). These required no real editing, being overseen in general by a cheerful spinster named Beatrice Bogert, whose chief interest was in things like playing golf. Beatie's most notable accomplishment, while I knew her, was in predicting almost to the minute when Quinn was going to fire *her*. Otherwise, the almost entirely mechanical work of putting the magazines together was done by the "art department," which meant whomever Quinn could press into service. Most of the puzzles, incidentally, were purchased from convicts, who "created" and submitted them in large batches.

*If* began to change with Paul Fairman's departure. Quinn's editorial for the first-anniversary issue was proud but restrained, and proclaimed that the following issue would lead off with "Jupiter

Five," a novelette by Arthur C. Clarke. I had nothing to do with choosing that story, but I was happy to see it in the inventory. It began to pave the way, to some extent, for "A Case of Conscience," which represented both a major change for the magazine and a breakthrough for the field when it appeared in the September 1953 issue.

Of course, it was also a hard act to follow. You don't find stories like that every day, even in a field that is maturing rapidly, as SF was at the time. I put out the word that I would welcome controversial stories, but I saw very few.

Maturity or no, there was a good deal of pessimism in the air in those days. The post–atomic doom stories, with their hideous mutants and the like, had just about run their course, but what might be called *Homo inferior* was a recurring motif.

To quote from the first example I come to, "The Lonely Ones" by Edward W. Ludwig, in the July '53 issue:

> The voice droned:
> "To those of Earth: Beings under the 4th stage of Galactic Development are restricted to the area of the landing field. We are sorry. In your primitive stage it would be unwise for you to learn the nature of our civilization. Knowledge of our science would be abused by your people, and used for the thing you call war. We hope that you have been inspired by what you have seen. However, neither we nor the other visitors to our planet are permitted to hold contact with you. It is suggested that you and your vessel depart."
> "Listen, you!" screamed Parker. "We've been nine years getting here! By Heaven, we won't leave now! We're . . ."
> "We have no time to discuss the matter. Beings under the 4th stage of Galactic . . ."

And so on. The Sevagram says you can't park here. God says you can't explore here. The Galactic Futurian League says get back in the ghetto, Earthies! There were plenty of other examples.

That same July issue contained "A Bottle of Old Wine" by Richard O. Lewis, blurbed as "A grim tale of a future in which everyone is desperate to escape reality, and a hero who wants to have his wine and drink it, too"; "One Martian Afternoon," about a sweet little old Martian lady who baked apple cobbler and sliced up the children of the Earth colonists; and similar cheerful tales.

By contrast if nothing else, I thought "Celebrity" by James McKimmey, Jr., an honestly optimistic little two-pager (it could have been done almost as well as a cartoon with no words at all), was a relief and a real gem.

I didn't deliberately try to buck any trends, but I favored the upbeat when possible and I did try to inject a little more variety. It wasn't terribly difficult, since we were getting some of the early work of writers who later became the field's biggest stars: Alan E. Nourse, Mark Clifton, Jack Vance, James E. Gunn, and even (bless him!) Harry Harrison, who had a delightfully zany short called "Navy Day" in the January 1954 issue. There were also good, solid backup men like Kris Neville and H. B. Fyfe, the latter an underrated storyteller.

Of course, some of them were writing up their own early small storms, and couldn't sell everything they produced to *Astounding*. And any time one of them turned out something that wasn't strictly a "Campbell story," we stood a good chance of getting second crack at it.

Finally, there were names like Robert Ernest Gilbert and Arthur Dekker Savage, writers whose early stories caused me to expect great things of them, but who vanished after seeing print a handful of times apiece. I would include the already mentioned Jim McKimmey with this group, except that he is still around, competently crafting mysteries but rarely dabbling in SF or fantasy anymore.

And then there was S. A. Lombino. . . .

At this point we do a flashback to the offices of Scott Meredith, sometime in early 1952. Circumstances find me alone in those offices with S. A. Lombino, who later changed his name to Evan Hunter. I did not find Sal terribly likable, but was polite when he showed me a copy of his first published story, a short called "Welcome Martians" in the May 1952 issue of *If*. And I was polite enough to read it. Although I thought it was pure imitation Bradbury (of which there was also a glut about then), I didn't want to hurt Sal's feelings by saying so. I said something to the effect that it was very well written, but contained a basic scientific flaw that rendered it impossible.

Sal looked me in the eye and said something along the lines of, "Oh well, it's *only* science fiction."

After that, I liked Lombino even less.

I did use a Lombino story in the July '53 issue. I wasn't happy about it, but Quinn liked it and I had more important things to argue about. Besides, it was only three and a half pages, and a noticeable improvement over Sal's first story.

It wasn't so much of an improvement, however, that I was prepared for "Malice in Wonderland" by Evan Hunter.

Scott Meredith bypassed me and sent the manuscript of this short novel directly to Quinn. Quinn was impressed by it as well as by Scott's sales pitch, and obviously glad to have the chance to prove that he could find controversial stories too. So he was already sold on it before he gave it to me to read.

I reacted with mixed feelings. Compared to earlier stories, it was a masterpiece. Some of the ideas and some of the writing were on the dazzling side. In some ways—its treatment of sex, for example—it was advanced for its time. (Parts of it, I'm sure, would have shocked Quinn if he had understood them.) But the science (what there was of it) was shaky, the thinking simplistic, and the resolution unsatisfactory, I felt.

Quinn and I discussed it, without heat. I was somewhat reluctant, but I had asked for controversial stories, and you can't expect perfection every time, if ever. If the story had flaws, I told myself, the readers would find them. So it went on the schedule.

Anyway, it was only science fiction.

Life in Kingston was pleasant at best, undemanding at worst. I couldn't be as enthusiastic as Quinn, but there were unique attractions, like the small candy shop that made its own superb chocolate and turned it into such items as a chocolate model of *The Spirit of St. Louis*, with the name of your choice in white icing on the wing.

I found a one-room apartment in a huge old former mansion, which had originally been patterned after a castle. Yes, unquestionably a mansion once; the former carriage house had been turned into apartments too. My "one room" was an enormous chamber on the third floor, under the "battlements," with good-sized kitchenette, bathroom with bookshelves (for *me*, they were bookshelves . . .) on all four walls, and two walk-in closets so cavernous they could almost have passed as rooms in a New York City tenement. For this, I paid fourteen dollars a week at most; it may have been less.

The only visitors I ever had there were Lester and Edith Feldman, friends from New York who were no SF types. Jim

Blish drove me home from Milford, which formed a triangle with Kingston and New York, one Sunday night and stayed for a few drinks at a local bar, but didn't really count as a visitor.

The only other Kingston resident I met who could talk about science fiction at all was one Ed Grecious, a pleasant sort who had left New York to work for Quinn for a while and then departed to set up his own advertising/public relations studio. Ed had brains and talent, but Kingston had little need of him, and he eventually returned to Manhattan too.

I spent more weekends than not in New York, driving the '37 Chevy until it blew its engine on the road south and I sold it for seven dollars, which happened to equal the towing fee. Trailways was cheap and quick, and it wasn't difficult to survive in Kingston without a car, since no conceivable destination was more than fifteen minutes away on foot.

I did buy another car, though, to explore the surrounding territory. There was supposed to be an art colony at nearby Woodstock, a village where both Ted Sturgeon and Mack Reynolds had lived at different times. I never saw any artists, who apparently spent most of their time hiding from the tourists, but I did find a roadhouse that had been Mack's favorite hangout. He was remembered fondly by the host and other guests, with some awe at his drinking capacity.

I did meet one writer who lived in Kingston: Dr. Comstock, my dentist, who was also an alcoholic. He had written a novel about black bears, told almost entirely from the viewpoint of one battle-scarred old black bear, except for a couple of chapters that switched to the viewpoint of the human hunters. I read the entire manuscript as a favor to him, and tried to convince him that the viewpoint switch was a mistake, but was unsuccessful.

There was not a great deal of office space available in town, and Quinn by preference rented the second floor of a good-sized house. The first such place was rather decrepit, and appeared to be threatening to slide down the hill at its rear at any moment. Quinn found another, similar but not quite as old, and put quite a bit of work into refurbishing it. It was comfortable and fine for its purpose, which was to provide plenty of working space with no frills to impress visitors, who of course were rare.

I remember only two people who came to see me at the office—a writer and an artist, respectively. The artist was one whose work I liked, but who had decaying teeth and the worst breath I have ever smelled. He kept edging closer to me to spread out the sample from his portfolio, and I kept backing away until there was no farther to go. By the time he left I was gasping for air.

In the other case, let's make it "writer." The gentleman had obviously never had anything published, and what he showed me was a mixture of newspaper clippings, rough notes, diagrams, and whatnot. The newspapers had reported someone's theory that there could be a planet somewhere that was invisible to eye and telescope because it absorbed light instead of reflecting it. The gentleman, who slobbered slightly when he got excited, thought there was a great idea for a story in that. He also thought that such a planet would be completely impossible to detect, and for the purposes of his story he wanted to place it in an orbit between Earth and the moon. Needless to say, he hadn't gotten much further than that with his "story"; he had no plot or characters, just the idea. Like an idiot, I argued with him. . . .

Operating from Kingston also meant assigning most of the illustrations by mail, with the artists working from synopses I wrote. This system is never ideal—I learned long ago that any artist worth his salt will find more and better visual possibilities in a story than I will—and produced some disappointments. I learned as much as possible on good old reliable Paul Orban (one of the most genial and obliging people I've met anywhere) and Frank Kelly Freas, doing his early work. Kelly's vivid imagination and breathtaking rendering more than made up for his occasionally shaky perspective. I liked him (and Polly) enormously in person, too, and we were rapidly becoming close friends.

It will probably not surprise anyone that I saw very little of Quinn outside the office. I visited the apartment where he and his wife lived exactly once. I forget the reason, but I remember that it was Sunday. They had celebrated Quinn's birthday the evening before, and, still in a festive spirit, he served me a glass of pink champagne. They had had about half the bottle left over from the party and had kept it, standing open, in the refrigerator overnight.

I went to the 1953 Worldcon in Philadelphia—at my own expense, of course. Quinn surprised me by dropping in briefly, and I introduced him to Dick and Doris (Leslie Perri) Wilson. Quinn's teeth, mentioned briefly before, were almost unbelievable in their whiteness and perfection, and set in a face that was handsome if you like the window-dummy type. Quinn showed them as often as possible, in a smile that tended to turn into a grimace. Although he had published stories by both Dick and Doë, he showed no recognition of their names; but he did flash his smile. In that instant, he became "Teeth" Quinn to them, and that is the only way they ever referred to him afterward.

Quinn's attitude toward women teetered somewhere between awe and lasciviousness. He liked women writers. Before I left Kingston, he informed me that he had arranged for a professional rewrite of the Helen Huber story "I'll Kill You Tomorrow," and was going to print it after all. I read it when it came out, and could detect no change from the version I had rejected. Immediately after I left, someone named Eve P. Wulff was listed as assistant editor, and Quinn published a novelette called "The First Day of Spring" by Mari Wolf ("Here is a love story of two young people who met under the magic of festival time. She was Trina, whose world was a gentle make-believe Earth. The other was Max, handsome spaceman, whose world was the infinite universe of space . . .").

A certain West Coast literary agent had either spotted Quinn's fondness for femininity somehow or happened to be lucky. He had formed the habit of including, with manuscripts he submitted, small black-and-white photographs of naked women. These were the kind you could buy for a dollar or two in cellophane packets in any Times Square porno store (and presumably in Los Angeles), but such a place would be far out of Quinn's ken. As a result, the stories in question received immediate attention, and quite a few were purchased. As another result, Quinn got me aside one day and asked, surreptitiously and without explanation (I wasn't supposed to know about the photos), "Larry, is Forry Ackerman a nudist?"

As lip service to science, Quinn saddled *If* with departments like "Personalities in Science" and "What Is Your Science I.Q.?" I wanted to drop these, but Quinn wouldn't budge on them. It wasn't his fault, however, that I failed to build up a larger and livelier letter column. I wanted to, but in spite of Paul Fairman's 624 pieces of mail on the first issue, we were lucky to get two or three letters to the magazine in any given month.

We maintained our separate orbits for the months I was in Kingston (mine involving a wonderful corner saloon, called The Hofbrau and run by a family named Provenzano), and associated with different people. Those I encountered, if they knew anything about Quinn at all, were puzzled as to why he had dropped the publication of Handi-Books, a very early line of original paperbacks selling at first for twenty cents a copy (or perhaps even fifteen cents in the beginning) and eventually soaring to a quarter, in favor of a couple of magazines that weren't remotely interesting to anybody. Quinn mentioned Handi-Books himself a couple of times, a little wistfully, I thought. They had, he said, done quite well for several years, with good market acceptance and virtually no competition. But he had made a deal giving a certain New York City agent (not Scott Meredith) the exclusive right to supply all the books, and this, in some obscure fashion, had killed the line.

I sometimes wonder what some of those folks who stopped and gabbed with Quinn in the middle of the street would have thought if one of his favorite daydreams had materialized. At one end of town the highway entered Kingston on a long bridge over the Hudson River; crossing this, you inevitably saw a very large billboard, which was without a tenant most of the time. Quinn talked about renting it and putting up a sign advertising *If,* informing anyone entering the small city on the banks of the Hudson that a real-live science-fiction magazine was published there. It would have been quite a sight, but I suspect people would have wondered. . . .

Quinn did follow through on one project we had talked about off and on while I was there, a contest for the best science-fiction stories written by college students. I was afraid that the best manuscripts he would get in such a contest wouldn't be worth publishing, but that didn't seem to bother him. He asked me to suggest some possible judges; I suggested the science editor of the New York *Herald-Tribune;* he said, "*That* pinko sheet!" and I shut up. He went ahead with the idea, and eventually announced the winners in the November 1954 issue (first prize went to one Andy Offut). Obviously, too, Quinn must have paid out the two thousand dollars in prize money, but he never did publish any of the winning stories. As I said, improbable.

I was expecting him to fire me, and he did so abruptly, his only stated reason being that he didn't need a science-fiction editor. And again, it was impossible to argue with him. There wasn't that much work involved in getting the magazine out; and Quinn, being Quinn, would never find a better editor than himself.

As I said, the last time I checked he was still publishing crossword-puzzle magazines, but from somewhere in Florida. I hope he is happy. He didn't actually dislike science fiction; he just didn't understand most of it. He had a rough idea of the difference between a good and a bad story, but he always had more important things to think about—like whether to buy a new Cadillac or a Lincoln Continental.

# THE GOLDEN MAN

## APRIL 1954

## PHILIP K. DICK

## (1928-1982)

One of a handful of American science fiction writers to enjoy a greater reputation in Europe (especially in France) than in his native country, the late Philip K. Dick amassed an immense and impressive body of work which totals more than thirty novels and five collections of short stories. His outstanding books include the Hugo Award–winning *The Man in the High Castle* (1963), *The Three Stigmata of Palmer Eldritch* (1965), *Ubik* (1969), and *Do Androids Dream of Electric Sheep?* (1968).

As he indicates in his memoir, *If* was an important early market for him, and he contributed several notable stories to the magazine, especially "Progeny" (November 1954), "The Impossible Planet" (October 1953), and the brilliant "Captive Market" (April 1955).

## MEMOIR BY PHILIP K. DICK

In the early fifties much American science fiction dealt with human mutants and their glorious superpowers and superfaculties by which they would presently lead mankind to a higher state of existence, a sort of Promised Land. John W. Campbell, Jr., editor of *Analog*, demanded that the stories he bought deal with such wonderful mutants, and he also insisted that the mutants always be shown as (1) good and (2) firmly in charge. When I wrote "The Golden Man" I intended to show that (1) the mutant might not be good, at least good for the rest of mankind, for us ordinaries, and (2) not in charge but sniping at us as a bandit would, a feral mutant who potentially would do us more harm than good. This was specifically the view of psionic mutants that Campbell loathed, and the theme in fiction that he refused to publish . . . so my story appeared in *If*.

We SF writers of the fifties liked *If* because it had high-quality paper and illustrations; it was a classy magazine. And, more important, it would take a chance with unknown authors. A fairly large number of my early stories appeared in *If*; for me it was a major market. The editor of *If* at the beginning was Paul W. Fairman. He would take a badly written story by you and rework it until it was okay—which I appreciated. Later James L. Quinn, the publisher, became himself the editor, and then Frederik Pohl. I sold to all three of them.

In the issue of *If* that followed the publishing of "The Golden Man" appeared a two-page editorial consisting of a letter by a lady schoolteacher complaining about "The Golden Man." Her complaints consisted of John W. Campbell, Jr.'s, complaint: she upbraided me for presenting mutants in a negative light and she offered the notion that certainly we could expect mutants to be (1) good and (2) firmly in charge. So I was back to square one.

My theory as to why people took this view is: I think these people secretly imagined they were themselves early manifestations of these kindly, wise, superintelligent *Übermenschen* who would guide the stupid—i.e., the rest of us—to the Promised Land. A power fantasy was involved here, in my opinion. The idea of the psionic superman taking over was a role that appeared originally in Stapleton's *Odd John* and in A. E. van Vogt's *Slan*. "We are persecuted now," the message ran, "and despised and rejected. But later on, boy oh boy, will we show them!"

As far as I was concerned, for psionic mutants to rule us would be to put the fox in charge of the henhouse. I was reacting to what I considered a dangerous hunger for power on the part of neurotic people, a hunger which I felt John W. Campbell, Jr., was pandering to—and deliberately so. *If*, on the other hand, was not committed to selling any one particular idea; it was a magazine devoted to genuinely new ideas, willing to take any side of an issue. Its several editors should be commended, inasmuch as they understood the real task of science fiction: to look in *all* directions without restraint.

# THE GOLDEN MAN

"Is it always hot like this?" the salesman demanded. He addressed everybody at the lunch counter and in the shabby booths against the wall. A middle-aged fat man with a good-natured smile, rumpled gray suit, sweat-stained white shirt, a drooping bowtie, and a panama hat.

"Only in the summer," the waitress answered.

None of the others stirred. The teen-age boy and girl in one of the booths, eyes fixed intently on each other. Two workmen, sleeves rolled up, arms dark and hairy, eating bean soup and rolls. A lean, weathered farmer. An elderly businessman in a blue-serge suit, vest and pocket watch. A dark rat-faced cab driver drinking coffee. A tired woman who had come in to get off her feet and put down her bundles.

The salesman got out a package of cigarettes. He glanced curiously around the dingy café, lit up, leaned his arms on the counter, and said to the man next to him: "What's the name of this town?"

The man grunted. "Walnut Creek."

The salesman sipped at his Coke for a while, cigarette held loosely between plump white fingers. Presently he reached in his coat and brought out a leather wallet. For a long time he leafed thoughtfully through cards and papers, bits of notes, ticket stubs, endless odds and ends, soiled fragments—and finally a photograph.

He grinned at the photograph, and then began to chuckle, a low moist rasp. "Look at this," he said to the man beside him.

The man went on reading his newspaper.

"Hey, look at this." The salesman nudged him with his elbow and pushed the photograph at him. "How's that strike you?"

Annoyed, the man glanced briefly at the photograph. It showed a nude woman, from the waist up. Perhaps thirty-five years old. Face turned away. Body white and flabby. With eight breasts.

"Ever seen anything like that?" The salesman chuckled, his little red eyes dancing. His face broke into lewd smiles and again he nudged the man.

"I've seen that before." Disgusted, the man resumed reading his newspaper.

The salesman noticed the lean old farmer was looking at the picture. He passed it genially over to him. "How's that strike you, pop? Pretty good stuff, eh?"

The farmer examined the picture solemnly. He turned it over, studied the creased back, took a second look at the front, then tossed it to the salesman. It slid from the counter, turned over a couple of times, and fell to the floor face up.

The salesman picked it up and brushed it off. Carefully, almost tenderly, he restored it to his wallet. The waitress' eyes flickered as she caught a glimpse of it.

"Damn nice," the salesman observed, with a wink. "Wouldn't you say so?"

The waitress shrugged indifferently. "I don't know. I saw a lot of them around Denver. A whole colony."

"That's where this was taken. Denver DCA Camp."

"Any still alive?" the farmer asked.

The salesman laughed harshly. "You kidding?" He made a short, sharp swipe with his hand. "Not any more."

They were all listening. Even the high school kids in the booth had stopped holding hands and were sitting up straight, eyes wide with fascination.

"Saw a funny kind down near San Diego," the farmer said. "Last year, sometime. Had wings like a bat. Skin, not feathers. Skin and bone wings."

The rat-eyed taxi driver chimed in. "That's nothing. There was a two-headed one in Detroit. I saw it on exhibit."

"Was it alive?" the waitress asked.

"No. They'd already euthed it."

"In sociology," the high school boy spoke up, "we saw tapes of a whole lot of them. The winged kind from down south, the big-headed one they found in Germany, an awful-looking one with sort of cones, like an insect. And—"

"The worst of all," the elderly businessman stated, "are those English ones. That hid out in the coal mines. The ones they didn't find until last year." He shook his head. "Forty years, down there in the mines, breeding and developing. Almost a hundred of them. Survivors from a group that went underground during the War."

"They just found a new kind in Sweden," the waitress said. "I was reading about it. Controls minds at a distance, they said. Only a couple of them. The DCA got there plenty fast."

"That's a variation of the New Zealand type," one of the workmen said. "It reads minds."

"Reading and controlling are two different things," the businessman said. "When I hear something like that I'm plenty glad there's the DCA."

"There was a type they found right after the War," the farmer said. "In Siberia. Had the ability to control objects. Psychokinetic ability. The Soviet DCA got it right away. Nobody remembers that any more."

"I remember that," the businessman said. "I was just a kid, then. I remember because that was the first deeve I ever heard of. My father called me into the living room and told me and my brothers and sisters. We were still rebuilding the house. That was in the days when the DCA inspected everyone and stamped their arms." He held up his thin, gnarled wrist. "I was stamped there sixty years ago."

"Now they just have the birth inspection," the waitress said. She shivered. "There was one in San Francisco this month. First in over a year. They thought it was over, around here."

"It's been dwindling," the taxi driver said. "Frisco wasn't too bad hit. Not like some. Not like Detroit."

"They still get ten or fifteen a year in Detroit," the high school boy said. "All around there. Lots of pools still left. People go into them, in spite of the robot signs."

"What kind was this one?" the salesman asked. "The one they found in San Francisco."

The waitress gestured. "Common type. The kind with no toes. Bent-over. Big eyes."

"The nocturnal type," the salesman said.

"The mother had hid it. They say it was three years old. She got the doctor to forge the DCA chit. Old friend of the family."

The salesman had finished his Coke. He sat playing idly with his cigarette, listening to the hum of talk he had set into motion. The high school boy was leaning excitedly toward the girl across from him, impressing her with his fund of knowledge. The lean farmer and the businessman were huddled together, remembering the old days, the last years of the War, before the first Ten-Year Reconstruction Plan. The taxi driver and the two workmen were swapping yarns about their own experiences.

The salesman caught the waitress' attention. "I guess," he said thoughtfully, "that one in Frisco caused quite a stir. Something like that happening so close."

"Yeah," the waitress murmured.

"This side of the Bay wasn't really hit," the salesman continued. "You never get any of them over here."

"No." The waitress moved abruptly. "None in this area. Ever." She scooped up dirty dishes from the counter and headed toward the back.

"Never?" the salesman asked, surprised. "You've never had any deeves on this side of the Bay?"

"No. None." She disappeared into the back, where the fry cook stood by his burners, white apron and tattooed wrists. Her voice was a little too loud, a little too harsh and strained. It made the farmer pause suddenly and glance up.

Silence dropped like a curtain. All sound cut off instantly. They were all gazing down at their food, suddenly tense and ominous.

"None around here," the taxi driver said, loudly and clearly, to no one in particular. "None ever."

"Sure," the salesman agreed genially. "I was only—"

"Make sure you get that straight," one of the workmen said.

The salesman blinked. "Sure, buddy. Sure." He fumbled nervously in his pocket. A quarter and a dime jangled to the floor and he hurriedly scooped them up. "No offense."

For a moment there was silence. Then the high school boy spoke up, aware for the first time that nobody was saying anything. "I heard something," he began eagerly, voice full of importance. "Somebody said they saw something up by the Johnson farm that looked like it was one of those—"

"*Shut up,*" the businessman said, without turning his head.

Scarlet-faced, the boy sagged in his seat. His voice wavered and broke off. He peered hastily down at his hands and swallowed unhappily.

The salesman paid the waitress for his Coke. "What's the quickest road to Frisco?" he began. But the waitress had already turned her back.

The people at the counter were immersed in their food. None of them looked up. They ate in frozen silence. Hostile, unfriendly faces, intent on their food.

The salesman picked up his bulging briefcase, pushed open the screen door, and stepped out into the blazing sunlight. He moved toward his battered 1978 Buick, parked a few meters up. A blue-shirted traffic cop was standing in the shade of an awning, talking languidly to a young woman in a yellow silk dress that clung moistly to her slim body.

The salesman paused a moment before he got into his car. He waved his hand and hailed the policeman. "Say, you know this town pretty good?"

The policeman eyed the salesman's rumpled gray suit, bowtie, his sweat-stained shirt. The out-of-state license. "What do you want?"

"I'm looking for the Johnson farm," the salesman said. "Here to see him about some litigation." He moved toward the policeman, a small white card between his fingers. "I'm his attorney—from the New York Guild. Can you tell me how to get out there? I haven't been through here in a couple of years."

Nat Johnson gazed up at the noonday sun and saw that it was good. He sat sprawled out on the bottom step of the porch, a pipe between his yellowed teeth, a lithe, wiry man in red-checkered shirt and canvas jeans, powerful hands, iron-gray hair that was still thick despite sixty-five years of active life.

He was watching the children play. Jean rushed laughing in front of him, bosom heaving under her sweat shirt, black hair streaming behind her. She was sixteen, bright-eyed, legs strong and straight, slim young body bent slightly forward with the weight of the two horseshoes. After her scampered Dave, fourteen, white teeth and black hair, a handsome boy, a son to be proud of. Dave caught up with his sister, passed her, and reached the far peg. He stood waiting, legs apart, hands on his hips, his two horseshoes gripped easily. Gasping, Jean hurried toward him.

"Go ahead!" Dave shouted. "You shoot first. I'm waiting for you."

"So you can knock them away?"

"So I can knock them closer."

Jean tossed down one horseshoe and gripped the other with both hands, eyes on the distant peg. Her lithe body bent, one leg slid back, her spine arched. She took careful aim, closed one eye, and then expertly tossed the shoe. With a clang the shoe struck the distant peg, circled briefly around it, then bounced off again and rolled to one side. A cloud of dust rolled up.

"Not bad," Nat Johnson admitted, from his step. "Too hard, though. Take it easy." His chest swelled with pride as the girl's glistening, healthy body took aim and again threw. Two powerful, handsome children, almost ripe, on the verge of adulthood. Playing together in the hot sun.

And there was Cris.

Cris stood by the porch, arms folded. He wasn't playing. He was watching. He had stood there since Dave and Jean had begun playing, the same half-intent, half-remote expression on his finely cut face. As if he were seeing past them, beyond the two of them. Beyond the field, the barn, the creek bed, the rows of cedars.

"Come on, Cris!" Jean called, as she and Dave moved across the field to collect their horseshoes. "Don't you want to play?"

No, Cris didn't want to play. He never played. He was off in a world of his own, a world into which none of them could come. He never joined in anything, games or chores or family activities. He was by himself always. Remote, detached, aloof. Seeing past everyone and everything—that is, until all at once something clicked and he momentarily rephased, reentered their world briefly.

Nat Johnson reached out and knocked his pipe against the step. He refilled it from his leather tobacco pouch, his eyes on his eldest son. Cris was now moving into life. Heading out onto the field. He walked slowly, arms folded calmly, as if he had, for the moment, descended from his own world into theirs. Jean didn't see him; she had turned her back and was getting ready to pitch.

"Hey," Dave said, startled. "Here's Cris."

Cris reached his sister, stopped, and held out his hand. A great dignified figure, calm and impassive. Uncertainly, Jean gave him one of the horseshoes. "You want this? You want to play?"

Cris said nothing. He bent slightly, a supple arc of his incredibly graceful body, then moved his arm in a blur of speed. The shoe sailed, struck the far peg, and dizzily spun around it. Ringer.

The corners of Dave's mouth turned down. "What a lousy darn thing."

"Cris," Jean reproved. "You don't play fair."

No, Cris didn't play fair. He had watched half an hour—then come out and thrown once. One perfect toss, one dead ringer.

"He never makes a mistake," Dave complained.

Cris stood, face blank. A golden statue in the mid-day sun. Golden hair, skin, a light down of gold fuzz on his bare arms and legs—

Abruptly he stiffened. Nat sat up, startled. "What is it?" he barked.

Cris turned in a quick circle, magnificent body alert. "Cris!" Jean demanded. "What—"

Cris shot forward. Like a released energy beam he bounded across the field, over the fence, into the barn and out the other side. His flying figure seemed to skim over the dry grass as he descended into the barren creek bed, between the cedars. A momentary flash of gold—and he was gone. Vanished. There was no sound. No motion. He had utterly melted into the scenery.

"What was it this time?" Jean asked wearily. She came over to her father and threw herself down in the shade. Sweat glowed on her smooth neck and upper lip; her sweat shirt was streaked and damp. "What did he see?"

"He was after something," Dave stated, coming up.

Nat grunted. "Maybe. There's no telling."

"I guess I better tell Mom not to set a place for him," Jean said. "He probably won't be back."

Anger and futility descended over Nat Johnson. No, he wouldn't be back. Not for dinner and probably not the next day—or the one after that. He'd be gone God only knew how long. Or where. Or why. Off by himself, alone someplace. "If I thought there was any use," Nat began, "I'd send you two after him. But there's no—"

He broke off. A car was coming up the dirt road toward the farmhouse. A dusty, battered old Buick. Behind the wheel sat a plump red-faced man in a gray suit, who waved cheerfully at them as the car sputtered to a stop and the motor died into silence.

"Afternoon," the man nodded, as he climbed out of the car. He tipped his hat pleasantly. He was middle-aged, genial-looking, perspiring freely as he crossed the dry ground toward the porch. "Maybe you folks can help me."

"What do you want?" Nat Johnson demanded hoarsely. He was frightened. He watched the creek bed out of the corner of his eye, praying silently. God, if only he *stayed* away. Jean was breathing quickly, sharp little gasps. She was terrified. Dave's face was expressionless, but all color had drained from it. "Who are you?" Nat demanded.

"Name's Baines. George Baines." The man held out his hand but Johnson ignored it. "Maybe you've heard of me. I own the Pacifica Development Corporation. We built all those little bomb-proof houses just outside of town. Those little round ones you see as you come up the main highway from Lafayette."

"What do you want?" Johnson held his hands steady with an effort. He'd never heard of the man, although he'd noticed the housing tract. It couldn't be missed—a great ant-heap of ugly pill-boxes straddling the highway. Baines looked like the kind of man who'd own them. But what did he want here?

"I've bought some land up this way," Baines was explaining. He rattled a sheaf of crisp papers. "This is the deed, but I'll be damned if I can find it." He grinned good-naturedly. "I know it's around this way, someplace, this side of the State road. According to the clerk at the County Recorder's Office, a mile or so this side of that hill over there. But I'm no damn good at reading maps."

"It isn't around here," Dave broke in. "There's only farms around her. Nothing for sale."

"This is a farm, son," Baines said genially. "I bought it for myself and my missus. So we could settle down." He wrinkled his pug nose. "Don't get the wrong idea—I'm not putting up any tracts around here. This is strictly for myself. An old farm house, twenty acres, a pump and a few oak trees—"

"Let me see the deed." Johnson grabbed the sheaf of papers, and while Baines blinked in astonishment, he leafed rapidly through them. His face hardened and he handed them back. "What are you up to? This deed is for a parcel fifty miles from here."

"Fifty miles!" Baines was dumbfounded. "No kidding? But the clerk told me—"

Johnson was on his feet. He towered over the fat man. He was in top-notch physical shape—and he was plenty damn suspicious. "Clerk, hell. You get back into your car and drive out of here. I don't know what you're after, or what you're here for, but I want you off my land."

In Johnson's massive fist something sparkled. A metal tube that gleamed ominously in the mid-day sunlight. Baines saw it—and gulped. "No offense, mister." He backed nervously away. "You folk sure are touchy. Take it easy, will you?"

Johnson said nothing. He gripped the lash-tube tighter and waited for the fat man to leave.

But Baines lingered. "Look, buddy. I've been driving around this furnace five hours, looking for my damn place. Any objection to my using your—facilities?"

Johnson eyed him with suspicion. Gradually the suspicion turned to disgust. He shrugged. "Dave, show him where the bathroom is."

"Thanks." Baines grinned thankfully. "And if it wouldn't be too much trouble, maybe a glass of water. I'd be glad to pay you for it." He chuckled knowingly. "Never let the city people get away with anything, eh?"

"Christ." Johnson turned away in revulsion as the fat man lumbered after his son, into the house.

"Dad," Jean whispered. As soon as Baines was inside she hurried up onto the porch, eyes wide with fear. "Dad, do you think he—"

Johnson put his arm around her. "Just hold on tight. He'll be gone, soon."

The girl's dark eyes flashed with mute terror. "Every time the man from the water company, or the tax collector, some tramp, children, *anybody* come around, I get a terrible stab of pain— here." She clutched at her heart, hand against her breasts. "It's been that way thirteen years. How much longer can we keep it going? *How long?*"

The man named Baines emerged gratefully from the bathroom. Dave Johnson stood silently by the door, body rigid, youthful face stony.

"Thanks, son," Baines sighed. "Now where can I get a glass of cold water?" He smacked his thick lips in anticipation. "After you've been driving around the sticks looking for a dump some red-hot real estate agent stuck you with—"

Dave headed into the kitchen. "Mom, this man wants a drink of water. Dad said he could have it."

Dave had turned his back. Baines caught a brief glimpse of the mother, gray-haired, small, moving toward the sink with a glass, face withered and drawn, without expression.

Then Baines hurried from the room down a hall. He passed through a bedroom, pulled a door open, found himself facing a closet. He turned and raced back, through the living room, into a dining room, then another bedroom. In a brief instant he had gone through the whole house.

He peered out a window. The back yard. Remains of a rusting truck. Entrance of an underground bomb shelter. Tin cans. Chickens scratching around. A dog, asleep under a shed. A couple of old auto tires.

He found a door leading out. Soundlessly, he tore the door open and stepped outside. No one was in sight. There was a barn, a leaning, ancient wood structure. Cedar trees beyond, a creek of some kind. What had once been an outhouse.

Baines moved cautiously around the side of the house. He had perhaps thirty seconds. He had left the door of the bathroom closed; the boy would think he had gone back in there. Baines looked into the house through a window. A large closet, filled with old clothing, boxes and bundles of magazines.

He turned and started back. He reached the corner of the house and started around it.

Nat Johnson's gaunt shape loomed up and blocked his way. "All right, Baines. You asked for it."

A pink flash blossomed. It shut out the sunlight in a single blinding burst. Baines leaped back and clawed at his coat pocket.

The edge of the flash caught him and he half-fell, stunned by the force. His suit-shield sucked in the energy and discharged it, but the power rattled his teeth and for a moment he jerked like a puppet on a string. Darkness ebbed around him. He could feel the mesh of the shield glow white, as it absorbed the energy and fought to control it.

His own tube came out—and Johnson had no shield. "You're under arrest," Baines muttered grimly. "Put down your tube and your hands up. And call your family." He made a motion with the tube. "Come on, Johnson. Make it snappy."

The lash-tube wavered and then slipped from Johnson's fingers. "You're still alive." Dawning horror crept across his face. "Then you must be—"

Dave and Jean appeared. *"Dad!"*

"Come over here," Baines ordered. "Where's your mother?"

Dave jerked his head numbly. "Inside."

"Get her and bring her here."

"You're DCA," Nat Johnson whispered.

Baines didn't answer. He was doing something with his neck, pulling at the flabby flesh. The wiring of a contact mike glittered as he slipped it from a fold between two chins and into his pocket. From the dirt road came the sound of motors, sleek purrs that rapidly grew louder. Two teardrops of black metal came gliding up and parked beside the house. Men swarmed out, in the dark gray-green of the Government Civil Police. In the sky swarms of black dots were descending, clouds of ugly flies that darkened the sun as they spilled out men and equipment. The men drifted slowly down.

"He's not here," Baines said, as the first man reached him. "He got away. Inform Wisdom back at the lab."

"We've got this section blocked off."

Baines turned to Nat Johnson, who stood in dazed silence, uncomprehending, his son and daughter beside him. "How did he know we were coming?" Baines demanded.

"I don't know," Johnson muttered. "He just—knew."

"A telepath?"

"I don't know."

Baines shrugged. "We'll know, soon. A clamp is out, all around here. He can't get past, no matter what the hell he can do. Unless he can dematerialize himself."

"What'll you do with him when you—if you catch him?" Jean asked huskily.

"Study him."

"And then kill him?"

"That depends on the lab evaluation. If you could give me more to work on, I could predict better."

"We can't tell you anything. We don't know anything more." The girl's voice rose with desperation. "He doesn't talk."

Baines jumped. "*What?*"

"He doesn't talk. He never talked to us. Ever."

"How old is he?"

"Eighteen."

"No communication." Baines was sweating. "In eighteen years there hasn't been any semantic bridge between you? Does he have *any* contact? Signs? Codes?"

"He—ignores us. He eats here, stays with us. Sometimes he plays when we play. Or sits with us. He's gone days on end. We've never been able to find out what he's doing—or where. He sleeps in the barn—by himself."

"Is he really gold-colored?"

"Yes."

"Skin, eyes, hair, nails. Everything."

"And he's large? Well formed?"

It was a moment before the girl answered. A strange emotion stirred her drawn features, a momentary glow. "He's incredibly beautiful. A god come down to earth." Her lips twisted. "You won't find him. He can do things. Things you have no comprehension of. Powers so far beyond your limited—"

"You don't think we'll get him?" Baines frowned. "More teams are landing all the time. You've never seen an Agency clamp in operation. We've had sixty years to work out all the bugs. If he gets away it'll be the first time—"

Baines broke off abruptly. Three men were quickly approaching the porch. Two green-clad Civil Police. And a third man between them. A man who moved silently, lithely, a faintly luminous shape that towered above them.

"*Cris!*" Jean screamed.

"We got him," one of the police said.

Baines fingered his lash-tube uneasily. "Where? How?"

"He gave himself up," the policeman answered, voice full of awe. "He came to us voluntarily. Look at him. He's like a metal statue. Like some sort of—god."

The golden figure halted for a moment beside Jean. Then it turned slowly, calmly, to face Baines.

"Cris!" Jean shrieked. *"Why did you come back?"*

The same thought was eating at Baines, too. He shoved it aside—for the time being. "Is the jet out front?" he demanded quickly.

"Ready to go," one of the CP answered.

"Fine." Baines strode past them, down the steps and onto the dirt field. "Let's go. I want him taken directly to the lab." For a moment he studied the massive figure who stood calmly between the two Civil Policemen. Beside him, they seemed to have shrunk, become ungainly and repellent. Like dwarves . . . What had Jean said? *A god come to earth.* Baines broke angrily away. "Come on," he muttered brusquely. "This one may be tough; we've never run up against one like it before. We don't know what the hell it can do."

The chamber was empty, except for the seated figure. Four bare walls, floor and ceiling. A steady glare of white light relentlessly etched every corner of the chamber. Near the top of the far wall ran a narrow slot, the view windows through which the interior of the chamber was scanned.

The seated figure was quiet. He hadn't moved since the chamber locks had slid into place, since the heavy bolts had fallen from outside and the rows of bright-faced technicians had taken their places at the view windows. He gazed down at the floor, bent forward, hands clasped together, face calm, almost expressionless. In four hours he hadn't moved a muscle.

"Well?" Baines said. "What have you learned?"

Wisdom grunted sourly. "Not much. If we don't have him doped out in forty-eight hours we'll go ahead with the euth. We can't take any chances."

"You're thinking about the Tunis type," Baines said. He was, too. They had found ten of them, living in the ruins of the abandoned North African town. Their survival method was simple. They killed and absorbed other life forms, then imitated them and took their places. *Chameleons,* they were called. It had cost sixty lives, before the last one was destroyed. Sixty top-level experts, highly trained DCA men.

"Any clues?" Baines asked.

"He's different as hell. This is going to be tough." Wisdom thumbed a pile of tape-spools. "This is the complete report, all the material we got from Johnson and his family. We pumped them with the psych-wash, then let them go home. Eighteen years—and no semantic bridge. Yet, he looks fully developed.

Mature at thirteen—a shorter, faster life-cycle than ours. But why the mane? All the gold fuzz? Like a Roman monument that's been gilded."

"Has the report come in from the analysis room? You had a wave-shot taken, of course."

"His brain pattern has been fully scanned. But it takes time for them to plot it out. We're all running around like lunatics while he just sits there!" Wisdom poked a stubby finger at the window. "We caught him easily enough. He can't have *much*, can he? But I'd like to know what it is. Before we euth him."

"Maybe we should keep him alive until we know."

"Euth in forty-eight hours," Wisdom repeated stubbornly. "Whether we know or not. I don't like him. He gives me the creeps."

Wisdom stood chewing nervously on his cigar, a red-haired, beefy-faced man, thick and heavy-set, with a barrel chest and cold, shrewd eyes deep-set in his hard face. Ed Wisdom was Director of DCA's North American Branch. But right now he was worried. His tiny eyes darted back and forth, alarmed flickers of gray in his brutal, massive face.

"You think," Baines said slowly, "this is *it*?"

"I always think so," Wisdom snapped. "I have to think so."

"I mean—"

"I know what you mean." Wisdom paced back and forth, among the study tables, technicians at their benches, equipment and humming computers. Buzzing tape-slots and research hookups. "This thing lived eighteen years with his family and *they* don't understand it. *They* don't know what it has. They know what it does, but not how."

"What does it do?"

"It knows things."

"What kind of things?"

Wisdom grabbed his lash-tube from his belt and tossed it on a table. "Here."

"What?"

"Here." Wisdom signalled, and a view window was slid back an inch. "Shoot him."

Baines blinked. "You said forty-eight hours."

With a curse, Wisdom snatched up the tube, aimed it through the window directly at the seated figure's back, and squeezed the trigger.

A blinding flash of pink. A cloud of energy blossomed in the center of the chamber. It sparkled, then died into dark ash.

"Good God!" Baines gasped. "You—"

He broke off. The figure was no longer sitting. As Wisdom fired, it had moved in a blur of speed, away from the blast, to the corner of the chamber. Now it was slowly coming back, face blank, still absorbed in thought.

"Fifth time," Wisdom said, as he put his tube away. "Last time Jamison and I fired together. Missed. He knew exactly when the bolts would hit. And where."

Baines and Wisdom looked at each other. Both of them were thinking the same thing. "But even reading minds wouldn't tell him where they were going to hit," Baines said. "When, maybe. But not where. Could you have called your own shots?"

"Not mine," Wisdom answered flatly. "I fired fast, damn near at random." He frowned. "*Random*. We'll have to make a test of this." He waved a group of technicians over. "Get a construction team up here. On the double." He grabbed paper and pen and began sketching.

While construction was going on, Baines met his fiancée in the lobby outside the lab, the great central lounge of the DCA Building.

"How's it coming?" she asked. Anita Ferris was tall and blonde, blue eyes and a mature, carefully cultivated figure. An attractive, competent-looking woman in her late twenties. She wore a metal-foil dress and cape—with a red and black stripe on the sleeve, the emblem of the A Class. Anita was Director of the Semantics Agency, a top-level Government Coordinator. "Anything of interest, this time?"

"Plenty." Baines guided her from the lobby, into the dim recess of the bar. Music played soft in the background, a shifting variety of patterns formed mathematically. Dim shapes moved expertly through the gloom, from table to table. Silent, efficient robot waiters.

As Anita sipped her Tom Collins, Baines outlined what they had found.

"What are the chances," Anita asked slowly, "that he's built up some kind of deflection-cone? There was one kind that warped their environment by direct mental effort. No tools. Direct mind to matter."

"Psychokinetics?" Baines drummed restlessly on the table top. "I doubt it. The thing has ability to predict, not to control. He can't stop the beams, but he can sure as hell get out of the way."

"Does he jump between the molecules?"

Baines wasn't amused. "This is serious. We've handled these things sixty years—longer than you and I have been around added together. Eighty-seven types of deviants have shown up, real mutants that could reproduce themselves, not mere freaks. This is the eighty-eighth. We've been able to handle each of them in turn. But this—"

"Why are you so worried about this one?"

"First, it's eighteen years old. That in itself is incredible. Its family managed to hide it that long."

"Those women around Denver were older than that. Those ones with—"

"They were in a Government camp. Somebody high up was toying with the idea of allowing them to breed. Some sort of industrial use. We withheld euth for years. But Cris Johnson stayed alive *outside our control*. Those things at Denver were under constant scrutiny."

"Maybe he's harmless. You always assume a deeve is a menace. He might even be beneficial. Somebody thought those women might work in. Maybe this thing has something that would advance the race."

"*Which* race? Not the human race. It's the old 'the operation was a success but the patient died' routine. If we introduce a mutant to keep us going it'll be mutants, not us, who'll inherit the earth. It'll be mutants surviving for their own sake. Don't think for a moment we can put padlocks on them and expect them to serve us. If they're really superior to Homo sapiens, they'll win out in even competition. To survive, we've got to cold-deck them right from the start."

"In other words, we'll know Homo superior when he comes—by definition. He'll be the one we won't be able to euth."

"That's about it," Baines answered. "Assuming there *is* a Homo superior. Maybe there's just Homo peculiar. Homo with an improved line."

"The Neanderthal probably thought the Cro-Magnon man had merely an improved line. A little more advanced ability to conjure up symbols and shape flint. From your description, this thing is more radical than a mere improvement."

"This thing," Baines said slowly, "has an ability to predict. So far, it's been able to stay alive. It's been able to cope with situations better than you or I could. How long do you think we'd stay alive in that chamber, with energy beams blazing down at us? In a sense it's got the ultimate survival ability. If it can always be accurate—"

A wall-speaker sounded. "Baines, you're wanted in the lab. Get the hell out of the bar and upramp."

Baines pushed back his chair and got to his feet. "Come along. You may be interested in seeing what Wisdom has got dreamed up."

A tight group of top-level DCA officials stood around in a circle, middle-aged, gray-haired, listening to a skinny youth in a white shirt and rolled-up sleeves explaining an elaborate cube of metal and plastic that filled the center of the view-platform. From it jutted an ugly array of tube snouts, gleaming muzzles that disappeared into an intricate maze of wiring.

"This," the youth was saying briskly, "is the first real test. It fires at random—as nearly random as we can make it, at least. Weighted balls are thrown up in an air stream, then dropped free to fall back and cut relays. They can fall in almost any pattern. The thing fires according to their pattern. Each drop produces a new configuration of timing and position. Ten tubes, in all. Each will be in constant motion."

"And *nobody* knows how they'll fire?" Anita asked.

"Nobody." Wisdom rubbed his thick hands together. "Mind-reading won't help him, not with this thing."

Anita moved over to the view windows, as the cube was rolled into place. She gasped. "Is that him?"

"What's wrong?" Baines asked.

Anita's cheeks were flushed. "Why, I expected a—a *thing*. My God, he's beautiful! Like a golden statue. Like a deity!"

Baines laughed. "He's eighteen years old, Anita. Too young for you."

The woman was still peering through the view window. "Look at him. Eighteen? I don't believe it."

Cris Johnson sat in the center of the chamber, on the floor. A posture of contemplation, head bowed, arms folded, legs tucked under him. In the stark glare of the overhead lights his powerful body glowed and rippled, a shimmering figure of downy gold.

"Pretty, isn't he?" Wisdom muttered. "All right. Start it going."

"You're going to *kill* him?" Anita demanded.

"We're going to try."

"But he's—" She broke off uncertainly. "He's not a monster. He's not like those others, those hideous things with two heads, or those insects. Or those awful things from Tunis."

"What is he, then?" Baines asked.

"I don't know. But you can't just *kill* him. It's terrible!"

The cube clicked into life. The muzzles jerked, silently altered position. Three retracted, disappeared into the body of the cube. Others came out. Quickly, efficiently, they moved into position—and abruptly, without warning, opened fire.

A staggering burst of energy fanned out, a complex pattern that altered each moment, different angles, different velocities, a bewildering blur that cracked from the windows down into the chamber.

The golden figure moved. He dodged back and forth, expertly avoiding the bursts of energy that seared around him on all sides. Rolling clouds of ash obscured him; he was lost in a mist of crackling fire and ash.

"Stop it!" Anita shouted. "For God's sake, you'll destroy him!"

The chamber was an inferno of energy. The figure had completely disappeared. Wisdom waited a moment, then nodded to the technicians operating the cube. They touched guide buttons and the muzzles slowed and died. Some sank back into the cube. All became silent. The works of the cube ceased humming.

Cris Johnson was still alive. He emerged from the settling clouds of ash, blackened and singed. But unhurt. He had avoided each beam. He had weaved between them and among them as they came, a dancer leaping over glittering sword-points of pink fire. He had survived.

"No," Wisdom murmured, shaken and grim. "Not a telepath. Those were at random. No prearranged pattern."

The three of them looked at each other, dazed and frightened. Anita was trembling. Her face was pale and her blue eyes were wide. "What, then?" She whispered. "What is it? What does he have?"

"He's a good guesser," Wisdom suggested.

"He's not guessing," Baines answered. "Don't kid yourself. That's the whole point."

"No, he's not guessing." Wisdom nodded slowly. "He *knew.* He predicted each strike. I wonder . . . *Can* he err? *Can* he make a mistake?"

"We caught him," Baines pointed out.

"You said he came back voluntarily." There was a strange look on Wisdom's face. "Did he come back *after* the clamp was up?"

Baines jumped. "Yes, after."

"He couldn't have got through the clamp. So he came back."

Wisdom grinned wryly. "The clamp must actually have been perfect. It was supposed to be."

"If there had been a single hole," Baines murmured, "he would have known it—gone through."

Wisdom ordered a group of armed guards over. "Get him out of there. To the euth stage."

Anita shrieked. "Wisdom, you can't—"

"He's too far ahead of us. We can't compete with him." Wisdom's eyes were bleak. "We can only guess what's going to happen. He *knows*. For him, it's a sure thing. I don't think it'll help him at euth, though. The whole stage is flooded simultaneously. Instantaneous gas, released throughout." He signalled impatiently to the guards. "Get going. Take him down right away. Don't waste any time."

"Can we?" Baines murmured thoughtfully.

The guards took up positions by one of the chamber locks. Cautiously, the tower control slid the lock back. The first two guards stepped cautiously in, lash-tubes ready.

Cris stood in the center of the chamber. His back was to them as they crept toward him. For a moment he was silent, utterly unmoving. The guards fanned out, as more of them entered the chamber. Then—

Anita screamed. Wisdom cursed. The golden figure spun and leaped forward, in a flashing blur of speed. Past the triple line of guards, through the lock and into the corridor.

"Get him!" Baines shouted.

Guards milled everywhere. Flashes of energy lit up the corridor, as the figure raced among them up the ramp.

"No use," Wisdom said calmly. "We can't hit him." He touched a button, then another. "But maybe this will help."

"What—" Baines began. But the leaping figure shot abruptly at him, straight at him, and he dropped to one side. The figure flashed past. It ran effortlessly, face without expression, dodging and jumping as the energy beams seared around it

For an instant the golden face loomed up before Baines. It passed and disappeared down a side corridor. Guards rushed after it, kneeling and firing, shouting orders excitedly. In the bowels of the building, heavy guns were rumbling up. Locks slid into place as escape corridors were systematically sealed off.

"Good God," Baines gasped, as he got to his feet. "Can't he do anything but run?"

"I gave orders," Wisdom said, "to have the building isolated.

There's no way out. Nobody comes and nobody goes. He's loose here in the building—but he won't get out."

"If there's one exit overlooked, he'll know it," Anita pointed out shakily.

"We won't overlook any exit. We got him once; we'll get him again."

A messenger robot had come in. Now it presented its message respectfully to Wisdom. "From analysis, sir."

Wisdom tore the tape open. "Now we'll know how it thinks." His hands were shaking. "Maybe we can figure out its blind spot. It may be able to out-think us, but that doesn't mean it's invulnerable. It only predicts the future—it can't change it. If there's only death ahead, its ability won't . . ."

Wisdom's voice faded into silence. After a moment he passed the tape to Baines.

"I'll be down in the bar," Wisdom said. "Getting a good stiff drink." His face had turned lead-gray. "All I can say is *I hope to hell this isn't the race to come.*"

"What's the analysis?" Anita demanded impatiently, peering over Baines' shoulder. "How does it think?"

"It doesn't," Baines said, as he handed the tape back to his boss. "It doesn't think at all. Virtually no frontal lobe. It's not a human being—it doesn't use symbols. It's nothing but an animal."

"An animal," Wisdom said. "With a single highly developed faculty. Not a superior man. Not a man at all."

Up and down the corridors of the DCA Building, guards and equipment clanged. Loads of Civil Police were pouring into the building and taking up positions beside the guards. One by one, the corridors and rooms were being inspected and sealed off. Sooner or later the golden figure of Cris Johnson would be located and cornered.

"We were always afraid a mutant with superior intellectual powers would come along," Baines said reflectively. "A deeve who would be to us what we are to the great apes. Something with a bulging cranium, telepathic ability, a perfect semantic system, ultimate powers of symbolization and calculation. A development along our own path. A better human being."

"He acts by reflex," Anita said wonderingly. She had the analysis and was sitting at one of the desks studying intently. "Reflex—like a lion. A golden lion." She pushed the tapes aside, a strange expression on her face. "The lion god."

"Beast," Wisdom corrected tartly. "Blond beast, you mean."

"He runs fast," Baines said, "and that's all. No tools. He doesn't build anything or utilize anything outside himself. He just stands and waits for the right opportunity and then he runs like hell."

"This is worse than anything we've anticipated," Wisdom said. His beefy face was lead-gray. He sagged like an old man, his blunt hands trembling and uncertain. "To be replaced by an animal! Something that runs and hides. Something without a language!" He spat savagely. "That's why they weren't able to communicate with it. We wondered what kind of semantic system it had. It hasn't got any! No more ability to talk and think than a—dog."

"That means intelligence has failed," Baines went on huskily. "We're the last of our line—like the dinosaur. We've carried intelligence as far as it'll go. Too far, maybe. We've already got to the point where we know so much—think so much—we can't act."

"Men of thought," Anita said. "Not men of action. It's begun to have a paralyzing effect. But this thing—"

"This thing's faculty works better than ours ever did. We can recall past experiences, keep them in mind, learn from them. At best, we can make shrewd guesses about the future, from our memory of what's happened in the past. But we can't be certain. We have to speak of probabilities. Grays. Not blacks and whites. We're only guessing."

"Cris Johnson isn't guessing," Anita added.

"He can look ahead. See what's coming. He can—prethink. Let's call it that. He can see into the future. Probably he doesn't perceive it as the future."

"No," Anita said thoughtfully. "It would seem like the present. He has a broader present. But his present is ahead, not back. Our present is related to the past. Only the past is certain, to us. To him, the future is certain. And he probably doesn't remember the past, any more than any animal remembers what's happened."

"As he develops," Baines said, "as his race evolves, it'll probably expand its ability to prethink. Instead of ten minutes, thirty minutes. Then an hour. A day. A year. Eventually they'll be able to keep ahead a whole lifetime. Each one of them will live in a solid, unchanging world. There'll be no variables, no uncertainty. No motion! They won't have anything to fear. Their world will be perfectly static, a solid block of matter."

"And when death comes," Anita said, "they'll accept it. There won't be any struggle; to them, it'll already have happened."

"*Already have happened,*" Baines repeated. "To Cris, our shots had already been fired." He laughed harshly. "Superior survival doesn't mean superior man. If there were another world-wide flood, only fish would survive. If there were another ice age, maybe nothing but polar bears would be left. When we opened the lock, he had already seen the men, seen exactly where they were standing and what they'd do. A neat faculty—but not a development of mind. A pure physical *sense.*"

"But if every exit is covered," Wisdom repeated, "he'll see he can't get out. He gave himself up before—he'll give himself up again." He shook his head. "An animal. Without language. Without tools."

"With his new sense," Baines said, "he doesn't need anything else." He examined his watch. "It's after two. Is the building completely sealed off?"

"You can't leave," Wisdom stated. "You'll have to stay here all night—or until we catch the bastard."

"I meant her." Baines indicated Anita. "She's supposed to be back at Semantics by seven in the morning."

Wisdom shrugged. "I have no control over her. If she wants, she can check out."

"I'll stay," Anita decided. "I want to be here when he—when he's destroyed. I'll sleep here." She hesitated. "Wisdom, isn't there some other way? If he's just an animal couldn't we—

"A zoo?" Wisdom's voice rose in a frenzy of hysteria. "Keep it penned up in the zoo? Christ no! It's got to be killed!"

For a long time the great gleaming shape crouched in the darkness. He was in a store room. Boxes and cartons stretched out on all sides, heaped up in orderly rows, all neatly counted and marked. Silent and deserted.

But in a few moments people burst in and searched the room. He could see this. He saw them in all parts of the room, clear and distinct, men with lash-tubes, grim-faced, stalking with murder in their eyes.

The sight was one of many. One of a multitude of clearly etched scenes lying tangent to his own. And to each was attached a further multitude of interlocking scenes, that finally grew hazier and dwindled away. A progressive vagueness, each syndrome less distinct.

But the immediate one, the scene that lay closest to him, was clearly visible. He could easily make out the sight of the armed men. Therefore it was necessary to be out of the room before they appeared.

The golden figure got calmly to its feet and moved to the door. The corridor was empty; he could see himself already outside, in the vacant, drumming hall of metal and recessed lights. He pushed the door boldly open and stepped out.

A lift blinked across the hall. He walked to the lift and entered it. In five minutes a group of guards would come running along and leap into the lift. By that time he would have left it and sent it back down. Now he pressed a button and rose to the next floor.

He stepped out into a deserted passage. No one was in sight. That didn't surprise him. He couldn't be surprised. The element didn't exist for him. The positions of things, the space relationships of all matter in the immediate future, were as certain for him as his own body. The only thing that was unknown was that which had already passed out of being. In a vague, dim fashion, he had occasionally wondered where things went after he had passed them.

He came to a small supply closet. It had just been searched. It would be a half an hour before anyone opened it again. He had that long; he could see that far ahead. And then—

And then he would be able to see another area, a region farther beyond. He was always moving, advancing into new regions he had never seen before. A constantly unfolding panorama of sights and scenes, frozen landscapes spread out ahead. All objects were fixed. Pieces on a vast chess board through which he moved, arms folded, face calm. A detached observer who saw objects that lay ahead of him as clearly as those under foot.

Right now, as he crouched in the small supply closet, he saw an unusually varied multitude of scenes for the next half hour. Much lay ahead. The half hour was divided into an incredibly complex pattern of separate configurations. He had reached a critical region; he was about to move through worlds of intricate complexity.

He concentrated on a scene ten minutes away. It showed, like a three-dimensional still, a heavy gun at the end of the corridor, trained all the way to the far end. Men moved cautiously from door to door, checking each room again, as they had done repeatedly. At the end of the half hour they had reached the supply closet. A scene showed them looking inside. By that time he was gone, of course. He wasn't in that scene. He had passed on to another.

The next scene showed an exit. Guards stood in a solid line. No way out. He was in that scene. Off to one side, in a niche just inside the door. The street outside was visible, stars, lights, outlines of passing cars and people.

In the next tableau he had gone back, away from the exit. There was no way out. In another tableau he saw himself at other exits, a legion of golden figures, duplicated again and again, as he explored regions ahead, one after another. But each exit was covered.

In one dim scene he saw himself lying charred and dead; he had tried to run through the line, out of the exit.

But that scene was vague. One wavering, indistinct still out of many. The inflexible path along which he moved would not deviate in that direction. It would not turn him that way. The golden figure in that scene, the miniature doll in that room, was only distantly related to him. It was himself, but a far-away self. A self he would never meet. He forgot it and went on to examine the other tableau.

The myriad of tableaux that surrounded him were an elaborate maze, a web which he now considered bit by bit. He was looking down into a doll's house of infinite rooms, rooms without number, each with its furniture, its dolls, all rigid and unmoving. The same dolls and furniture were repeated in many. He, himself, appeared often. The two men on the platform. The woman. Again and again the same combinations turned up; the play was redone, frequently, the same actors and props moved around in all possible ways.

Before it was time to leave the supply closet, Cris Johnson had examined each of the rooms tangent to the one he now occupied. He had consulted each, considered its contents thoroughly.

He pushed the door open and stepped calmly out into the hall. He knew exactly where he was going. And what he had to do. Crouched in the stuffy closet, he had quietly and expertly examined each miniature of himself, observed which clearly etched configuration lay along his inflexible path, the one room of the doll house, the one set out of legions, toward which he was moving.

Anita slipped out of her metal-foil dress, hung it over a hanger, then unfastened her shoes and kicked them under the bed. She was just starting to unclip her bra when the door opened.

She gasped. Soundlessly, calmly, the great golden shape closed the door and bolted it after him.

Anita snatched up her lash-tube from the dressing table. Her hand shook; her whole body was trembling. "What do you want?" she demanded. Her fingers tightened convulsively around the tube. "I'll kill you."

The figure regarded her silently, arms folded. It was the first time she had seen Cris Johnson closely. The great dignified face, handsome and impassive. Broad shoulders. The golden mane of hair, golden skin, pelt of radiant fuzz—

"Why?" she demanded breathlessly. Her heart was pounding wildly. "What do you want?"

She could kill him easily. But the lash-tube wavered. Cris Johnson stood without fear; he wasn't at all afraid. Why not? Didn't he understand what it was? What the small metal tube could do to him?

"Of course," she said suddenly, in a choked whisper. "You can see ahead. You know I'm not going to kill you. Or you wouldn't have come here."

She flushed, terrified—and embarrassed. He knew exactly what she was going to do; he could see it as easily as she saw the walls of the room, the wall-bed with its covers folded neatly back, her clothes hanging in the closet, her purse and small things on the dressing table.

"All right." Anita backed away, then abruptly put the tube down on the dressing table. "I won't kill you. Why should I?" She fumbled in her purse and got out her cigarettes. Shakily, she lit up, her pulse racing. She was scared. And strangely fascinated. "Do you expect to stay here? It won't do any good. They've come through the dorm twice, already. They'll be back."

Could he understand her? She saw nothing on his face, only blank dignity. God, he was huge! It wasn't possible he was only eighteen, a boy, a child. He looked more like some great golden god, come down to earth.

She shook the thought off savagely. He wasn't a god. He was a beast. *The blond beast*, come to take the place of man. To drive man from the earth.

Anita snatched up the lash-tube. "Get out of here! You're an animal! A big stupid animal! You can't even understand what I'm saying—you don't even have a language. You're not human."

Cris Johnson remained silent. As if he were waiting. Waiting for what? He showed no sign of fear or impatience, even though the corridor outside rang with the sound of men searching, metal against metal, guns and energy tubes being dragged around, shouts and dim rumbles as section after section of the building was searched and sealed off.

"They'll get you," Anita said. "You'll be trapped here. They'll be searching this wing any moment." She savagely stubbed out her cigarette. "For God's sake, what do you expect *me* to do?"

Cris moved toward her. Anita shrank back. His powerful hands caught hold of her and she gasped in sudden terror. For a moment she struggled blindly, desperately.

"Let go!" She broke away and leaped back from him. His face was expressionless. Calmly, he came toward her, an impassive god advancing to take her. "Get away!" She groped for the lash-tube, trying to get it up. But the tube slipped from her fingers and rolled onto the floor.

Cris bent down and picked it up. He held it out to her, in the open palm of his hand.

"Good God," Anita whispered. Shakily, she accepted the tube, gripped it hesitantly, then put it down again on the dressing table.

In the half-light of the room, the great golden figure seemed to glow and shimmer, outlined against the darkness. A god—no, not a god. An animal. A great golden beast, without a soul. She was confused. Which was he—or was he both? She shook her head, bewildered. It was late, almost four. She was exhausted and confused.

Cris took her in his arms. Gently, kindly, he lifted her face and kissed her. His powerful hands held her tight. She couldn't breathe. Darkness, mixed with the shimmering golden haze, swept around her. Around and around it spiralled, carrying her senses away. She sank down into it gratefully. The darkness covered her and dissolved her in a swelling torrent of sheer force that mounted in intensity each moment, until the roar of it beat against her and at last blotted out everything.

Anita blinked. She sat up and automatically pushed her hair into place. Cris was standing before the closet. He was reaching up, getting something down.

He turned toward her and tossed something on the bed. Her heavy metal-foil traveling cape.

Anita gazed down at the cape without comprehension. "What do you want?"

Cris stood by the bed, waiting.

She picked up the cape uncertainly. Cold creepers of fear

plucked at her. "You want me to get you out of here," she said softly. "Past the guards and the CP."

Cris said nothing.

"They'll kill you instantly." She got unsteadily to her feet. "You can't run past them. Good God, don't you do anything but run? There must be a better way. Maybe I can appeal to Wisdom. I'm Class A—Director Class. I can go directly to the Full Directorate. I ought to be able to hold them off, keep back the euth indefinitely. The odds are a billion to one against us if we try to break past—"

She broke off.

"But you don't gamble," she continued slowly. "You don't go by odds. You *know* what's coming. You've seen the cards already." She studied his face intently. "No, you can't be cold-decked. It wouldn't be possible."

For a moment she stood deep in thought. Then with a quick, decisive motion, she snatched up the cloak and slipped it around her bare shoulders. She fastened the heavy belt, bent down and got her shoes from under the bed, snatched up her purse, and hurried to the door.

"Come on," she said. She was breathing quickly, cheeks flushed. "Let's go. While there are still a number of exits to choose from. My car is parked outside, in the lot at the side of the building. We can get to my place in an hour. I have a winter home in Argentina. If worst comes to worst we can fly there. It's in the back country, away from the cities. Jungle and swamps. Cut off from almost everything." Eagerly she started to open the door.

Cris reached out and stopped her. Gently, patiently, he moved in front of her.

He waited a long time, body rigid. Then he turned the knob and stepped boldly out into the corridor.

The corridor was empty. No one was in sight. Anita caught a faint glimpse, the back of a guard hurrying off. If they had come out a second earlier—

Cris started down the corridor. She ran after him. He moved rapidly, effortlessly. The girl had trouble keeping up with him. He seemed to know exactly where to go. Off to the right, down a side hall, a supply passage. Onto an ascent freight-lift. They rose, then abruptly halted.

Cris waited again. Presently he slid the door back and moved out of the lift. Anita followed nervously. She could hear sounds: guns and men, very close.

They were near an exit. A double line of guards stood directly ahead. Twenty men, a solid wall—and a massive heavy-duty robot gun in the center. The men were alert, faces strained and tense. Watching wide-eyed, guns gripped tight. A Civil Police officer was in charge.

"We'll never get past," Anita gasped. "We wouldn't get ten feet." She pulled back. "They'll—"

Cris took her by the arm and continued calmly forward. Blind terror leaped inside her. She fought wildly to get away, but his fingers were like steel. She couldn't pry them loose. Quietly, irresistibly, the great golden creature drew her along beside him, toward the double line of guards.

"*There he is!*" Guns went up. Men leaped into action. The barrel of the robot cannon swung around. "*Get him!*"

Anita was paralyzed. She sagged against the powerful body beside her, tugged along helplessly by his inflexible grasp. The lines of guards came nearer, a sheer wall of guns. Anita fought to control her terror. She stumbled, half-fell. Cris supported her effortlessly. She scratched, fought at him, struggled to get loose—

"Don't shoot!" she screamed.

Guns wavered uncertainly. "Who is she?" The guards were moving around, trying to get a sight on Cris without including her. "Who's he got there?"

One of them saw the stripe on her sleeve. Red and black. Director Class. Top-level.

"She's Class A." Shocked, the guards retreated. "Miss, get out of the way!"

Anita found her voice. "Don't shoot. He's—in my custody. You understand? I'm taking him out."

The wall of guards moved back nervously. "No one's supposed to pass. Director Wisdom gave orders—"

"I'm not subject to Wisdom's authority." She managed to edge her voice with a harsh crispness. "Get out of the way. I'm taking him to the Semantics Agency."

For a moment nothing happened. There was no reaction. Then slowly, uncertainly, one guard stepped aside.

Cris moved. A blur of speed, away from Anita, past the confused guards, through the breach in the line, out the exit, and onto the street. Bursts of energy flashed wildly after him. Shouting guards milled out. Anita was left behind, forgotten. The guards, the heavy-duty gun, were pouring out into the early morning darkness. Sirens wailed. Patrol cars roared into life.

Anita stood dazed, confused, leaning against the wall, trying to get her breath.

He was gone. He had left her. Good God—what had she done? She shook her head, bewildered, her face buried in her hands. She had been hypnotized. She had lost her will, her common sense. Her reason! The animal, the great golden beast, had tricked her. Taken advantage of her. And now he was gone, escaped into the night.

Miserable, agonized tears trickled through her clenched fingers. She rubbed at them futilely; but they kept on coming.

"He's gone," Baines said. "We'll never get him, now. He's probably a million miles from here."

Anita sat huddled in the corner, her face to the wall. A little bent heap, broken and wretched.

Wisdom paced back and forth. "But where can he go? Where can he hide? Nobody'll hide him! Everybody knows the law about deeves!"

"He's lived out in the woods most of his life. He'll hunt—that's what he's always done. They wondered what he was up to, off by himself. He was catching game and sleeping under trees." Baines laughed harshly. "And the first woman he meets will be glad to hide him—as *she* was." He indicated Anita with a jerk of his thumb.

"So all that gold, that mane, that god-like stance, was *for* something. Not just ornament." Wisdom's thick lips twisted. "He doesn't have just one faculty—he has two. One is new, the newest thing in survival methods. The other is as old as life." He stopped pacing to glare at the huddled shape in the corner. "Plumage. Bright feathers, combs for the roosters, swans, birds, bright scales for the fish. Gleaming pelts and manes for the animals. An animal isn't necessarily *bestial*. Lions aren't bestial. Or tigers. Or any of the big cats. They're anything but bestial."

"He'll never have to worry," Baines said. "He'll get by—as long as human women exist to take care of him. And since he can see ahead, into the future, he already knows he's sexually irresistible to human females."

"We'll get him," Wisdom muttered. "I've had the Government declare an emergency. Military and Civil Police will be looking for him. Armies of men—a whole planet of experts, the most advanced machines and equipment. We'll flush him, sooner or later."

"By that time it won't make any difference," Baines said. He put his hand on Anita's shoulder and patted her ironically. "You'll have company, sweetheart. You won't be the only one. You're just the first of a long procession."

"Thanks," Anita grated.

"The oldest survival method and the newest. Combined to form one perfectly adapted animal. How the hell are we going to stop him? We can put *you* through a sterilization tank—but we can't pick them all up, all the women he meets along the way. And if we miss one we're finished."

"We'll have to keep trying," Wisdom said. "Round up as many as we can. Before they can spawn." Faint hope glinted in his tired, sagging face. "Maybe his characteristics are recessive. Maybe ours will cancel his out."

"I wouldn't lay any money on that," Baines said. "I think I know already which of the two strains is going to turn up dominant." He grinned wryly. "I mean, I'm making a good *guess*. It won't be us."

# THE BATTLE

## SEPTEMBER 1954

## ROBERT SHECKLEY
## (B. 1928)

Although he was primarily associated with *If*'s companion magazine *Galaxy*, the taut and economic short stories of Robert Sheckley also graced the pages of the publication we are honoring in this book, particularly during its early days. Of these stories, three stand out: "The Academy" (August 1954), still one of the most powerful commentaries on what it means to be normal; "Carrier" (April 1954); and the present selection, which carries the unmistakable scent of pure Sheckley at his early best.

## MEMOIR BY ROBERT SHECKLEY

In the usual sort of a memoir, the author fondly remembers the time and circumstances in which he wrote the piece under examination. I can't write that sort of thing, because it made no particular impression on me at the time. I was just living my life as usual, and this idea came to me, and I sat down and wrote it.

I have a precarious relationship with my older stories. They live an independent existence of their own. My relationship to them is not close; second cousins twice removed would say it. I often resent the stories. Am I called upon to comment on them simply because I wrote them? But what has that got to do with anything? Writing takes place in its own time and space, and has no relationship to life. Yet we are connected in some way, these stories and I. I suppose I should have something to say about them. But I don't know what that something is.

If I knew what that something was, I would probably write a short story about it.

One of my tricks of the trade is the skillful use of ignorance. It is better for me as a writer not to be too loving toward my own work, not to be avuncular—here's this jolly little story that I did back in the golden days, et cetera. My relationship with these old stories has much more hate in it than love. When I read them, I see what went wrong, and this has more force with me than what went right.

Still, I feel I should say something. Readers are presumably interested in this sort of thing. The writer owes it to them to be autobiographical, anectdotal, jolly, a little sardonic, and filled, of course, with the wisdom that the years have brought to him. I would willingly speak of my wisdom if I could find any. I find, instead, approximation and uncertainty, I find chaos and madness, I find love and pain.

Sometimes, with considerable difficulty, I carve a story out of these elements, finding in a metaphor a way of discharging the strangeness of being a human being. To write a memoir, however, is frightening. It means speaking clearly about something, and I am clear on nothing. Thus, I wrote this, a pseudomemoir, and wish you enjoyment of the story. I will point out in its favor that it is short.

# THE BATTLE

Supreme General Fetterer barked "At ease!" as he hurried into the command room. Obediently, his three generals stood at ease.

"We haven't much time," Fetterer said, glancing at his watch. "We'll go over the plan of battle again."

He walked to the wall and unrolled a gigantic map of the Sahara desert.

"According to our best theological information, Satan is going to present his forces at these coordinates." He indicated the place with a blunt forefinger. "In the front rank there will be the devil, demons, succubi, incubi, and the rest of the ratings. Bael will command the right flank, Buer the left. His Satanic Majesty will hold the center."

"Rather medieval," General Dell murmured.

General Fetterer's aide came in, his face shining and happy with thought of the Coming.

"Sir," he said, "the priest is outside again."

"Stand at attention, soldier," Fetterer said sternly. "There's still a battle to be fought and won."

"Yes sir," the aide said, and stood rigidly, some of the joy fading from his face.

"The priest, eh?" Supreme General Fetterer rubbed his fingers together thoughtfully. Ever since the Coming, since the knowledge of the imminent Last Battle, the religious workers of the world had made a complete nuisance of themselves. They had stopped their bickering, which was commendable. But now they were trying to run military business.

"Send him away," Fetterer said. "He knows we're planning Armageddon."

"Yes sir," the aide said. He saluted sharply, wheeled, and marched out.

"To go on," Supreme General Fetterer said. "Behind Satan's first line of defense will be the resurrected sinners, and various elemental forces of evil. The fallen angels will act as his bomber corps. Dell's robot interceptors will meet them."

General Dell smiled grimly.

"Upon contact, MacFee's automatic tank corps will proceed toward the center of the line. MacFee's automatic tank corps will proceed toward the center," Fetterer went on, "supported by General Ongin's robot infantry. Dell will command the H-bombing of the rear, which should be tightly massed. I will thrust with the mechanized cavalry, here and here."

The aide came back, and stood rigidly at attention. "Sir," he said, "the priest refuses to go. He says he must speak with you."

Supreme General Fetterer hesitated before saying no. He remembered that this was the Last Battle, and that the religious workers *were* connected with it. He decided to give the man five minutes.

"Show him in," he said.

The priest wore a plain business suit, to show that he represented no particular religion. His face was tired but determined.

"General," he said, "I am a representative of all the religious workers of the world, the priests, rabbis, ministers, mullahs, and all the rest. We beg of you, General, to let us fight in the Lord's battle."

Supreme General Fetterer drummed his fingers nervously against his side. He wanted to stay on friendly terms with these men. Even he, the Supreme Commander, might need a good word, when all was said and done. . . .

"You can understand my position," Fetterer said unhappily. "I'm a general. I have a battle to fight."

"But it's the Last Battle," the priest said. "It should be the people's battle."

"It is," Fetterer said. "It's being fought by their representatives, the military."

The priest didn't look at all convinced.

Fetterer said, "You wouldn't want to lose this battle, would you? Have Satan win?"

"Of course not," the priest murmured.

"Then we can't take any chances," Fetterer said. "All the governments agreed on that, didn't they? Oh, it would be very nice to fight Armageddon with the mass of humanity. Symbolic, you might say. But could we be certain of victory?"

The priest tried to say something, but Fetterer was talking rapidly.

"How do we know the strength of Satan's forces? We simply *must* put forth our best foot, militarily speaking. And that means the automatic armies, the robot interceptors and tanks, the H-bombs."

The priest looked very unhappy. "But it isn't *right*," he said. "Certainly you can find some place in your plan for *people*?"

Fetterer thought about it, but the request was impossible. The plan of battle was fully developed, beautiful, irresistible. Any introduction of a gross human element would only throw it out of order. No living flesh could stand the noise of that mechanical attack, the energy potentials humming in the air, the all-enveloping fire power. A human being who came within a hundred miles of the front would not live to see the enemy.

"I'm afraid not," Fetterer said.

"There are some," the priest said sternly, "who feel that it was an error to put this in the hands of the military."

"Sorry," Fetterer said cheerfully. "That's defeatist talk. If you don't mind—" He gestured at the door. Wearily, the priest left.

"These civilians," Fetterer mused. "Well, gentlemen, are your troops ready?"

"We're ready to fight for Him," General MacFee said enthusiastically. "I can vouch for every automatic in my command. Their metal is shining, all relays have been renewed, and the energy reservoirs are fully charged. Sir, they're positively itching for battle!"

General Ongin snapped fully out of his daze. "The ground troops are ready, sir!"

"Air arm ready," General Dell said.

"Excellent," General Fetterer said. "All other arrangements have been made. Television facilities are available for the total population of the world. No one, rich or poor, will miss the spectacle of the Last Battle."

"And after the battle—" General Ongin began, and stopped. He looked at Fetterer.

Fetterer frowned deeply. He didn't know what was supposed to happen after The Battle. That part of it was presumably in the hands of the religious agencies.

"I suppose there'll be a presentation or something," he said vaguely.

"You mean we will meet—Him?" General Dell asked.

"Don't really know," Fetterer said. "But I should think so. After all—I mean, you know what I mean."

"But what should we wear?" General MacFee asked, in a sudden panic. "I mean, what *does* one wear?"

"What do the angels wear?" Fetterer asked Ongin.

"I don't know," Ongin said.

"Robes, do you think?" General Dell offered.

"No," Fetterer said sternly. "We will wear dress uniform, without decorations."

The generals nodded. It was fitting.

And then it was time.

Gorgeous in their battle array, the legions of Hell advanced over the desert. Hellish pipes skirled, hollow drums pounded, and the great host moved forward.

In a blinding cloud of sand, General MacFee's automatic tanks hurled themselves against the satanic foe. Immediately, Dell's automatic bombers screeched overhead, hurling their bombs on the massed horde of the damned. Fetterer thrust valiantly with his automatic cavalry.

Into this melee advanced Ongin's automatic infantry, and metal did what metal could.

The hordes of the damned overflowed the front, ripping apart tanks and robots. Automatic mechanisms died, bravely defending a patch of sand. Dell's bombers were torn from the skies by the fallen angels, led by Marchocias, his griffin's wings beating the air into a tornado.

The thin, battered line of robots held, against gigantic presences that smashed and scattered them, and struck terror into the

hearts of television viewers in homes around the world. Like
men, like heroes the robots fought, trying to force back the forces
of evil.

Astaroth shrieked a command, and Behemoth lumbered forward. Bael, with a wedge of devils behind him, threw a charge at
General Fetterer's crumbling left flank. Metal screamed, electrons howled in agony at the impact.

Supreme General Fetterer sweated and trembled, a thousand
miles behind the firing line. But steadily, nervelessly, he guided
the pushing of buttons and the throwing of levers.

His superb corps didn't disappoint him. Mortally damaged
robots swayed to their feet and fought. Smashed, trampled, destroyed by the howling fiends, the robots managed to hold their
line. Then the veteran Fifth Corps threw in a counterattack, and
the enemy front was pierced.

A thousand miles behind the firing line, the generals guided
the mopping-up operations.

"The battle is won," Supreme General Fetterer whispered,
turning away from the television screen. "I congratulate you,
gentlemen."

The generals smiled wearily.

They looked at each other, then broke into a spontaneous
shout. Armageddon was won, and the forces of Satan had been
vanquished.

But something was happening on their screens.

"Is that—is that—" General MacFee began, and then couldn't
speak.

For The Presence was upon the battlefield, walking among the
piles of twisted, shattered metal.

The generals were silent.

The Presence touched a twisted robot.

Upon the smoking desert, the robots began to move. The
twisted, scored, fused metals straightened.

The robots stood on their feet again.

"MacFee," Supreme General Fetterer whispered. "Try your
controls. Make the robots kneel or something."

The general tried, but his controls were dead.

The bodies of the robots began to rise in the air. Around them
were the angels of the Lord, and the robot tanks and soldiers and
bombers floated upward, higher and higher.

"He's saving them!" Ongin cried hysterically. "He's saving the
robots!"

"It's a mistake!" Fetterer said. "Quick. Send a messenger to—no! We will go in person!"

And quickly a ship was commanded, and quickly they sped to the field of battle. But by then it was too late, for Armageddon was over, and the robots gone, and the Lord and his host departed.

# LAST RITES

## OCTOBER 1955

## CHARLES BEAUMONT
## (1929–1967)

The tragic death of Charles Beaumont (Charles Nutt) in 1967 at the age of thirty-eight was a great loss to the field of speculative fiction. Primarily a horror/fantasy writer, he had a wonderful humorous touch that made his best stories the equal of those of writers like Richard Matheson, to whom he was frequently and favorably compared. Some of his best work can be found in the collections *The Hunter and Other Stories* (1958), especially his magnificent "The Vanishing American"; *Magic Man and Other Science-Fantasy Stories* (1965); and *Night Ride and Other Journeys* (1960). He was a literary mainstay of the "men's magazines," especially *Playboy*, during the 1950s.

Other *If* stories include "The Beautiful People" (September 1952) and "The Jungle" (December 1954).

# LAST RITES

Somewhere in the church a baby was shrieking. Father Courtney listened to it, and sighed, and made the Sign of the Cross. Another battle, he thought, dismally. Another grand tug of war. And who won this time, Lord? Me? Or that squalling infant, bless its innocence?

"In the Name of the Father, and of the Son, and of the Holy Ghost. Amen."

He turned and made his way down the pulpit steps, and told himself, Well, you ought to be used to it by now, Heaven knows. After all, you're a priest, not a monologist. What do you care about "audience reaction"? And besides, who ever listens to these sermons of yours, anyway—even under the best of conditions? A few of the ladies in the parish (though you're sure they never hear or understand a word), and, of course, Donovan. But who else?

Screech away, little pink child! Screech until you—no.

No, no. Ahhh!

He walked through the sacristy, trying to think of Donovan, or the big city churches with their fine nurseries, and sound-proof walls, and amplifiers that amplified . . .

One had what one had: It was God's will.

And were things really so bad? Here there was the smell of forests, wasn't there? And in what city parish could you see wild flowers growing on the hills like bright lava? Or feel the earth breathing?

He opened the door and stepped outside.

The fields were dark-silver and silent. Far above the fields, up near the clouds, a rocket launch moved swiftly, dragging its slow thunder behind it.

Father Courtney blinked.

Of course things were not so bad. Things would be just fine, he thought, and I would not be nervous and annoyed at little children, if only—

Abruptly he put his hands together. "Father," he whispered, "let him be well. Let that be Your will!"

Then, deciding not to wait to greet the people, he wiped his palms with a handkerchief and started for the rectory.

The morning was very cold. A thin film of dew coated each pebble along the path, and made them all glisten like drops of mercury. Father Courtney looked at the pebbles and thought of other walks down this path, which led through a wood to Hidden River, and of himself laughing; of excellent wine and soft cushions and himself arguing, arguing; of a thousand sweet hours in the past.

He walked and thought these things and did not hear the telephone until he had reached the rectory stairs.

A chill passed over him, unaccountably.

He went inside and pressed a yellow switch. The screen blurred, came into focus. The face of an old man appeared, filling the screen.

"Hello, Father."

"George!" The priest smiled and waved his fist, menacingly. "George, why haven't you contacted me?" He sputtered. "Aren't you out of that bed yet?"

"Not yet, Father."

"Well, I expected it. I knew it. *Now* will you let me call a doctor?"

"No—" The old man in the screen shook his head. He was thin and pale. His hair was profuse, but very white, and there was something in his eyes. "I think I'd like you to come over, if you could."

"I shouldn't," the priest said, "after the way you've been treating all of us. But, if there's still some of that Chianti left . . ."

George Donovan nodded. "Could you come right away?"

"Father Yoshida won't be happy about it."

"Please. Right away."

Father Courtney felt his fingers draw into fists. "Why?" he asked, holding onto the conversational tone. "Is anything the matter?"

"Not really," Donovan said. His smile was brief. "It's just that I'm dying."

"And I'm going to call Doctor Ferguson. Don't give me any argument either. This nonsense has gone far—"

The old man's face knotted. "No," he said loudly. "I forbid you to do that."

"But you're ill, man. For all we know, you're *seriously* ill. And if you think I'm going to stand around and watch you work yourself into the hospital just because you happen to dislike doctors, you're crazy."

"Father, listen—*please*. I have my reasons. You don't understand them, and I don't blame you. But you've got to trust me. I'll explain everything, if you'll promise me you won't call *anyone*."

Father Courtney breathed unsteadily; he studied his friend's face. Then he said, "I'll promise this much. I won't contact a doctor until I've seen you."

"Good." The old man seemed to relax.

"I'll be there in fifteen minutes."

"With your Little Black Bag?"

"Certainly not. You're going to be all right."

"Bring it, Father. Please. Just in case."

The screen blurred and danced and went white.

Father Courtney hesitated at the blank telephone.

Then he walked to a table and raised his fists and brought them down hard, once.

You're going to get well, he thought. It isn't going to be too late.

Because if you are dying, if you really are, and I could have prevented it . . .

He went to the closet and drew on his overcoat.

It was thick and heavy, but it did not warm him. As he returned to the sacristy he shivered and thought that he had never been so cold before in all his life.

The helicar whirred and dropped quickly to the ground. Father Courtney removed the ignition key, pocketed it, and thrust his bulk out the narrow door, wheezing.

A dull rumbling sifted down from the sky. The wake of fleets a mile away, ten miles, a hundred.

*It's raining whales in our backyard*, the priest thought, remembering how Donovan had described the sound once to a little girl.

A freshet of autumn leaves burst against his leg, softly, and for a while he stood listening to the rockets' dying rumble, watching the shapes of gold and red that scattered in the wind, like fire.

Then he whispered, "Let it be Your will," and pushed the picket gate.

The front door of the house was open.

He walked in, through the living room, to the study.

"George."

"In here," a voice answered.

He moved to the bedroom, and twisted the knob.

George Donovan lay propped on a cloudbank of pillows, his thin face white as the linen. He was smiling.

"I'm glad to see you, Father," he said, quietly.

The priest's heart expanded and shrank and began to thump in his chest.

"The Chianti's down here in the night-table." Donovan gestured. "Pour some: morning's a good enough time for a dinner wine."

"Not now, George."

"Please. It will help."

Father Courtney pulled out the drawer and removed the half-empty bottle. He got a glass from the bookshelf, filled it. Dutifully, according to ritual, he asked, "For you?"

"No," Donovan said. "Thank you all the same." He turned his head. "Sit over there, Father, where I can see you."

The priest frowned. He noticed that Donovan's arms were perfectly flat against the blanket, that his body was rigid, outlined beneath the covering. No part of the old man moved except the head and that slowly, unnaturally.

"That's better. But take off your coat—it's terribly hot in here. You'll catch pneumonia."

The room was full of cold winds from the open shutters.

Father Courtney removed his coat.

"You've been worried, haven't you?" Donovan asked.

The priest nodded. He tried to sense what was wrong, to smell the disease, if there was a disease, if there was anything.

"I'm sorry about that." The old man seemed to sigh. His eyes were misted, webbed with distance, lightly. "But I wanted to be alone. Sometimes you have to be alone, to think, to get things straight. Isn't that true?"

"Sometimes, I suppose, but—"

"No. I know what you're going to say, the questions you want to ask. But there's not enough time . . ."

Father Courtney arose from the chair, and walked quickly to the telephone extension. He jabbed a button. "I'm sorry, George," he said, "but you're going to have a doctor."

The screen did not flicker.

He pressed the button again, firmly.

"Sit down," the tired voice whispered. "It doesn't work. I pulled the wires ten minutes ago."

"Then I'll fly over to Milburn—"

"If you do, I'll be dead when you get back. Believe that: I know what I'm talking about."

The priest clenched and unclenched his stubby fingers, and sat down in the chair again.

Donovan chuckled. "Drink up," he said. "We can't have good wine going to waste, can we?"

The priest put the glass to his lips. He tried to think clearly. If he rushed out to Milburn and got Doctor Ferguson, perhaps there'd be a chance. Or— He took a deep swallow.

No. That wouldn't do. It might take hours.

Donovan was talking now; the words lost—a hum of locusts in the room, a far-off murmuring; then, like a radio turned up: "Father, how long have we been friends, you and I?"

"Why . . . twenty years," the priest answered. "Or more."

"Would you say you know me very well by now?"

"I believe so."

"Then tell me first, right now, would you say that I've been a good man?"

Father Courtney smiled. "There've been worse," he said and thought of what this man had accomplished in Mount Vernon, quietly, in his own quiet way, over the years. The building of a decent school for the children—Donovan had shamed the people into it. The new hospital—Donovan's doing, his patient campaigning. Entertainment halls for the young; a city fund for the poor; better teachers, better doctors—all, all because of the old man with the soft voice, George Donovan.

"Do you mean it?"

"Don't be foolish. And don't be treacly, either. Of course I mean it."

In the room, now, a strange odor fumed up, suddenly.

The old man said, "I'm glad." Still he did not move. "But I'm sorry I asked. It was unfair."

"I don't have the slightest idea what you're talking about."

"Neither do I, Father, completely. I thought I did, once, but I was wrong."

The priest slapped his knees, angrily. "Why won't you let me get a doctor? We'll have plenty of time to talk afterwards."

Donovan's eyes narrowed, and curved into what resembled a smile. "You're my doctor," he said. "The only one who can help me now."

"In what way?"

"By making a decision." The voice was reedy: it seemed to waver and change pitch.

"What sort of a decision?"

Donovan's head jerked up. He closed his eyes and remained this way for a full minute, while the acrid smell bellied and grew stronger and whirled about the room in invisible currents.

" '. . . the gentleman lay graveward with his furies . . .' Do you remember, that, Father?"

"Yes," the priest said. "Thomas, isn't it?"

"Thomas, He's been here with me, you know, really; and I've been asking him things. On the theory that poets aren't entirely human. But he just grins. 'You're dying of strangers,' he says; and grins. Bless him." The old man lowered his head. "He disappointed me."

Father Courtney reached for a cigarette, crumpled the empty pack, laced and unlaced his fingers. He waited, remembering the times he had come to this house, all the fine evenings. Ending now?

Yes. Whatever else he would learn, he knew that, suddenly: they were ending.

"What sort of a decision, George?"

"A theological sort."

Father Courtney snorted and walked to a window. Outside, the sun was hidden behind a curtain of gray. Birds sat black and still on the telephone lines, like notes of music; and there was rain.

"Is there something you think you haven't told me?" he asked.

"Yes."

"About yourself?"

"Yes."

"I don't think so, George." Father Courtney turned. "I've known about it for a long time."

The old man tried to speak.

"I've known very well. And now I think I understand why you've refused to see anyone."

"No," Donovan said. "You don't. Father, listen to me: it isn't what you think."

"Nonsense." The priest reverted to his usual gruffness. "We've been friends for too many years for this kind of thing. It's *exactly* what I think. You're an intelligent, well-read, mule-stubborn old man who's worried he won't get to Heaven because sometimes he has doubts."

"That isn't—"

"Well, rubbish! Do you think I don't ask questions, myself, once in a while? Just because I'm a priest, do you think I go blindly on, never wondering, not even for a minute?"

The old man's eyes moved swiftly, up and down.

"Every intelligent person doubts, George, once in a while. And we all feel terrible about it, and we're terribly sorry. But I assure you, if this were enough to damn us, Heaven would be a wilderness." Father Courtney reached again for a cigarette. "So you've shut yourself up like a hermit and worried and stewed and endangered your life, and all for nothing." He coughed. "Well, that's it, isn't it?"

"I wish it were," Donovan said sadly. His eyes kept dancing. There was a long pause; then he said, "Let me pose you a theoretical problem, Father. Something I've been thinking about lately."

Father Courtney recalled the sentence, and how many times it had begun the evenings of talk—wonderful talk! These evenings, he realized, were part of his life now. An important part. For there was no one else, no one of Donovan's intelligence, with whom you could argue any subject under the sun—from Frescobaldi to baseball, from colonization on Mars to the early French symbolists, to agrarian reforms, to wines, to theology. . . .

The old man shifted in the bed. As he did, the acrid odor diminished and swelled and pulsed. "You once told me," he said, "that you read imaginative fiction, didn't you?"

"I suppose so."

"And that there were certain concepts you could swallow—such as parallel worlds, mutated humans, and the like—but that other concepts you couldn't swallow at all. Artificial life, I believe you mentioned, and time travel, and a few others."

The priest nodded.

"Well, let's take one of these themes for our problem. Will you do that? Let's take the first idea."

"All right. Then the doctor."

"We have this man, Father," Donovan said, gazing at the ceiling. "He looks perfectly ordinary, you see, and it would occur to no one to doubt this; but he is not ordinary. Strictly speaking, he isn't even a man. For, though he lives, he isn't alive. You follow? He is a thing of wires and coils and magic, a creation of other men. He is a machine . . ."

"George!" The priest shook his head. "We've gone through this before: it's foolish to waste time. I came here to help you, not to engage in a discussion of science fiction themes!"

"But that's how you *can* help me," Donovan said.

"Very well," the priest sighed. "But you know my views on this. Even if there were a logical purpose to which such a creature might be put—and I can't think of any—I still say they will never create a machine that is capable of abstract thought. Human intelligence is a spiritual thing—and spiritual things can't be duplicated by men."

"You really believe that?"

"Of course I do. Extrapolation of known scientific advances is perfectly all right; but this is something else entirely."

"Is it?" the old man said. "What about Pasteur's discovery? Or the X ray? Did Roentgen correlate a lot of embryonic data, Father, or did he come upon something brand new? What do you think even the scientists themselves would have said to the idea of a machine that would see through human tissue? They would have said, It's fantastic. And it was, too, and is. Nevertheless, it exists."

"It's not the same thing."

"No . . . I suppose that's true. However, I'm not trying to convince you of my thesis. I ask merely that you accept it for the sake of the problem. Will you?"

"Go ahead, George."

"We have this man, then. He's artificial, but he's perfect: great pains have been taken to see to this. Perfect, no detail spared, however small. He looks human, and he acts human, and for all the world knows, he *is* human. In fact, sometimes even he, our man, gets confused. When he feels a pain in his heart, for instance, it's difficult for him to remember that he has no heart. When he sleeps and awakes refreshed, he must remind himself that this is all controlled by an automatic switch somewhere inside his brain, and that he doesn't *actually* feel refreshed. He must think, I'm not real, I'm not real, I'm not real!

"But this becomes impossible, after a while. Because he doesn't believe it. He begins to ask, Why? *Why* am I not real? Where is the difference, when you come right down to it? Humans eat and sleep—as I do. They talk—as I do. They move and work and laugh—as I do. What they think, I think, and what they feel, I feel. Don't I?

"He wonders, this mechanical man does, Father, what would happen if all the people on earth were suddenly to discover they were mechanical also. Would they feel any the less human? Is it likely that they would rush off to woo typewriters, and adding machines? Or would they think, perhaps, of revising their definition of the word 'Life.'?

"Well, our man thinks about it, and thinks about it, but he never reaches a conclusion. He doesn't believe he's nothing more than an advanced calculator, but he doesn't really believe he's human, either: not completely.

"All he knows is that the smell of wet grass is a fine smell to him, and that the sound of the wind blowing through trees is very sad and very beautiful, and that he loves the whole earth with an impossible passion . . ."

Father Courtney shifted uncomfortably in his chair. If only the telephone worked, he thought. Or if he could be sure it was safe to leave.

". . . other men made the creature, as I've said; but many more like him were made. However, of them all, let's say only he was successful."

"Why?" the priest asked, irritably. "Why would this be done in the first place?"

Donovan smiled. "Why did we send the first ship to the moon? Or bother to split the atom? For no very good reason, Father. Except the reason behind all of science: curiosity. My theoretical scientists were curious to see if it could be accomplished, that's all."

The priest shrugged.

"But perhaps I'd better give our man a history. That would make it a bit more logical. All right, he was born a hundred years ago, roughly. A privately owned industrial monopoly was his mother, and a dozen or so assorted technicians his father. He sprang from his electronic womb fully formed. But, as the result of an accident—lack of knowledge, what have you—he came out rather different from his unsuccessful brothers. A mutant! A mutated robot, Father—now there's an idea that ought to appeal to you! Anyway, *he* knew who, or what, he was. He remembered. And so—to make it brief—when the war interrupted the experiment and threw things into a general uproar, our man decided to escape. He wanted his individuality. He wanted to get out of the zoo.

"It wasn't particularly easy, but he did this. Once free, of course, it was impossible to find him. For one thing, he had been constructed along almost painfully, ordinary lines. And for another, they couldn't very well release the information that a mechanical man built by their laboratories was wandering the streets. It would cause a panic. And there was enough panic, what with the nerve gas and the bombs."

"So they never found him, I gather."

"No," Donovan said, wistfully. "They never found him. And they kept their secret well: it died when they died."

"And what happened to the creature?"

"Very little, to tell the truth. They'd given him a decent intelligence, you see—far more decent, and complex, than they knew—so he didn't have much trouble finding small jobs. A rather old-looking man, fairly strong—he made out. Needless to say, he couldn't stay in the same town for more than twenty years or so, because of his inability to age, but this was all right. Everyone makes friends and loses them. He got used to it."

Father Courtney sat very still now. The birds had flown away from the telephone lines, and were at the window, beating their wings, and crying harshly.

"But all this time, he's been thinking, Father. Thinking and reading. He makes quite a study of philosophy, and for a time he favors a somewhat peculiar combination of Russell and Schopenhauer—unbitter bitterness, you might say. Then this phase passes, and he begins to search through the vast theological and metaphysical literature. For what? He isn't sure. However, he is sure of one thing, now: He *is*, indubitably, human. Without breath, without heart, without blood or bone, artificially created, he thinks this and believes it, with a fair amount of firmness, too. Isn't that remarkable!"

"It is indeed," the priest said, his throat oddly tight and dry. "Go on."

"Well," Donovan chuckled, "I've caught your interest, have I? All right, then. Let us imagine that one hundred years have passed. The creature has been able to make minor repairs on himself, but—at last—he is dying. Like an ancient motor, he's gone on running year after year, until he's all paste and hairpins, and now, like the motor, he's falling apart. And nothing and no one can save him."

The acrid aroma burned and fumed.

"Here's the real paradox, though. Our man has become religious. Father! He doesn't have a living cell within him, yet he's concerned about his soul!"

Donovan's eyes quieted, as the rest of him did. "The problem," he said, "is this: Having lived creditably for over a century as a member of the human species, can this creature of ours hope for Heaven? Or will he 'die' and become only a heap of metal cogs?"

Father Courtney leapt from the chair, and moved to the bed. "George, in Heaven's name, let me call Doctor Ferguson!"

"Answer the question first. Or haven't you decided?"

"There's nothing to decide," the priest said, with impatience. "It's a preposterous idea. No machine can have a soul."

Donovan made the sighing sound, through closed lips. He said, "You don't think it's conceivable, then, that God could have made an exception here?"

"What do you mean?"

"That He could have taken pity on this theoretical man of ours, and breathed a soul into him after all? Is that so impossible?"

Father Courtney shrugged. "It's a poor word, impossible," he said. "But it's a poor problem, too. Why not ask me whether pigs ought to be allowed to fly?"

"Then you admit it's conceivable?"

"I admit nothing of the kind. It simply isn't the sort of question any man can answer."

"Not even a priest?"

"Especially not a priest. You know as much about Catholicism as I do, George; you ought to know how absurd the proposition is."

"Yes," Donovan said. His eyes were closed.

Father Courtney remembered the time they had argued furiously on what would happen if you went back in time and killed your own grandfather. This was like that argument. Exactly like it—exactly. It was no stranger than a dozen other discussions (What if Mozart had been a writer instead of a composer? If a person died and remained dead for an hour and were then revived, would he be haunted by his own ghost?). Plus, perhaps, the fact that Donovan might be in a fever. Perhaps and might and why do I sit here while his life may be draining away . . .

The old man made a sharp noise. "But you can tell me this much," he said. "If our theoretical man were dying, and you knew that he was dying, would you give him Extreme Unction?"

"George, you're delirious."

"No, I'm not: please, Father! Would you give this creature the Last Rites? If, say, you knew him? If you'd known him for years, as a friend, as a member of the parish?"

The priest shook his head. "It would be sacrilegious."

"But why? You said yourself that he might have a soul, that God might have granted him this. Didn't you say that?"

"I—"

"Father, remember, he's a friend of yours. You know him *well*. You and he, this creature, have worked together, side by side, for years. You've taken a thousand walks together, shared the same interests, the same love of art and knowledge. For the sake of the thesis, Father. Do you understand?"

"No," the priest said, feeling a chill freeze into him. "No, I don't."

"Just answer this, then. If your friend were suddenly to reveal himself to you as a machine, and he was dying, and wanted very much to go to Heaven—what would you do?"

The priest picked up the wine glass and emptied it. He noticed that his hand was trembling. "Why—" he began, and stopped, and looked at the silent old man in the bed, studying the face, searching for madness, for death.

*"What would you do?"*

An unsummoned image flashed through his mind. Donovan, kneeling at the altar for Communion Sunday after Sunday; Donovan, with his mouth firmly shut, while the others' yawned; Donovan, waiting to the last moment, then snatching the Host, quickly, dartingly, like a lizard gobbling a fly.

Had he ever seen Donovan eat?

Had he seen him take even one glass of wine, ever?

Father Courtney shuddered slightly, brushing away the images. He felt unwell. He wished the birds would go elsewhere.

*Well, answer him*, he thought. *Give him an answer. Then get in the helicar and fly to Milburn and pray it's not too late . . .*

"I think," the priest said, "that in such a case, I would administer Extreme Unction."

"Just as a precautionary measure?"

"It's all very ridiculous, but—I think that's what I'd do. Does that answer the question?"

"It does, Father. It does." Donovan's voice came from nowhere. "There is one last point, then I'm finished with my little thesis."

"Yes?"

"Let us say the man dies and you give him Extreme Unction; he does or does not go to Heaven, provided there is a Heaven. What happens to the body? Do you tell the townspeople they have been living with a mechanical monster all these years?"

"What do you think, George?"

"I think it would be unwise. They remember our theoretical man as a friend, you see. The shock would be terrible. Also, they would never believe he was the only one of his kind: they'd begin to suspect their neighbors of having clockwork interiors. And some of them might be tempted to investigate and see for sure. And, too, the news would be bound to spread, all over the world. I think it would be a bad thing to let anyone know, Father."

"How would I be able to suppress it?" the priest heard himself ask, seriously.

"By conducting a private autopsy, so to speak. Then, afterwards, you could take the parts to a junkyard and scatter them."

Donovan's voice dropped to a whisper. Again the locust hum.

". . . and if our monster had left a note to the effect he had moved to some unspecified place, you . . ."

The acrid smell billowed, all at once, like a steam, a hiss of blinding vapor.

"George."

Donovan lay unstirring on the cloud of linen, his face composed, expressionless.

"George!"

The priest reached his hand under the blanket and touched the heart-area of Donovan's chest. He tried to pull the eyelids up: they would not move.

He blinked away the burning wetness. "Forgive me!" he said, and paused, and took from his pocket a small white jar and a white stole.

He spoke softly, under his breath, in Latin. While he spoke, he touched the old man's feet and head with glistening fingertips.

Then, when many minutes had passed, he raised his head.

Rain sounded in the room, and swift winds and far-off rockets.

Father Courtney grasped the edge of the blanket.

He made the Sign of the Cross, breathed, and pulled downward, slowly.

After a long while he opened his eyes.

# GAME PRESERVE

## (OCTOBER 1957)

## ROG PHILLIPS

## (1909–1965)

The late Rog Phillips (Roger Phillips Graham) is now largely forgotten. But his stories appeared frequently in the SF magazines in the 1945–1960 period, especially in *Amazing,* for which he wrote "The Club House," a popular regular feature on fanzines and fandom. Although much of his work was indifferent, he wrote two outstanding stories: the often reprinted "The Yellow Pill" (1958), still one of the finest treatments of the nature of reality in science fiction, and the strangely neglected "Game Preserve," a powerful story that we are proud to restore to print.

## GAME PRESERVE

"Hi-hi-hi!" Big One shouted, and heaved erect with the front end of It.

"Hi-hi-hi," Fat One and the dozen others echoed more mildly, lifting wherever they could get a hold on It.

It was lifted and borne forward in a half-crouching trot.

"Hi-hi hi-hi-hihihi," Elf chanted, running and skipping along-side the panting men and their massive burden.

It was carried forward through the lush grass for perhaps fifty feet.

"Ah-ah-ah," Big One sighed loudly, slowly letting the front end of It down until it dug into the soft black soil.

"Ahhh," Fat One and the others sighed, letting go and standing up, stretching aching back muscles, rubbing cramped hands.

"Ah-ah-ah-ah-ah-ah," Elf sang, running around and in between the resting men. He came too close to Big One and was sent sprawling by a quick, good-humored push.

Everyone laughed, Big One laughing the loudest. Then Big

One lifted Elf to his feet and patted him on the back affection-
ately, a broad grin forming a toothy gap at the top of his bushy
black beard.

Elf answered the grin with one of his own, and at that moment
his ever present yearning to grow up to be the biggest and the
strongest like Big One flowed through him with new strength.

Abruptly Big One leaped to the front of It, shouting "Hi,
hi-HI!"

"Hi-hi-hi," the others echoed, scrambling to their places. Once
again It was borne forward for fifty feet—and again and again,
across the broad meadowland.

A vast matting of blackberry brambles came into view off to one
side. Big One veered his course toward it. The going was uphill
now, so the forward surges shortened to forty feet, then thirty. By
the time they reached the blackberries they were wet and glossy
with sweat.

It was a healthy patch, loaded with large ripe berries. The men
ate hungrily at first, then more leisurely, pointing to one another's stained beards and laughing. As they denuded one area they
leaped to It, carried it another ten feet, and started stripping
another section, never getting more than a few feet from It.

Elf picked his blackberries with first one then another of the
men. When his hunger was satisfied he became mischievous,
picking a handful of berries and squashing them against the back
or the chest of the nearest man and running away, laughing. It
was dangerous sport, he knew, because if one of them caught him
he would be tossed into the brambles.

Eventually they all had their fill, and thanks to Elf looked as
though they were oozing blackberry juice from every pore. The
sun was in its mid-afternoon position. In the distance a line of
white-barked trees could be seen—evidence of a stream.

"Hi-hi-hi!" Big One shouted.

The journey toward the trees began. It was mostly downhill, so
the forward spurts were often as much as a hundred feet.

Before they could hear the water they could smell it. They
grunted their delight at the smell, a rich fish odor betokening
plenty of food. Intermingled with this odor was the spicy scent of
eucalyptus.

They pushed forward with renewed zeal so that the sweat ran
down their skins, dissolving the berry juices and making rivulets
that looked like purple blood.

When less than a hundred yards from the stream, which was

still hidden beyond the tall grasses and the trees lining its bank, they heard the sound of voices, high pitched—women's voices. They became uneasy and nervous. Their surges forward shortened to ten feet, their rest periods became longer, they searched worriedly for signs of motion through the trees.

They changed their course to arrive a hundred yards downstream from the source of the women's voices. Soon they reached the edge of the tree belt. It was more difficult to carry It through the scatterings of bushes. Too, they would get part way through the trees and run into trees too close together to get It past them, and have to back out and try another place. It took almost two hours to work through the trees to the bank of the stream.

Only Elf recognized the place they finally broke through as the place they had left more than two days before. In that respect he knew he was different, not only from Big One and other grownups, but also all other Elfs except one, a girl Elf. He had known it as long as he could remember. He had learned it from many little things. For example, he had recognized the place when they reached it. Big One and the others never remembered anything for long. In getting It through the trees they blundered as they always had, and got through by trial and error with no memory of past blunderings.

Elf was different in another way, too. He could make more sounds than the others. Sometimes he would keep a little It with him until it gave him a feeling of security almost as strong as the big It, then wander off alone with It and play with making sounds, "Bz-bz. Walla-walla-walla-rue-rue-la-lo-hi. Da!" and all kinds of sounds. It excited him to be able to make different sounds and put them together so that they pleased his hearing, but such sounds made the others avoid him and look at him from a safe distance, with worried expressions, so he had learned not to make *different* sounds within earshot of others.

The women and Elfs were upstream a hundred yards, where they always remained. From the way they were milling around and acting alarmed it was evident to Elf they could no more remember the men having been here a few days before than the men could remember it themselves. It would be two or three days before they slowly lost their fear of one another. It would be the women and their Elfs who would cautiously approach, holding their portable Its clutched for security, until finally losing all fear, they would join into one big group for a while.

Big One and the others carried It right to the water's edge so

they could get into the water without ever being far from It. They
shivered and shouted excitedly as they bathed. Fat One screamed
with delight as he held a squirming fish up for the others to see.
He bit into it with strong white teeth, water dripping from his
heavy brown beard. Renewed hunger possessed him. He gobbled
the fish and began searching for another. He always caught two
fish for any other man's one, which was why he was fat.

Elf himself caught a fish. After eating it he lay on the grassy
bank looking up at the white billowing clouds in the blue sky. The
sun was now near the horizon, half hidden behind a cloud,
sending divergent ramps of light downward. The clouds on the
western horizon were slowly taking on color until red, orange, and
green separated into definite areas. The soft murmur of the
stream formed a lazy background to the excited voices of the
men. From upstream, faintly, drifted the woman and Elf sounds.

Here, close to the ground, the rich earthy smell was stronger
than that of the stream. After a time a slight breeze sprang up,
bringing with it other odors, that of distant pines, the pungent
eucalyptus, a musky animal scent.

Big One and the others were out of the water finally. Half
asleep, Elf watched them move It up to dry ground. As though
that were what the sun had been waiting for, it sank rapidly
below the horizon.

The clouds where the sun had been seemed now to blaze for a
time with a smoldering redness that cooled to black. The stars
came out, one by one.

A multitude of snorings erupted into the night. Elf crept among
the sleeping forms until he found Big One, and settled down for
the night, his head against Big One's chest, his right hand resting
against the cool smooth metal of It.

Elf awoke with the bright morning sun directly in his eyes. Big
One was gone, already wading in the stream after fish. Some of
the others were with him. A few were still sleeping.

Elf leaped to his feet, paused to stretch elaborately, then
splashed into the stream. As soon as he caught a fish he climbed
out onto the bank and ate it. Then he turned to his search for a
little It. There were many lying around, all exactly alike. He
studied several, not touching some, touching and even nudging
others. Since they all looked alike it was more a matter of *feel*
than any real difference that he looked for. One and only one
seemed to be the It. Elf returned his attention to it several times.

Finally he picked it up and carried it over to the big It, and hid it underneath. Big One, with shouts of sheer exuberance, climbed up onto the bank dripping water. He grinned at Elf.

Elf looked in the direction of the women and other Elfs. Some of them were wandering in his direction, each carrying an It of some sort, many of them similar to the one he had chosen.

In sudden alarm at the thought that someone might steal his new It, Elf rescued it from its hiding place. He tried to hide it behind him when any of the men looked his way. They scorned an individual It and, as men, preferred an It too heavy for one person.

As the day advanced, women and Elfs approached nearer, pretending to be unaware at times that the men were here, at other times openly fleeing back, overcome by panic.

The men never went farther than twenty feet from the big It. But as the women came closer the men grew surly toward one another. By noon two of them were trying to pick a fight with anyone who would stand up to them.

Elf clutched his little It closely and moved cautiously down-stream until he was twenty feet from the big It. Tentatively he went another few feet—farther than any of the men dared go from the big It. At first he felt secure, then panic overcame him and he ran back, dropping the little It. He touched the big It until the panic was gone. After a while he went to the little It and picked it up. He walked around, carrying it, until he felt secure with it again. Finally he went downstream again, twenty feet, twenty-five feet, thirty . . . He felt panic finally, but not overwhelmingly. When it became almost unendurable, he calmly turned around and walked back.

Confidence came to him. An hour later he went downstream until he was out of sight of the big It and the men. Security seemed to flow warmly from the little It.

Excitement possessed Elf. He ran here and there, clutching It closely so as not to drop it and lose it. He felt *free*.

"Bdlboo," he said aloud, experimentally. He liked the sounds. "Bdlboo-bdlboo-bdlboo." He saw a berry bush ahead and ran to it to munch on the delicious fruit. "Riddle piddle biddle," he said. It sounded nice.

He ran on, and after a time he found a soft grassy spot and stretched out on his back, holding It carelessly in one hand. He looked up and up, at a layer of clouds going in one direction and another layer above it going in another direction.

Suddenly he heard voices.

At first he thought the wind must have changed so that it was carrying the voices of the men to him. He lay there, listening. Slowly he realized these voices were different. They were putting sounds together like those he made himself.

A sense of wonder possessed him. How could there be anyone besides himself who could do that?

Unafraid, yet filled with caution, he clutched It closely to his chest and stole in the direction of the sounds.

After going a hundred yards he saw signs of movement through the trees. He dropped to the ground and lay still for a moment, then gained courage to rise cautiously, ready to run. Stooping low, he stole forward until he could see several moving figures. Darting from tree to tree he moved closer to them, listening with greater excitement than he had ever known to the smoothly flowing variety of beautiful sounds they were making.

This was something new, a sort of game they must be playing. One voice would make a string of sounds then stop, another would make a string of different sounds and stop, a third would take it up. They were good at it, too.

But the closer he got to them the more puzzled he became. They were shaped somewhat like people, they carried Its, they had hands and faces like people. That's as far as the similarity went. Their feet were solid, their arms, legs, and body were not skin at all but strangely colored and unliving in appearance. Their faces were smooth like women's, their hair short like babies', their voices deep like men's.

And the Its they carried were unlike any Elf had ever seen. Not only that, each of them carried more than one.

*That* was an *idea!* Elf became so excited he almost forgot to keep hidden. If you had more than one It, then if something happened to one you would still feel secure!

He resisted the urge to return to the stream and search for another little It to give him extra security. If he did that he might never again find these creatures that were so like men and yet so different. So instead, he filed the idea away to use at the earliest opportunity and followed the strange creatures, keeping well hidden from them.

Soon Elf could hear the shouts of the men in the distance. From the behavior of the creatures ahead, they had heard those shouts too. They changed their direction so as to reach the stream a hundred yards or more downstream at about the spot where Elf had left. They made no voice sounds now that Elf could hear. They clutched their strangely shaped long Its before them tensely as though feeling greater security that way, their heads turning this way and that as they searched for any movement ahead.

They moved purposefully. An overwhelming sense of kinship brought tears to Elf's eyes. These creatures were *his kind.* Their differences from him were physical and therefore superficial, and even if those differences were greater it wouldn't have mattered.

He wanted, suddenly, to run to them. But the thought of it sent fear through him. Also they might run in panic from him if he suddenly revealed himself.

It would have to be a mutual approach, he felt. He was used to seeing them now. In due time he would reveal himself for a brief moment to them. Later he would stay in the open and watch them, making no move to approach until they got used to his being around. It might take days, but eventually, he felt sure, he could join them without causing them to panic.

After all, there had been the time when he absented himself from the men for three whole days and when he returned they had forgotten him, and his sudden appearance in their midst had sent even Big One into spasms of fear. Unable to flee from the security of the big It, and unable to bear his presence among them without being used to him, they had all fallen on the ground in a fit. He had had to retreat and wait until they recovered. Then, slowly, he had let them get used to his being in sight before approaching again. It had taken two full days to get to the point where they would accept him once more.

That experience, Elf felt, would be valuable to remember now. He wouldn't want to plunge these creatures into fits or see them scatter and run away.

Also, he was too afraid right now to reveal himself even though every atom of his being called for their companionship.

Suddenly he made another important discovery. Some of the Its these creatures carried had something like pliable vines attached to them so they could be hung about the neck! The thought was so staggering that Elf stopped and examined his It to see if that could be done to it. It was twice as long as his hand and round one way, tapering to a small end that opened to the hollow inside. It was too smooth to hold with a pliable vine unless— He visualized pliable vines woven together to hold it. He wasn't sure how it could be done, but maybe it could.

He set the idea aside for the future and caught up with the

creatures again, looking at them with a new emotion, awe. The ideas he got just from watching them were so staggering he was getting dizzy!

Another new thought hit him. He rejected it at once as being too fantastic. It returned. Leaves are thin and pliable and can be wrapped around small objects like pebbles. Could it be that these creatures were really men of some sort, with bodies like men, covered with something thin like leaves are thin? It was a new and dizzy height in portable securities, and hardly likely. No. He rejected the idea with finality and turned his mind to other things.

He knew now where they could reach the stream. He decided to circle them and get ahead of them. For the next few minutes this occupied his full attention, leaving no room for crazy thoughts.

He reached the stream and hid between some bushes where he would have a quick line of retreat if necessary. He clutched It tightly and waited. In a few moments he saw the first of the creatures emerge a hundred feet away. The others soon joined the first. Elf stole forward from concealment to concealment until he was only fifteen feet from them. His heart was pounding with a mixture of fear and excitement. His knuckles were white from clutching It.

The creatures were still carrying on their game of making sounds, but now in an amazing new way that made them barely audible. Elf listened to the incredibly varied sounds, enraptured.

"This colony seems to have remained pure."

"You never can tell."

"No, you never can tell. Get out the binoculars and look, Joe."

"Not just yet, Harold. I'm looking to see if I can spot one whose behavior shows intelligence."

Elf ached to imitate some of the beautiful combinations of sounds. He wanted to experiment and see if he could make the softly muted voices. He had an idea how it might be done, not make a noise in your throat but breathe out and form the sounds with your mouth just like you were uttering them aloud.

One of the creatures fumbled at an It hanging around his neck. The top of it hinged back. He reached in and brought out a gleaming It and held it so that it covered his eyes. He was facing toward the men upstream and stood up slowly.

"See something, Joe?"

Suddenly Elf was afraid. Was this some kind of magic? He had often puzzled over the problem of whether things were there when he didn't look at them. He had experimented, closing his eyes then opening them suddenly to see if things were still there, and they always were; but maybe this was magic to make the men not be there. Elf waited, watching upstream, but Big One and the others did not vanish.

The one called Joe chuckled. "The toy the adult males have would be a museum piece if it were intact. A 1960 Ford, I think. Only one wheel on it, right front."

Elf's attention jerked back. One of the creatures was reaching over his shoulder, lifting on the large It fastened there. The top of the It pulled back. He reached inside, bringing out something that made Elf almost exclaim aloud. It was shaped exactly like the little It Elf was carrying, but it glistened in the sunlight and its interior was filled with a richly brown fluid.

"Anyone else want a Coke?"

"This used to be a picnic area," the one called Joe said, not taking his eyes from the binoculars. "I can see a lot of pop bottles lying around in the general area of that wreck of a Ford."

While Elf watched, breathless, the creature reached inside the skin of his hip and brought out a very small It and did something to the small end of the hollow It. Putting the very small It back under the skin of his hip, he put the hollow It to his lips and tilted it. Elf watched the brown liquid drain out. Here was magic. Such an It—the very one he carried—could be filled with water from the stream and carried around to drink any time!

When the It held no more liquid the creature dropped it to the ground. Elf could not take his eyes from it. He wanted it more than he had ever wanted anything. They might forget it. Sometimes the women dropped their Its and forgot them, picking up another one instead, and these creatures had beardless faces like women. Besides, each of them carried so many Its that they would feel just as secure without this one.

So many Its! One of the creatures held a flat white It in one hand and a very slim It shaped like a straight section of a bush stem, pointed at one end, with which he scratched on the white It at times, leaving black designs.

"There're fourteen males," the one called Joe whispered. The other wrote it down.

The way these creatures did things, Elf decided, was very similar to the way Big One and the other men went at moving the big It. They were very much like men in their actions, these creatures.

"Eighty-five or -six females."

"See any sign of intelligent action yet?"

"No. A couple of the males are fighting. Probably going to be a mating free-for-all tomorrow or next day. There's one! Just a minute, I want to make sure. It's a little girl, maybe eight or nine years old. Good forehead. Her eyes definitely lack the large marble-like quality of the submoron parent species. She's intelligent all right. She's drawing something in the sand with a stick. Give me your rifle, Bill, it's got a better telescope sight on it than mine, and I don't want her to suffer."

That little It, abandoned on the ground. Elf wanted it. One of the creatures would be sure to pick it up. Elf worried. He would never get it then. If only the creatures would go, or not notice him. If only—

The creature with the thing over his eyes put it back where he had gotten it out of the thing hanging from his shoulder. He had taken one of the long slim things from another of the creatures and placed the thick end against his shoulder, the small end pointed upstream. The others were standing, their backs to Elf, all of them looking upstream. If they would remain that way, maybe he could dart out and get the little It. In another moment they might lose interest in whatever they were watching.

Elf darted out from his concealment and grabbed the It off the ground, and in the same instant an ear-shattering sound erupted from the long slim thing against the creature's shoulder.

"Got her!" the creature said.

Paralyzed with fright, Elf stood motionless. One of the creatures started to turn his way. At the last instant Elf darted back to his place of concealment. His heart was pounding so loudly he felt sure they would hear it.

"You sure, Joe?"

"Right through the head. She never knew what happened."

Elf held the new It close to him, ready to run if he were discovered. He didn't dare look at it yet. It wouldn't notice if he just held it and felt it without looking at it. It was cold at first, colder than the water in the stream. Slowly it warmed. He dared to steal a quick glance at it. It gleamed at him as though possessed of inner life. A new feeling of security grew within him, greater than he had ever known. The other It, the one half filled with dried mud, and deeply scratched from the violent rush of water over it when the stream went over its banks, lay forgotten at his feet.

"Well, that finishes the survey trip for this time."

Elf paid little attention to the voice whispers now, too wrapped up in his new feelings.

"Yes, and quite a haul. Twenty-two colonies—three more than ten years ago. Fourteen of them uncontaminated, seven with only one or two intelligent offspring to kill, only one colony so contaminated we had to wipe it out altogether. And one renegade."

"The renegades are growing scarcer every time. Another ten or twenty years and they'll be extinct."

"Then there won't be any more intelligent offspring in these colonies."

"Let's get going. It'll be dark in another hour or so."

The creatures were hiding some of their Its under their skin, in their carrying cases. There was a feeling about them of departure. Elf waited until they were on the move, back the way they had come, then he followed at a safe distance.

He debated whether to show himself now or wait. The sun was going down in the sky now. It wouldn't be long until it went down for the night. Should he wait until in the morning to let them get their first glimpse of him?

He smiled to himself. He had plenty of time. Tomorrow and tomorrow. He would never return to Big One and the other men. Men or creatures, he would join with these new and wonderful creatures. They were *his kind*.

He thought of the girl Elf. They were her kind, too. If he could only get her to come with him.

On sudden impulse he decided to try. These creatures were going back the same way they had come. If he ran, and if she came right with him, they could catch up with the creatures before they went so far they would lose them.

He turned back, going carefully until he could no longer see the creatures, then he ran. He headed directly toward the place where the women and Elfs stayed. They would not be so easily alarmed as the men because there were so many of them they couldn't remember one another, and one more or less of the Elfs went unnoticed.

When he reached the clearing he slowed to a walk, looking for her. Ordinarily he didn't have to look much. She would see him and come to him, smiling in recognition of the fact that he was the only one like her.

He became a little angry. Was she hiding? Then he saw her. He went to her. She was on her stomach, motionless as though asleep, but something was different. There was a hole in one side of her head, and on the opposite side it was torn open, red and grayish white, with— He knelt down and touched her. She had the same inert feel to her that others had had who never again moved.

He studied her head curiously. He had never seen anything like this. He shook her. She remained limp. He sighed. He knew what would happen now. It was already happening. The odor was very faint yet, but she would not move again, and day after day the odor would get stronger. No one liked it.

He would have to hurry or he would lose the creatures. He turned and ran, never looking back. Once he started to cry, then stopped in surprise. Why had he been crying, he wondered. He hadn't hurt himself.

He caught up with the creatures. They were hurrying now, their long slender Its balanced on one shoulder, the big end resting in the palm of the hand. They no longer moved cautiously. Shortly it was new country. Elf had never been this far from the stream;. Big One more or less led the men, and always more or less followed the same route in cross-country trips.

The creatures didn't spend hours stumbling along impossible paths. They looked ahead of them and selected a way, and took it. Also they didn't have a heavy It to transport, fifty feet at a time. Elf began to sense they had a destination in mind. Probably the place they lived.

Just ahead was a steep bank, higher than a man, running in a long line. The creatures climbed the bank and vanished on the other side. Cautiously Elf followed them, heading toward a large stone with It qualities at the top of the bank from whose concealment he could see where they had gone without being seen. He reached it and cautiously peeked around it. Just below him were the creatures, but what amazed Elf was the sight of the big It.

It was very much like the big It the men had, except that there were differences in shape, and instead of one round thing at one corner, it had one at each corner and rested on them so that it was held off the ground. It glistened instead of being dull. It had a strange odor that was quite strong.

The creatures were putting some of their Its into it, two of them had actually climbed into it—something neither Elf nor the men had ever dared to do with their own big It.

Elf took his eyes off of it for a moment to marvel at the ground. It seemed made of stone, but such stone as he had never before seen. It was an even width with edges going in straight lines that paralleled the long narrow hill on which he stood, and on the other side was a similar hill, extending as far as the eye could see.

He returned his attention to the creatures and their big It. The creatures had all climbed into it now. Possibly they were settling down for the night, though it was still early for that. . . .

No matter. There was plenty of time. Tomorrow and tomorrow. Elf would show himself in the morning, then run away. He would come back again after a while and show himself a little longer, giving them time to get used to him so they wouldn't panic.

They were playing their game of making voice sounds to one another again. It seemed their major preoccupation. Elf thought how much fun it would be to be one of them, making voice sounds to his heart's content.

"I don't see why the government doesn't wipe out the whole lot," one of them was saying. "It's hopeless to keep them alive. Feeble-mindedness is dominant in them. They can't be absorbed into the race again, and any intelligent offspring they get from mating with a renegade would start a long line of descendants, at least one fourth of whom would be mindless idiots."

"Well," another of them said, "it's one of those things where there is no answer. Wipe them out, and next year it would be all the blond-haired people to be wiped out to keep the race of dark-haired people pure, or something. Probably in another hundred years nature will take care of the problem by wiping them out for us. Meanwhile we game wardens must make the rounds every two years and weed out any of them we can find that have intelligence." He looked up the embankment but did not notice Elf's head, concealed partially by the grass around the concrete marker. "It's an easy job. Any of them we missed seeing this time, we'll probably get next time. In the six or eight visits we make before the intelligent ones can become adults and mate we always find them."

"What I hate is when they see us, those intelligent ones," a third voice said. "When they walk right up to us and want to be friends with us it's too much like plain murder, except that they can't talk, and only make moronic sounds like 'Bdl-bdl-bdl.' Even so, it gets me when we kill them." The others laughed.

Suddenly Elf heard a new sound from the big It. It was not a voice sound, or if it was it was one that Elf felt he could not possibly match exactly. It was a growling, "RRrrRRrrRRrr." Suddenly it was replaced by still a different sound, a "p-p-p-p-p" going very rapidly. Perhaps it was the way these creatures snored. It was not unpleasant. Elf cocked his head to one side, listening to the sound, smiling. How exciting it would be when he could join with these creatures! He wanted to so much.

The big It began to move. In the first brief second Elf could not believe his senses. How could it move without being carried? But it was moving, and the creatures didn't seem to be aware of it! Or perhaps they were too overcome by fear to leap out!

Already the big It was moving faster than a walk, and was moving faster with every heartbeat. How could they remain unaware of it and not leap to safety?

Belatedly Elf abandoned caution and leaped down the embankment to the flat ribbon of rock, shouting. But already the big It was over a hundred yards away, and moving faster now than birds in flight!

He shouted, but the creatures didn't hear him—or perhaps they were so overcome with fright that they were frozen. Yes, that must be it.

Elf ran after the big It. If he could only catch up with it he would gladly join the creatures in their fate. Better to die with them than to lose them!

He ran and ran, refusing to believe he could never overtake the big It, even when it disappeared from view, going faster than the wind. He ran and ran until his legs could lift no more.

Blinded by tears, he tripped and sprawled full length on the wide ribbon of stone. His nose bled from hitting the hard surface. His knees were scraped and bleeding. He was unaware of this.

He was aware only that the creatures were gone, to what unimaginable fate he could not guess, but lost to him, perhaps forever.

Sobs welled up within him, spilled out, shaking his small naked body. He cried as he hadn't cried since he was a baby.

And the empty Coca-Cola bottle, clutched forgotten in his hand, glistened with the rays of the setting sun. . . .

# THE BURNING OF THE BRAIN
## (OCTOBER 1958)
## CORDWAINER SMITH
## (1913–1966)

The Instrumentality stories of Cordwainer Smith (Paul Myron Anthony Linebarger) constitute one of the most remarkable series in science fiction, both for their settings and their memorable characters. Their author was just as remarkable, a professor of Asiatic studies at Johns Hopkins University who also worked for the United States government. Although primarily a *Galaxy* writer, Smith had several important stories in *If*, including "Western Science Is So Wonderful" (December 1958), "No, No, Not Rogov!" (February 1959), and "The Burning of the Brain," which captures all of the sense of wonder that made its author a legend.

# THE BURNING OF THE BRAIN

## I
## DOLORES OH

I tell you, it is sad, it is more than sad, it is fearful—for it is a dreadful thing to go into the Up-and-Out, to fly without flying, to move between the stars as a moth may drift among the leaves on a summer night.

Of all the men who took the great ships into planoform none was braver, none stronger, than Captain Magno Taliano.

Scanners had been gone for centuries and the jonasoidal effect had become so simple, so manageable, that the traversing of light-years was no more difficult to most of the passengers of the great ships than to go from one room to the other.

Passengers moved easily.

Not the crew.

Least of all the captain.

The captain of a jonasoidal ship which had embarked on an

interstellar journey was a man subject to rare and overwhelming strains. The art of getting past all the complications of space was far more like the piloting of turbulent waters in ancient days than like the smooth seas which legendary men once traversed with sails alone.

Go-Captain on the *Wu-Feinstein*, finest ship of its class, was Magno Taliano.

Of him it was said, "He could sail through hell with the muscles of his left eye alone. He could plow space with his living brain if the instruments failed. . . ."

Wife to the Go-Captain was Dolores Oh. The name was Japonical, from some nation of the ancient days. Dolores Oh had been once beautiful, so beautiful that she took men's breath away, made wise men into fools, made young men into nightmares of lust and yearning. Wherever she went men had quarreled and fought over her.

But Dolores Oh was proud beyond all common limits of pride. She refused to go through the ordinary rejuvenescence. A terrible yearning a hundred or so years back must have come over her. Perhaps she said to herself, before that hope and terror which a mirror in a quiet room becomes to anyone:

"Surely I am me. There must be a *me* more than the beauty of my face; there must be a something other than the delicacy of skin and the accidental lines of my jaw and my cheekbone.

"What have men loved if it wasn't me? Can I ever find out who I am or what I am if I don't let beauty perish and live on in whatever flesh age gives me?"

She had met the Go-Captain and had married him in a romance that left forty planets talking and half the ship lines stunned.

Magno Taliano was at the very beginning of his genius. Space, we can tell you, is rough—rough like the wildest of storm-driven waters, filled with perils which only the most sensitive, the quickest, the most daring of men can surmount.

Best of them all, class for class, age for age, out of class, beating the best of his seniors, was Magno Taliano.

For him to marry the most beautiful beauty of forty worlds was a wedding like Héloise and Abelard's or like the unforgettable romance of Helen America and Mr. Grey-no-more.

The ships of the Go-Captain Magno Taliano became more beautiful year by year, century by century.

As ships became better he always obtained the best. He maintained his lead over the other Go-Captains so overwhelmingly that it was unthinkable for the finest ship of mankind to sail out amid the roughness and uncertainties of two-dimensional space without himself at the helm.

Stop-Captains were proud to sail space beside him. (Though the Stop-Captains had nothing more to do than to check the maintenance of the ship, its loading and unloading when it was in normal space, they were still more than ordinary men in their own kind of world, a world far below the more majestic and adventurous universe of the Go-Captains.)

Magno Taliano had a niece who in the modern style used a place instead of a name: she was called "Dita from the Great South House."

When Dita came aboard the *Wu-Feinstein* she had heard much of Dolores Oh, her aunt by marriage who had once captivated the men in many worlds. Dita was wholly unprepared for what she found.

Dolores greeted her civilly enough, but the civility was a sucking pump of hideous anxiety, the friendliness was the driest of mockeries, the greeting itself an attack.

*What's the matter with the woman?* thought Dita.

As if to answer her thought, Dolores said aloud and in words: "It's nice to meet a woman who's not trying to take Taliano from me. I love him. Can you believe that? Can you?"

"Of course," said Dita. She looked at the ruined face of Dolores Oh, at the dreaming terror in Dolores' eyes, and she realized that Dolores had passed all limits of nightmare and had become a veritable demon of regret, a possessive ghost who sucked the vitality from her husband, who dreaded companionship, hated friendship, rejected even the most casual of acquaintances, because she feared forever and without limit that there was really nothing to herself, and feared that without Magno Taliano she would be more lost than the blackest of whirlpools in the nothing between the stars.

Magno Taliano came in.

He saw his wife and niece together.

He must have been used to Dolores Oh. In Dita's eyes Dolores was more frightening than a mud-caked reptile raising its wounded and venomous head with blind hunger and blind rage. To Magno Taliano the ghastly woman who stood like a witch beside him was somehow the beautiful girl he had wooed and had married one hundred sixty-four years before.

He kissed the withered cheek, he stroked the dried and stringy hair, he looked into the greedy terror-haunted eyes as though they were the eyes of a child he loved. He said, lightly and gently, "Be good to Dita, my dear."

He went on through the lobby of the ship to the inner sanctum of the planoforming room.

The Stop-Captain waited for him. Outside on the world of Sherman the scented breezes of that pleasant planet blew in through the open windows of the ship.

*Wu-Feinstein*, finest ship of its class, had no need for metal walls. It was built to resemble an ancient, prehistoric estate named Mount Vernon, and when it sailed between the stars it was encased in its own rigid and self-renewing field of force.

The passengers went through a few pleasant hours of strolling on the grass, enjoying the spacious rooms, chatting beneath a marvelous simulacrum of an atmosphere-filled sky.

Only in the planoforming room did the Go-Captain know what happened. The Go-Captain, his pinlighters sitting beside him, took the ship from one compression to another, leaping hotly and frantically through space, sometimes one light-year, sometimes a hundred light-years, jump, jump, jump, jump until the ship, the light touches of the captain's mind guiding it, passed the perils of millions upon millions of worlds, came out at its appointed destination, and settled as lightly as one feather resting upon others, settled into an embroidered and decorated countryside where the passengers could move as easily away from their journey as if they had done nothing more than to pass an afternoon in a pleasant old house by the side of a river.

## II
## THE LOST LOCKSHEET

Magno Taliano nodded to his pinlighters. The Stop-Captain bowed obsequiously from the doorway of the planoforming room. Taliano looked at him sternly, but with robust friendliness. With formal and austere courtesy he asked, "Sir and colleague, is everything ready for the jonasoidal effect?"

The Stop-Captain bowed even more formally. "Truly ready, sir and master."

"The locksheets in place?"

"Truly in place, sir and master."

"The passengers secure?"

"The passengers are secure, numbered, happy, and ready, sir and master."

Then came the last and most serious of questions. "Are my pinlighters warmed with their pin-sets and ready for combat?"

"Ready for combat, sir and master." With these words the Stop-Captain withdrew. Magno Taliano smiled to his pinlighters. Through the minds of all of them there passed the same thought.

*How could a man that pleasant stay married all those years to a hag like Dolores Oh? How could that witch, that horror, have ever been a beauty? How could that beast have ever been a woman, particularly the divine and glamorous Dolores Oh whose image we still see in four-di every now and then?*

Yet pleasant he was, though long he may have been married to Dolores Oh. Her loneliness and greed might suck at him like a nightmare, but his strength was more than enough strength for two.

Was he not the captain of the greatest ship to sail between the stars?

Even as the pinlighters smiled their greetings back to him, his right hand depressed the golden ceremonial lever of the ship. This instrument alone was mechanical. All other controls in the ship had long since been formed telepathically or electronically.

Within the planoforming room the black skies became visible and the tissue of space shot up around them like boiling water at the base of a waterfall. Outside that one room the passengers still walked sedately on scented lawns.

From the wall facing him, as he sat rigid in his Go-Captain's chair, Magno Taliano sensed the forming of a pattern which in three or four hundred milliseconds would tell him where he was and would give him the next clue as to how to move.

He moved the ship with the impulses of his own brain, to which the wall was a superlative complement.

The wall was a living brickwork of locksheets, laminated charts, one hundred thousand charts to the inch, the wall preselected and preassembled for all imaginable contingencies of the journey which, each time afresh, took the ship across half-unknown immensities of time and space. The ship leapt, as it had before.

The new star focused.

Magno Taliano waited for the wall to show him where he was, expecting (in partnership with the wall) to flick the ship back into the pattern of stellar space, moving it by immense skips from source to destination.

This time nothing happened.

*Nothing?*

For the first time in a hundred years his mind knew panic.

It couldn't be nothing. Not *nothing*. Something had to focus. The locksheets always focused.

His mind reached into the locksheets and he realized with a devastation beyond all limits of ordinary human grief that they were lost as no ship had ever been lost before. By some error never before committed in the history of mankind, the entire wall was made of duplicates of the same locksheet.

Worst of all, the Emergency Return sheet was lost. They were amid stars none of them had ever seen before, perhaps as little as five hundred million miles, perhaps as far as forty parsecs.

And the locksheet was lost.

And they would die.

As the ship's power failed coldness and blackness and death would crush in on them in a few hours at the most. That then would be all, all of the *Wu-Feinstein*, all of Dolores Oh.

## III

## THE SECRET OF THE OLD DARK BRAIN

Outside of the planoforming room of the *Wu-Feinstein* the passengers had no reason to understand that they were marooned in the nothing-at-all.

Dolores Oh rocked back and forth in an ancient rocking chair. Her haggard face looked without pleasure at the imaginary river that ran past the edge of the lawn. Dita from the Great South House sat on a hassock by her aunt's knees.

Dolores was talking about a trip she had made when she was young and vibrant with beauty, a beauty which brought trouble and hate wherever it went.

". . . so the guardsman killed the captain and then came to my cabin and said to me, 'You've got to marry me now. I've given up everything for your sake,' and I said to him, 'I never said that I loved you. It was sweet of you to get into a fight, and in a way I suppose it is a compliment to my beauty, but it doesn't mean that I belong to you the rest of my life. What do you think I am, anyhow?' "

Dolores Oh sighed a dry, ugly sigh, like the crackling of subzero winds through frozen twigs. "So you see, Dita, being beautiful the way you are is no answer to anything. A woman has got to be herself before she finds out what she is. I know that my lord and husband, the Go-Captain, loves me because my beauty is gone, and with my beauty gone there is nothing but *me* to love, is there?"

An odd figure came out on the verandah. It was a pinlighter in full fighting costume. Pinlighters were never supposed to leave the planoforming room, and it was most extraordinary for one of them to appear among the passengers.

He bowed to the two ladies and said with the utmost courtesy: "Ladies, will you please come into the planoforming room? We have need that you should see the Go-Captain now."

Dolores' hand leapt to her mouth. Her gesture of grief was as automatic as the striking of a snake. Dita sensed that her aunt had been waiting a hundred years and more for disaster, that her aunt had craved ruin for her husband the way that some people crave love and others crave death.

Dita said nothing. Neither did Dolores, apparently at second thought, utter a word.

They followed the pinlighter silently into the planoforming room.

The heavy door closed behind them.

Magno Taliano was still rigid in his Captain's chair.

He spoke very slowly, his voice sounding like a record played too slowly on an ancient parlophone.

"*We are lost in space, my dear,*" said the frigid, ghostly voice of the Captain, still in his Go-Captain's trance. "*We are lost in space and I thought that perhaps if your mind aided mine we might think of a way back.*"

Dita started to speak.

A pinlighter told her: "Go ahead and speak, my dear. Do you have any suggestion?"

"Why don't we just go back? It would be humiliating, wouldn't it? Still it would be better than dying. Let's use the Emergency Return Locksheet and go on right back. The world will forgive Magno Taliano for a single failure after thousands of brilliant and successful trips."

The pinlighter, a pleasant enough young man, was as friendly and calm as a doctor informing someone of a death or of a mutilation. "The impossible has happened, Dita from the Great South House. All the locksheets are wrong. They are all the same one. And not one of them is good for emergency return."

With that the two women knew where they were. They knew that space would tear into them like threads being pulled out of a fiber so that they would either die bit by bit as the hours passed and as the material of their bodies faded away a few molecules here and a few there. Or, alternatively, they could die all at once in a flash if the Go-Captain chose to kill himself and the ship rather than to wait for a slow death. Or, if they believed in religion, they could pray.

The pinlighter said to the rigid Go-Captain, "We think we see a familiar pattern at the edge of your own brain. May we look in?"

Taliano nodded very slowly, very gravely.

The pinlighter stood still.

The two women watched. Nothing visible happened, but they knew that beyond the limits of vision and yet before their eyes a great drama was being played out. The minds of the pinlighters probed deep into the mind of the frozen Go-Captain, searching amid the synapses for the secret of the faintest clue to their possible rescue.

Minutes passed. They seemed like hours.

At last the pinlighter spoke. "We can see into your midbrain, Captain. At the edge of your paleocortex there is a star pattern which resembles the upper left rear of our present location."

The pinlighter laughed nervously. "We want to know can you fly the ship home on your brain?"

Magno Taliano looked with deep tragic eyes at the inquirer. His slow voice came out at them once again since he dared not leave the half-trance which held the entire ship in stasis. *"Do you mean can I fly the ship on a brain alone? It would burn out my brain and the ship would be lost anyhow. . . ."*

"But we're lost, lost, lost," screamed Dolores Oh. Her face was alive with hideous hope, with a hunger for ruin, with a greedy welcome of disaster. She screamed at her husband, "Wake up, my darling, and let us die together. At least we can belong to each other that much, that long, forever!"

"Why die?" said the pinlighter softly. "You tell him, Dita."

Said Dita, "Why not try, sir and uncle?"

Slowly Magno Taliano turned his face toward his niece. Again his hollow voice sounded. *"If I do this I shall be a fool or a child or a dead man but I will do it for you."*

Dita had studied the work of the Go-Captains and she knew well enough that if the paleocortex was lost the personality became intellectually sane, but emotionally crazed. With the most ancient part of the brain gone the fundamental controls of hostility, hunger, and sex disappeared. The most ferocious of animals and the most brilliant of men were reduced to a common level—a level of infantile friendliness in which lust and playfulness and gentle, unappeasable hunger became the eternity of their days.

Magno Taliano did not wait.

He reached out a slow hand and squeezed the hand of Dolores Oh. "*As I die you shall at last be sure I love you.*"

Once again the women saw nothing. They realized they had been called in simply to give Magno Taliano a last glimpse of his own life.

A quiet pinlighter thrust a beam-electrode so that it reached square into the paleocortex of Captain Magno Taliano.

The planoforming room came to life. Strange heavens swirled about them like milk being churned in a bowl.

Dita realized that her partial capacity of telepathy was functioning even without the aid of a machine. With her mind she could feel the dead wall of the locksheets. She was aware of the rocking of the *Wu-Feinstein* as it leapt from space to space, as uncertain as a man crossing a river by leaping from one ice-covered rock to the other.

In a strange way she even knew that the paleocortical part of her uncle's brain was burning out at last and forever, that the star patterns which had been frozen in the locksheets lived on in the infinitely complex pattern of his own memories, and that with the help of his own telepathic pinlighters he was burning out his brain cell by cell in order for them to find a way to the ship's destination. This indeed was his last trip.

Dolores Oh watched her husband with a hungry greed surpassing all expression.

Little by little his face became relaxed and stupid.

Dita could see the midbrain being burned blank, as the ship's controls with the help of the pinlighters searched through the most magnificent intellect of its time for a last course into harbor.

Suddenly Dolores Oh was on her knees, sobbing by the hand of her husband.

A pinlighter took Dita by the arm.

"We have reached destination," he said.

"And my uncle?"

The pinlighter looked at her strangely.

She realized he was speaking to her without moving his lips—speaking mind-to-mind with pure telepathy.

"Can't you see it?"

She shook her head dazedly.

The pinlighter thought his emphatic statement at her once again.

"As your uncle burned out his brain, you picked up his skills. Can't you sense it? You are a Go-Captain yourself and one of the greatest of us."

"And he?"

The pinlighter thought a merciful comment at her.

Magno Taliano had risen from his chair and was being led from the room by his wife and consort, Dolores Oh. He had the amiable smile of an idiot, and his face for the first time in more than a hundred years trembled with shy and silly love.

# THE MAN WHO TASTED ASHES
## (FEBRUARY 1959)
## ALGIS BUDRYS
## (B. 1931)

Algis Budrys broke into science fiction in 1952 with a story in *Astounding*. A year later, he became an editorial assistant at *Galaxy*, where he was later to achieve respect as one of the finest critics in SF, a reputation that is still climbing as these words are written. His best-known novels are *Who?* (1958), the widely acclaimed *Rogue Moon* (1960), and *Michaelmas* (1977), but his generally excellent shorter fiction is shamefully unavailable except for one collection, *Blood and Burning* (1978).

He had one novel serialized in *If, Amsirs and the Iron Thorn* (1967, as "The Iron Thorn"), which also published his excellent novelette "Die, Shadow!" in the May 1963 issue.

## MEMOIR BY ALGIS BUDRYS

My awareness of *If* as a force in the science-fiction community came and went, undergoing peculiar metamorphoses. This subjective picture more or less matched the evolutions in the magazine.

Its earliest years coincided with the beginning of my professional career; I sold my first stories in the same month it first appeared. But it appeared in upstate New York, initiated by a man no one had ever heard of in SF circles—James Quinn, a publisher of crossword-puzzle magazines—and most of us were trudging back and forth only among editorial offices in New York City.

It was possible to gather from its contents that Quinn was a capital-letter Humanist. Most of the stories he published were sharply opposed to the gloss and glitter of contemporary consumer technology; he especially seemed to have it in for cars and the undeniable dehumanizing aspects of the burgeoning highway culture. Other favorite targets were network TV in particular and the mass entertainment industry in general. Pop hedonism infuriated *If*, and presumably Quinn. All were laudable foresights, as it happens, but reading story after polemical story in issue after issue cast a certain pall.

There were high spots. I remember—unfortunately not in detail—a short story in which a returning white astronaut finds the U.S. firmly in the hands of blacks. The blacks were depicted as rather middle-class types, given to three-piece suits and lip-service liberalism, which made their ineradicable basic antiwhite racial bias all the more poignant. The whites were called "sharkies"—this was long before the common use of "honky," or of "black" for "Negro"—and the story was altogether—uncomfortably altogether—out of place in the early 1950s.

At the time, it was clear to (almost) everyone that the Negroes were being swiftly and easily assimilated into the only culture that counted—the urban, enlightened civilization of the future which had already come into being in the North. Many SF stories, such as Fredric Brown's and Mack Reynolds's contemporaneous *Galaxy* piece, "Dark Interlude," casually assumed that the Earthman of the future would be slightly, attractively, cocoa-and-milk in color, rather like Lena Horne in MGM makeup. The indignant and effective liberalism of "Interlude" did directly attack Southern rural anti-Negro bias, by showing its protagonist murderously opposed to the romanticized miscegenation which I think we all believed would, over the generations, solve that sociopolitical problem in the nicest possible way.

But Quinn succeeded himself as editor by appointing Paul Fairman, a man tainted in most New York City minds by a past association with the Chicago *Amazing* and *Fantastic Adventures*, and that did not improve the magazine's credentials downtown. Fairman was too much the pro, not sufficiently the individual in print, and, from his recent writings in such media as *Startling Stories* and *Thrilling Wonder*, hardly the deep thinker. At a time when *The Magazine of Fantasy & Science Fiction* and *Galaxy Science Fiction* were at the forefront of what was new, and *Astounding* was still essentially unimpaired in presenting the best of what was old, Quinn's publication seemed not specially considerable.

I'm not aware that anyone in New York—which meant everyone of any importance to SF—ever contemplated writing for *If* directly. It was a salvage market, to which writers sent the material rejected by the Big Three, because *If* at least looked like a decently produced magazine and paid about two-thirds of what the top markets offered. Larry Shaw's great coup as an editor, for instance, came when he got James Blish's "A Case of Conscience" novella ahead of *F&SF* after *Galaxy* had in effect rejected it by demanding a heavy rewrite.

Shaw had succeeded Fairman, and although he moved to Poughkeepsie to work on the magazine, he was frequently in New York, and was a friend of mine. From time to time, we talked about my writing for *If*, but nothing came of that. (The relationship bore fruit when Shaw became the founding editor of *Infinity* years later, but that was years later.)

Actually, it was Frank Kelly Freas, my illustrator friend, who first convinced me there was something in particular to be said for *If*.

One of my early novelettes had finally found a home there. "The Strangers" is from my complicated period, which resulted in a series of extremely involved, talky, and sententious long pieces that fell through the top of the market like lard dumplings. Published in the June 1955 issue, it was unexpectedly given a Freas cover, which is clearly the best thing about it, and had been purchased by Quinn after Shaw had departed because, like all other editors of the Poughkeepsie *If*, he had never found a way to make the magazine show much of any profit.

I've never been able to understand why Quinn liked that story, or what in it he found sufficiently promising to outweigh its complex faults. Time was soon to prove I hadn't solved that puzzle. But meanwhile it was two hundred fifty dollars or thereabouts that I'd had no right to expect, and perhaps some sort of vindication of the thinking that had led to my writing it in the first place. When Kelly told me he had been talking me up to Quinn as a promising new writer, and that he himself found Quinn a gentleman and an intellect, I began to modify my view of the whole matter.

Kelly and I, and our new respective wives, were very close at the time, each family conscious of a need to establish a firm foothold on the SF landscape, neither so secure that working for an out-of-town account was out of the question. A particularly fruitful working relationship had established itself between Kelly and myself. I was always delighted when he was assigned to illustrate one of my stories because he always did such a good job. If in any doubt about the tone of what I'd meant—for *ASF*, for instance, he often had to work from editorial synopses, rather than actual manuscripts—he'd talk it over with me, or borrow my carbon, and then would find some way of not only illustrating but illuminating my idea.

Conversely, finished Freas art, or comprehensive sketches for art he was in the process of selling, had sparked some of my best stories. These were days when magazines often bought art either to run as completely independent pieces or as bases from which writers would be assigned to do stories to fit. I had written the original short story for "Who?" around a Freas *Fantastic Universe* cover, and the first story in the then-promising Doncaster Industrial Linens series for a Freas *Future* painting, and it was obvious there was a particularly effective harmony between Kelly and myself.

So when Kelly showed me a comprehensive sketch he was doing for *If,* everything seemed right. It showed a fellow in a toreador suit, made up and bejeweled, wearing a curly blond wig and attentively cleaning a gun. The finished painting, with its fine detail, would be done after Quinn approved the sketch. But meanwhile it was instantly clear to me that the absurd and ill-fitting wig was directly analogous to British judicial wigs, and from that it was no trouble to visualize a culture in which trial by combat had taken on butchy overtones. At some very early point— perhaps because Kelly had already scrawled "The Executioner" on the back of the sketch, perhaps because it was so inevitable a name for the resulting twin works—we had decided on that title without any need for discussion. In taking the sketch up to Poughkeepsie (perhaps it was Schenectady or Newburgh or Rochester or Ithaca, what difference?) Kelly would ask Quinn whether he'd like to see a matching novelette from me. It transpired that not only would he but there would be a little something extra in the rate for doing a story no other magazine had seen beforehand.

Having written a story—which is still fondly recalled in some quarters, and anthologized reasonably often—I sent it off to Quinn and waited for the check. What I got was a rejection, with vague but clearly disappointed references to "all that philosophy stuff" in it, an utterance I still haven't decoded in the light of "The Strangers" and the magazine's track record under Quinn. He may have thought I had a sincere interest in the story's overlay of religiosity, or he may have reacted badly to a discovery that I was a cryptoatheist; as I say, I have never gotten a firm handle on what went wrong, and I knew from the start this was in fact one of my major pieces of work. It was sent over to John Campbell at

*ASF*, and purchased at once with complimentary remarks and a little something extra in the rate, which meant that Quinn's loss was not only my spiritual but material gain.

It appeared as the lead novelette in the January 1956 *ASF*, with Freas interior illustrations which struck me as particularly well done and may be seen in Kelly's own book of his work. The cover for that issue was an SF Christmas card by Van Dongen, unrelated to the story. Which was just as well, because on the stands next month was the April 1956 issue of *If*, with the finished Freas cover illustrating a short story called "The Executioner" by Frank Riley, written around the cover and with some very good interior illustrations by Frank Kelly Freas.

The dimensions of the resulting brouhaha can be imagined and are best not recounted in detail. I have to wonder what Riley felt, since we never had any contact then or at any other time, but I was in no doubt on the feelings of anyone else involved. Campbell, as I recall, spent most of his discussion time in nearly helpless laughter, but Quinn did not.

It was one of those episodes, peculiar to the way SF was written and packaged in those days, which never had a clear resolution, and no lasting animosities anyone could put a finger on. Not too long afterward, Quinn picked up another novelette from me, "The Barbarians" (by John A. Sentry), for the September 1953 issue, so the wounds were not fatal or even festering. ("The Barbarians" was proficiently illustrated by Ed Emshwiller. It is memorable to me mainly because it was sparked by my assertion that the Elizabethan folk song "Barbry Allen" is actually a development of a love/fear relationship with a "cruel, barb'rous Ellen." I manage to conceal this in the written text of the story, which is neither very good nor bad as a story but is set somewhere in an earlier or perhaps later segment of the "Executioner" universe. This is a fact I have never hitherto pointed out to anyone, let alone Quinn in 1953.)

The thing about the Quinn *If* was that when it got an editor who could communicate with what the rest of the world's magazine SF was like, it couldn't relate to him. It lost Shaw before he got fairly started. Then it lost Damon Knight even quicker than that.

Knight was Quinn's last editor, doing most of his work out of the same rickety Milford, Pennsylvania, farmhouse from which he had run most of the moves leading up to the first Milford Conference of professional writers. Earlier stints at Hillman Periodicals'

*Worlds Beyond,* and at *Super Science* and *Astonishing,* had qualified him for here-today-gone-tomorrow conditions, although not
voluntarily. In his brief tenure, he made a serious attempt to get
something special out of the magazine, as if he didn't know Quinn
was searching for a buyer, for sound business reasons, and as if he
didn't know that whatever he did would take longer to be
noticed by the readers than Quinn was apt to give him time for.

"The Man Who Tasted Ashes" was delivered to him in Milford
toward the end of that doomed brief flowering. It was written for
him specifically, because I had the idea he respected me, because
I certainly respected him, and because I expected to be paid
almost immediately. Those were the three best reasons, in the
proper priority order, for doing good SF in those days.

It was written for *delivery* to him specifically, I should have
said. There hadn't been time for an *If* tone to develop. It had
always been a magazine short on personality except when Quinn
was editing it himself, probably because he couldn't communicate
with his editors but could obstruct their communications. So all I
had to go on was what little I knew of Knight's past editing
technique; I decided to simply give him the best story I could. In
1958–59, that meant I would write him a *Venture* story.

*Venture* was the failing sister of *F&SF*. Its editor, Robert Mills,
had in some way caused me to stop writing essentially Campbellian
SF and begin rousting about for other kinds of stories to do. One
means of expressing that was to begin writing stories in which I
knew the beginning and the central character, but not necessarily
the end . . . for me, a totally revolutionary approach.

Sometimes it worked. Some of my favorite and most anthologized stories come from that time. They're all distinguished by
not having the thumper endings visible on my immediately previous work for *ASF.* They're essentially character studies, and they
have the characteristic of simply ending; the protagonist comes to
some break-point in his life, but the world goes on, unsaved,
unshriven, and just about as addled as it was when he began
participating in the events of the story.

So it was with the tale of Ralph Redfern, of which I'll say no
more than it is without a doubt the best work of mine ever
published in *If* at less than novel length. I can also assure you that
almost everyone else in the SF community would not only agree
but would want to take away that terminal qualifier, inasmuch as
the novel I did for Fred Pohl is often cited as a less than absolute
success.

Having been sold to the Guinn Company, *If* became a stable-mate of Frederik Pohl's *Galaxy*, and found a consistent identity at last.

Its sterling record in this period of stability—dynamic stability; terminal stability—needs no recounting here, since I presume it's described elsewhere in this volume.

I'm gradually beginning to realize that Fred Pohl is the hidden Prometheus of SF; he has done more crucial things at more places and times in the history of newsstand science fiction than any other individual. He has also been my literary agent, my opponent at the poker table, my editor, my drinking companion, and my mentor, and my friend, over all the years since 1952. He put me in the business of writing book-review columns, permitted me to court my very best friend under his roof—she having been room-mates at the Modern School of Fashion and Design with Carol Pohl—and lent me cars and money.

For some time, we lived within a few miles of each other in New Jersey. But in late 1961 I had moved to a Chicago suburb, where I still am, and saw Fred only on his infrequent trips through town. Each time, I was moved to write a story, either for *If* or *Galaxy*; a rare thing to do, for at this time I was employed in a variety of salaried positions which cut my free-lance writing time to nearly zero.

For Fred's *If* I wrote the Leigh Brackett novelette I had always wanted to do—"Die, Shadow!" in the May 1963 issue. It would be improved if I had had the sense to let its ten thousand words run out to their natural length of something like twelve thousand words, but, compressed and slighted though some of its elements are, it was still a great deal of fun to play with, although I would not seriously compare it to even workaday Brackett.

And finally, sometime in 1965, Fred worked me around to writing him a novel. This became a four-part serial called "The Iron Thorn," eventually published in paperback as *The Amsirs and the Iron Thorn* by the same Gold Medal Books editor who had had the wit to change the title of my *The Death Machine* to *Rogue Moon*, both times without consultation or permission.

Writing "The Iron Thorn" was a peculiar experience. Large chunks of it were dictated as rough draft into a tape recorder; the typist's transcripts were then gone over more or less meticulously. Often enough, there were puns, homonyms, or other errata caused by this working method. I kept the ones I liked better than my intended statements, and dedicated half the book to her.

Many signatures of the old pulp days cropped up during the experience. For one thing, Fred began running it before it was finished, which accounts for the fact that an announced three-part serial became a four-parter. For another, although Gray Morrow was the illustrator, the Gray Morrow cover for the serial was a found piece; just an odd painting Morrow had offered to Fred, and which fit with material I had coincidentally put into the first installment. For a third, I detested Morrow's interior art for the story, and so was able to take a slap at it while writing the fourth installment.

Opinion on "The Iron Thorn" is decidedly mixed. It appeared to many immediate readers as a story which promised to go one way and then went another. Perhaps. In my own opinion, it's exactly the story I'd been intending to write all along: a tale of the artist brought down by artifice. I'm sure that critics of the next century, or perhaps the one after that, will see its subtleties of nuance and subtext and accord it its proper place in Western literature. Well may they marvel!

But however that will all work out, the thing I most remember about the experience of working for the Pohl *If* was the relaxed venturesomeness of it all; of working for a magazine which differentiated itself from the Big Three by being less than Cosmic in many of its ways; a place that ran good, crisp tales swiftly told, that tried out new writers as a matter of policy, and whose circulation rose and rose while the SF community awards came in. It was, from just about the start of Fred's editing it until its eventual demise in the collapse of Universal Publishing's empire, a very well *liked* magazine. Better liked, as distinguished from institutionalized, than the Big Three. It had finally found the thing it had been looking for since its inception: a viable alternative position in the field.

I rather think that any of *If*'s editors would have published "The Man Who Tasted Ashes," which is another reason for its inclusion here. I'm not so sure about "Die, Shadow!" or "The Iron Thorn" which is to me another indicator that in its final incarnation it had acquired a more distinct personality. But never at any time in its existence had it been without excellences, some more rigidly defined than others, a few antithetical to each other, but each an excellence.

It appeared in the market at a time when an SF boom gave

birth to tens and scores of short-lived magazines from unlikely publishers, and it lived longer—far longer—than most. Of all the unlikely publishers, Quinn was certainly one of the less likely, and yet one of the best in his way. Almost all his peers were simple money-grubbers, riding a trend, putting out packages, folding up and stealing away when the market softened without having done a thing for it or for their readers. That, emphatically, is not what Quinn tried to do or wanted to do. He spent money on higher-quality printing and paper when even the Big Three saw no especial need to embody their contents in more than the bare minimum. He wanted the magazine to carry a flag for something beyond mere wordsmithing. And in the end he chose to sell it rather than cheapen it, which was an option very few around him would even contemplate, much less execute.

If he and Fred had found each other, the result would have been as short-lived and unsatisfactory as what happened when he found Shaw, or Knight; he was not a man to let go the reins sufficiently. But when his magazine and Fred found each other, that was a happier story. And as for James Quinn, he may not have known that much about what the SF world was really like, but he knew a thing or two about the real world, and he knew how to comport himself with dignity and rectitude within it. That's not all bad.


# THE MAN WHO TASTED ASHES

The car he'd stolen was a beautifully groomed thing: all polished lacquer and chrome, with almost brand-new dual tread whitewall tires on the nickeled wire wheels. But the transmission was bad, the brake drums scraped, and there was a short circuit in the wiring somewhere, so that he had to keep over sixty miles per hour or the generator would not charge at all. He would have stolen another one if he could, but he had got onto the turnpike before he realized just how unreliable this one was. If he changed cars at a restaurant, it would be reported and the police would stop him when he tried to leave the turnpike.

No, he was trapped with what he had. Hunched over the wheel of his roaring cage, the yellowish headlights reflecting white from the lane markers, Redfern swept his eyes systematically over the instruments: ammeter, fuel gauge, oil pressure, water temperature, speedometer, odometer. He thought of himself as doing it systematically, every ten minutes, like a professionally trained driver. Actually, he was dividing his attention almost equally between the road and the odometer. A hundred and ten miles covered, seventy miles to go, ninety minutes before the ship was due to take off, with or without him, average speed required: 46.6, approx.; round off to allow for stopping the car at the exit toll booth, for covering two miles of back roads, for leaving the car and running an unknown distance across a weed-grown field to the ship's airlock—they would take off on schedule with him six inches from the slamming airlock door; they would not stay themselves a microsecond to accommodate him—say fifty miles per hour, average. Then allow for speedometer error. Say fifty-five miles per hour, indicated, average. Allow for odome-ter error. Say sixty miles per hour, indicated, average. Allow for unforeseen delays. Sixty-five miles per hour.

Redfern's foot trembled on the accelerator pedal. His thigh ached from hours of unremitting pressure. His car flashed by signboards, wove continually around immense trailer trucks in the slow lane. His mind raced to keep up with the changing figures on the odometer. He wished he weren't feeling a slight miss in the engine whenever he eased up on the accelerator. He cursed the car's owner for his false-front prodigality with wax and whitewalls.

He looked at his watch again. Four in the morning. He turned the radio on, ignoring his fear that something else might happen to the car's wiring.

"—And that's the news," the announcer's professionally relaxed voice said. "After a word about United Airlines, we'll hear, first, Carl Orff's *Carmina Burana*, followed by—"

His watch was slow.

Five minutes? Fifteen minutes? How long did the news take?

He held the watch to his ear. It was an expensive one, wafer thin, beautifully crafted, left over from his younger days—he could barely hear it running. Was it running at all?

Redfern was a leathery man, his yellowish-white hair brushed back from angular temples, a scruffy Guards moustache over his nearly invisible lips. His suits were made for him by a London tailor, from measurements taken in 1925; they were gored and belted in the backs of the jackets. Outdoors, he wore a Burberry and carried a briefcase. People who saw him on the street in

Washington always took him for someone with diplomatic connections. But since Redfern was always seen afoot, these connections perforce had to be minor. Was he an assistant attaché of sorts, perhaps? At his age? Looking at Redfern, people would wonder about it.

People. But the man who'd sat easily on the edge of Redfern's lumpy bed in the wallpapered hotel room—that man, now . . .

That man had coal-black hair, broad, flat cheekbones above a sharply narrowing chin, oval, maroon-pupiled eyes and cyanotic lips. He smiled easily and agreeably across the room.

Redfern sat in the one chair, sipping at the water tumbler half-full of gin. The bottle his visitor had brought up was standing on the bureau. His visitor, who had given the name of Charlie Spence, was not drinking.

"You don't look like a Charlie," Redfern said abruptly over the tumbler's rim. "You look as cold as ice."

Spence laughed, his small mouth stretching as far as it could. "Maybe I'm made of it," he said. "But then, you're nothing but a lump of coal. Carbon." He brushed his fingertips together.

"But then," Redfern mocked sharply, "*I* don't pretend to be gregarious."

"Oh, I don't pretend—don't pretend at all. I *am* gregarious. I love the company of people. I've been moving about among them for several years, now."

"All right," Redfern said sharply, "we've already settled that. Let's let it be. I don't care where you come from—I don't really care what you're made of. It may surprise you, but I've thought for some time that if people were coming to this world from other places, they'd be bound to get in touch with me sooner or later."

"Why on Earth should we try to get in touch with you?" Spence asked, nonplused.

"Because if you people have been coming here for years, then you're not here openly. You've got purposes of your own. People with purposes of their own generally come to me."

Charlie Spence began to chuckle. "I like you," he laughed. "I really do. You're a rare type."

"Yes," said Redfern, "and now let's get down to business." He gestured toward the bureau top. "Pour me some more of that." Alcohol affected him swiftly but not deeply. Once it had stripped him of the ordinary inhibitions, he could go on drinking for some time before his intellect lost its edge. Since he always took two aspirins and went straight to bed at that point, it was not a serious sort of weakness. But without his inhibitions he was a very unpleasant man.

"It's a simple business," Charlie Spence was saying a little later. "The ambassador will land at National Airport and be met by the usual sort of reception committee. Red carpet, band, dignitaries, and so forth. But the red carpet will be a little shabby, the band won't be first-rate, and the reception committee will not be quite as high-ranking as it might be. After all, the ambassador's country is definitely on the other side of the fence."

"Yes," Redfern drawled. "The protocol of prejudice."

"Oh, no, no, nothing deliberate," Spence said, with a hand raised. "Diplomats pride themselves on equal courtesy to all. But the employee in charge of caring for the carpets simply won't do his best. The band won't play with any great enthusiasm. And any of your officials who happen to be ill, with colds or similar afflictions, will honestly decide their health precludes the effort of attending. This is simply human nature, and any snub will be completely unintended."

"I heard you the first time. What's all this to do with me?"

"Well, now," Charlie Spence explained, "the ambassador's not from a particularly large nation in their bloc. It seems doubtful they'd bother to send along any of their own security police. The only guards present will likely be American Secret Service personnel, extending courtesy protection."

"Yes."

"So. In the first place, the ambassador is really a small fish. In the second place, no American, even a trained professional sworn to his duty, is apt to be quite as devoted to the ambassador's life as he would be to that of, say, any American congressman. Those two factors represent a potential assassin's margin of safety."

"And what're you meddling in our politics for?" Redfern growled.

"*Your* politics? Redfern, my dear fellow, it may or may not be your planet, but it's most assuredly our solar system."

The neck of the bottle tinked against the lip of Redfern's glass. "And I'm your assassin?"

"You are."

"What makes you think I'll do it?" Redfern cocked his head and looked narrowly at Spence.

"A compulsive need to meddle in human history."

"Oh?"

Charlie Spence laughed. "You were cashiered from your country's foreign service in nineteen hundred and thirty-two. But you've never stopped mixing into international situations. Gun running, courier work, a little export-import, a little field work for foreign development corporations . . . and, now and then, a few more serious escapades. Don't tell me you don't enjoy it, Redfern. It's a very hard life, all told. No one would stay in it as long as you have if it didn't satisfy his need for power."

Redfern pinched his lips together even more tightly, in the fleeting reflex with which he always acknowledged the truth. "I wasn't cashiered," he said. "I resigned without prejudice."

"Oh, yes; yes, you did. Being unpleasant to one's superiors doesn't disgrace a man—it merely makes him unemployable. Except for special purposes that don't require a pukka sahib. And here I am, as you said, with a special purpose. Ten thousand dollars, on completion, Redfern, and the satisfaction of having started World War III."

Redfern's eyes glittered. "All over one little ambassador?" he asked carefully.

"Over one little ambassador. In life, he's not considered worth the trouble of protecting him. And no one but a rather stout and liverish woman in the Balkans will mourn him in death. But when he dies, his side will suddenly discover a great and genuine moral indignation. Why? Because they will be truly shocked at such a thing happening in America."

"World War III," Redfern said ruminatively.

"Exactly. You'll shake the ambassador's hand. An hour later, when he's already safe inside his embassy refreshing himself after his trip, he'll fall into a sudden coma. The embassy will close its doors, issue a misleading statement, and call its doctor."

"Yes."

"Very well. The embassy staff has taken routine steps, and waits for the ambassador to recover. But, just to allow for all eventualities, the unofficial courier service is already transmitting a notification to the government at home. The doctor examines the patient and discovers an inflamed puncture on his right hand. Another message goes home. The ambassador dies, and tests indicate poison. Obviously, it was hoped the puncture would go unnoticed and the cause of death, which resembles cerebral occlusion, would be mistaken. But the tiny needle must not have been quite sterilized, by accident, and the clever doctor has penetrated the scheme—and another message goes home, before the American State Department even suspects anything serious."

"Hmm. I'll simply shake his hand?"

Charlie Spence reached into his pocket. "Wearing this." He held out a crumpled something, the size of a handkerchief. Redfern took it and unfolded it. "A mask," Spence said. "Drawn over your head, it will mold new features for you. It'll be devilish uncomfortable, but you won't have to wear it long."

"It'll make me look like someone entitled to be on the field?"

Spence grinned the grin of a Renaissance Florentine. "Better than that. It will give you the composite features of six people entitled to be on the field. You will look like none of them, but you will look superficially familiar to anyone who knows any of them. The subsequent questioning of witnesses will yield amusing results, I think."

"Very clever. Good technique. Confuse and obscure. But then, you've practiced it a long time." Redfern pushed himself abruptly out of the chair and went into the adjoining bathroom, keeping the door open. "Excuse me," he said perfunctorily.

"Lord, you're a type!" Charlie Spence said. "Will you do it?"

"What?" Redfern said from the bathroom.

"Will you do it?" Spence repeated, raising his voice.

Redfern came out, picking up the gin bottle, and sat back down in the chair. He tipped the bottle over the glass. "Maybe."

"I've told you too much for you to back out now," Spence said with a frown.

"Rubbish!" Redfern spat. "Don't try to bully me. You don't care what any of the natives tell each other about you. There are dozens of people living off their tales about you. It's to your advantage to hire native helpers wherever you can—if they're caught, who cares what wild tales they tell? You'd be insane to risk losing one of your own people." He looked sharply into Charlie Spence's eyes. "I don't suppose you fancy the thought of a dissecting table."

Charlie Spence licked his lips with a flicker of his tongue. "Don't be too sure of yourself," he said after a moment, in a more careful tone of voice.

Redfern snorted. "If I acted only on what I was sure of, I'd still be an embassy clerk."

"And you wouldn't like that, I suppose?" Charlie Spence, recovered, was looking around the room. "Sometimes? At night, when you can't sleep?"

"I want an out," Redfern said brusquely. "I won't do it without accident insurance."

"Oh?" Charlie Spence's eyebrows quivered.

"If I'm caught in the field, I'm caught and that's it. I'll protect you."

"Professionalism. I like that. Go on—what if you get away from the field?"

"If I get away, but there's trouble, I want a rendezvous with one of your ships."

"Oh, ho!" Charlie Spence said. "You do, do you?"

"I'll cover my tracks, if you think it's important, but I want a rendezvous. I want to be off this planet if there's trouble. Change that—I want to be off it in any case, and if there's no trouble, I can always be brought back."

"Oh, ho!" Charlie Spence repeated with a grin. "Yes, I'd think you *would* want to watch the next war from some safe place." It was easy to see he'd been expecting Redfern to lead up to this all along.

"Have it your way," Redfern said ungraciously.

Charlie Spence was laughing silently, his eyes aslit. "All right, Redfern," he said indulgently. He reached into his card case, took out a photograph of a dumpy blonde woman and a string-haired man on the porch of a Middle Western farmhouse, and carefully split it with his thumbnails. Out of the center, he took a bit of tissue paper, and stuck the front and back of the photograph together again. Replacing the card case in his pocket, he handed the slip of paper to Redfern.

"Dip it in your drink," he said.

He watched while Redfern complied, but kept his eyes away from the short handwritten directions the alcohol brought up. "Don't repeat the location aloud. I don't know it, and don't want to. Memorize it and destroy it. And I tell you now, Redfern, if the ambassador doesn't die, there'll be no ship." He smiled. "For that matter, you have no guarantee there'll be any ship at all."

Redfern growled. "I know."

"Lord, what meager hopes you live on, Redfern!"

"You're through here now, aren't you?" Redfern said.

"Yes . . ." Charlie Spence said with pursed lips.

"Then get out." He took the palm hypodermic Charlie Spence handed him in its green pasteboard box, and closed the hotel room door behind his visitor.

Thirty-five miles to go. His watch now read 4:30. It hadn't stopped, but was merely slow. If he'd thought to have it cleaned by a jeweler, last year or even the year before that, it would be accurate now. As it was, he had less than an hour, and he would be off the turnpike fairly soon, onto roads that were paved but had been laid out in the days of horse-drawn wagons.

He tried another station on the radio, but that was playing popular music. A third was conducting some sort of discussion program about water fluoridation. And that was all. The rest of the dial yielded only hisses or garbled snatches from Minneapolis or Cincinnati. His ammeter showed a steady discharge as long as the radio was on, no matter how fast he drove. He turned it off and steered the car, his face like a graven image. He was seething with anger, but none of it showed. As an adolescent, he had made the mistake of equating self-possession with maturity, and had studiously practiced the mannerism, with the inevitable result that he had only learned to hide his feelings from himself. He was the prisoner of his practice now, to the extent that he often had to search deep to find what emotion might be driving him at any particular time. Often he found it only in retrospect, when it was too late.

That lunch with Dick Farleagh this afternoon . . .

It had been difficult even to reach him; a call to the embassy—"*Who* shall I tell Mr. Farleagh is calling? Mr. Redfern?" and then the barely muffled aside, a whispered "Oh, dear." Then the pause, and finally, with a sigh: "Mr. Farleagh will speak to you now, Mr. Redfern," as though the secretary thought a bad mistake was being made.

"Dickie," Redfern said with tension.

"What is it, Ralph?" Farleagh's voice was too neutral. Obviously, he had taken the call only out of curiosity, because he had not heard directly from Redfern in nearly fifteen years. But he must already be regretting it—probably he didn't like being called Dickie, now that his junior clerk days were well behind him. Redfern ought to have thought of that, but he was in a hurry, and hurry, like liquor, always took away his social graces.

"I have to speak to you."

"Yes?"

Redfern waited. Only after a moment did he understand that Farleagh had no intention of meeting him in person.

"I can't do it over the telephone."

"I see." Now the voice was crisp, as Farleagh decided he could meet the situation with routine procedure. "I'll ask my secretary to make an appointment. She'll call you. Can you leave a number?"

"No, no, no!" Redfern was shouting into the telephone. "I won't be fobbed off like that!" His words and actions were registering on his consciousness in only the haziest way. He had no idea he was shouting. "This is too important for your blasted conventionalities! I won't put up with it! I have to see you." His voice was wheedling, now, though he did not realize that, either. "Today. No later than lunch."

Farleagh said with quiet shock, "There's no need to rave at me. Now, take hold of yourself, Ralph, and perhaps we can talk this out sensibly."

"Will you come or won't you?" Redfern demanded. "I'll be at the Grosvenor bar in an hour. I'm warning you you'll regret it if you don't come."

There was a long pause, during which there was a sudden buzz in the phone, and the sound of Redfern's coin being collected. In a moment, the operator would be asking for another dime.

"Are you there?" Farleagh asked with maddening detachment. "See here, Redfern—" now the tenor of his thinking was unmistakeable in his voice, even before he continued—"if it's a matter of a few dollars or so, I can arrange it, I suppose. I'll mail you a check. You needn't bother to return it.'

"Deposit ten cents for the next three minutes, please," the operator said at that moment.

"To hell with your blasted money!" Redfern cried. "I have to see you. Will you be there?"

"I—" Farleagh had begun when the operator cut them off.

Redfern stared in bafflement at the telephone. Then he thrust it back on its cradle and walked briskly out of the booth.

He waited in the Grosvenor bar for an hour and a half, rationing his drinks out of a sense that he ought to keep his head. He was not a stupid man. He knew that he always got into quarrels whenever he'd been drinking.

He rationed his drinks, but after the first one he did so out of a spiteful feeling that he ought to, to please that stuffed shirt Farleagh. He already knew that if Farleagh appeared at all, their meeting would not do the slightest good. Hunched over his drink, glowering at the door, he now only wanted to be able to say, afterwards, that he had made the utmost effort to do the right thing.

Farleagh came, at last, looking a great deal beefier than he had when he and Redfern were in public school together. His hand-shake was perfunctory—his maddeningly level gray eyes cata-logued the changes in Redfern's face with obvious disapproval—and he practically shepherded Redfern to the farthest and darkest table. Obviously, he did not relish being seen in a public place with a man of Redfern's character. Redfern drawled: "You've gone to fat."

Farleagh's eyes remained steady. "And you to lean. What is it you want, Redfern?"

"If it isn't money?" Redfern's mouth curled. He turned and signaled to a waiter. "What will you have, Dickie?"

"None for me, thank you," Farleagh said in an impassive drone. "I'm pressed for time."

"Are you? You've no idea, do you, that I might be on a close schedule myself." Redfern glanced at his watch. The ambassador's plane was due at National Airport in two hours, and there was a great deal still to be done. "You've kept me waiting." He waved the waiter away in sudden irritation, without ordering. "Now, you listen to me," he told Farleagh. "I'm going to be at a definite place and time tonight. Here." He flicked the balled bit of tissue paper across the table into Farleagh's lap.

Farleagh picked it out and transferred it to a side pocket. He would have been a very bad diplomat if he had ignored it. But it was plain he was merely providing for an extremely remote possibility. "Redfern," he said, "if you're attempting to involve my government in some scheme of yours, that will be the end. You'll have gone too far."

"*Our* government, Dickie," Redfern almost snarled. "I still carry my passport."

"Precisely," Farleagh said. "I'm sure the American authorities would deport you, at our request. If you stand trial at home, you'll not get off easily."

"There's nothing in my past record that breaks the law at home."

"There's a great deal about you that breaks laws more popular than those in books."

"Damn you, Farleagh," Redfern said in a voice he did not know was high and almost tearful, "you'd better be there tonight."

"Why?"

"Because if you aren't, and I do get involved in something, it'll be found out soon enough that you could have been there. I warn you now, Farleagh, if I go down, it won't be easily. Perhaps it won't matter to *you* if *your* career's smashed. I tell you now, there's a great deal more involved in this than your career."

Farleagh was still not taking his eyes away from Redfern's face, nor moderating the set of his mouth. He gave the appearance, sitting there in his expensive suit, with his graying black hair combed down sleekly, of enormous patience nearly at an end.

"Very well, then!" Redfern exclaimed. "I don't care if you believe me or not." He thrust his chair back. "But if someone gets ill who shouldn't, today, you'd better believe me!" He stalked away, his Burberry flapping from his arm, his briefcase banging into the backs of chairs, his face an unhealthy red.

He drove vengefully, in a rage that included the car and the radio, his watch, Farleagh, Charlie Spence, and the world.

Five o'clock, by his watch. He turned into the exit ramp with a squealing from the tires, and one part of his mind was hoping there would be a blowout, just to prove something to the car's owner. He touched the brakes almost reluctantly, and at the same time cursed their criminal softness. He fumbled on the seat beside him for the toll ticket, and searched in his nearly empty wallet. He had had to spend a good deal of money today—more than he'd expected, for the drug and the explosive. It had never been his intention to steal a car, but rental had been out of the question. He knew, and damned the fact, that another man might have gotten better prices with his suppliers. But what sort of logic was there in making up to criminals, slapping their backs and buying them drinks, talking to them on an equal basis, when he could not even see the need to do that sort of thing in his dealings with respectable people?

He slapped the ticket and his two remaining dollar bills into the toll attendant's palm, and accelerated again without bothering even to look toward the man. He had seen no sign of drawn-up police cars anywhere around the toll plaza. That was the important thing, the only important thing at the moment.

Now that he was off the turnpike, he forgot he had been so afraid of being stopped for automobile theft. It had been another in a succession of thin-edged risks which could be shown to extend back to the beginning of his independent life. He forgot it as he had forgotten his fears concerning all the others—as he had forgotten that he had been afraid something would go wrong at the airport this afternoon, or that he would be caught as he hung about in Washington for hours afterward, until he was sure the embassy was acting as if something were wrong behind its doors.

As he drove now, forcing his car around the twisting mountain corners, he had other things to be afraid of.

Farleagh might not be there—might have been stubborn, or unaccountably stupid, or simply too slow, in spite of the margin Redfern had allowed him. He looked at his watch again as he turned off onto a dirt track leading almost straight up the hill. Five-twenty by his watch. He had perhaps five minutes.

He took one deep breath—one, and no more, just as he had done at the airport gate this afternoon, and as he had done on other occasions in his life—and drove the car into a tangle of shrubbery just past a mortared-stone culvert that was his position marker. He shut off the ignition and sat as if stupefied by the engine's silence. Almost instantly, the headlights were no more than a sickly orange glow upon the leaves pressed against the car's grille. He shut them off, picked up his briefcase, and abandoned the car. Burberry flapping around his thighs, he trotted across the road and plunged down a slight decline into a stand of tamaracks. It was dark except for the remaining light of a low half-moon seeping through the overcast.

He moved with practiced efficiency through the trees, keeping his direction by paralleling the brook that had trickled through the culvert, until he emerged without warning into an open and long-neglected field, choked with proliferating brush, entirely sur-rounded by evergreens, with the spaceship, tall as an oil refin-ery's cracking tower, standing in its center.

The airlock door in the side of it was open. Redfern began to force his way through the brush, toward the extended ladder which connected the airlock with the ground. There was a single light in the lock chamber. No other lights were visible—the ship was a complex silhouette of struts and vanes, given the reality of depth only by that open door, and what that door might lead to, Redfern could not really guess.

As he struggled up to the ladder, he was arming the satchel charge in his briefcase.

There was still no sign of life from inside the ship. But as he climbed the ladder, hoisting himself awkwardly with his one free hand, the ladder began to retract with the sound of metal sliding into metal, and other mechanical sounds resonated out of the hull, like generators coming up to speed, and relays in a sequence of switching operations. He looked up and saw the airlock door quiver and begin to turn on its massive hinges.

With a strained motion of his arm, he threw the charge overarm into the airlock, and let go the ladder. He heard the briefcase thump to the deck in the lock chamber, while he himself was falling ten or twelve feet back to the ground. When the explosion came, he was sprawled on the ground, rearing up on his out-thrust arms, and he stared in fascination at the flame-shot billow of orange smoke gouting through the still half-open lock.

He rolled, off to one side, as the outer door rebounded from the hull. He was afraid it might fall on him, but then he saw it was still hanging, like a broken gate.

The starting-noises inside the ship came to a complete stop. He had done what he had hoped to do—breached the hull, and activated the safety cut-offs in the controls. The ship was caught, earthbound, possibly not for very long, but perhaps for long enough.

The brush crackled and plucked at his pasage. He could not bring himself to look away from the ship, and he blundered through the undergrowth with his arms behind him, feeling his way. The light in the airlock chamber was off now, but something was still burning in there, with a dull smoldering red flicker.

A hand placed itself flat between his shoulderblades. "All right, easy now, sir," a voice said.

He turned convulsively, his face contorted as if by pain, and made out a tall, huskily built young man in a narrow-brimmed hat, who was holding a short-barreled revolver in his other hand. The brush was parting all around him—there were many men here—and suddenly a portable floodlight shot up a beam to strike the airlock.

"We were just about ready to send a man aboard when you crippled them, sir," the young man said with his trained politeness.

"Is Farleagh here?" Redfern demanded.

"Yes, sir, Mr. Farleagh's back among the trees, with the chief."

A man had stepped up to the base of the ship, where the ladder had rested. Like Redfern's young man, he wore a civilian suit as if it had been made by a uniform manufacturer. "Aboard the ship!" he shouted up through cupped hands. "Can you hear me? Do you speak English? This is the Secret Service."

There was a grating sound up in the lock chamber, as someone forced open the balky inner door. Then a man stumbled up to the edge and looked down, his white coveralls smudged and a strained look on his face. He squinted at the Secret Service man.

"Jesus Christ, yes, I speak English," he said in outrage. "Who threw that bomb? This is a goddamn Air Force project, and there's gonna be all kinds of hell."

"Oh, no, you don't!" Redfern shouted, mortally afraid things could still go wrong. "It won't wash—not with me to testify against you."

The Secret Service man at the base of the ship turned his head in Redfern's direction long enough to show his exasperation. Then he pointed his pistol up at the man in the lock, "Jump down, you."

There was the sound of someone heavy coming toward them through the brush. After a moment, Farleagh said: "There you are."

"Hullo, Dickie," Redfern grinned at Farleagh in the spottily reflected light. "Now you know."

"Know what?" Farleagh asked heavily.

Redfern shifted his feet nervously. "Why I got myself cashiered years ago. You see, I knew they were coming here—at least, I believed they were—and I decided what sort of human being they would be mostly likely to contact."

Rage crossed Farleagh's face at last, and shocked Redfern. "Stop it, Redfern," he said savagely. "For once in your life, admit you're the sort of man you are."

After that, no one seemed to look at him. An improvised ladder was brought up, and Secret Service men went into the ship and came down again escorting sullen, blue-lipped men.

# KINGS WHO DIE
## (MARCH 1962)
## POUL ANDERSON
## (B. 1926)

Poul Anderson is a prolific and excellent writer who has built up an impressive body of work since he entered science fiction in 1947. He is best known for his series characters Dominic Flandry and Nicholas van Rijn, but he has written many other notable stories, including the award-winning "The Longest Voyage" (1960), "The Queen of Air and Darkness" (1971), and "Hunter's Moon" (1978). For *If*, he contributed memorable works such as "The Critique of Impure Reason" (November 1962) and the present selection.

## MEMOIR BY POUL ANDERSON

If memory serves, this story was written around a cover. That is, an artist had painted a scene out of his own imagination and sold it to a magazine, whose editor then persuaded a writer to produce a narrative it would illustrate. The practice was quite common in the pulps, and did not necessarily lead to bad text. Indeed, often the need to explain—or explain away—such a picture generated an interesting plot. I even remember that once, when in the mood to do a short story but without any idea that struck a spark, I asked my wife to create an assignment for me by visualizing and describing a piece of cover art that would not appear to make much sense. The result was "The Critique of Impure Reason," a bit of humor that, as a matter of fact, got published in *Worlds of If*.

"Kings Who Die" came out rather different, of course. The painting showed a combat in space. For some time I had been speculating about interplanetary war. Experts long before me had shown that, under any remotely realistic assumptions, its strategy, tactics, and maneuvers could not be like those of Earthbound conflict, whether ground, naval, or airborne. But what were the possibilities? Here was a chance to consider a few of them.

This in turn led me to direct linkages between human and computer. In those days the idea was unheard of, except in places like the Stanford Research Institute where an occasional scientist was quietly looking into it. (I was surprised to learn that, after I had turned in my manuscript.) Nowadays it is fast approaching reality, and I have tried to explore it further in a novel, *The Avatar*.

A second theme, still more important, also insisted on attention. Why have space wars? Why have any wars?

I am not a pacifist. On the contrary, for at least twenty years I have tried to warn Americans that unless they make adequate preparation to fight *and win* wars of every kind and magnitude, including the all-out nuclear one, American society does not have much longer to live. Yet at the same time, the insanity is obvious. War pays off, but only for a few among the victors, mostly in their power-hungry officialdom. For the rest of us, it is at best a lesser evil than submission to an alien officialdom. Otherwise we gain nothing except death, maiming, impoverishment, unfreedom, and misery, as do our enemies. Why does the little girl's famous prophecy never come true, that someday they'll give a war and nobody will come?

Many answers have been offered, and no doubt most contain a bit of truth, but I suspect that none has yet gotten to the core of the matter. Behavior so strange—to the conscious, logical mind— must have wellsprings very far down in the darknesses beneath our awareness. War will no more go away because we piously declare it should than cancer will. If ever we come to a measure of understanding of the phenomenon, we may discover that all we can do is contain it—as has happened once in a while in history. My story raises questions of this sort.

Reviewing a collection where it was earlier reprinted, an ultrafeminist critic objected to the subordinate status of the women in it. I refrained then from pointing out, but do now, that the protagonist would not likely know any other kind. As far as my information goes, there are just two nations that have put women in combat units, Israel and the Soviet Union. Both soon abandoned the practice. The implication seems clear enough to me, in real life and in the narrative, that here an instinct has asserted itself, declaring women too important—not alone as mothers but as human beings—to squander in battle.

Lest the foregoing paragraphs seem pretentious, let me finish by remarking that this is simply a story, a yarn spun for what I hope will be your entertainment.

# KINGS WHO DIE

Luckily, Diaz was facing the other way when the missile exploded. It was too far off to blind him permanently, but the retinal burns would have taken a week or more to heal. He saw the glare reflected in his view lenses. As a ground soldier he would have hit the rock and tried to claw himself a hole. But there was no ground here, no up or down, concealment or shelter, on a slice of spaceship orbiting through the darkness beyond Mars.

Diaz went loose in his armor. Countdown: brow, jaw, neck, shoulders, back, chest, belly . . . No blast came, to slam him against the end of his lifeline and break any bones whose muscles were not relaxed. So it had not been a shaped-charge shell, firing a cone of atomic-powered concussion through space. Or if it was, he had not been caught in the danger zone. As for radiation, he needn't worry much about that. Whatever particles and gamma photons he got at this distance should not be too big a dose for the anti-X in his body to handle the effects.

He was alive.

He drew a breath which was a good deal shakier than the Academy satorist would have approved of. ("If your nerves twitch, cadet-san, then you know yourself alive and they need not twitch. Correct?" To hell with that, except as a technique.) Slowly, he hauled himself in until his boots made magnetic contact and he stood, so to speak, upon his raft.

Then he turned about for a look.

*"Nombre de Dios,"* he murmured, a hollow noise in the helmet. Forgotten habit came back, with a moment's recollection of his mother's face. He crossed himself.

Against blackness and a million wintry stars, a gas cloud expanded. It glowed in many soft hues, the center still bright, edges fading into vacuum. Shaped explosions did not behave like that, thought the calculator part of Diaz; this had been a standard fireball type. But the cloud was nonspherical. Hence a ship had been hit. A big ship. But whose?

Most of him stood in wonder. A few years ago he'd spent a furlough at Antarctic Lodge. He and some girl had taken a snowcat out to watch the aurora, thinking it would make a romantic

119

background. But then they saw the sky and forgot about each other for a long time. There was only the aurora.

The same awesome silence was here, as that incandescence which had been a ship and her crew swelled and vanished into space.

The calculator in his head proceeded with its business. Of those American vessels near the *Argonne* when first contact was made with the enemy, only the *Washington* was sufficiently massive to go out in a blast of yonder size and shape. If that was what had happened, Captain Martin Diaz of the United States Astromilitary Corps was a dead man. The other ships of the line were too distant, traveling on vectors too unlike his own, for their scoutboats to come anywhere close to where he was.

On the other hand, it might well have been a Unasian battle-wagon. Diaz had small information on the dispositions of the enemy fleet. He'd had his brain full just directing the torp launchers under his immediate command. If that had indeed been a hostile dreadnaught which got clobbered, surely none but the *Washington* could have delivered the blow, and its boats would be near—

There!

For half a second Diaz was too stiffened by the sight to react. The boat ran black across waning clouds, accelerating on a streak of its own fire. The wings and sharp shape that were needed in atmosphere made him think of a marlin he had once hooked off Florida, blue lightning under the sun. . . . Then a flare was in his hand; he squeezed the igniter and radiance blossomed.

Just an attention-getting device, he thought, and laughed unevenly as he and Bernie Sternthal had done, acting out the standard irreverences of high school students toward the psych course. But Bernie had left his bones on Ganymede, three years ago, and in this hour Diaz's throat was constricted and his nostrils full of his own stench.

He skyhooked the flare and hunkered in its harsh illumination by his radio transmitter. Clumsy in their gauntlets, his fingers adjusted controls, set the revolving beams on SOS. If he had been noticed, and if it was physically possible to make the velocity changes required, a boat would come for him. The Corps looked after its own.

Presently the flare guttered out. The pyre cloud faded to nothing.

The raft deck was between Diaz and the shrunken sun, but the stars that crowded on every side gave ample soft light. He al-

lowed his gullet, which felt like sandpaper, a suck from his one
water flask. Otherwise he had several air bottles, an oxygen
reclaim unit and a ridiculously large box of Q rations. His raft was
a section of inner plating, torn off when the *Argonne* encountered
the ball storm. She was only a pursuit cruiser, unarmored against
such weapons. At thirty miles per second, relative, the little steel
spheres tossed in her path by some Unasian gun had not left
much but junk and corpses. Diaz had found no other survivors.
He'd lashed what he could salvage onto this raft, including a
shaped torp charge that rocketed him clear of the ruins. This far
spaceward, he didn't need screen fields against solar-particle
radiation. So he had had a small hope of rescue. Maybe bigger
than small, now.

Unless an enemy craft spotted him first.

His scalp crawled with that thought. His right arm, where the
thing lay buried which he might use in the event of capture,
began to itch.

But no, he told himself, don't be sillier than regulations require. That scoutboat was positively American. The probability of
a hostile vessel being in detection range of his flare and radio—or
able to change vectors fast enough—or giving a damn about him in
any event—approached so close to zero as to make no difference.

"Wish I'd found our bottle in the wreckage," he said aloud. He
was talking to Carl Bailey, who'd helped him smuggle the Scotch
aboard at Shepard Field when the fleet was alerted for departure.
The steel balls had chewed Carl to pieces, some of which Diaz
had seen. "It gripes me not to empty that bottle. On behalf of us
both, I mean. Maybe," his voice wandered on, "a million years
hence, it'll drift into another planetary system and owl-eyed critters will pick it up in boneless fingers, eh, Carl, and put it in a
museum."

He realized what he was doing and snapped his mouth shut.
But his mind continued. *The trouble is, those critters won't know
about Carl Bailey, who collected antique jazz tapes, and played a
rough game of poker, and had a D.S.M. and a gimpy leg from
rescuing three boys whose patroller crashed on Venus, and went
on the town with Martin Diaz one evening not so long ago
when— What did happen that evening, anyhow?*

*He dreamed . . .*

There was a joint down in the Mexican section of San Diego
which Diaz remembered was fun. So they caught a giro outside

the Hotel Kennedy, where the spacemen were staying—they could afford swank, and felt they owed it to the Corps—and where they had bought their girls dinner. Diaz punched the cantina's name. The autopilot searched its directory and swung the cab onto the Embarcadero–Balboa skyrail.

Sharon sighed and snuggled into the curve of his arm. "How beautiful," she said. "How nice of you to show me this." He felt she meant a little more than polite banality. The view through the bubble really was great tonight. The city winked and blazed, a god's hoard of jewels, from horizon to horizon. Only in one direction was there anything but light: westward, where the ocean lay aglow. A nearly full moon stood high in the sky. He pointed out a tiny distant glitter on its dark edge.

"Vladimir Base."

"Ugh," said Sharon. "Unasians." She stiffened a trifle.

"Oh, they're decent fellows," Bailey said from the rear seat.

"How do you know?" asked his own date, Naomi, a serious-looking girl and quick on the uptake.

"I've been there a time or two." He shrugged.

"What?" Sharon exclaimed. "When we're at *war?*"

"Why not?" Diaz said. "The Ambassador of United Asia gave a party for our President just yesterday. I watched on the newscreen. Big social event."

"But that's different," Sharon protested. "The war goes on in space, not on Earth, and—"

"We don't blow up each other's lunar bases either," Bailey said. "Too close to home. So once in a while we have occasion to, uh, 'parley' is the official word. Actually, the last time I went over—couple years ago now—it was to return a craterbug we'd borrowed and bring some alga-blight antibiotic they needed. They poured me full of very excellent vodka."

"I'm surprised you admit this so openly," said Naomi.

"No secret, my dear," purred Diaz in his best grandee manner, twirling an imaginary mustache. "The newscreens simply don't mention it. Wouldn't be popular, I suppose."

"Oh, people wouldn't care, seeing it was the Corps," Sharon said.

"That's right," Naomi smiled. "The Corps can do no wrong."

"Why, thankee kindly." Diaz grinned at Sharon, chucked her under the chin and kissed her. She held back an instant, having met him only this afternoon. But of course she knew what a date with a Corpsman usually meant, and he knew she knew, and she knew he knew, so before long she relaxed and enjoyed it.

The giro stopped those proceedings by descending to the street and rolling three blocks to the cantina. They entered a low, noisy room hung with bullfight posters and dense with smoke. Diaz threw a glance around and wrinkled his nose. "*Sanabiche!*" he muttered. "The tourists have discovered this place."

"Uh-huh," Bailey answered in the same disappointed *sotto voce*. "Loud tunics, lard faces, 3V and a juke wall. But let's have a couple drinks, at least, seeing we're here."

"That's the trouble with being in space two or three years at a time," Diaz said. "You lose track. Well—" They found a booth.

The waiter recognized him, even after so long a lapse, and called the proprietor. The old man bowed nearly to the floor and begged they accept tequila from his private stock. "*No, no, Señor Capitán, conserva el dinero, por favor.*" The girls were delighted. Picturesqueness seemed harder to come by each time Diaz made Earthfall. The evening was off to a good start in spite of everything.

But then someone paid the juke.

The wall came awake with a scrawny blonde fourteen-year-old, the latest fashion in sex queens, wearing a grass skirt and three times life size:

> *Bingle-jingle-jungle-bang-POW!*
> *Bingle-jingle-jangle-bang-UGH!*
> *Uh'm uh red-hot Congo gal an' Uh'm lookin' fuh a pal*
> *Tuh share mah bingle-jingle-bangle-jungle-ugh-YOW!*

"What did you say?" Sharon called through the saxophones.

"Never mind," Diaz grunted. "They wouldn't've included it in your school Spanish anyway."

"Those things make me almost wish World War Four would start," Naomi said bitterly.

Bailey's mouth tightened. "Don't talk like that," he said. "Wasn't Number Three a close enough call for the race? Without even accomplishing its aims, for either side. I've seen . . . Any war is too big."

Lest they become serious, Diaz said thoughtfully above the racket: "You know, it should be possible to do something about those Kallikak walls. Like, maybe, an oscillator. They've got oscillators these days which'll even goof a solid-state apparatus at close range."

"The FCC wouldn't allow that," Bailey said. "Especially since it'd interfere with local 3V reception."

"That's bad? Besides, you could miniaturize the oscillator so it'd be hard to find. Make it small enough to carry in your pocket. Or even in your body, if you could locate a doctor who'd, uh, perform an illegal operation. I've seen uplousing units no bigger than—"

"You could strew 'em around town," Bailey said, getting interested. "Hide 'em in obscure corners and—"

"*Ugga-wugga-wugga, hugga me, do!*"

"I *wish* it would stop," Naomi said. "I came here to get to know you, Carl, not that thing."

Bailey sat straight. One hand, lying on the table, shaped a fist. "Why not?" he said.

"Eh?" Diaz asked.

Bailey rose. "Excuse me a minute." He bowed to the girls and made his way through the dancers to the wall control. There he switched the record off.

Silence fell like a meteor. For a moment, voices were stilled too. Then a large tourist came barreling off his bar stool and yelled, "Hey, wha' d'yuh think you're—"

"I'll refund your money, sir," Baily said mildly. "But the noise bothers the lady I'm with."

"Huh? Hey, who d'yuh think yuh are, you—"

The proprietor came from around the bar. "If the lady weeshes it off," he declared, "off it stays."

"What kinda discrimination is this?" roared the tourist. Several other people growled with him.

Diaz prepared to go help, in case things got rough. But his companion pulled up the sleeve of his mufti tunic. The ID bracelet gleamed into view. "First Lieutenant Carl H. Bailey, United States Astromilitary Corps, at your service," he said; and a circular wave of quietness expanded around him. "Please forgive my action. I'll gladly stand the house a round."

But that wasn't necessary. The tourist fell all over himself apologizing and begged to buy the drinks. Then someone else bought them, and someone after him. Nobody ventured near the booth, where the spacemen obviously wanted privacy. But from time to time, when Diaz glanced out, he got many smiles and a few shy waves. It was almost embarrassing.

"I was afraid for a minute we'd have a fight," he said.

"N-no," Bailey answered. "I've watched our prestige develop

exponentially, being stateside while my leg healed. I doubt if there's an American alive who'd lift a finger against a Corpsman these days. But I admit I was afraid of a scene. That wouldn't've done the name of the Corps any good. As things worked out, though—"

"We came off too bloody well," Diaz finished. "Now there's not even any pseudo life in this place. Let's haul mass. We can catch the transpolar shuttle to Paris if we hurry."

But at that moment the proprietor's friends and relations, who also remembered him, began to arrive. They must have been phoned the great news. Pablo was there, Manuel, Carmen with her castanets, Juan with his guitar, Tio Rico waving a bottle in each enormous fist; and they welcomed Diaz back with embraces, and soon there was song and dancing, and the fiesta ended in the rear courtyard watching the moon set before dawn, and everything was just like the old days, for Señor Capitán Diaz's sake.

That had been a hell of a good furlough. . . .

Another jet splashed fire across the Milky Way. Closer this time, and obviously reducing relative speed.

Diaz croaked out a cheer. He had spent weary hours waiting. The hugeness and aloneness had eaten further into his defenses than he wished to realize. He had begun to understand what some people told him, that it disturbed them to see the stars on a clear mountain night. (Where wind went soughing through pines whose bark smelled like vanilla if you laid your head close, and a river flowed cold and loud over stones—oh, Christ, how beautiful Earth was!) He shoved such matters aside and reactivated his transmitter.

The streak winked out and the stars crowded back into his eyes. But that was all right. It meant the boat had decelerated as much as necessary, and soon there would be a scooter homing on his beam, and water and food and sleep, and a new ship and eventually certain letters to write. That would be the worst part. But not for months or years yet, not till one side or the other conceded the present phase of the war. Diaz found himself wishing most for a cigarette.

He hadn't seen the boat's hull this time, of course; there had been no rosy cloud to silhouette its blackness. Nor did he see the scooter until it was almost upon him. That jet was very thin, since it need only drive a few hundred pounds of mass on which two spacesuited men sat. They were little more than a highlight and a shadow. Diaz's pulse filled the silence. "Hallo!" he called in his helmet mike. "Hallo, there!"

They didn't answer. The scooter matched velocities a few yards off. One man tossed a line with a luminous bulb at the end. Diaz caught it and made fast. The line was drawn taut. Scooter and raft bumped together and began gently rotating.

Diaz recognized those helmets.

He snatched for a sidearm he didn't have. A Unasian sprang to one side, lifeline unreeling. His companion stayed mounted, a chucker gun cradled in his arms. The sun rose blindingly over the raft edge.

There was nothing to be done. Yet. Diaz fought down a physical nausea of defeat, "raised" his hands and let them hang free. The other man came behind him and deftly wired his wrists together. Both Unasians spent a few minutes inspecting the raft. The man with the gun tuned in on the American band.

"You make very clever salvage, sir," he said.

"Thank you," Diaz whispered, helpless and stunned.

"Come, please." He was lashed to the carrier rack. Weight tugged at him as the scooter accelerated.

They took an hour or more to rendezvous. Diaz had time to adjust his emotions. The first horror passed into numbness; then there was a sneaking relief, that he would get a reasonably comfortable vacation from war until the next prisoner exchange; and then he remembered the new doctrine, which applied to all commissioned officers whom there had been time to operate on.

*I may never get the chance*, he thought frantically. *They told me not to waste myself on anything less than a cruiser; my chromosomes and several million dollars spent in training me make me that valuable to the country, at least. I may go straight to Pallas, or wherever their handiest prison base is, in a lousy scoutboat or cargo ship.*

*But I may get a chance to strike a blow that'll hurt. Have I got the guts? I hope so. No, I don't even know if I hope it. This is a cold place to die.*

The feeling passed. Emotional control, drilled into him at the Academy and practiced at every refresher course, took over. It was essentially psychosomatic, a matter of using conditioned reflexes to bring muscles and nerves and glands back toward normal. If the fear symptoms, tension, tachycardia, sweat, decreased salivation and the rest, were alleviated, then fear itself was. Far down under the surface, a four-year-old named Martin woke from nightmare and screamed for his mother, who did not come; but Diaz grew able to ignore him.

The boat became visible, black across star clouds. No, not a boat. A small ship . . . abnormally large jets and light guns, a modified *Panyushkin* . . . what had the enemy been up to in his asteroid shipyards? Some kind of courier vessel, maybe. Recognition signals must be flashing back and forth. The scooter passed smoothly through a lock that closed again behind. Air was pumped in. Diaz went blind as frost condensed on his helmet. Several men assisted him out of the armor. They hadn't quite finished when an alarm rang, engines droned and weight came back. The ship was starting off at about half a gee.

Short bodies in green uniforms surrounded Diaz. Their immaculate appearance reminded him of his own unshaven filthiness, how much he ached and how sandy his brain felt. "Well," he mumbled, "where's your interrogation officer?"

"You go more high, Captain," answered a man with colonel's insignia. "Forgive us we do not attend your needs at once, but he says very important."

Diaz bowed to the courtesy, remembering what had been planted in his arm and feeling rather a bastard. Though it looked as if he wouldn't have occasion to use the thing. Dazed by relief and weariness, he let himself be escorted along corridors and tubes, until he stood before a door marked with great black Cyrillic warnings and guarded by two soldiers. Which was almost unheard of aboard a spaceship; he thought joltingly.

There was a teleye above the door. Diaz barely glanced at it. Whoever sat within the cabin must be staring through it at him. He tried to straighten his shoulders. "Martin Diaz," he husked, "Captain, U.S.A.C., serial number—"

Someone yelled from the loudspeaker beside the pick-up. Diaz half understood. He whirled about. His will gathered itself and surged. He began to think the impulses that would destroy the ship. A guard tackled him. A rifle butt came down on his head. And that was that.

They told him forty-eight hours passed while he was in sick bay. "I wouldn't know," he said dully. "Nor care." But he was again in good physical shape. Only a bandage sheathing his lower right arm, beneath the insignleless uniform given him, revealed that surgeons had been at work. His mind was sharply aware of its

environment—muscle play beneath his own skin, pastel bulkheads and cold fluorescence, faint machine-quiver underfoot, gusts
from ventilator grilles, odors of foreign cooking. And always the
men, with alien faces and carefully expressionless voices, who had
caught him.

At least there was no abuse. They might have been justified in
resenting his attempt to kill them. Some would call it treacher-
ous. But they gave him the treatment due an officer and, except
for supplying his needs, left him alone in his tiny bunk cubicle.
Which in some respects was worse than punishment. Diaz was
actually glad when he was at last summoned for an interview.

They brought him to the guarded door and gestured him through.
It closed behind him.

For a moment Diaz noticed only the suite itself. Even a fleet
commander didn't get this much space and comfort. The ship had
long ceased accelerating, but spin provided a reasonable weight.
The suite was constructed within a rotatable shell, so that the
same deck was "down" as when the jets were in operation. Diaz
stood on a Persian carpet, looking past low-legged furniture to a
pair of arched doorways. One revealed a bedroom, lined with
microspools—ye gods, there must be ten thousand volumes! The
other showed part of an office, a desk and a great enigmatic
control panel and—

The man seated beneath the Monet reproduction got up and
made a slight bow. He was tall for a Unasian, with a lean mobile
face whose eyes were startlingly blue against a skin as white as a
Swedish girl's. His undress uniform was neat, but carelessly worn.
No rank insignia was visible, for a gray hood, almost a coif,
covered his head and fell over the shoulders.

"Good day, Captain Diaz," he said, speaking English with little
accent. "Permit me to introduce myself: General Leo Ilyitch
Rostock, Cosmonautical Service of the People of United Asia."

Diaz went through the rituals automatically. Most of him was
preoccupied with how quiet this place was. How very quiet. But
the layout was serene. Rostock must be fantastically important if
his comfort rated this much mass. Diaz's gaze flickered to the
other man's waist. Rostock bore a sidearm. More to the point,
though, one loud holler would doubtless be picked up by the
teleye mike and bring in the guards outside.

Diaz tried to relax. *If they haven't kicked my teeth in so far,
they don't plan to. I'm going to live.* But he couldn't believe that.
Not here, in the presence of this hooded man. Even more so, in

his drawing room. Its existence beyond Mars was too eerie. "No, sir, I have no complaints," he heard himself saying. "You run a good ship. My compliments."

"Thank you," Rostock had a charming, almost boyish smile. "Although this is not my ship, actually. Colonel Sumoro commands the *Ho Chi Minh*. I shall convey your appreciation to him."

"You may not be called the captain," Diaz said bluntly, "but the vessel is obviously your instrument."

Rostock shrugged. "Will you not sit down?" he invited, and resumed his own place on the couch. Diaz took a chair across the table from him, feeling knobby and awkward. Rostock pushed a box forward. "Cigarettes?"

"Thank you." Diaz struck and inhaled hungrily.

"I hope your arm does not bother you."

Diaz's belly muscles tightened. "No. It's all right."

"The surgeons left the metal ulnar bone in place, as well as its nervous and muscular connections. Complete replacement would have required more hospital equipment than a spaceship can readily carry. We did not want to cripple you by removing the bone. After all, we were only interested in the cartridge."

Diaz gathered courage and snapped: "The more I see of you, General, the sorrier I am that it didn't work. You're big game."

Rostock chuckled. "Perhaps. I wonder, though, if you are as sorry as you would like to feel you are. You would have died too, you realize."

"Uh-huh."

"Do you know what the weapon embedded in you was?"

"Yes. *We* tell our people such things. A charge of isotopic explosive, with a trigger activated by a particular series of motor nerve pulses. Equivalent to about ten tons of TNT." Diaz gripped the chair arms, leaned forward, and said harshly: "I'm not blabbing anything you don't now know. I daresay you consider it a violation of the customs of war. Not me! I gave no parole—"

"Certainly, certainly." Rostock waved a deprecating hand. "There are—what is your idiom?—no hard feelings. The device was ingenious. We have already dispatched a warning to our Central, whence the word can go out through the fleet, so your effort, the entire project, has gone for nothing. But it was a rather gallant attempt."

He leaned back, crossed one leg over the other, and regarded the American candidly. "Of course, as you implied, we would have proceeded somewhat differently," he said. "Our men would not have known what they carried, and the explosion would have been trigered posthypnotically, by some given class of situations, rather than consciously. In that way, there would be less chance of betrayal."

"How did you know, anyway?" Diaz sighed.

Rostock gave him an impish grin. "As the villain of this particular little drama, I shall only say that I have my methods." Suddenly he was grave. "One reason we made such an effort to pick you up before your own rescue party arrived was to gather data on what you have been doing, you people. You know how comparatively rare it is to get a prisoner in space warfare; and how hard to get spies into an organization of high morale which maintains its own laboratories and factories off Earth. Divergent developments can go far these days, before the other side is aware of them. The miniaturization involved in your own weapon, for example, astonished our engineers."

"I can't tell you anything else," Diaz said.

"Oh, you could," Rostock answered gently. "You know as well as I what can be done with a shot of babble juice. Not to mention other techniques—nothing melodramatic, nothing painful or disabling, merely applied neurology—in which I believe Unasia is ahead of the Western countries. But don't worry, Captain, I shall not permit any such breach of military custom.

"However, I do want you to understand how much trouble we went to, to get you. When combat began, I reasoned that the ships auxilary to a dreadnaught would be the likeliest to suffer destruction of the type which leaves a few survivors. From the pattern of action in the first day, I deduced the approximate orbits and positions of several American capital ships. Unasian tactics throughout the second day were developed with two purposes: to inflict damage, of course, but also to get the *Ho* so placed that we would be likely to detect any distress signals. This cost us the *Genghis*—a calculated risk which did not pay off—I am not omniscient. But we did hear your call.

"You are quite right about the importance of this ship here. My superiors will be horrified at my action. But of necessity, they have given me *carte blanche*. And since the *Ho* itself takes no direct part in any engagement, if we can avoid it, the probability of our being detected and attacked was small."

Rostock's eyes held Diaz's. He tapped the table, softly and repeatedly, with one fingernail. "Do you appreciate what all this means, Captain?" he asked. "Do you see how badly you were wanted?"

Diaz could only wet his lips and nod.

"Partly," Rostock said, smiling again, "there was the desire I have mentioned, to—er—check up on American activities during the last cease-fire period. But partly, too, there was a wish to bring you up to date on what we have been doing."

"*Huh?*" Diaz half scrambled from his chair, sagged back, and gaped.

"The choice is yours, Captain," Rostock said. "You can be transferred to a cargo ship when we can arrange it, and so to an asteroid camp, and in general receive the normal treatment of a war prisoner. Or you may elect to hear what I would like to discuss with you. In the latter event, I can guarantee nothing. Obviously, I can't let you go home, in a routine prisoner exchange with a prime military secret of ours. You will have to wait until it is no longer a secret. Until American Intelligence has learned the truth, and we know that they have. That may take years. It may take forever: because I have some hope that the knowledge will change certain of your own attitudes.

"No, no, don't answer now. Think it over. I will see you again tomorrow. In twenty-four hours, that is to say."

Rostock's eyes shifted past Diaz, as if to look through the bulkheads. His tone dropped suddenly to a whisper, "Have you ever wondered, like me, why we carry Earth's rotation period to space with us? Habit; practicality; but is there not also an element of magical thinking? A hope that somehow we can create our own sunrises? The sky is very black out there. We need all the magic we can invent. Do we not?"

Some hours later, alarms sounded, voices barked over the intercoms, spin was halted but weight came quickly back as the ship accelerated.

Diaz knew just enough Mandarin to understand from what he overheard that radar contact had been made with American units and combat would soon resume. The guard who brought him dinner in his cubicle confirmed it, with many a bow and hissing smile. Diaz had gained enormous face by his audience with the man in the suite.

He couldn't sleep, though the racket soon settled down to a purposeful murmur with few loud interruptions. Restless in his bunk harness, he tried to reconstruct a total picture from what clues he had. The primary American objective was the asteroid base system of the enemy. But astromilitary tactics were too complicated for one brain to grasp. A battle might go on for months, flaring up whenever hostile units came near enough in their enormous orbitings to exchange fire. Eventually, Diaz knew, if everything went well—that is, didn't go too badly haywire— Americans would land on the Unasian worldlets. That would be the rough part. He remembered ground operations on Mars and Ganymede much too well.

As for the immediate situation, though, he could only make an educated guess. The leisurely pace at which the engagement was developing indicated that ships of dreadnaught mass were involved. Therefore no mere squadron was out there, but an important segment of the American fleet, perhaps the task force headed by the *Alaska*. But if this was true, then the *Ho Chi Minh* must be directing a flotilla of comparable size.

Which wasn't possible! Flotillas and subfleets were bossed from dreadnaughts. A combat computer and its human staff were just too big and delicate to be housed in anything less. And the *Ho* was not even as large as the *Argonne* had been.

Yet what the hell was this but a command ship? Rostock had hinted as much. The activity aboard was characteristic, the repeated sound of courier boats coming and going, intercom calls, technicians hurrying along the corridors, but no shooting.

Nevertheless—

Voices jabbered beyond the cell door. Their note was triumphant. Probably they related a hit on an American vessel. Diaz recalled brushing aside chunks of space-frozen meat that had been his Corps brothers. Sammy Yoshida was in the *Utah Beach*, which was with the *Alaska*—Sammy who'd covered for him back at the Academy when he crawled in dead drunk hours after taps, and some years later had dragged him from a shell-struck foxhole on Mars and shared oxygen till a rescue squad happened by. Had the *Utah Beach* been hit? Was that what they were giggling about out there?

*Prisoner exchange, in a year or two or three, will get me back for the next round of the war,* Diaz thought in darkness. *But I'm only one man. And I've goofed somehow, spilled a scheme which might've cost the Unies several ships before they tumbled. It's hardly conceivable I could smuggle out whatever information Rostock wants to give me. But there'd be some tiny probability that I could, somehow, sometime. Wouldn't there?*

*I don't want to. Dios mio, how I don't want to! Let me rest a while, and then be swapped, and go back for a long furlough on Earth, where anything I ask for is mine and mainly I ask for sunlight and ocean and flowering trees. But Carl liked those things too, didn't he? Liked them and lost them forever.*

There came a lull in the battle. The fleets had passed each other, decelerating as they fired. They would take many hours to turn around and get back within combat range. A great quietness descended on the *Ho*. Walking down the passageways, which thrummed with rocketblast, Diaz saw how the technicians slumped at their posts. The demands on them were as hard as those on a pilot or gunner or missile chief. Evolution designed men to fight with their hands, not with computations and push buttons. Maybe ground combat wasn't the worst kind.

The sentries admitted Diaz through the door of the warning. Rostock sat at the table again. His coifed features looked equally drained, and his smile was automatic. A samovar and two teacups stood before him.

"Be seated, Captain," he said tonelessly. "Pardon me if I do not rise. This has been an exhausting time."

Diaz accepted a chair and a cup. Rostock drank noisily, eyes closed and forehead puckered. There might have been an extra stimulant in his tea, for before long he appeared more human. He refilled the cups, passed out cigarettes and leaned back on his couch with a sigh.

"You may be pleased to know," he said, "that the third pass will be the final one. We shall refuse further combat and proceed instead to join forces with another flotilla near Pallas."

"Because that suits your purposes better," Diaz said.

"Well, naturally. I compute a higher likelihood of ultimate success if we follow a strategy of— No matter now."

Diaz leaned forward. His heart slammed. "'So this *is* a command ship," he exclaimed. "I thought so."

The blue eyes weighed him with care. "If I give you any further information," Rostock said—softly, but the muscles tightened along his jaw—"you must accept the conditions I set forth."

"I do," Diaz got out.

"I realize that you do so in the hope of passing on the secret to your countrymen," Rostock said. "You may as well forget about that. You won't get the chance."

"Then why do you want to tell me? You won't make a Unie out of me, General." The words sounded too stuck-up, Diaz decided.

"That is, I respect your people and, and so forth, but, uh, my loyalties lie elsewhere."

"Agreed. I don't hope or plan to change them. At least, not in an easterly direction." Rostock drew hard on his cigarette, let smoke stream from his nostrils and squinted through it. "The microphone is turned down," he remarked. "We cannot be overheard unless we shout. I must warn you, if you make any attempt to reveal what I am about to say to you to any of my own people, I shall not only deny it but order you sent out the airlock. It is that important."

Diaz rubbed his hands on his trousers. The palms were wet. "Okay," he said.

"Not that I mean to browbeat you, Captain," said Rostock hastily. "What I offer is friendship. In the end, maybe, peace." He sat a while longer looking at the wall, before his glance shifted back to Diaz's. "Suppose you begin the discussion. Ask me what you like."

"Uh—" Diaz floundered about, as if he'd been leaning on a door that was thrown open. "Uh . . . well, was I right? Is this a command ship?"

"Yes. It performs every function of a flag dreadnaught, except that it seldom engages in direct combat. The tactical advantages are obvious. A smaller, lighter vessel can get about much more readily, hence be a correspondingly more effective directrix. Furthermore, if due caution is exercised, we are not likely to be detected and fired at. The massive armament of a dreadnaught is chiefly to stave off the missiles which can annihilate the command post within. Ships of this class avoid the whole problem by avoiding attack in the first place."

"But your computer! You, uh, you must have developed a combat computer as . . . small and rugged as an autopilot—I thought miniaturization was our specialty."

Rostock laughed.

"And you'd still need a large human staff," Diaz protested. "Bigger than the whole crew of this ship!

"Wouldn't you?" he finished weakly.

Rostock shook his head. "No." His smile faded. "Not under this new system. I am the computer."

"What?"

"Look." Rostock pulled off his hood.

The head beneath was hairless, not shaved but depilated. A dozen silvery plates were set into it, flush with the scalp; there were outlets in them. Rostock pointed toward the office. "The rest of me is in there," he said. "I need only plug the jacks into the appropriate points of myself, and I become—no, not part of the computer. *It* becomes part of *me*."

He fell silent again, gazing now at the floor. Diaz hardly dared move, until his cigarette burned his fingers and he must stub it out. The ship pulsed around them. Monet's picture of sunlight caught in young leaves was like something seen at the far end of a tunnel.

"Consider the problem," Rostock said at last, low. "In spite of much loose talk about giant brains, computers do not think, except perhaps on an idiot level. They merely perform logical operations, symbol-shuffling, according to instructions given them. It was shown long ago that there are infinite classes of problems which no computer can solve: the classes dealt with in Godel's theorem, that can only be solved by the nonlogical process of creating a metalanguage. Creativity is not logical and computers do not create.

"In addition, as you know, the larger a computer becomes, the more staff it requires to perform such operations as data coding, programming, retranslation of the solutions into practical terms, and adjustment of the artificial answer to the actual problem. Yet your own brain does this sort of thing constantly . . . because it is creative. Moreover, the advanced computers are heavy, bulky, fragile things. They use cryogenics and all the other tricks, but that involves elaborate ancillary apparatus. Your brain weighs a kilogram or so, is very adequately protected in the skull and needs less than a hundred kilos of outside equipment—your body.

"I am not being mystical. There is no reason why creativity cannot someday be duplicated in an artificial structure. But I think that structure will look very much like a living organism; will, indeed, be one. Life has had a billion years to develop these techniques.

"Now, if the brain has so many advantages, why use a computer at all? Obviously, to do the uncreative work, for which the brain is not specifically designed. The brain visualizes a problem of, say, orbits, masses, and tactics, and formulates it as a set of matrix equations. Then the computer goes swiftly through the millions of idiot counting operations needed to produce a numerical solution. What we have developed here, we Unasians, is nothing but a direct approach. We eliminate the middle man, as you Americans would say.

"In yonder office is a highly specialized computer. It is built from solid-state units, analogous to neurones, but in spite of being able to treat astromilitary problems, it is a comparatively small, simple, and sturdy device. Why? Because it is used in connection with my brain, which directs it. The normal computer must have its operational patterns built in. Mine develops synapse pathways as needed, just as a man's lower brain can develop skills under the direction of the cerebral cortex. And these pathways are modifiable by experience; the system is continually restructuring itself. The normal computer must have elaborate failure detection systems and arrangement for re-routing. I, in the hookup here, sense any trouble directly, and am no more disturbed by the temporary disability of some region than you are disturbed by the fact that most of your brain cells at any given time are resting.

"The human staff becomes superfluous here. My technicians bring me the data, which need not be reduced to standardized format. I link myself to the machine and—think about it—there are no words. The answer is worked out in no more time than any other computer would require. But it comes to my consciousness not as a set of figures, but in practical terms, decisions about what to do. Furthermore, the solution is modified by my human awareness of those factors too complex to go into physical condition— men and equipment, morale, long-range questions of logistics and strategy and ultimate goals. You might say this is a computer system with common sense. Do you understand, Captain?"

Diaz sat still for a long time before he said, "Yes. I think I do."

Rostock had gotten a little hoarse. He poured himself a fresh cup of tea and drank half, struck another cigarette, and said earnestly: "The military value is obvious. Were that all, I would never have revealed this much to you. But something else developed as I practiced and increased my command of the system. Something quite unforeseen. I wonder if you will comprehend." He finished his cup. "That repeated experience changed me. I am no longer human. Not really."

The ship whispered, driving through darkness.

"I suppose a hookup like that would affect the emotions," Diaz ventured. "How does it feel?"

"There are no words," Rostock repeated, "except those I have made for myself." He rose and walked restlessly across the subdued rainbows in the carpet, hands behind his back, eyes focused on nothing Diaz could see. "As a matter of fact, the only emotional effect may be a simple intensification. Although . . . there are myths about mortals who became gods. How did it feel to them? I think they hardly noticed the palaces and music and feasting on Olympus. What mattered was how, piece by piece, as he mastered his new capacities, the new god won a god's understanding. His perception, involvement, detachment, totalness . . . there *are* no words."

Back and forth he paced, feet noiseless but metal and energies humming beneath his low and somehow troubled voice. "My cerebrum directs the computer," he said, "and the relationship becomes reciprocal. True, the computer part has no creativity of its own but it endows mine with a speed and sureness you cannot imagine. After all, a great part of original thought consists merely in proposing trial solutions. The scientist hypothesizes, the artist draws a charcoal line, the poet scribbles a phrase. Then they test them to see if they work. By now, to me, this mechanical aspect of imagination is back down on the subconscious level where it belongs. What my awareness senses is the final answer, springing to life almost simultaneously with the question, and yet with a felt reality to it such as comes only from having pondered and tested the issue for thousands of times.

"Also, the amount of sense data I can handle is fantastic. Oh, I am blind and deaf and numb away from my machine half! So you will realize that over the months I have tended to spend more and more time in the linked state. When there was no immediate command problem to solve, I would sit and savor it."

In a practical tone: "That is how I perceived that you were about to sabotage us, Captain. Your posture alone betrayed you. I guessed the means at once and ordered the guards to knock you unconscious. I think, also, that I detected in you the potential I need. But that demands closer examination. Which is easily given. When I am linked, you cannot lie to me. The least insincerity is written across your whole organism."

He paused, to stand a little slumped, looking at the bulkhead. For a moment Diaz's legs tensed. *Three jumps and I can be there and get his gun!* But no, Rostock wasn't any brain-heavy dwarf. The body in that green uniform was young and trained. Diaz took another cigarette. "Okay," he said. "What do you propose?"

"First," Rostock said, turning about—and his eyes kindled—"I want you to understand what you and I are. What the spacemen of both factions are."

"Professional soldiers," Diaz grunted uneasily. Rostock waited. Diaz puffed hard and plowed on, since he was plainly expected to: "The only soldiers left. You can't count those ornamental regiments on Earth, nor the guys sitting by the big missiles. Those missiles will never be fired. World War Three was a large enough dose of nucleonics. Civilization was lucky to survive. Terrestrial life would be lucky to survive, next time around. So war has moved into space. Uh . . . professionalism . . . the old traditions of mutual respect and so forth have naturally revived." He made himself look up. "What more clichés need I repeat?"

"Suppose your side completely annihilated our ships," Rostock said. "What would happen?"

"Why . . . that's been discussed theoretically . . . by damn near every political scientist, hasn't it? The total command of space would not mean total command of Earth. We could destroy the whole eastern hemisphere without being touched. But we wouldn't because Unasia would fire its cobalt weapons while dying, and there'd be no western hemisphere to come home to either. Not that that situation will ever arise. Space is too big. There are too many ships and fortresses scattered around; combat is too slow a process. Neither fleet can wipe out the other."

"Since we have this perpetual stalemate, then," Rostock pursued, "why is there perpetual war?"

"Well, uh, partial victories are possible. Like our capture of Mars, or your destruction of three dreadnaughts in one month, on different occasions. The balance of power shifts. Rather than let its strength continue being whittled down, the side which is losing asks for a parley. There are negotiations, which end to the relative advantage of the stronger side. Meanwhile the arms race continues. Pretty soon a new dispute arises, the cease-fire ends, and maybe the other side is lucky that time."

"Is this situation expected to be eternal?"

"No!" Diaz stopped, thought a minute, and grinned with one corner of his mouth. "That is, they keep talking about an effective international organization. Trouble is, the two cultures are too far apart by now. They can't live together."

"I used to believe that myself," Rostock said. "Lately I have not been sure. A world federalism could be devised which would let both civilizations keep their identities. There have in fact been many such proposals, as you know. None has gotten beyond the talking stage. None ever will. Because, you see, what maintains the war is not the difference between our two cultures, but their similarity."

"Whoa, there!" Diaz bristled. "I resent that."

"Please," Rostock said. "I pass no moral judgments. For the sake of argument, at least, I can concede you the moral superiority, remarking only in parenthesis that Earth holds billions of people who not only fail to comprehend what you mean by freedom but would not like it if you gave it to them. The similarity I am talking about is technological. Both civilizations are based on the machine, with all the high organization and dynamism which this implies."

"So?"

"So war is a necessity— Wait! I am not talking about 'merchants of death,' or 'dictators needing an outside enemy,' or whatever the current propaganda lines are. I mean that conflict is built into the culture. There *must* be an outlet for the destructive emotions generated in the mass of the people by the type of life they lead. A type of life for which evolution never designed them.

"Have you ever heard about L. F. Richardson? No? He was an Englishman in the last century, a Quaker, who hated war but, being a scientist, realized the phenomenon must be understood clinically before it can be eliminated. He performed some brilliant theoretical and statistical analyses which showed, for example, that the rate of deadly quarrels was very nearly constant over the decades. There could be many small clashes or a few major ones, but the result was the same. Why were the United States and the Chinese Empire so peaceful during the nineteenth century? The answer is that they were not. They had their Civil War and Taiping Rebellion, which devastated them as much as required. I need not multiply examples. We can discuss this later in detail. I have carried Richardson's work a good deal further and have studied the problem more rigorously. I say to you now only that civilized societies must have a certain rate of immolations."

Diaz listened to silence for a minute before he said: "Well, I've sometimes thought the same. I suppose you mean we spacemen are the goats these days?"

"Exactly. War fought out here does not menace the planet. By our deaths we keep Earth alive."

Rostock sighed. His mouth drooped. "Magic works, you know," he said: "works on the emotions of the people who practice it. If a primitive witch doctor told a storm to go away, the storm did not hear, but the tribe did and took heart. The ancient analogy to us, though, is the sacrificial king in the early agricultural societies: a god in mortal form, who was regularly slain that the fields might bear fruit. This was not mere superstition. You must realize that. It worked—on the people. The rite was essential to the operation of their culture, to their sanity and hence to their survival.

"Today the machine age has developed its own sacrificial kings. We are the chosen of the race. The best it can offer. None gainsays us. We may have what we choose, pleasure, luxury, women, adulation—only not the simple pleasures of wife and child and home, for we must die that the people may live."

Again silence, until: "Do you seriously mean that's why the war goes on?" Diaz breathed.

Rostock nodded.

"But nobody—I mean, people wouldn't—"

"They do not reason things out, of course. Traditions develop blindly. The ancient peasant did not elaborate logical reasons why the king must die. He merely knew this was so, and left the syllogism for modern anthropologists to expound. I did not see the process going on today until I had had the chance to . . . to become more perceptive than I had been," Rostock said humbly.

Diaz couldn't endure sitting down any longer. He jumped to his feet. "Assuming you're right," he snapped, "and you may be, what of it? What can be done?"

"Much," Rostock said. Calm descended on his face like a mask. "I am not being mystical about this, either. The sacrificial king has reappeared as the end product of a long chain of cause and effect. There is no reason inherent in natural law why this must be. Richardson was right in his basic hope, that when war becomes understood, as a phenomenon, it can be eliminated. This would naturally involve restructuring the entire terrestrial culture. Gradually, subtly. Remember—" His hand shot out, seized Diaz's shoulder, and gripped painfully hard. "There is a new element in history today. Us. The kings. We are not like those who spend their lives under Earth's sky. In some ways we are more, in other ways less, but always we are different. You and I are more akin to each other than to our planet-dwelling countrymen. Are we not?

"In the time and loneliness granted me, I have used all my new powers to think about this. Not only think; this is so much more than cold reason. I have tried to feel. To love what is, as the Buddhists say. I believe a nucleus of spacemen like us, slowly and secretly gathered, wishing the good of everyone on Earth and the harm of none, gifted with powers and insights they cannot really imagine at home—I believe we may accomplish something. If not us, then our sons. Men ought not to kill each other, when the stars are waiting."

He let go, turned away and looked at the deck. "Of course," he mumbled, "I, in my peculiar situation, must first destroy a number of your brothers."

They had given Diaz a whole pack of cigarettes, an enormous treasure out here, before they locked him into his cubicle for the duration of the second engagement. He lay in harness, hearing clang and shout and engine roar through the vibrating bulkheads, stared at blackness and smoked until his tongue was foul. Sometimes the *Ho* accelerated, mostly it ran free and he floated. Once a tremor went through the entire hull, near miss by a shaped charge. Doubtless gamma rays, ignoring the magnetic force screens, sleeted through the men and knocked another several months off their life expectancies. Not that that mattered. Spacemen rarely lived long enough to worry about degenerative diseases. Diaz hardly noticed.

*He's not lying, Rostock. Why should he? What could he gain? He may be a nut, of course. But he doesn't act like a nut either. He wants me to study his statistics and equations, satisfy myself that he's right. And he must be damn sure I will be convinced, to tell me as much as he has.*

*How many are there like him? Only a very few, I'm sure. The man-machine symbiosis is obviously new, or we'd've had some inkling ourselves. This is the first field trial of the system. I wonder if the others have reached the same conclusions as Rostock. No, he said he doubts that. Their psychology impressed him as being more deeply channeled than his. He's a lucky accident.*

*Lucky? Now how can I tell? I'm only a man. I've never experienced an IQ of 1,000, or whatever the figure may be. A god's purposes aren't necessarily what a man would elect.*

The eventual end to war? Well, other institutions had been ended, at least in the Western countries; judicial torture, chattel slavery, human sacrifice— No, wait, according to Rostock human sacrifice had been revived.

"But is our casualty rate high enough to fit your equations?" Diaz had argued. "Space forces aren't as big as old-time armies. No country could afford that."

"Other elements than death must be taken into account," Rostock answered. "The enormous expense is one factor. Taxpaying is a form of symbolic self-mutilation. It also tends to direct civilian resentments and aggressions against their own government, thus taking some pressure off international relations.

"Chiefly, though, there is the matter of emotional intensity. A spaceman not only dies, he usually dies horribly; and that moment is the culmination of a long period under grisly conditions. His groundling brothers, administrative and service personnel, suffer vicariously: 'sweat it out,' as your idiom so well expresses the feeling. His kinfolk, friends, women, are likewise racked. When Adonis dies—or Osiris, Tammuz, Baldur, Christ, Tlaloc, whichever of his hundred names you choose—the people must in some degree share his agony. That is part of the sacrifice."

Diaz had never thought about it just that way. Like most Corpsmen, he had held the average civilian in thinly disguised contempt. But . . . from time to time, he remembered, he'd been glad his mother died before he enlisted. And why did his sister hit the bottle so hard? Then there had been Lois, she of the fire-colored hair and violet eyes, who wept as if she would never stop weeping when he left for duty. He'd promised to get in touch with her on his return, but of course he knew better.

Which did not erase memories of men whose breath and blood came exploding from burst helmets; who shuddered and vomited and defecated in the last stages of radiation sickness; who stared without immediate comprehension at a red spurt which a second ago had been an arm or a leg; who went insane and must be gassed because psychoneurosis is catching on a six months' orbit beyond Saturn; who— Yeah, Carl had been lucky.

You could talk as much as you wished about Corps brotherhood, honor, tradition, and gallantry. It remained sentimental guff . . .

No, that was unjust. The Corps had saved the people, their lives and liberties. There could be no higher achievement—for the Corps. But knighthood had once been a noble thing, too. Then, lingering after its day, it became a yoke and eventually a farce. The warrior virtues were not ends in themselves. If the warrior could be made obsolete—

Could he? How much could one man, even powered by a machine, hope to do? How much could he even hope to understand?

The moment came upon Diaz. He lay as if blinded by shellburst radiance.

As consciousness returned, he knew first, irrelevantly, what it meant to get religion.

"By God," he told the universe, "we're going to try!"

The battle would resume very shortly. At any moment, in fact, some scoutship leading the American force might fire a missile. But when Diaz told his guard he wanted to speak with General Rostock, he was taken there within minutes.

The door closed behind him. The living room lay empty, altogether still except for the machine throb, which was not loud since the *Ho* was running free. Because acceleration might be needful on short notice, there was no spin. Diaz hung weightless as fog. And the Monet flung into his eyes all Earth's sunlight and summer forests.

"Rostock?" he called uncertainly.

"Come," said a voice, almost too low to hear. Diaz gave a shove with his foot and flew toward the office.

He stopped himself by grasping the doorjamb. A semicircular room lay before him, the entire side taken up by controls and meters. Lights blinked, needles wavered on dials, buttons and switches and knobs reached across black paneling. But none of that was important. Only the man at the desk mattered, who free-sat with wires running from his head to the wall.

Rostock seemed to have lost weight. Or was that an illusion? The skin was drawn taut across his high cheekbones and gone a dead, glistening white. His nostrils were flared and the colorless lips held tense. Diaz looked into his eyes, once, and then away again. He could not meet them. He could not even think about them. He drew a shaken breath and waited.

"You made your decision quickly," Rostock whispered. "I had not awaited you until after the engagement."

"I . . . I didn't think you would see me till then."

"This is more important." Diaz felt as if he were being probed with knives. He could not altogether believe it was his imagination. He stared desperately at the paneled instruments. Their nonhumanness was like a comforting hand. *They must only be for the benefit of maintenance techs*, he thought in a very distant part of himself. *The brain doesn't need them.*

"You are convinced," Rostock said in frank surprise.

"Yes," Diaz answered.

"I had not expected that. I only hoped for your reluctant agreement to study my work." Rostock regarded him for a still century. "You were ripe for a new faith," he decided. "I had not taken you for the type. But then, the mind can only use what data are given it, and I have hitherto had little opportunity to meet Americans. Never since I became what I am. You have another psyche from ours."

"I need to understand your findings, sir," Diaz said. "Right now I can only believe. That isn't enough, is it?"

Slowly, Rostock's mouth drew into a smile of quite human warmth. "Correct. But given the faith, intellectual comprehension should be swift."

"I . . . I shouldn't be taking your time . . . now, sir," Diaz stammered. "How should I begin? Should I take some books back with me?"

"No." Acceptance had been reached. Rostock spoke resonantly, a master to his trusted servant. "I need your help here. Strap into yonder harness. Our first necessity is to survive the battle upon us. You realize that this means sacrificing many of your comrades. I know how much that will hurt you. Afterward we shall spend our lives repaying our people—both our peoples. But today I shall ask you questions about your fleet. Any information is valuable, especially details of construction and armament which our intelligence has not been able to learn."

*Doña mia.* Diaz let go the door, covered his face and fell free, endlessly. *Help me.*

"It is not betrayal," said the superman. "It is the ultimate loyalty you can offer."

Diaz made himself look at the cabin again. He shoved against the bulkhead and stopped by the harness near the desk.

"You cannot lie to me," said Rostock. "Do not deny how much pain I am giving you." Diaz glimpsed his fists clamping together. "Each time I look at you, I share what you feel."

Diaz clung to his harness. There went an explosion through him.

NO, BY GOD!

Rostock screamed.

"Don't," Diaz sobbed. "I don't want—" But wave after wave ripped outward. Rostock flopped about in his harness and shrieked. The scene came back, ramming home like a bayonet.

\* \* \*

"We like to put an extra string on our bow," the psych officer said. Lunar sunlight, scarcely softened by the dome, blazed off his bronze eagles, wings and beaks. "You know that your right ulna will be replaced with a metal section in which there is a nerve-triggered nuclear cartridge. But that may not be all, gentlemen."

He bridged his fingers. The young men seated on the other side of his desk stirred uneasily. "In this country," the psych officer said, "we don't believe humans should be turned into puppets. Therefore you will have voluntary control of your bombs; no posthypnosis, Pavlov reflex or any such insult. However, those of you who are willing will receive a rather special extra treatment, and that fact will be buried from the consciousness of all of you.

"Our reasoning is that if and when the Unasians learn about the prisoner weapon, they'll remove the cartridge by surgery but leave the prosthetic bone in place. And they will, we hope, not examine it in microscopic detail. Therefore they won't know what it contains an oscillator, integrated with the crystal structure. Nor will you; because what you don't know, you can't babble under anesthesia.

"The opportunity may come, if you are captured and lose your bomb, to inflict damage by this reserve means. You may find yourself near a crucial electronic device, for example a spaceship's autopilot. At short range, the oscillator will do an excellent job of bollixing it. Which will at least discomfit the enemy, and may even give you a chance to escape.

"The posthypnotic command will be such that you'll remember about this oscillator when conditions seem right for using it. Not before. Of course, the human mind is a damned queer thing, that twists and turns and bites its own tail. In order to make an opportunity to strike this blow, your subsconscious may lead you down strange paths. It may even have you seriously contemplating treason, if treason seems the only way of getting access to what you can wreck. Don't let that bother you afterward, gentlemen. Your superiors will know what happened.

"Nevertheless, the experience may be painful. And posthypnosis is, at best, humiliating to a free man. So this aspect of the program is strictly volunteer. Does anybody want to go for broke?"

The door flung open. The guards burst in. Diaz was already behind the desk, next to Rostock. He yanked out the general's sidearm and fired at the soldiers. Free fall recoil sent him back against the computer panel. He braced himself, fired again and used his left elbow to smash the nearest meter face.

Rostock clawed at the wires in his head. For a moment Diaz guessed what it must be like to have random oscillations in your brain, amplified by an electronic engine that was part of you. He laid the pistol to the screaming man's temple and fired once more.

Now to get out! He shoved hard, arrowing past the sentries, who rolled through the air in a crimson galaxy of blood globules. Confusion boiled in the corridor beyond. Someone snatched at him. He knocked the fellow aside and dove along a tubeway. Somewhere hearabouts should be a scooter locker—there, and nobody around!

He didn't have time to get on a spacesuit, even if a Unasian one would have fitted, but he slipped on an air dome over the scooter. That, with the heater unit and oxy reclaim, would serve. He didn't want to get off anywhere en route; not before he'd steered the machine through an American hatch.

With luck, he'd do that. Their command computer gone, the enemy were going to get smeared. American ships would close in as the slaughter progressed. Eventually one should come within range of the scooter's little radio.

He set the minilock controls, mounted the saddle, dogged the air dome and waited for ejection. It came none to soon. Three soldiers had just appeared down the passageway. Diaz applied full thrust and jetted away from the *Ho*. Its blackness was soon lost among the star clouds.

Battle commenced. The first Unasian ship to be destroyed must have been less than fifty miles distant. Luckily, Diaz was facing the other way when the missile exploded.

# FORTRESS SHIP

## (JANUARY 1963)

## FRED SABERHAGEN

## (B. 1930)

The giant killer machines called berserkers were one of the most popular "characters" to appear in the pages of *If*, and their creator has become closely identified with them in the minds of science-fiction writers. This has had its disadvantages, since Fred Saberhagen is a fine writer of considerable range (see, for example, his *The Dracula Tape,* 1975), one who is finally getting the recognition long due him.

Many of the Berserker tales appeared in *If*, as did the novel *Berserker's Planet* (serialized in 1974, the year of the magazine's death). "Fortress Ship" is one of the best in the series, a story of evil and virtue in conflict.

## A MEMOIR BY FRED SABERHAGEN

A look back through the files tells me something that I find surprising. Between 1961, when I started writing professionally, and 1974 my name appeared on the title page of *Worlds of If* no less than nineteen times. This is probably not a record of any kind, but it certainly was fun.

As far as I know, *Worlds of If* never invited any pretensions or made any claims of literary flavor or breathtaking writing style. It just used stories wherein beings faced problems, and more often than not solved them, adjusting the world to fit themselves a little better. I wouldn't claim this as the only basis on which a good story can be written, but following such a philosophy is not necessarily a drawback, either. I have a theory about art: Thinking a lot about art does not produce it, but trying to do a good job may. The writers and editors who performed in the old *If* tried. Imagine, "Gods of all Space," a story (by Christopher Anvil) that got me to write in to the letter column! (I've nothing against letter columns, it's only writing letters that I dislike.)

Imagine Poul Anderson, Lester del Rey, Fritz Leiber . . . and Shaw, Asimov, Niven, Pohl, Schmitz, Reynolds . . . no need to go on. You have the idea in hand already, with this book.

As for "Fortress Ship," it's the start of what publishers' blurbs are now calling the Berserker Saga. It's also my champion story in terms of number of times reprinted, both under this title and under another one that I like a little better. But this is Fred Pohl's book, as *If* was once his magazine, and he has my whole-hearted blessing this time to use whatever title he likes.

# FORTRESS SHIP

The machine was a vast fortress, containing no life, set by its long-dead masters to destroy anything that lived. It and many others like it were the inheritance of Earth from some war fought between unknown interstellar empires, in some time that could hardly be connected with any Earthly calendar.

One such machine could hang over a planet colonized by men and in two days pound the surface into a lifeless cloud of dust and steam, a hundred miles deep. This particular machine had already done just that.

It used no predictable tactics in its dedicated, unconscious war against life. The ancient, unknown gamesmen had built it as a random factor, to be loosed in the enemy's territory to do what damage it might. Men thought its plan of battle was chosen by the random disintegrations of atoms in a block of some long-lived isotope buried deep inside it, and so was not even in theory predictable by opposing brains, human or electronic.

Men called it a berserker.

Del Murray, sometime computer specialist, had called it other names than that; but right now he was too busy to waste breath, as he moved in staggering lunges around the little cabin of his one-man fighter, plugging in replacement units for equipment damaged by the last near-miss of a berserker missile. An animal resembling a large dog with an ape's forelegs moved around the cabin too, carrying in its nearly human hands a supply of emergency sealing patches. The cabin air was full of haze. Wherever movement of the haze showed a leak to an unpressurized part of the hull, the dog-ape moved to apply a patch.

"Hello, Foxglove!" the man shouted, hoping that his radio was again in working order.

"Hello, Murray, this is Foxglove," said a sudden loud voice in the cabin. "How far did you get?"

Del was too weary to show much relief that his communications were open again. "I'll let you know in a minute. At least it's stopped shooting at me for a while. Move, Newton." The alien animal, pet and ally, called an *aiyan*, moved away from the man's feet and kept singlemindedly looking for leaks.

After another minute's work Del could strap his body into the deep-cushioned command chair again, with something like an operational panel before him. That last near-miss had sprayed the whole cabin with fine penetrating splinters. It was remarkable that man and *aiyan* had come through unwounded.

His radar working again, Del could say: "I'm about ninety miles out from it, Foxglove. On the opposite side from you." His present position was the one he had been trying to achieve since the battle had begun.

The two Earth ships and the berserker were half a light-year from the nearest sun. The berserker could not leap out of normal space, toward the defenseless colonies of the planets of that sun, while the two ships stayed close to it. There were only two men aboard Foxglove. They had more machinery working for them than did Del, but both manned ships were mites compared to their opponent.

Del's radar showed him an ancient ruin of metal, not much smaller in cross section than New Jersey. Men had blown holes in it the size of Manhattan Island, and melted puddles of slag as big as lakes upon its surface.

But the berserker's power was still enormous. So far no man had fought it and survived. Now, it could squash Del's little ship like a mosquito; it was wasting its unpredictable subtlety on him. Yet there was a special taste of terror in the very difference of it. Men could never frighten this enemy, as it frightened them.

Earthmen's tactics, worked out from bitter experience against other berserkers, called for a simultaneous attack by three ships. Foxglove and Murray made two. A third was supposedly on the way, but still about eight hours distant, moving at C-plus velocity, outside of normal space. Until it arrived, Foxglove and Murray must hold the berserker at bay, while it brooded unguessable schemes.

It might attack either ship at any moment, or it might seek to disengage. It might wait hours for them to make the first move—though it would certainly fight if the men attacked it. It had learned the language of Earth's spacemen—it might try to talk with them. But always, ultimately, it would seek to destroy them and every other living thing it met. That was the basic command given it by the ancient warlords.

A thousand years ago, it would easily have swept ships of the type that now opposed it from its path, whether they carried fusion missiles or not. Now, it was in some electrical way conscious of its own weakening by accumulated damage. And perhaps in long centuries of fighting its way across the galaxy it had learned to be wary.

Now, quite suddenly, Del's detectors showed force fields forming in behind his ship. Like the encircling arms of a huge bear they blocked his path away from the enemy. He waited for some deadly blow, with his hand trembling over the red button that would salvo his atomic missiles at the berserker—but if he attacked alone, or even with Foxglove, the infernal machine would parry their missiles, crush their ships, and go on to destroy another helpless planet. Three ships were needed to attack. The red firing button was now only a last desperate resort.

Del was reporting the force fields to Foxglove when he felt the first hint in his mind of another attack.

"Newton!" he called sharply, leaving the radio connection with Foxglove open. They would hear and understand what was going to happen.

The *aiyan* bounded instantly from its combat couch to stand before Del as if hypnotized, all attention riveted on the man. Del had sometimes bragged: "Show Newton a drawing of different-colored lights, convince him it represents a particular control panel, and he'll push buttons or whatever you tell him, until the real panel matches the drawing."

But no *aiyan* had the human ability to learn and to create on an abstract level; which was why Del was now going to put Newton in command of his ship.

He switched off the ship's computers—they were going to be as useless as his own brain under the attack he felt gathering—and said to Newton: "Situation Zombie."

The animal responded instantly as it had been trained, seizing Del's hands with firm insistence and dragging them one at a time down beside the command chair to where the fetters had been installed.

Hard experience had taught men something about the berserkers' mind weapon, although its principles of operation were still unknown. It was slow in its onslaught, and its effects could not be steadily maintained for more than about two hours, after which a berserker was evidently forced to turn it off for an equal time. But while in effect, it robbed any human or electronic brain of the ability to plan or to predict—and left it unconscious of its own incapacity.

It seemed to Del that all this had happened before, maybe more than once. Newton, that funny fellow, had gone too far with his pranks; he had abandoned the little boxes of colored beads that were his favorite toys, and was moving the controls around at the lighted panel. Unwilling to share the fun with Del, he had tied the man to his chair somehow. Such behavior was really intolerable, especially when there was supposed to be a battle in progress. Del tried to pull his hands free, and called to Newton.

Newton whined earnestly, and stayed at the panel.

"Newt, you dog, come lemme loose. I know what I have to say: Fourscore and seven . . . hey, Newt, where're your toys? Lemme see your pretty beads." There were hundreds of tiny boxes of the varicolored beads, leftover trade goods that Newton loved to sort out and handle. Del peered around the cabin, chuckling a little at his own cleverness. He would get Newton distracted by the beads, and then . . . the vague idea faded into other crackbrained grotesqueries.

Newton whined now and then but stayed at the panel moving controls in the long sequence he had been taught, taking the ship through the feinting, evasive maneuvers that might fool a berserker into thinking it was still competently manned. Newton never put a hand near the big red button. Only if he felt deadly pain himself, or found a dead man in Del's chair, would he reach for that.

"Ah, roger, Murray," said the radio from time to time, as if acknowledging a message. Sometimes Foxglove added a few words or numbers that might have meant something. Del wondered what the talking was about.

At last he understood that Foxglove was trying to help maintain the illusion that there was still a competent brain in charge of

Del's ship. The fear reaction came when he began to realize that he had once again lived through the effect of the mind weapon. The brooding berserker, half genius, half idiot, had forborne to press the attack when success would have been certain—perhaps deceived, perhaps following the strategy that avoided predictability at almost any cost.

"Newton." The animal turned, hearing a change in his voice. Now Del could say the words that would tell Newton it was safe to set his master free, a sequence too long for anyone under the mind weapon to recite.

"—shall not perish from the earth," he finished. With a yelp of joy Newton pulled the fetters from Del's hands. Del turned instantly to the radio.

"Effect has evidently been turned off, Foxglove," said Del's voice through the speaker in the cabin of the larger ship."

The Commander let out a sigh. "He's back in control!"

The Second Officer—there was no third—said: "That means we've got some kind of fighting chance, for the next two hours. I say let's attack now!"

The Commander shook his head, slowly but without hesitation. "With two ships, we don't have any real chance. Less than four hours until Gizmo gets here. We have to stall until then, if we want to win."

"It'll attack the next time it gets Del's mind scrambled! I don't think we fooled it for a minute . . . we're out of range of the mind beam here, but Del can't withdraw now. And we can't expect that *aiyan* to fight his ship for him. We'll really have no chance, with Del gone."

The Commander's eyes moved ceaselessly over his panel. "We'll wait. We can't be sure it'll attack the next time it puts the beam on him . . ."

The berserker spoke suddenly, its radioed voice plain in the cabins of both ships: "I have a proposition for you, little ship." Its voice had a cracking, adolescent quality, because it strung together words and syllables recorded from the voices of human prisoners of both sexes and different ages. Bits of human emotion, sorted and fixed like butterflies on pins, thought the Commander. There was no reason to think it had kept the prisoners alive after learning the language from them.

"Well?" Del's voice sounded tough and capable by comparison.

"I have invented a game which we will play," it said. "If you play well enough, I will not kill you right away."

"Now I've heard everything," murmured the Second Officer.

After three thoughtful seconds the Commander slammed a fist on the arm of his chair. "It means to test his learning ability, to run a continuous check on his brain while it turns up the power of the mind beam and tries different modulations. If it can make sure the mind beam is working, it'll attack instantly. I'll bet my life on it. That's the game it's playing this time."

"I will think over your proposition," said Del's voice coolly.

The Commander said: "It's in no hurry to start. It won't be able to turn on the mind beam again for almost two hours."

"But we need another two hours beyond that."

Del's voice said: "Describe the game you want to play."

"It is a simplified version of the human game called checkers."

The Commander and the Second looked at each other, neither able to imagine Newton able to play checkers. Nor could they doubt that Newton's failure would kill them within a few hours, and leave another planet open to destruction.

After a minute's silence, Del's voice asked: "What'll we use for a board?"

"We will radio our moves to one another," said the berserker equably. It went on to describe a checkers-like game, played on a smaller board with less than the normal number of pieces. There was nothing very profound about it; but, of course, playing would seem to require a functional brain, human or electronic, able to plan and to predict.

"If I agree to play," said Del slowly, "how'll we decide who gets to move first?"

"He's trying to stall," said the Commander, gnawing a thumbnail. "We won't be able to offer any advice, with that thing listening. Oh, stay sharp, Del boy!"

"To simplify matters," said the berserker. "I will move first in every game."

Del could look forward to another hour free of the mind weapon when he finished rigging the checkerboard. When the pegged pieces were moved, appropriate signals would be radioed to the berserker; lighted squares on the board would show him where its pieces were moved. If it spoke to him while the mind weapon was on, Del's voice would answer from a tape, which he had stocked with vaguely aggressive phrases, such as: "Get on with the game," or "Do you want to give up now?"

He hadn't told the enemy how far along he was with his preparations because he was still busy with something the enemy must not know—the system that was going to enable Newton to play a game of simplified checkers.

Del gave a soundless little laugh as he worked, and glanced over to where Newton was lounging on his couch, clutching toys in his hands as if he drew some comfort from them. This scheme was going to push the *aiyan* near the limit of his ability, but Del saw no reason why it should fail.

Del had completely analyzed the miniature checker game, and diagrammed every position that Newton could possibly face— playing only even-numbered moves, thank the random berserker for that specification!—on small cards. Del had discarded some lines of play that would arise from some poor early moves by Newton, further simplifying his job. Now, on a card showing each possible remaining position, Del indicated the best possible move with a drawn-in arrow. Now he could quickly teach Newton to play the game by looking at the appropriate card and making the move shown by the arrow—

"Oh, oh," said Del, as his hands stopped working and he stared into space. Newton whined at the tone of his voice.

Once Del had sat at one board in a simultaneous chess exhibition, one of sixty players opposing the world champion, Blankenship. Del had held his own into the middle game. Then, when the great man paused again opposite his board, Del had shoved a pawn forward, thinking he had reached an unassailable position and could begin a counterattack. Blankenship had moved a rook to an innocent-looking square and strolled on to the next board— and then Del had seen the checkmate coming at him, four moves away but one move too late for him to do anything about it.

The Commander suddenly said a foul phrase in a loud distinct voice. Such conduct on his part was extremely rare, and the Second Officer looked round in surprise. "What?"

"I think we've had it." The Commander paused. "I hoped that Murray could set up some kind of a system over there, so that Newton could play the game—or appear to be playing it. But it won't work. Whatever system Newton plays by rote will always have him making the same move in the same position. It may be a perfect system—but a man doesn't play any game that way, damn it. He makes mistakes, he changes strategy. Even in a game this simple there'll be room for that. Most of all, a man *learns* a game as he plays it. He gets better as he goes along.

That's what'll give Newton away, and that's what our bandit wants. It's probably heard about *aiyans*. Now as soon as it can be sure it's facing a dumb animal over there, and not a man or computer . . ."

After a little while the Second Officer said: "I'm getting signals of their moves. They've begun play. Maybe we should've rigged up a board so we could follow along with the game."

"We better just be ready to go at it when the time comes." The Commander looked hopelessly at his salvo button, and then at the clock that showed two hours must pass before Gizmo could reasonably be hoped for.

Soon the Second Officer said: "That seems to be the end of the first game; Del lost it, if I'm reading their scoreboard signal right." He paused. "Sir, here's that signal we picked up the last time it turned the mind beam on. Del must be starting to get it again."

There was nothing for the Commander to say. The two men waited silently for the enemy's attack, hoping only that they could damage it in the seconds before it would overwhelm them and kill them.

"He's playing the second game," said the Second Officer, puzzled. "And I just heard him say, 'Let's get on with it.' "

"His voice could be recorded. He must have made some plan of play for Newton to follow; but it won't fool the berserker for long. It can't."

Time crept unmeasurably past them.

The Second said: "'He's lost the first four games. But he's *not* making the same moves every time. I wish we'd made a board. . . ."

"Shut up about the board! We'd be watching it instead of the panel. Now stay alert, Mister."

After what seemed a long time, the Second said: "Well, I'll be!"

"What?"

"Our side got a draw in that game."

"Then the beam can't be on him. Are you sure . . ."

"It is! Look, here, the same indication we got last time. It's been on him the better part of an hour now, and getting stronger."

The Commander stared in disbelief; but he knew and trusted his Second's ability. And the panel indications were convincing. He said: "Then someone—or something—with no functioning mind is learning how to play a game, over there. Ha, ha," he added, as if trying to remember how to laugh.

*     *     *

The berserker won another game. Another draw. Another win for the enemy. Then three drawn games in a row.

Once the Second Officer heard Del's voice ask coolly: "Do you want to give up now?" On the next move he lost another game. But the following game ended in another draw. Del was plainly taking more time than his opponent to move, but not enough to make the enemy impatient.

"It's trying different modulations of the mind beam," said the Second. "And it's got the power turned way up."

"Yeah," said the Commander. Several times he had almost tried to radio Del, to say something that might keep the man's spirits up—and also to relieve his own feverish inactivity, and to try to find out what could possibly be going on. But he could not take the chance. Any interference might upset the miracle.

He could not believe the inexplicable success could last, even when the checker match turned gradually into an endless successions of drawn games between two perfect players. Hours ago the Commander had said good-bye to life and hope, and he still waited for the fatal moment.

And he waited.

"—not perish from the earth!" said Del Murray, and Newton's eager hands flew to loose his right arm from its shackle.

A game, unfinished on the little board before him, had been abandoned seconds earlier. The mind beam had been turned off at the same time, when Gizmo had burst into normal space right in position and only five minutes late; and the berserker had been forced to turn all its energies to meet the immediate all-out attack of Gizmo and Foxglove.

Del saw his computers, recovering from the effect of the beam, lock his aiming screen onto the berserker's scarred and bulging midsection, as he shot his right arm forward, scattering pieces from the game board.

"Checkmate!" he roared out hoarsely, and brought his fist down on the big red button.

"I'm glad it didn't want to play chess," Del said later, talking to the Commander in Foxglove's cabin. "I could never have rigged that up."

The ports were cleared now, and the men could look out at the cloud of expanding gas, still faintly luminous, that had been a berserker; metal fire-purged of the legacy of ancient evil.

But the Commander was watching Del. "You got Newt to play

by following diagrams, I see that. But how could he *learn* the game?"

Del grinned. "He couldn't, but his toys could. Now wait before you slug me." He called the *aiyan* to him and took a small box from the animal's hand. The box rattled faintly as he held it up. On the cover was pasted a diagram of one possible position in the simplified checker game, with a different-colored arrow indicating each possible move of Del's pieces.

"It took a couple of hundred of these boxes," said Del. "This one was in the group that Newt examined for the fourth move. When he found a box with a diagram matching the position on the board, he picked the box up, pulled out one of these beads from inside, without looking—that was the hardest part to teach him in a hurry, by the way," said Del, demonstrating. "Ah, this one's blue. That means, make the move indicated on the cover by a blue arrow. Now the orange arrow leads to a poor position, see?" Del shook all the beads out of the box into his hand. "No orange beads left; there were six of each color when we started. But every time Newton drew a bead, he had orders to leave it out of the box until the game was over. Then, if the scoreboard indicated a loss for our side, he went back and threw away all the beads he had used. All the bad moves were gradually eliminated. In a few hours, Newt and his boxes learned to play the game perfectly."

"Well," said the Commander. He thought for a moment, then reached down to scratch Newton behind the ears. "I never would have come up with that idea."

"I should have thought of it sooner. The basic idea's a couple of centuries old. And computers are supposed to be my business."

"This could be a big thing," said the Commander. "I mean your basic idea might be useful to any task force that has to face a berserker's mind beam."

"Yeah." Del grew reflective. "Also . . ."

"What?"

"I was thinking of a guy I met once. Named Blankenship. I wonder if I *could* rig something up. . . ."

# FATHER OF THE STARS
## NOVEMBER 1964
## FREDERIK POHL
## (B. 1919)

Fred Pohl not only edited *If* during its greatest years, but he also contributed some fine science fiction to the magazine, both before and after his editorial tenure, including "The Engineer" (February 1956, with C. M. Kornbluth), "Doomship" (April 1973), "The Martian in the Attic" (July 1960), "The Merchants of Venus" (August 1972), and three novels written with Jack Williamson, *The Reefs of Space* (1963), *Starchild* (1965), and *Rogue Star* (1968).

# FATHER OF THE STARS

Norman Marchand sat in the wings of the ballroom's small stage, on a leather hassock someone had found for him. There were fifteen hundred people outside in the ballroom, waiting to do him honor.

Marchand remembered the ballroom very well. He had once owned it. Forty . . . no, it wasn't forty. Not even fifty. Sixty years ago it had been, sixty and more years ago that he and Joyce had danced in that ballroom. Then the hotel was the newest on Earth and he was the newly married son of the man who had built it, and the party was the reception for his wedding to Joyce. Of course, none of these people would know about that. But Marchand remembered . . . *Oh, Joyce, my very dear!* But she had been dead a long time now.

It was a noisy crowd. He peered out through the wings, and could see the head table filling up. There was the Vice President of the United States shaking hands with the Governor of Ontario as though, for the moment, they had forgotten they were of different parties. There was Linfox, from the Institute, obligingly helping a chimpanzee into the chair next to what, judging by the microphones ranked before it, would probably be Marchand's own. Linfox seemed a little ill at ease with the chimp. The chimpanzee had no doubt been smithed, but the imposition of human intelligence did not lengthen its ape's legs.

Then Dan Fleury appeared, up the steps from the floor of the ballroom where the rest of the fifteen hundred diners were taking their places.

Fleury didn't look well at all, Marchand thought—not without a small touch of satisfaction, since Fleury was fifteen years younger than himself. Still, Marchand wasn't jealous. Not even of the young bellman who had brought him the hassock, twenty years at the most and built like a fullback. One life was enough for a man to live. Especially when you had accomplished the dream you had set out to bring to fruition. Or almost.

Of course, it cost him everything his father left. But what else was money for?

"It's time to go in, sir. May I help you?" It was the young fullback nearly bursting his bellman's uniform with the huge hard muscles of youth. He was very solicitous. One of the nice things about having this testimonial dinner in a Marchand hotel was that the staff was as deferential to him as though he still owned the place. Probably that was why the committee had picked it, Marchand ruminated, quaint and old-fashioned as the hotel must seem now. Though at one time—

He recollected himself. "I'm sorry, young man. I was—wool-gathering. Thank you."

He stood up, slowly but not very painfully, considering that it had been a long day. As the fullback walked him onto the stage the applause was enough to drive down the automatic volume control on his hearing aid.

For that reason he missed the first words from Dan Fleury. No doubt they were complimentary. Very carefully he lowered himself into his chair, and as the clapping eased off he was able to begin to hear the words.

Dan Fleury was still a tall man, built like a barrel, with bushy eyebrows and a huge mane of hair. He had helped Marchand's mad project for thrusting man into space from its very beginnings. He said as much now. "Man's grandest dream!" he roared. "The conquering of the stars themselves! And here is the one man who taught us how to dream it, Norman Marchand!"

Marchand bowed to the storm of applause.

Again his hearing aid saved his ears and cost him the next few words: "—and now that we are on the threshold of success,"

Fleury was booming, "it is altogether fitting that we should gather here tonight . . . to join in fellowship and in the expression of that grand hope . . . to rededicate ourselves to its fulfillment . . . and to pay our respects, and give of our love, to the man who first showed us what dream to have!"

While the AVC registered the power of Dan Fleury's oratory Marchand smiled out on the foggy sea of faces. It was, he thought, almost cruel of Fleury to put it like that. The threshold of success indeed! How many years now had they waited on it patiently? —and the door still locked in their faces. Of course, he thought wryly, they must have calculated that the testimonial dinner would have to be held soon unless they wanted a cadaver for a guest. But still . . . There was something in his tone. Was there— Could there be—

There could not, he told himself firmly. There was no news, no breakthrough, no report from one of the wandering ships, no dream come true at last. He would have been the first to know. Not for anything would they have kept a thing like that from him. And he did not know that thing.

"—and now," Fleury was saying, "I won't keep you from your dinners. There will be many a long, strong speech to help your digestions afterwards, I promise you! But now, let's eat!"

Laughter. Applause. A buzz and clash of forks.

The injunction to eat did not, of course, include Norman Marchand. He sat with his hands in his lap, watching them dig in, smiling and feeling just a touch deprived, with the wry regret of the very old. He didn't envy the young people anything *really*, he told himself. Not their health, their youth or their life expectancy. But he envied them the bowls of ice.

He tried to pretend he enjoyed his wine and the huge pink shrimp in crackers and milk. According to Asa Czerny, who ought to know since he had kept Marchand alive this long, he had a clear choice. He could eat whatever he chose, or he could stay alive. For a while. And ever since Czerny had been good enough, or despairing enough, to give him a maximum date for his life expectancy, Marchand had in idle moments tried to calculate just how much of those remaining months he was willing to give up for one really good meal. He rather believed that when Czerny looked up at him after the weekly medical checkup and said that only days were left, he would take those last days and trade them in for a sauerbraten with potato pancakes and sweet-sour red cabbage on the side. But that time was not yet. With any kind of luck he still had a month. Perhaps as much as two. . . . "I beg your—pardon," he said, half-turning to the chimpanzee. Even smithed, the animal spoke so poorly that Marchand had not at first known that he was being addressed.

He should not have turned.

His wrist had lost its suppleness; the spoon in his hand tilted: the soggy crackers fell. He made the mistake of trying to move his knee out of the way—it was bad enough to be old, he did not want to be sloppy—and he moved too quickly.

The chair was at the very edge of the little platform. He felt himself going over.

Ninety-six is too old to be falling on your head, he thought; if I was going to do this sort of thing I might just as well have eaten some of those shrimp. . . . But he did not kill himself.

He only knocked himself unconscious. And not for very long at that, because he began to wake up while they were still carrying him back to his dressing room behind the stage.

Once upon a time, Norman Marchand had given his life to a hope.

Rich, intelligent, married to a girl of beauty and tenderness, he had taken everything he owned and given it to the Institute for Colonizing Extra-Solar Planets. He had, to begin with, given away several million dollars.

That was the whole of the personal fortune his father had left him, and it was nowhere near enough to do the job. It was only a catalyst. He had used it to hire publicity men, fund-raisers, investment counselors, foundation managers. He had spent it on documentary films and on TV commercials. With it he had financed cocktail parties for United States senators and prize contests for the nation's sixth grades, and he had done what he set out to do.

He had raised money. A very great deal of money.

He had taken all the money he had begged and teased out of the pockets of the world and used it to finance the building of twenty-six great ships, each the size of a dozen ocean liners, and he had cast them into space like a farmer sowing wheat upon the wind.

I tried, he whispered to himself, returning from the darkest place he had ever seen. I wanted to see man reach out and touch a new home . . . and I wanted to be the one to guide him there. . . .

And someone was saying: "—he knew about it, did he? But we were trying to keep it quiet—" Someone else told the first person to shut his mouth. Marchand opened his eyes.

Czerny was there, unsmiling. He saw that Marchand was conscious. "You're all right," he said, and Marchand knew that it was true, since Czerny was scowling angrily at him. If the news had been bad he would have smiled— "No you don't!" cried Czerny, catching him by the shoulder. "You stay right there. You're going home to bed."

"But you said I was all right."

"I meant you were still breathing. Don't push it, Norm."

Marchand protested, "But the dinner—I ought to be there—"

Asa Czerny had cared for Marchand for thirty years. They had gone fishing together, and once or twice they had gotten drunk. Czerny would not have refused for nothing. He only shook his head.

Marchand slumped back. Behind Czerny the chimpanzee was squatting silently on the edge of a chair, watching. He's worried, Marchand thought. Worried because he feels it's his fault, what happened to me. The thought gave him enough strength to say: "Stupid of me to fall like that, Mr.—I'm sorry."

Czerny supplied the introduction. "This is Duane Ferguson, Norman. He was supernumerary on the *Copernicus*. Smithed. He's attending the dinner in costume, as it were." The chimpanzee nodded but did not speak. He was watching that silver-tongued orator, Dan Fleury, who seemed upset. "Where is that ambulance?" demanded Czerny, with a doctor's impatience with internes, and the fullback in bellman's uniform hurried silently away to find out.

The chimpanzee made a barking sound, clearing his throat. "Ghwadd," he said—more or less: the German *ich* sound followed by the word "what"—"Ghwadd did jou mee-an aboud evdial, Midda Vleury?"

Dan Fleury turned and looked at the chimp blankly. But not, Marchand thought suddenly, as though he didn't know what the chimp was talking about. Only as if he didn't intend to answer.

Marchand rasped. "What's this 'evdial,' Dan?"

"Search me. Look, Mr. Ferguson, perhaps we'd better go outside."

"Ghwadd?" The harsh barking voice struggled against the simian body it occupied, and came closer to the sounds it meant to emit. "*What* did you bean—did you *mean?*"

He was a rude young man, Marchand thought irritably. The fellow was tiring him.

Although there was something about that insistent question—

Marchand winced and felt for a moment as though he were going to throw up. It passed, leaving him wobbly. It wasn't possible he had broken anything, he told himself. Czerny would not lie about that. But he felt as if he had.

He lost interest in the chimp-man, did not even turn his head as Fleury hurried him out of the room, whispering to him in an agitated and low-pitched chirrup like the scratching of a cricket's legs.

If a man wanted to abandon his God-given human body and put his mind, thoughts and—yes—soul into the corpus of an anthropoid, there was nothing in that to entitle him to any special consideration from Norman Marchand.

Of course not! Marchand rehearsed the familiar argument as he waited for the ambulance. Men who volunteered for the interstellar flights he had done so much to bring about knew what they were getting into. Until some frabjous super-Batman invented the mythical FTL drive it would always be so. At possible speeds— less than light's 186,000 mps crawl—it was a matter of decades to reach almost every worthwhile planet that was known.

The Smith process allowed these men to use their minds to control chimpanzee bodies—easily bred, utterly expendable—while their own bodies rested in the deep-freeze for all the long years between the stars.

It took brave men, naturally. They were entitled to courtesy and consideration.

But so was he, and it was not courteous to blather about "evdial," whatever that was, while the man who had made their trip possible was seriously injured. . . .

Unless . . .

Marchand opened his eyes again.

"Evdial." Unless "evdial" was the closest chimpanzee vocal chords and chimpanzee lips could come to—to—unless what they had been talking about, while he was unconscious, was that utterly impossible, hopeless and fantastic dream that he, Marchand, had turned his back upon when he began organizing the colonization campaign.

Unless someone had really found the way to FTL travel.

## II

As soon as he was able the next day, Marchand got himself into a wheelchair—all by himself; he didn't want any help in this—and rolled it out into the chart room of the home the Institute had given him rent-free for all of his life. (He had, of course, given it in the first place to the Institute.)

The Institute had put three hundred thousand dollars into the chart room. Stayed and guywired stars flecked the volume of a forty-foot ballroom, representing in scale all the space within fifty-five light-years of Sol. Every star was mapped and tagged. They had even moved a few of them slightly, a year ago, to correct for proper motion: it was that carefully done.

The twenty-six great starships the Institute had financed were there, too, or such of them as were still in space. They were out of scale, of course, but Marchand understood what they represented. He rolled his chair down the marked path to the center of the room and sat there, looking around, just under yellow Sol.

There was blue-white Sirius dominating them all. Procyon hanging just above. The two of them together were incomparably the brightest objects in the room, though red Altair was brighter in its own right than Procyon. In the center of the chamber Sol and Alpha Centauri A made a brilliant pair.

He gazed with rheuming eyes at the greatest disappointment of his life, Alpha Centauri B. So close. So right. So sterile. It was an ironic blunder of creation that the nearest and best chance of another home had never formed planets . . . or had formed them and swept them into the Bode-area traps set by itself and its two companions.

But there were other hopes. . . .

Marchand sought and found Tau Ceti, yellow and pale. Only eleven light-years away, the colony should be definitely established by now. In another decade or less they should have an answer . . . if, of course, it had planets Man could live on.

That was the big question, to which they had already received so many nos. But Tau Ceti was still a good bet, Marchand told himself stoutly. It was a dimmer, cooler sun than Sol. But it was type G, and according to spectropolarimetry, almost certainly planetiferous. And if it were another disappointment—

Marchand turned his eyes to 40 Eridani A, even dimmer, even farther away. The expedition to 40 Eridani A had been, he remembered, the fifth ship he had launched. It ought to be reaching its destination soon—this year, or perhaps next. There was no sure way of estimating time when the top velocity was so close to light's own. . . .

But now of course the top velocity was more.

The sudden wash of failure almost made him physically ill. Faster than light travel—why, how dared they!

But he didn't have time to waste on that particular emotion, or indeed on any emotion at all. He felt time draining away from him and sat up straight again, looking around. At ninety-six you dare not do anything slowly, not even daydream.

He glanced at, and dismissed, Procyon. They had tried Procyon lately—the ship would not be even halfway. They had tried almost everything. Even Epsilon Eridani and Groombridge 1618; even, far down past the probably good bets among the spectroscopic classes, 61 Cygni A and Epsilon Indi, a late and despairing try at Proxima Centauri (though they were very nearly sure it was wasted: the Alpha Centauri expedition had detected nothing like viable planets).

There had been twenty-six of them in all. Three ships lost, three returned, one still Earthbound. Nineteen were still out there.

Marchand looked for comfort at the bright green arrow that marked where the *Tycho Brahe* rode its jets of ionized gas, the biggest of his ships, three thousand men and women. It seemed to him that someone had mentioned the *Tycho Brahe* recently. When? Why? He was not sure, but the name stuck in his mind.

The door opened and Dan Fleury walked in, glancing at the arrayed stars and ships and not seeing them. The chart room had never meant anything to Fleury. He scolded, "Damn it, Norman, you scared us witless! Why you're not in the hospital now—"

"I was in the hospital, Dan. I wouldn't stay. And finally I got it through Asa Czerny's head that I meant it, so he said I could come home if I would stay quiet and let him look in. Well, as you see, I'm quiet. And I don't care if he looks in. I only care about finding out the truth about FTL."

"Oh, cripes, Norm! Honestly, you shouldn't worry yourself—"

"Dan, for thirty years you've never used the word 'honestly' except when you were lying to me. Now give. I sent for you this morning because you know the answer. I want it.

*"For God's sake, Dan."*

Fleury glanced around the room, as though he were seeing the glowing points of light for the first time . . . perhaps he was, Marchand thought.

He said at last, "Well, there is something."

Marchand waited. He had had a great deal of practice at waiting.

"There's a young fellow," said Fleury, starting over again. "He's named Eisele. A mathematician, would you believe it? He's got an idea."

Fleury pulled over a chair and sat down.

"It's far from perfect," he added.

"In fact," he said, "a lot of people think it won't work at all. You know the theory, of course. Einstein, Lorentz, Fitzgerald, the whole roster—they're all against it. It's called—get this!—poly-nomiation."

He waited for a laugh, hopelessly. Then he said, "Although I must say he appears to have something, since the tests—"

Marchand said gently and with enormous restraint: "Dan, will you please spit it out? Let's see what you said so far. There's this fellow named Eisele and he has something and it's crazy but it works."

"Well—yes."

Marchand slowly leaned back and closed his eyes. "So that means that we were all wrong. Especially me. And all our work—"

"Look, Norman! Don't *ever* think like that. Your work has made it all the difference. If it weren't for you, people like Eisele never would have had the chance. Don't you know he was working under one of our grants?"

"No. I didn't know that." Marchand's eyes went out to the *Tycho Brahe* for a moment. "But it doesn't help much. I wonder if fifty-odd thousand men and women who have given most of their lives to the deep-freeze because of—my work—will feel the way you do. But thanks. You've told me what I want to know."

When Czerny entered the chart room an hour later Marchand said at once, "Am I in good enough shape to stand a smith?"

The doctor put down his bag and took a chair before he answered. "We don't have anyone available, Norman. There hasn't been a volunteer for years."

"No. I don't mean smithed into a human body. I don't want any would-be suicide volunteer donors; you said yourself the smithed bodies sometimes suicided anyway. I'll settle for a chimp. Why should I be any better than that young fellow—what's his name?"

"You mean Duane Ferguson."

"Sure. Why should I be any better than he is?"

"Oh, cut it out, Norman. You're too old. Your phosopholipids—"

"I'm not too old to die, am I? And that's the worst that could happen."

"It wouldn't be stable! Not at your age; you just don't understand the chemistry. I couldn't promise you more than a few weeks."

Marchand said joyously, "Really! I didn't expect that much. That's more than you can promise me now."

The doctor argued, but Marchand had held up his end of many a hard-fought battle in ninety-six years, and besides he had an advantage over Czerny. The doctor knew even better than Marchand himself that getting into a passion would kill him. At the moment when Czerny gauged the risk of a smith translation less than the risk of going on arguing about it, he frowned, shook his head grudgingly and left.

Slowly Marchand wheeled after him.

He did not have to hurry to what might be the last act of his life. There was plenty of time. In the Institute they kept a supply of breeding chimpanzees, but it would take several hours to prepare one.

One mind had to be sacrificed in the smith imposition. The man would ultimately be able to return to his own body, his risk less than one chance in fifty of failure. But the chimp would never be the same. Marchand submitted to the beginnings of the irradiation, the delicate titration of his body fluids, the endless strapping and patching and clamping. He had seen it done and there were no surprises in the procedure. . . . He had not known, however, that it would hurt so much.

## III

Trying not to walk on his knuckles (but it was hard; the ape body was meant to crouch, the arms were too long to hang comfortably along his sides), Marchand waddled out into the pad area and bent his rigid chimp's spine back in order to look up at the hated thing.

Dan Fleury came toward him. "Norm?" he asked tentatively. Marchand attempted to nod: it was not a success, but Fleur understood. "Norman," he said, "this is Sigmund Eisele. He invented the FTL drive."

Marchand raised one long arm and extended a hand that resisted being opened: it was used to being clawed into a fist. "Congradulazhuns," he said, as clearly as he could. Virtuously he did not squeeze the hand of the young dark-eyed man who was being introduced to him. He had been warned that chimpanzee strength maimed human beings. He was not likely to forget, but it was tempting to allow himself to consider it for a moment.

He dropped the hand and winced as pain flooded through him.

Czerny had warned him to expect it. *Unstable, dangerous, won't last* had rumbled through his conversation; *and don't forget, Norman, the sensory equipment is set high for you; you're not used to so much input: it will hurt.*

But Marchand had assured the doctor he would not mind that, and indeed he didn't. He looked at the ship again. *"Zo thads id,"* he grumbled, and again bent the backbone, the whole barrel chest of the brute he occupied, to stare at the ship on the pad. It was perhaps a hundred feet tall. "Nod mudge," he said scornfully. *"De Zirian,* dad was our firzd, zdood nine hoonderd feed dall and garried a dousand beople to Alpha Zendauri."

"And it brought a hundred and fifty back alive," said Eisele. He didn't emphasize the words in any way, but he said it quite clearly. "I want to tell you I've always admired you, Dr. Marchand. I hope you won't mind my company. I understand you want to go along with me out to the *Tycho Brahe.*"

"Why zhould I mind?" He did, of course. With the best will in the world, this young fellow had thrown seventy years of dedication, plus a handsome fortune—eight million dollars of his own, countless hundreds of millions that Marchand had begged from millionaires, from government handouts, from the pennies of school children—tossed them all into the chamber pot and flushed them into history. They would say: *A nonce figure of the early twenty-first century, Norman Marchand, or Marquand, attempted stellar colonization with primitive rocket-propelled craft. He was of course unsuccessful, and the toll of life and wealth in his ill-conceived venture enormous. However, after Eisele's faster-than-light became practicable . . .* They would say that he was a failure. And he was.

When *Tycho Brahe* blasted off to the stars massed bands of five hundred pieces played it to its countdown and television audiences all over the world watched it through their orbiting satellites. A president, a governor and half the senate were on hand.

When Eisele's little ship took off to catch it and tell its people their efforts had been all in vain, it was like the departure of the 7:17 ferry for Jersey City. To that extent, thought Marchand, had Eisele degraded the majesty of star-flight. Yet he would not have missed it for anything. Not though it meant forcing himself as supercargo on Eisele, who had destroyed his life, and on the other smithed chimpanzee, Duane Ferguson, who was for some reason deemed to have special privileges in regard to the *Brahe*.

They shipped an extra FTL unit—Marchand heard one of the men call it a polyflecter, but he would not do it the honor of asking anyone what that meant—for some reason. Because it was likely to break down, so spares were needed? Marchand dismissed the question, realizing that it had not been a fear but a hope. Whatever the reason he didn't care; he didn't want even to be here, he only regarded it as his inescapable duty.

And he entered Eisele's ship.

The interior of Eisele's damned ship was built to human scale, nine-foot ceilings and broad acceleration couches, but they had brought hammocks scaled to a chimpanzee torso for himself and Duane Ferguson. Doubtless they had looted the hammocks from the new ship. The one that would never fly—or at least not on streams of ionized gas. And doubtless this was almost the last time that a man's mind would have to leave Earth in an ape's body.

What Eisele's damned ship rode to the stars on in place of ionized gas Marchand did not understand. The whatchaflecter, whatever the damned thing was named, was so tiny. The whole ship was a pigmy.

There was no room for reaction mass, or at least only for enough to get it off-Earth. Then the little black box—it was not really little, since it was the size of a grand piano; and it was not black but gray; but it was a box, all right—would work its magic. They called that magic "polynomiation." What polynomiation was Marchand did not try to understand, beyond listening, or seeming to listen, to Eisele's brief, crude attempt to translate mathematics into English. He heard just enough to recognize a few words. Space was N dimensional. All right, that answered the whole question, as far as he was concerned, and he did not hear Eisele's tortuous efforts to explain how one jacked oneself up, so to speak, into a polynomial dimension—or no, not that, but translated the existing polynomial extensions of a standard 4-space mass into higher orders—he didn't hear. He didn't hear any of it.

What he was listening to was the deep liquid thump of the great ape's heart that now was sustaining his brain.

Duane Ferguson appeared, in the ape's body that he would never leave now. That was one more count of Marchand's self-indictments; he had heard them say that the odds had worked against Ferguson, and his body had died in the imposition.

As soon as he had heard what Eisele was up to, Marchand had seized on it as a chance for expiation. The project was very simple. A good test for Eisele's drive, and a mission of mercy, too. They intended to fleet after the plodding, long-gone *Tycho Brahe* and catch it in mid-space . . . for even now, thirty years after it had left Port Kennedy, it was still decelerating to begin its search orbit around Groombridge 1618. As Marchand strapped himself in, Eisele was explaining it all over again. He was making tests on his black box and talking at the same time: "You see, sir, we'll try to match course and velocity, but frankly that's the hard part. Catching them's nothing: we've got the speed. Then we'll transfer the extra polyflecter to the *Tyco Brahe*—"

"Yez, thanggs," said Marchand politely, but he still did not listen to the talk about the machine. As long as it existed he would use it, his conscience would not let him off that, but he didn't want details.

Because the thing was, there were all those wasted lives.

Every year in the *Tycho Brahe*'s deep-freeze means a month off the life of the body that lay there. Respiration was slowed, but it was not stopped. The heart did not beat but blood was perfused through a pump; tubes dripped sugar and minerals into the torpid blood, catheters carried wastes away. And Groombridge 1618 was a flight of ninety years.

The best a forty-year-old man could hope for on arriving was to be restored into a body whose biological age was nearly fifty—while behind him on the Earth was nothing but a family long dead, friends turned into dust.

It had been worth it. Or so the colonists had thought. Driven by the worm that wriggled in the spine of the explorer, the itch that drove him on; because of the wealth and the power and the freedom that a new world could give them, and because of the place they would have in the history books—not Washington's place, or even Christ's. They would have the place of an Adam and an Eve.

It had been worth it, all those thousands had thought when

they volunteered and set out. But what would they think when they landed!

If they landed without knowing the truth, if some ship like Eisele's did not reach and tell them in mid-space, they would find the greatest disappointment any man had ever borne. The Groombridge 1618 expedition aboard the *Tycho Brahe* still had forty years to go on its original trip plan. With Eisele's invention driving faster-than-light commerce, there would be a planet populated by hundreds of thousands of people, factories at work, roads built, the best land taken, the history books already into their fifth chapter . . . and what would the three thousand aging adventurers think then?

Marchand moaned and shook, not entirely because the ship was taking off and the acceleration squeezed his rib cage down against his spine.

When they were in the polyflecter's grip he floated across the pilot room to join the others. "I was never in zpaze bevore," he said.

Eisele said with great deference, "Your work was on the Earth."

"Vas, yez." But Marchand left it at that. A man whose whole life was a failure owed something to humanity, and one of the things he owed was the privilege of allowing them to overlook it.

He watched carefully while Eisele and Ferguson read their instruments and made micrometric settings on the polyflecter. He did not understand anything about the faster-than-light drive, but he understood that a chart was a chart. Here there was a doubly profiled representation of the course-line of the Groombridge star in distance, which meant something under three-quarters of the way in time.

"Mass detectors, Dr. Marchand," said Eisele cheerfully, pointing to the charts. "Good thing they're not much closer, or they wouldn't have mass enough to show." Marchand understood: the same detectors that would show a sun or a planet would also show a mere million-ton ship if its speed were great enough to add sufficient mass. "And a good thing," added Eisele, looking worried, "that they're not much farther away. We're going to have trouble matching their velocity now, even though they've been decelerating for nine years. . . . Let's get strapped in."

From the hammock Marchand braced himself for another surge of acceleration. But it was not that, it was something different and far worse.

It was a sausage-grinder, chewing his heart and sinews and spitting them out in strange crippled shapes.

It was a wine-press, squeezing his throat, collapsing his heart.

It was the giddy nausea of a roller-coaster or a small craft in a typhoon. Wherever it took them, the stars on the profile charts slipped and slid and flowed into new positions.

Marchand, absorbed in the most crushing migraine of all but a century, hardly knew what was happening, but he knew that in the hours they found the *Tycho Brahe*, after giving it a thirty-year start.

# IV

The captain of the *Tycho Brahe* was a graying, yellow-fanged chimp named Lafcadio, his brown animal eyes hooded with shock, his long, stringy arms still quivering with the reaction of seeing a ship—a ship—and human beings.

He could not take his eyes off Eisele, Marchand noted, and looked? It had been thirty years in an ape's body for the captain. The ape was old now. Lafcadio would be thinking himself more than half chimp already, the human frame only a memory that blurred against the everyday reminders of furry-backed hands and splayed prehensile feet. Marchand himself could feel the ape's mind stealing back, though he knew it was only imagination.

Or was it imagination? Asa Czerny had said the imposition would not be stable—something to do with the phospholipids—he could not remember. He could not, in fact, remember anything with the clarity and certainty he could wish, and it was not merely because his mind was ninety-six years old.

Without emotion Marchand realized that his measured months or weeks had dwindled to a few days.

It could, of course, be the throbbing pain between his temples that was robbing him of reason. But Marchand only entertained that thought to dismiss it; if he had courage enough to realize that his life's work was wasted, he could face the fact that pain was only a second-order derivative of the killer that stalked his ape's body. But it made it hard for him to concentrate. It was through a haze that he heard the talk of the captain and his crew—the twenty-two smithed chimpanzees who superintended the running of the *Tycho Brahe* and watched over the three thousand frozen bodies in its hold. It was over a deep, confusing roar that he heard Eisele instruct them in the transfer of the FTL unit from his tiny ship to the great, lumbering ark that his box could make fleet enough to span the stars in a day's journey.

He was aware that they looked on him, from time to time, with pity.

He did not mind their pity. He only asked that they allow him to live with them until he died, knowing as he knew that that would be no long time; and he passed, while they were still talking, into a painful, dizzying reverie that lasted until—he did not know the measure of the time—until he found himself strapped in a hammock in the control room of the ship, and felt the added crushing agony that told him they were once again slipping through the space of other dimensions.

"Are you all right?" said a familiar thick, slurred voice.

It was the other, last victim of his blundering, the one called Ferguson. Marchand managed to say that he was.

"We're almost there," said Ferguson. "I thought you'd like to know. There's a planet. Inhabitable, they think."

From Earth the star called Groombridge 1618 was not even visible to the naked eye. Binoculars might make it a tiny flicker of light, lost among countless thousands of farther, but brighter, stars. From Groombridge 1618 Sol was not much more.

Marchand remembered struggling out of his hammock, over-ruling the worry on Ferguson's simian face, to look back at the view that showed Sol. Ferguson had picked it out for him, and Marchand looked at light that had been fifteen years journeying from his home. The photons that impinged on his eyes now had paused to drench the Earth in the colors of sunset when he was in his seventies and his wife only a few years mourned. . . . He did not remember getting back to his hammock.

He did not remember, either, at what moment of time some-one told him about the planet they hoped to own. It hung low around the little orange disk of Groombridge 1618—by solar standards, at least. The captain's first approximation made its orbit quite irregular, but at its nearest approach it would be less than ten million miles from the glowing fire-coal of its primary. Near enough. Warm enough. Telescopes showed it a planet with oceans and forests, removing the lingering doubts of the captain, for its orbit could not freeze it even at greatest remove from its star, or char it at closest—or else the forest could not have grown. Spectroscopes, thermocouples, filarometers showed more, the instruments racing ahead of the ship, now in orbit and compelled to creep at rocket speeds the last little inch of its journey. The atmosphere could be breathed, for the ferny woods had flushed out the poisons and filled it with oxygen. The gravity was more than Earth's—a drag on the first generation, to be sure, and an expense in foot troubles and lumbar aches for many more—but nothing that could not be borne. The world was fair.

Marchand remembered nothing of how he learned this, or of the landing, or of the hurried, joyful opening of the freezing crypts, the awakening of the colonists, the beginning of life on the planet . . . he only knew that there was a time when he found himself curled on a soft, warm hammock, and he looked up and saw sky.

# V

The protuberant hairy lip and sloping brows of a chimpanzee were hovering over him. Marchand recognized that young fellow Ferguson. "Hello," he said. "How long have I been unconscious?"

The chimp said, with embarrassment, "Well—you haven't been unconscious at all, exactly. You've been—" His voice trailed off.

"I see," said Marchand, and struggled up. He was grateful for the strength of the slope-shouldered, short-legged body he had borrowed, for this world he had come to had an uncomfortably powerful grip. The effort made him dizzy. A pale sky and thin clouds spiraled around him; he felt queer flashes of pain and pleasure, remembered tastes he had never experienced, felt joys he had never known. . . . With an effort he repressed the vestigial ape and said, "You mean I've been—what would you call it? Unstable? The smithing didn't quite take." But he didn't need confirmation from Ferguson. He knew; and knew that the next time he slipped away would be the last. Czerny had warned him. The phospholipids, wasn't that it? It was almost time to go home . . .

Off to one side he saw men and women, *human* men and women, on various errands and it made him ask: "You're still an ape?"

"I will be for a while, Dr. Marchand. My body's gone, you know."

Marchand puzzled over that for a while. His attention wandering, he caught himself licking his forearm and grooming his round belly. "No!" he shouted, and tried to stand up.

Ferguson helped him, and Marchand was grateful for the ape's strong arm. He remembered what had been bothering him. "Why?" he asked.

"Why what, Dr. Marchand?"

"Why did you come?"

Ferguson said anxiously, "I wish you'd sit down till the doctor gets here. I came because there's someone on the *Tycho Brahe* I wanted to see."

A girl? thought Marchand wonderingly. "And did you see her?"

"Not her, them. Yes, I saw them. My parents. You see, I was two years old when the *Tycho Brahe* left. My parents were good breeding stock—volunteers were hard to get then, they tell me— oh, of course, you'd know better than I. Anyway they—I was adopted by an aunt. They left me a letter to read when I was old enough . . . Dr. Marchand! What's the matter?"

Marchand reeled and fell; he could not help it, he knew he was a spectacle, could feel the incongruous tears rheuming out of his beast eyes; but this last and unexpected blow was too harsh. He had faced the fact of fifty thousand damaged lives and accepted guilt for them, but one abandoned baby, left to an aunt and the apology of a letter, broke his heart.

"I wonder why you don't kill me," he said.

"Dr. Marchand! I don't know what you're talking about."

"If only," said Marchand carefully, "I don't expect any favors, but if only there were some way I could *pay*. But I can't. I have nothing left, not even enough life to matter. But I'm sorry, Mr. Ferguson, and that will have to do."

Ferguson said, "Dr. Marchand, if I'm not mistaken, you're saying that you apologize for the Institute." Marchand nodded. "But—oh, I'm not the one to say this, but there's no one else. Look. Let me try to make it clear. The first thing the colonists did yesterday was choose a name for the planet. The vote was unanimous. Do you know what they called it?"

Marchand only looked at him dully.

"Please listen, Dr. Marchand. They named it after the man who inspired all their lives. Their greatest hero. They named it Marchand."

Marchand stared at him, and stared longer, and then without changing expression closed his eyes. "Dr. Marchand!" said Ferguson tentatively, and then, seriously worried at last, turned and scuttled ape-like, legs and knuckles bearing him rapidly across the ground, to get the ship's doctor who had left him with strict orders to call him as soon as the patient showed any signs of life.

When they got back the chimp was gone. They looked at the fronded forest and at each other.

"Wandered off, I expect," said the doctor. "It may be just as well."

"But the nights are cold! He'll get pneumonia. He'll die."

"Not any more," said the doctor, as kindly as he could. "He's already dead in every way that matters."

He bent and rubbed his aching thighs, worn already from the struggle against this new Eden's gravity, then straightened and looked at the stars in the darkening western sky. A bright green one was another planet of Groombridge 1618's, farther out, all ice and copper salts. One of the very faintest ones, perhaps, was Sol. "He gave us these planets," said the doctor, and turned back toward the city. "Do you know what being a good man means, Ferguson? It means being better than you really are—so that even your failures carry someone a little farther to success—and that's what he did for us. I hope he heard what you were trying to tell him. I hope he remembers it when he dies," the doctor said.

"If he doesn't," said Ferguson very clearly, "the rest of us always will."

The next day they found the curled-up body.

It was the first funeral ever held on the planet, and the one that the history books describe. That is why, on the planet called Marchand, the statue at the spaceport has a small bas-relief carved over the legend:

## THE FATHER OF THE STARS

The bas-relief is the shape of a chimpanzee, curled on itself and looking out with blind, frightened eyes upon the world, for it was the chimpanzee's body that they found, and the chimpanzee's body that they buried under the monument. The bas-relief and the body, they are ape. But the statue that rises above them is a god's.

# TRICK OR TREATY
## (AUGUST 1965)
## KEITH LAUMER
### (B. 1925)

The success enjoyed by *If* during the 1960s, a decade which saw the magazine win an impressive three Hugo Awards in a row, was due to a number of factors. But one factor certainly was the more than two dozen appearances of Keith Laumer's creation Retief, an intergalactic diplomat who became (and continued to be) one of the most popular series characters in the history of science fiction. His adventures have been collected in many books, including *Retief of the C.D.T.* (1971), *Galactic Diplomat* (1965), and *Retief: Ambassador to Space* (1969). In addition, the novel *Retief's War* was serialized in the magazine in 1965 and 1966.

Non-Retief novels that appeared in *If* include *Earthblood* (with the late and lamented George Rosel Brown, 1966), *Galactic Odyssey* (as "Spaceman," 1967), and *A Plague of Demons* (as "The Hounds of Hell," 1965).

# TRICK OR TREATY

A large green-yolked egg splattered across the flexglas panel as it slammed behind Retief. Across the long, narrow lobby, under a glare-sign reading HOSTELRY RITZ-KRUDLU, the Gaspierre room clerk looked up, then came quickly around the counter, long-bodied, short-legged, an expression as of one detecting a bad odor on his flattened, leathery-looking face. He spread six of the eight arms attached to his narrow shoulders like a set of measuring spoons, twitching the other two in a cramped shrug.

"The hotel, he is fill!" he wheezed. "To some other house you convey your custom, yes?"

"Stand fast," Retief said to the four Terrans who had preceded him through the door. "Hello, Strupp," he nodded to the agitated clerk. "These are friends of mine. See if you can't find them a room."

"As I comment but now, the rooms, he is occupy!" Strupp pointed to the door. "Kindly facilities provide by management to place selves back outside use!"

A narrow panel behind the registration desk popped open; a second Gaspierre slid through, took in the situation, emitted a sharp hiss. Strupp whirled, his arms semaphoring an unreadable message.

"Never mind that, Strupp," the newcomer snapped in accentless Terran. He took out a strip of patterned cloth, mopped under the breathing orifices set in the sides of his neck, looked at the group of Terrans, and then back at Retief. "Ah, something I can do for you, Mr. Retief?"

"Evening Hrooze," Retief said. "Permit me to introduce Mr. Julius Mulvihill, Miss Suzette La Flamme, Wee Willie and Professor Fate, just in from out-system. There seems to be a room shortage in town. I thought perhaps you could accommodate them."

Hrooze eyed the door through which the Terrans had entered, twitched his nictating eyelids in a nervous gesture.

"You know the situation here, Retief!" he said. "I have nothing against Terries personally, of course, but if I rent to these people—"

"I was thinking you might fix them up with free rooms, just as a sort of good-will gesture."

"If we these Terries to the Ritz-Krudlu admit, the repercussions political out of business us will put!" Strupp expostulated.

"The next ship out is two days from now," Retief said. "They need a place to stay until then."

Hrooze looked at Retief, mopped his neck again. "I owe you a favor, Retief," he said. "Two days, though, that's all!"

"But—" Strupp began.

"Silence!" Hrooze sneezed. "Put them in twelve-oh-three and four!"

He drew Retief aside as a small bell-hop in a brass-studded harness began loading baggage on his back.

"How does it look?" he inquired. "Any hope of getting that squadron of Peace Enforcers to stand by out-system?"

"I'm afraid not; Sector HQ seems to feel that might be interpreted by the Krultch as a war-like gesture."

"Certainly it would! That's exactly what the Krultch can understand—"

"Ambassador Sheepshorn has great faith in the power of words," Retief said soothingly. "He has a reputation as a great verbal karate expert; the Genghis Khan of the conference table."

"But what if you lose? The cabinet votes on the Krultch treaty tomorrow! If it's signed, Gaspierre will be nothing but a fueling station for the Krultch battle fleet! And you Terries will end up slaves!"

"A sad end for a great oral athlete," Retief said. "Let's hope he's in good form tomorrow."

In the shabby room on the twelfth level, Retief tossed a thick plastic coin to the baggage slave, who departed emitting the thin squeaking that substituted in his species for a jaunty whistle. Mulvihill, a huge man with a handlebar mustache, looked around, plumped his vast, bulging suitcase to the thin carpet, and mopped at the purple-fruit stain across his red plastiweve jacket.

"I'd like to get my hands on the Gasper that threw that," he growled in a bullfrog voice.

"That's a mean crowd out there," said Miss La Flamme, a shapely redhead with a tattoo on her left biceps. "It was sure a break for us the Ambassador changed his mind about helping us out. From the look the old sourpuss gave me when I kind of bumped up against him, I figured he had ground glass where his red corpuscles ought to be."

"I got a sneaking hunch Mr. Retief swung this deal on his own, Suzie," the big man said. "The Ambassador's got bigger things on his mind than out-of-work variety acts."

"This is the first time the Marvelous Merivales have ever been flat out of luck on tour," commented a whiskery little man no more than three feet tall, dressed in an old-fashioned frock coat and a checkered vest, in a voice like the yap of a Pekinese. "How come we got to get mixed up in politics?"

"Shut up, Willie," the big man said. "It's not Mr. Retief's fault we came here."

"Yeah," the midget conceded. "I guess you fellows in the CDT got it kind of rough too, trying to pry the Gaspers outa the Krultch's hip pocket. Boy, I wish I could see the show tomorrow when the Terry Ambassador and the Krultch brass slug it out to see whose side the Gasper'll be neutral on."

"Neutral, ha!" the tall, cadaverous individual looming behind Wee Willie snorted. "I caught a glimpse of that ferocious war vessel at the port, openly flying the Krultch battleflag! It's an open breach of interworld custom—"

"Hey, Professor, leave the speeches to the CDT," the girl said.

"Without free use of Gaspierre ports, the Krultch plans for expansion through the Gloob cluster would come to naught. A firm stand—"

"Might get 'em blasted right off the planet," the big man growled. "The Krultch play for keeps."

"And the Gaspers aim to be on the winning side," the midget piped. "And all the smart money is on the Krultch battle-wagon to put up the best argument."

"Terries are fair game around here, it looks like, Mr. Retief," Mulvihill said. "You better watch yourself going back."

Retief nodded. "Stay close to your rooms; if the vote goes against us tomorrow, we may all be looking for a quick way home."

# II

Outside on the narrow elevated walkway that linked the gray slab-like structures of the city, thin-featured Gaspierre natives shot wary looks at Retief, some skirting him widely, others jostling him as they crowded past. It was a short walk to the building where the Terrestrial delegation occupied a suite. As Retief neared it, a pair of Krultch sailors emerged from a shop, turned in his direction. They were short-coupled centauroid quadrupeds, with deep, narrow chests, snouted faces with businesslike jaws and fringe beards, dressed in the red-striped livery of the Krultch Navy, complete with side-arms and short swagger sticks.

Retief altered course to the right to give them passing room; they saw him, nudged each other, and spaced themselves to block the walk. Retief came on without slowing, started between them. The Krultch closed ranks. Retief stepped back, started around the sailor on the left. The creature sidled, still blocking his path.

"Oh-hoh, Terry loose in street," he said in a voice like sand in a gear-box. "You lost, Terry?"

The other Krultch crowded Retief against the rail. "Where you from, Terry? What you do—?"

Without warning, Retief slammed a solid kick to the shin of the Krultch before him, simultaneously wrenched the stick from the alien's grip, cracked it down sharply across the wrist of the other sailor as he went for his gun. The weapon clattered, skidded off the walk and was gone. The one whom Retief had kicked was hopping on three legs, making muffled sounds of agony. Retief stepped quickly to him, jerked his gun from its holster, aimed it negligently at the other Krultch.

"Better get your buddy back to the ship and have that leg looked at," he said. "I think I broke it."

A ring of gaping Gaspierre had gathered, choking the walk. Retief thrust the pistol into his pocket, turned his back on the Krultch, pushed through the locals. A large coarsehided Gaspierre policeman made as if to block his way; Retief rammed an elbow in his side, chopped him across the side of the neck as he doubled up, thrust him aside and kept going. A mutter was rising from the crowd behind him.

The Embassy was just ahead now. Retief turned off toward the entry; two yellow-uniformed Gaspierre moved into sight under the marquee, eyed him as he came up.

"Terran, have you not heard of the curfew?" one demanded in shrill but accurate Terran.

"Can't say that I have," Retief replied. "There wasn't any, an hour ago."

"There is now!" the other snapped. "You Terries are not popular here. If you insist in inflaming the populace by walking abroad, we cannot be responsible for your safety—" He broke off as he saw the Krultch pistol protruding from Retief's pocket.

"Where did you get that?" he demanded in Gaspierran, then switched to pidgin Terran: "Where you-fella catch um bang-bang?"

"A couple of lads were playing with it in the street," Retief said in the local dialect. "I took it away from them before someone got hurt." He started past them.

"Hold on there," the policeman snapped. "We're not finished with you yet, fellow. We'll tell you when you can go. Now . . ." He folded his upper elbows. "You're to go to your quarters at once. In view of the tense interplanetary situation, you Terries are to remain inside until further notice. I have my men posted on all approaches to, ah, provide protection."

"You're putting a diplomatic mission under arrest?" Retief inquired mildly.

"I wouldn't call it that. Let's just say that it wouldn't be safe for foreigners to venture abroad."

"Threats too?"

"This measure is necessary in order to prevent unfortunate incidents!"

"How about the Krultch? They're foreigners; are you locking them in their bedrooms?"

"The Krultch are old and valued friends of the Gaspierre," the police captain said stiffly. "We—"

"I know; ever since they set an armed patrol just outside Gaspierran atmosphere, you've developed a vast affection for them. Of course, their purchasing missions help too."

The captain smirked, "We Gaspierre are nothing if not practical." He held out his claw-like two-fingered hand. "You will now give me the weapon."

Retief handed it over silently.

"Come; I will escort you to your room," the cop said.

Retief nodded complacently, followed the Gaspierre through the entry cubicle and into the lift.

"I'm glad you've decided to be reasonable," the cop said. "After all, if you Terries *should* convince the cabinet, it will be much nicer all around if there have been no incidents."

"How true," Retief murmured.

He left the car at the twentieth floor.

"Don't forget, now," the cop said, watching Retief key his door. "Just stay inside and all will yet be well." He signaled to a policeman standing a few yards along the corridor.

"Keep an eye on the door, Klosta."

Inside, Retief picked up the phone, dialed the Ambassador's room number. There was a dry buzz, no answer. He looked around the room. There was a tall, narrow window set in the wall opposite the door with a hinged section that swung outward. Retief opened it, leaned out, looked down at the dizzying stretch of blank facade that dropped sheer to the upper walkway seventy yards below. Above, the wall extended up twenty feet to an overhanging cornice. He went to the closet, yanked a blanket from the shelf, ripped it in four wide strips, knotted them together, and tied one end to a chair which he braced below the window.

Retief swung his legs outside the window, grasped the blanket-rope, and slid down.

The window at the next level was closed and shuttered. Retief braced himself on the sill, delivered a sharp kick to the panel; it shattered with an explosive sound. He dropped lower, reached through, released the catch, pulled the window wide, knocked the shutter aside, and scrambled through into a darkened room.

"Who's there?" a sharp voice barked. A tall, lean man in a

ruffled shirt with an unknotted string tie hanging down the front
gaped at Retief from the inner room.

"Retief! How did you get here? I understood that none of the
staff were to be permitted—that is, I agreed that protective
custody—er, it seems . . ."

"The whole staff is bottled up here in the building, Mr. Ambassador. I'd guess they mean to keep us here until after the cabinet
meeting. It appears the Krultch have the fix in."

"Nonsense! I have a firm commitment from the Minister that no
final commitment will be made until we've been heard—"

"Meanwhile, we're under house arrest—just to be sure we don't
have an opportunity to bring any of the cabinet around to our
side."

"Are you suggesting that I've permitted illegal measures to be
taken without a protest?" Ambassador Sheepshorn fixed Retief
with a piercing gaze which wilted, and slid aside. "The place was
alive with armed gendarmes," he sighed. "What could I do?"

"A few shrill cries of outrage might have helped," Retief pointed
out. "It's not too late. A fast visit to the Foreign Office—"

"Are you out of your mind? Have you observed the temper of
the populace? We'd be torn to shreds!"

Retief nodded. "Quite possibly; but what do you think our chances
are tomorrow, after the Gaspierre conclude a treaty with the
Krultch?"

Sheepshorn made two tries, then swallowed hard. "Surely, Retief,
you don't—"

"I'm afraid I do," Retief said. "The Krultch need a vivid symbol
of their importance—and they'd also like to involve the Gaspierre
in their skulduggery, just to insure their loyalty. Packing a clutch
of Terry diplomats off to the ice mines would do both jobs."

"A great pity," the Ambassador sighed. "And only nine months
to go till my retirement."

"I'll have to be going now," Retief said. "There may be a posse
of annoyed police along at any moment, and I'd hate to make it
too easy for them."

"Police? You mean they're not even waiting until after the
cabinet's decision?"

"Oh, this is just a personal matter; I damaged some Krultch
naval property and gave a Gaspierre cop a pain in the neck."

"I've warned you about your personality, Retief," Sheepshorn
admonished. "I suggest you give yourself up, and ask for clem-

ency; with luck, you'll get to go along to the mines with the rest of us. I'll personally put in a good word!"

"That would interfere with my plans, I'm afraid," Retief said. He went to the door. "I'll try to be back before the Gaspierre do anything irrevocable. Meanwhile hold the fort here. If they come for you, quote regulations at them; I'm sure they'll find that discouraging."

"Plans? Retief, I positively forbid you to—"

Retief stepped through the door and closed it behind him, cutting off the flow of Ambassadorial wisdom. A fat policeman, posted a few feet along the corridor, came to the alert.

"All right, you can go home now," Retief said in brisk Gaspierran. "The chief changed his mind; he decided violating a Terran Embassy's quarters was just asking for trouble. After all, the Krultch haven't won yet."

The cop stared at him, then nodded. "I wondered if this wasn't kind of getting the rickshaw before the coolie . . ." He hesitated. "But what do *you* know about it?"

"I just had a nice chat with the captain, one floor up."

"Well, if he let you come down here, I guess it's all right."

"If you hurry, you can make it back to the barracks before the evening rush begins." Retief waved airily and strolled away along the corridor.

# III

Back at ground level, Retief went along a narrow service passage leading to the rear of the building, stepped out into a deserted-looking courtyard. There was another door across the way. He went to it, followed another hall to a street exit. There were no cops in sight. He took the sparsely peopled lower walkway, set off at a brisk walk.

Ten minutes later, Retief surveyed the approaches to the Hostelry Ritz-Krudlu from the shelter of an inter-level connecting stair. There was a surging crowd of Gaspierre blocking the walkway, with a scattering of yellow police uniforms patrolling the edge of the mob. Placards lettered TERRY GO HOME and KEEP GASPIERRE BROWN bobbed above the sea of flattened heads. Off to one side, a heavily braided Krultch officer stood with a pair of age-tarnished locals, looking on approvingly.

Retief retraced his steps to the debris-littered ground level twenty feet below the walkway, found an eighteen-inch-wide airspace leading back between buildings. He inched along it, came to a door, found it locked. Four doors later, a latch yielded to his touch.

He stepped inside, made out the dim outlines of an empty storage room. The door across the room was locked. Retief stepped back, slammed a kick against it at latch level; it bounced wide.

After a moment's wait for the sound of an alarm which failed to materialize, Retief moved off along the passage, found a rubbish-heaped stair. He clambered over the debris, and started up.

At the twelfth level, he emerged into the corridor. There was no one in sight. He went quickly along to the door numbered 1203, tapped lightly. There was a faint sound from inside; then a bass voice rumbled, "Who's there?"

"Retief. Open up before the house dick spots me."

Bolts clattered and the door swung wide; Julius Mulvihill's mustached face appeared; he seized Retief's hand and pumped it.

"Cripes, Mr. Retief, we were worried about you. Right after you left, old Hrooze called up here and said there was a riot starting up!"

"Nothing serious; just a few enthusiasts out front putting on a show for the Krultch."

"What's happened?" Wee Willie chirped, coming in from the next room with lather on his chin. "They throwing us out already?"

"No, you'll be safe enough right here. But I need your help."

The big man nodded, flexed his hands.

Suzette La Flamme thrust a drink into Retief's hand. "Sit down and tell us about it."

"Glad you came to us, Retief," Wee Willie piped.

Retief took the offered chair, sampled the drink, then outlined the situation.

"What I have in mind could be dangerous," he finished.

"What ain't?" Willie demanded.

"It calls for a delicate touch and some fancy footwork," Retief added.

The professor cleared his throat. "I am not without a certain dexterity—" he started.

"Let him finish," the redhead said.

"And I'm not even sure it's possible," Retief stated.

The big man looked at the others. "There's a lot of things that look impossible—but the Marvelous Merivales do 'em anyway. That's what's made our act a wow on a hundred and twelve planets."

The girl tossed her red hair. "The way it looks, Mr. Retief, if somebody doesn't do something, by this time tomorrow this is going to be mighty unhealthy territory for Terries."

"The ones the mob don't get will be chained to an oar in a Krultch battle-wagon," Willie piped.

"With the Mission pinned down in their quarters, the initiative appears to rest with us," Professor Fate intoned. The others nodded.

"If you're all agreed then," Retief said, "here's what I have in mind . . ."

The corridor was empty when Retief emerged, followed by the four Terrans.

"How are we going to get out past that crowd out front?" Mulvihill inquired. "I've got a feeling they're ready for something stronger than slogans."

"We'll try the back way."

There was a sudden hubbub from the far end of the corridor; half a dozen Gaspierre burst into view, puffing hard from a fast climb. They hissed, pointed, and started for the Terrans at a short-legged trot. At the same moment, a door flew wide at the opposite end of the hallway; more locals popped into view, closed in.

"Looks like a neck-tie party," Wee Willie barked. "Go get 'em Julie!" He put his head down and charged. The oncoming natives slowed, skipped aside. One, a trifle slow, bounced against the wall as the midget rammed him at knee level. The others whirled, grabbing at Wee Willie as he skidded to a halt. Mulvihill roared, took three giant steps, caught two Gaspierre by the backs of their leathery necks, lifted them and tossed them aside.

The second group of locals, emitting wheezes of excitement, dashed up, eager for the fray. Retief met one with a straight right, knocked two more aside with a sweep of his arm, sprinted for the door through which the second party of locals had appeared. He looked back to see Mulvihill toss another Gaspierre aside, pluck Wee Willie from the melee.

"Down here, Julie!" the girl called. "Come on, Professor!"

The tall, lean Terran, backed against the wall by three hissing locals, stretched out a yard-long arm, flapped his hand. A large white pigeon appeared, fluttered, squawking and snorting. Professor Fate plunged through them, grabbed the bird by the legs as he passed, dashed for the door where Retief and the girl waited.

There was a sound of pounding feet from the stairwell; a fresh contingent of locals came charging into view on stub legs. Retief took two steps, caught the leader full in the face with a spread hand, sent him among his followers, as Mulvihill appeared, Wee Willie over his shoulder yelling and kicking.

"There's more on the way," Retief called. "We'll have to go up."

The girl nodded, started up, three steps at a time. Mulvihill dropped the midget, who scampered after her. Professor Fate tucked his bird away, disappeared up the stairs in giant strides, Mulvihill and Retief behind him.

On the roof, Retief slammed the heavy door, shot the massive bolt. It was late evening now; cool blue air flowed across the unrailed deck; faint crowd-sounds floated up from the street twenty stories below.

"Willie, go secure that other door," Mulvihill commanded. He went to the edge of the roof, looked down, shook his head, started across toward another side. The redhead called to him.

"Over here, Julie . . ."

Retief joined Mulvihill at her side. A dozen feet down and twenty feet distant across a narrow street was the slanted roof of an adjacent building. A long ladder was clamped to brackets near the ridge.

"Looks like that's it," Mulvihill nodded. Suzette unlimbered a coil of light line from a clip at her waist, gauged the distance to a projecting ventilator intake, swung the rope, and let it fly. The broad loop spread, slapped the opposite roof, and encircled the target. With a tug, the girl tightened the noose, quickly whipped the end around a four-inch stack. She stopped, pulled off her shoes, tucked them in her belt, tried the taut rope with one foot.

"Take it easy, baby," Mulvihill muttered. She nodded, stepped out on the taut, down-slanting cable, braced her feet, spread her arms, and in one smooth swoop, slid along the line and stepped off the far end, turned and executed a quick curtsey.

"This is no time to ham it up," Mulvihill boomed.

"Just habit," the girl said. She went up the roof, freed the ladder, released the catch that caused an extensible section to slide out, then came back to the roof's edge, deftly raised the ladder to a vertical position.

"Catch!" She let it lean toward Mulvihill and Retief; as it fell both men caught it, lowered it the last foot.

"Hey, you guys," Willie called, "I can't get this thing locked!"

"Never mind that now," Mulvihill rumbled. "Come on, Prof," he said to the lean prestidigitator. "You first."

The professor's Adam's apple bobbed as he swallowed. He peered down at the street far below, then threw his shoulders back, clambered up onto the ladder, and started across on all fours.

"Don't look down, Professor," Suzie called. "Look at me."

"Let's go, Willie!" Mulvihill called over his shoulder. He freed the rope, tossed it across, then stepped up on the ladder, started across, one small step at a time. "This isn't my strong suit," he muttered, teeth together. The professor had reached the far side. Mulvihill was halfway. There was a sudden yelp from Willie. Retief turned. The midget was struggling against a door which was being forced open from inside.

"Hey!" Mulvihill boomed. Suzie squealed. Retief sprinted for the embattled midget, caught him as he was hurled backward as the door flew open, disgorging three Gaspierre who staggered for balance, and went down as Retief thrust out a foot. He thrust Wee Willie aside, picked up the nearest native, pitched him back inside, followed with the other two, then slammed the door, and tried the bolt.

"It's sprung," he said. "Let go, Willie!" He caught up the small man, ran for the ladder where Mulvihill still stood, halfway across.

"Come on, Julie!" the girl cried. "It won't hold both of you!"

There were renewed breathy yells from the site of the scuffle. The door had burst open and more Gaspierre were spilling from it. Mulvihill snorted, finished the crossing in two jumps, scrambled for footing on the slanting roof. Retief stepped out on the limber ladder, started across, Willie under his arm.

"Look out!" Suzette said sharply. The rungs jumped under Retief's feet. He reached the roof, dropped the midget, and turned to see a huddle of Gaspierre tugging at the ladder. One, rendered reckless in his zeal, started across. Retief picked up the end of the ladder, shook it; the local squeaked, scrambled back. Retief hauled the ladder in.

"Up here," the girl called. Retief went up the slope, looked down at an open trap door in the opposite slope. He followed the others down through it into a musty loft, latched it behind him. The loft door opened into an empty hall. They followed it, found a lift, rode it down to ground level. Outside in a littered alley, the crowd noises were faint.

"We appear to have outfoxed the ruffians," Professor Fate said, adjusting his cuffs.

"The Gaspers ain't far behind," Wee Willie shrilled. "Let's make tracks."

"We'll find a spot and hide out until dark," Retief said. "Then we'll make our try."

## IV

A faint gleam from Gaspierre's three bright-star-sized moons dimly illuminated the twisting alley along which Retief led the four Terrans.

"The port is half a mile from the city wall," he said softly to Mulvihill at his side. "We can climb it between watchtowers, and circle around and hit the ramp from the east."

"They got any guards posted out there?" the big man asked.

"Oh-oh, here's the wall . . ." The barrier loomed up, twelve feet high. Suzette came forward, looked it over.

"I'll check the top," she said. "Give me a boost, Julie." He lifted her, raised her to arm's length. She put a foot on the top of his head, stepped up.

Mulvihill grunted. "Watch out some Gasper cop doesn't spot you."

"Coast is clear." She pulled herself up. "Come on, Willie, I'll give you a hand." Mulvihill lifted the midget, who caught the girl's hand, and scrambled up. Mulvihill bent over, and Retief stepped in his cupped hands, then to the big man's shoulders, and reached the top of the wall. The girl lowered her rope for Mulvihill. He clambered up, swearing softly, with Retief's help hoisted his bulk to the top of the wall. A moment later the group was moving off quietly across open ground toward the south edge of the port.

Lying flat at the edge of the ramp, Retief indicated a looming, light-encrusted silhouette.

"That's her," he said. "Half a million tons, crew of three hundred."

"Big enough, ain't she?" Wee Willie chirped.

"Hsst! There's a Krultch!" Mulvihill pointed.

Retief got to his feet. "Wait until I get in position behind that fuel monitor." He pointed to a dark shape crouching fifty feet distant. "Then make a few suspicious noises."

"I better go with you, Retief," Mulvihill started, but Retief was gone. He moved forward silently, reached the shelter of the heavy apparatus, watched the Krultch sentinel move closer, stepping daintily as a deer on its four sharp hooves. The alien had reached a point a hundred feet distant when there was a sharp *ping!* from behind Retief. The guard halted; Retief heard the snick of a power gun's action. The Krultch turned toward him. He could hear the cli-clack, cli-clack of the hooves now. At a distance of ten feet, the quadruped slowed, came to a halt. Retief could see the vicious snout of the gun aimed warily into the darkness. There was another sound from Mulvihill's position. The guard plucked something from the belt rigged across his chest, and started toward the source of the sound. As he passed Retief he shied suddenly, and grabbed for his communicator. Retief leaped, landed a haymaker on the bony face, and caught the microphone before it hit the pavement. The Krultch, staggering back from the blow, went to his haunches and struck out with knife-edged forefeet. Retief ducked aside, chopped hard at the collar bone. The Krultch collapsed with a choked cry. Mulvihill appeared at a run, seized the feebly moving guard, pulled off the creature's belt, trussed his four legs together, and then, using other straps to bind the hands, he gagged the powerful jaws.

"Now what?" Wee Willie inquired. "You gonna cut his throat?"

"Shove him back of the monitor," Mulvihill said.

"Now let's see how close we can get to the ship without getting spotted," Retief said.

The mighty Krultch war vessel, a black column towering into the night, was ablaze with varicolored running and navigation lights. Giant floods mounted far up on the ship's sleek sides cast puddles of blue-white radiance on the tarmac; from the main cabin amidships, softer light gleamed through wide view windows.

"All lit up like a party," Mulvihill growled.

"A tough party to crash," Wee Willie said, looking up the long slant of the hull.

"I think I see a route, Mr. Retief," the girl said. "What's the little square opening up there, just past the gun emplacement?"

"It looks as though it might be a cargo hatch. It's not so little, Miss La Flamme! it's a long way up—"

"You reckon I could get through it?"

Retief nodded, looking up at the smooth surface above. "Can you make it up there?"

"They used to bill me as the human lady-bug. Nothing to it."

"If you get in," Retief said, "try to find your way back down into the tube compartment. If you can open one of these access panels, we're in."

Suzette nodded, took out her rope, tossed a loop over a projection fifteen feet above, and clambered quickly up the landing jack to its junction with the smooth metal of the hull. She put her hands flat against the curving, slightly in-slanting wall before her, planted one crepe-soled shoe against a tiny weld seam and started up the sheer wall.

Ten minutes passed. From the deep shadow at the ship's stern, Retief watched as the slim girl inched her way up, skirting a row of orange glare panels spelling out the name of the vessel in blocky Krultch ideographs, taking advantage of a ventilator outlet for a minute's rest, then going on up, up, thirty feet now, forty, forty-five . . .

She reached the open hatch, raised her head cautiously for a glance inside, then swiftly pulled up and disappeared through the opening.

Julius Mulvihill heaved a sign of relief. "That was as tough a climb as Suzie ever made," he rumbled.

"Don't get happy yet," Wee Willie piped up. "Her troubles is just starting."

"I'm sure she'll encounter no difficulty," Professor Fate said anxiously. "Surely there'll be no one on duty aft, here in port."

More minutes ticked past. Then there was a rasp of metal, a gentle clatter. A few feet above ground, a panel swung out: Suzie's face appeared, oil streaked.

"Boy, this place needs a good scrubbing," she breathed. "Come on; they're all having a shindig up above, sounds like."

Inside the echoing, gloomy vault of the tube compartment, Retief studied the layout of equipment, the placement of giant cooling baffles, and the contour of the bulkheads.

"This is a Krultch-built job," he said. "But it seems to be a pretty fair copy of an old Concordiat cruiser of the line. That means the controls are all the way forward."

"Let's get started!" Wee Willie went to the wide-runged catwalk designed for goat-like Krultch feet, started up. The others followed. Retief glanced around, reached for the ladder. As he did, a harsh Krultch voice snapped, "Halt where you are, Terrans!"

Retief turned slowly. A dirt-smeared Krultch in baggy coveralls stepped from the concealment of a massive ion-collector, a grim-looking power gun aimed. He waited as a second and third sailor followed him, all armed.

"A nice catch, Udas," one said admiringly in Krultch. "The

captain said we'd have Terry labor to do the dirty work on the run back, but I didn't expect to see 'em volunteering."

"Get 'em down here together, Jesau," the first Krultch barked. His partner came forward, motioned with the gun.

"Retief, you savvy Fustian?" Mulvihill muttered.

"Uh-huh," Retief answered.

"You hit the one on the left; I'll take the bird on the right. Professor—"

"Not yet," Retief said.

"No talk!" the Krultch barked in Terran. "Come down!"

The Terrans descended to the deck, stood in a loose group.

"Closer together!" the sailor said; he poked the girl with the gun to emphasize the command. She smiled at him sweetly. "You bat-eared son of a goat, just wait till I get a handful of your whiskers!"

"No talk!"

Professor Fate edged in front of the girl. He held out both hands toward the leading Krultch, flipped them over to show both sides, then twitched his wrists, fanned two sets of playing cards. He waved them under the astounded nose of the nearest gunman, and with a flick they disappeared.

The two rearmost sailors stepped closer, mouths open. The professor snapped his fingers; flame shot from the tip of each pointed forefinger. The Krultch jumped. The tall Terran waved his hands, whipped a gauzy blue handkerchief from nowhere, swirled it around; now it was red. He snapped it sharply, and a shower of confetti scattered around the dumbfounded Krultch. He doubled his fists, popped them open; whoofed into the aliens' faces. A final wave, and a white bird was squawking in the air.

"Now!" Retief said, and took a step, uppercut the leading sailor; the slender legs buckled as the creature went down with a slam. Mulvihill was past him, catching Krultch number two with a roundhouse swipe. The third sailor made a sound like tearing sheet metal, brought his gun to bear on Retief as Wee Willie, hurtling forward, hit him at the knees. The shot melted a furrow in the wall as Mulvihill floored the hapless creature with a mighty blow.

"Neatly done," Professor Fate said, tucking things back into his cuffs. "Almost a pity to lose such an appreciative audience."

With the three Krultch securely strapped hand and foot in their own harnesses, Retief nudged one with his foot.

"We have important business to contract in the control room," he said. "We don't want to disturb anyone, Jesau, so we'd prefer a nice quiet approach via the back stairs. What would you suggest?"

The Krultch made a suggestion.

Retief said, "Professor, perhaps you'd better give him a few more samples."

"Very well." Professor Fate stepped forward, waved his hands; a slim-bladed knife appeared in one. He tested the edge with his thumb, which promptly dripped gore. He stroked the thumb with another finger; the blood disappeared. He nodded.

"Now, fellow," he said to the sailor. "I've heard you rascals place great store by your beards; what about a shave?" He reached—

The Krultch made a sound like glass shattering. "The port catwalk!" he squalled. "But you won't get away with this!"

"Oh, no?" The professor smiled gently, made a pass in the air, plucked a small cylinder from nowhere.

"I doubt if anyone will be along this way for many hours," he said. "If we fail to return safely in an hour, this little device will detonate with sufficient force to distribute your component atoms over approximately twelve square miles." He placed the object by the Krultch, who rolled horrified eyes at it.

"Oh—on second thought, try the service catwalk behind the main tube," he squeaked.

"Good enough," Retief said. "Let's go."

# V

The sounds of Krultch revelry were loud in the cramped passage.

"Sounds like they're doing a little early celebrating for tomorrow's big diplomatic victory," Mulvihill said. "You suppose most of them are in there?"

"There'll be a few on duty," Retief said. "But that sounds like a couple of hundred out of circulation for the moment—until we trip something and give the alarm."

"The next stretch is all right," Professor Fate said, coming back dusting off his hands. "Then I'm afraid we shall have to emerge into the open."

"We're not far from the command deck now," Retief said. "Another twenty feet, vertically, ought to do it."

The party clambered on up, negotiated a sharp turn, came to an exit panel. Professor Fate put his ear against it.

"All appears silent," he said. "Shall we sally forth?"

Retief came to the panel, eased it open, glanced out; then he stepped through, motioned the others to follow. It was quieter here; there was a deep-pile carpeting underfoot, an odor of alien food and drug-smoke in the air.

"Officers' country," Mulvihill muttered.

Retief pointed toward a door marked with Krultch lettering. "Anybody read that?" he whispered.

There were shakes of the head and whispered negatives.

"We'll have to take a chance." Retief went to the door, gripped the latch, and yanked it suddenly wide. An obese Krultch in uniform belt but without his tunic looked up from a brightly colored magazine on the pages of which Retief glimpsed glossy photos of slender-built Krultch mares flirting saucy derrieres at the camera.

The alien stuffed the magazine in a desk slot, came to his feet, gaping, then whirled and dived for a control panel across the narrow passage in which he was posted. He reached a heavy lever and hauled it down just as Retief caught him with a flying tackle. Man and Krultch hit the deck together; Retief's hand chopped; the Krultch kicked twice and lay still.

"That lever—you suppose—" Wee Willie started.

"Probably an alarm," Retief said, coming to his feet. "Come on!" He ran along the corridor; it turned sharply to the right. A heavy door was sliding shut before him. He leaped to it, wedged himself in the narrowing opening, braced against the thrust of the steel panel. It slowed, with a groaning of machinery. Mulvihill charged up, grasped the edge of the door and heaved. Somewhere, metal creaked. There was a loud *clunk!* and a clatter of broken mechanism.

The door slid freely back.

"Close," Mulvihill grunted. "For a minute there—" He broke off at a sound from behind him. Ten feet back along the passage a second panel had slid noiselessly out, sealing off the corridor. Mulvihill jumped to it, heaved against it.

Ahead, Retief saw a third panel, this one standing wide open. He plunged through it; skidded to a halt. A braided Krultch officer was waiting, a foot-long purple cigar in his mouth, a power gun in each hand. He kicked a lever near his foot. The door whooshed shut behind Retief.

"Ah, welcome aboard, Terran," the captain grated. "You can be the first of your kind to enjoy Krultch hospitality.

"I have been observing your progress on my inspection screen here." The captain nodded toward a small panel which showed a view of the four Terrans pushing fruitlessly against the doors that had closed to entrap them.

"Interesting," Retief commented.

"You are surprised at the sophistication of the equipment we Krultch can command?" The captain puffed out smoke, showed horny gums in a smile-like grimace.

"No, anybody who can steal the price can buy a Groaci spy-eye system," Retief said blandly. "But I find it interesting that you had to spend all that cash just to keep an eye on your crew. Not too trustworthy, eh?"

"What? Any of my crew would die at my command!"

"They'll probably get the chance, too," Retief nodded agreement. "How about putting one of the guns down—unless you're afraid of a misfire."

"Krultch guns never misfire." The captain tossed one pistol aside. "But I agree: I am overprotected against the paltry threat of a single Terran."

"You're forgetting—I have friends."

The Krultch made a sound like fingernails on a blackboard. "They are effectively immobilized," he said. "Now, tell me, what did you hope to accomplish by intruding here?"

"I intend to place you under arrest," Retief said. "Mind if I sit down?"

The Krultch captain made laughing noises resembling a flawed drive bearing; he waved a two fingered claw-hand.

"Make yourself comfortable—while you can," he said. "Now, tell me, how did you manage to get your equipment up to my ship without being seen? I shall impale the slackers responsible, of course."

"Oh, we have no equipment," Retief said breezily. He sniffed. "That's not a Lovenbroy cigar, is it?"

"Never smoke anything else," the Krultch said. "Care for one?"

"Don't mind if I do," Retief admitted. He accepted an eighteen-inch stogie, lit up.

"Now, about the equipment," the captain persisted. "I assume you used fifty-foot scaling ladders, though I confess I don't see how you got them onto the port—"

"Ladders?" Retief smiled comfortably. "We Terrans don't need ladders; we just sprouted wings."

"Wings?"

"Oh, we're versatile, we Terries."

The captain was wearing an expression of black disapproval now. "If you had no ladders, I must conclude that you breached my hull at ground level," he snapped. "What did you use? It would require at least a fifty K-T-Second power input to penetrate two inches of flint-steel—"

Retief shook his head, puffing out scented smoke. "Nice," he said. "No, we just peeled back a panel bare-handed. We Terrans—"

"Blast you Terrans! Nobody could." The captain clamped his jaws, puffed furiously. "Just outside, in the access-control chamber you sabotaged the closure mechanism. Where is the hydraulic jack you used for this?"

"As I said, we Terrans—"

"You entered the secret access passage almost as soon as you boarded my vessel!" the captain screeched. "My men are inoculated against every talk-drug known! What did you use on the traitor who informed you!"

Retief held up a hand. "We Terrans can be very persuasive, Captain. At this very moment, you yourself, for example, are about to be persuaded of the futility of trying to out-maneuver us."

The Krultch commander's mouth opened and closed. "*Me!*" he burst out. "You think that you can divert a Krultch officer from the performance of his duty?"

"Sure," a high voice piped from above and behind the captain. "Nothing to it."

The Krultch's hooves clattered as he whirled, froze at the sight of Wee Willie's small, round face smiling down at him from the ventilator register above the control panel. In a smooth motion, Retief cracked the alien across the wrist, and twitched the gun from his nerveless hand.

"You see?" he said as the officer stared from him to the midget and back. "Never underestimate us Terrans."

The captain drooped in his chair, mopping at his face with a polka-dotted hanky provided by Wee Willie.

"This interrogation is a gross illegality!" he groaned. "I was assured that all your kind did was talk—"

"We're a tricky lot," Retief conceded. "But surely a little innocent deception can be excused, once you understand our natures. We love strife, and this seemed to be the easiest way to stir up some action."

"Stir up action?" the Krultch croaked.

"There's something about an apparently defenseless nincompoop that brings out the opportunist in people," Retief said. "It's a simple way for us to identify troublemakers, so they can be dealt with expeditiously. I think you Krultch qualify handsomely. It's convenient timing, because we have a number of new planet-wrecking devices we've been wanting to field-test."

"You're bluffing!" the Krultch bleated.

Retief nodded vigorously. "I have to warn you, but you don't have to believe me. So if you still want to try conclusions—"

There was a sharp buzz from the panel; a piercing yellow light blinked rapidly. The captain's hand twitched as he eyed the phone.

"Go ahead, answer it," Retief said. "But don't say anything that might annoy me. We Terrans have quick tempers."

The Krultch flipped a key.

"Exalted one," a rapid Krultch voice babbled from the panel. "We have been assassinated by captives! I mean, captivated by assassins! There were twelve of them, or perhaps twenty! Some were as high as a hundred-year Fufu tree, and others smaller than hoof-nits! One had eyes of live coals, and flames ten feet long shot from his hands, melting all they touched, and another—"

"Silence!" the captain roared. "Who are you? Where are you? What in the name of the Twelve Devils is going on here!" He whirled on Retief. "Where are the rest of your commandos? How did they evade my surveillance system? What—"

"Ah-ah," Retief clucked. "I'm asking the questions now. First, I'll have the names of all Gaspierre officials who accepted your bribes."

"You think I would betray my compatriots to death at your hands?"

"Nothing like that; I just need to know who the cooperative ones are so I can make them better offers."

A low brackk! sounded; this time a baleful blue light winked. The Krultch officer eyed it warily.

"That's my outside hot line to the Foreign Office," he said. "When word reaches the Gaspierre government of the piratical behavior you allegedly peaceful Terries indulged in behind the facade of diplomacy—"

"Go ahead, tell them," Retief said. "It's time they discovered they aren't the only ones who understand the fine art of the triple-cross."

The Krultch lifted the phone. "Yes?" he snapped. His expression stiffened. He rolled an eye at Retief, then at Wee Willie.

"What's that?" he barked into the communicator. "Flew through the air? Climbed where? What do you mean, giant white birds!"

"Boy," Wee Willie exclaimed. "Them Gaspers sure exaggerate!"

The captain eyed the tiny man in horror, comparing his height with Retief's six-three.

He shuddered.

"I know," he said into the phone.

"They're already here. . . ." He dropped the instrument back on its hook, glanced at his panel, idly reached—

"That reminds me," Retief said. He pointed the gun at the center of the captain's chest. "Order all hands to assemble amidships," he said.

"They—they're already there," the Krultch said unsteadily, his eyes fixed on the gun.

"Just make sure."

The captain depressed a key, cleared his throat.

"All hands to the central feeding area, on the double," he said.

There was a moment's pause. Then a Krultch voice came back: "All except the stand-by crews in power section and armaments, I guess you mean, Exalted One."

"I said all hands, damn you!" the officer snarled. He flipped off the communicator, "I don't know what you think you'll accomplish with this," he barked. "I have three hundred fearless warriors aboard this vessel; you'll never get off this ship alive!"

Two minutes passed. The communicator crackled. "All hands assembled, sir."

"Willie, you see that big white lever?" Retief said mildly. "Just pull it down, and the next one to it."

The captain made as if to move. The gun jumped at him. Willie went past the Krultch, wrestled the controls down. Far away, machinery rumbled. A distinct shock ran through the massive hull, then a second.

"What was that?" Willie asked.

"The disaster bulkheads, sliding shut," Retief said. "The three hundred fearless warriors are nicely locked in between them."

The captain slumped, looking stricken. "How do you know so much about the operation of my vessel?" he demanded, "It's classified . . ."

"That's the result of stealing someone else's plans; the wrong people may have been studying them. Now, Willie, go let Julius and the rest of the group in; then I think we'll be ready to discuss surrender terms."

"This is a day that will live in the annals of treachery," the captain grated hollowly.

"Oh, I don't think it needs to get into the annals," Retief said. "Not if we can come to a private understanding, just between gentlemen."

# VI

It was an hour past sunrise when the emergency meeting of the Gaspierre cabinet broke up. Ambassador Sheepshorn, emerging from the chamber deep in amiable conversation with an uncomfortable-looking Krultch officer in elaborate full dress uniform, halted as he spied Retief.

"Ah, there, my boy! I was a trifle concerned when you failed to return last evening; but, as I was just pointing out to the Captain here, it was really all just a dreadful misunderstanding. Once the Krultch position was made clear—that they really preferred animal husbandry and folk dancing to any sort of war-like adventure—the cabinet was able to come to a rapid and favorable decision on the Peace-and-Friendship Treaty, giving Terrans full Most Favored Nation status."

"I'm glad to hear that, Mr. Ambassador," Retief said, nodding to the stony-faced Krultch commander. "I'm sure we'd all rather engage in friendly competition than have to demonstrate our negotiating ability any further."

There was a stir at the end of the corridor; a harried-looking Krultch officer with a grimy Krultch yeoman in tow appeared, came up to the captain, and saluted.

"Exalted One, this fellow has just escaped from some sort of magical paralysis."

"It was that one." The sailor indicated Retief. "Him and the others." He looked reproachfully at Retief. "That was a dirty trick, telling us that was a bomb you were planting; we spent a rough night before we found out it was just a dope-stick."

"Sorry," Retief said.

"Look, Exalted One," the sailor went on in a stage whisper. "What I wanted to warn you about, that Terry—the long one, with the pointed tail and the fiery breath; he's a warlock; he waves his hands and giant white flying creatures appear—"

"Silence, idiot!" the captain bellowed. "Have you no power of observation? They don't merely *produce* birds; any fool could do

*that*! They transform themselves! Not get out of my sight! I plan
to enter a monastery as soon as we return home, and I want to get
started on my meditating!" He nodded curtly and clattered away.

"Odd sort of chap," Sheepshorn commented. "I wonder what
he was talking about?"

"Just some sort of in-group joke, I imagine," Retief said. "By the
way, about that group of distressed Terrans I mentioned to you—"

"Yes. I may have been a bit abrupt with them, Retief; but of
course I was busy planning my strategy for today's meeting.
Perhaps I was hasty. I hereby authorize you to put in a good word
for them."

"I took the liberty of going a little farther than that," Retief
said. "Since the new treaty calls for Terran cultural missions, I
signed a six months' contract with them to put on shows here on
Gaspierre."

Sheepshorn frowned. "You went a bit beyond your authority,
Retief," he snapped. "I'd thought we might bring in a nice group
or two to read classic passages from the Congressional Record, or
perform some of the new silent music; and I had halfway promised the Garoci Minister I'd have one of his nose-flute troupes—"

"I thought it might be a good idea to show Terran solidarity,
just at this juncture," Retief pointed out. "Then, too, a demonstration of sword-swallowing, prestidigitation, fire-eating, juggling,
tight-rope walking, acrobatics and thaumaturgics might be just
the ticket for dramatizing versatility."

Sheepshorn considered with pursed lips, then nodded. "You
may have a valuable point there, my boy; we Terrans *are* a
versatile breed. Speaking of which, I wish you'd been there to see
my handling of the negotiation this morning! One moment I was
all fire and truculence; the next, as smooth as Yill silk."

"A brilliant performance, I daresay, Mr. Ambassador."

"Yes, indeed," Sheepshorn rubbed his hands together, chuckling. "In a sense, Retief, diplomacy itself might be thought of as a
branch of show business, eh? Thus, these performers might be
considered colleagues of a sort."

"True, but I wouldn't mention it when they're within earshot."

"Yes, it might go to their heads. Well, I'm off, Retief. My
report on this morning's work will become a classic study of
Terran diplomatic subtlety."

He hurried away. A Gaspierre with heavy bifocal lenses edged
up to Retief.

"I'm with the *Gaspierre Morning Exhalation*," he wheezed. "Is it true, sire, that you Terries can turn into fire-breathing dragons at will?"

A second reporter closed in. "I heard you read minds," he said. "And about this ability to walk through walls—"

"Just a minute, boys." Retief held up a hand. "I wouldn't want to be quoted on this, of course, but just between you and me, here's what actually happened: As soon as the Ambassador had looked into his crystal ball . . ."

# NINE HUNDRED GRANDMOTHERS
## (FEBRUARY 1966)
## R. A. LAFFERTY
## (B. 1914)

Raymond A. Lafferty only started writing science fiction in his mid-forties, but his work was anything but conventional or middle-aged. In fact, we are not exactly sure what his stories are, except that they are unique, often charming, and always thought-provoking. The best of his shorter work can be found in the collections *Strange Doings* (1972) and *Does Anyone Else Have Anything Further to Add?* (1974). He had a dozen or so appearances in *If*, including "Seven-Day Terror" (March 1962—one of his best early stories), "Ride a Tin Can" (April 1970), "The Man Underneath" (January 1971), and "Guesting Time" (May 1965).

## MEMOIR BY R. A. LAFFERTY

In the years when *Galaxy* was counted as the best science-fiction magazine by a disproportionate number of science-fiction readers, there was the paradox that *Worlds of If*, the little brother of *Galaxy*, consistently published better fiction than *Galaxy* did. This was a fairly open secret, and yet at least one, and possibly two, of the editors of the magazines did not seem to be aware of it. But if a magazine is better than the best, should it not be accounted as the best? Probably not, not if it's *If*.

*Galaxy* had the features, the better reviews, the science articles (including the wonderful pieces by Willy Ley for some of those years). And it was apparently *intended* to have the best fiction. It had the name writers, it had the hokum, it had the pomposity; all those things count heavily with the readers. And *Galaxy* had much the better art. But *Worlds of If* did have the better fiction.

I was fortunate in selling quite a few stories to each of the magazines. Whenever one of them was taken by *Galaxy* I knew that it was a little bit lacking; but I also knew that I would get more money for it than I would if it were taken by *If*.

"Nine Hundred Grandmothers" is a story that doesn't have any story line and doesn't have any ending. In those years, the preachers preached that a story should have both of these things. For a while I was almost, but not quite, convinced that they were right. They weren't, of course. A story line and an ending, if handled right, will not hurt a story, may even help it; but they are not essential. Stories without these two things could sometimes be published in *If*. There was no way they could have been published in *Galaxy*.

"Nine Hundred Grandmothers" is a good story. And I don't see any way that *Worlds of If: A Retrospective Anthology* wouldn't be a good book. A bucket could be dipped down almost anywhere into the hundred or so issues of *If* and it couldn't help but bring up a couple of good stories. There would be no danger of it bringing up any of the Royal Turkeys that *Galaxy* often had in those years, though it never had them to the extent that *Astounding* or the *Magazine of Fantasy & Science Fiction* had them. Almost anywhere in *If* there are real treasures to be lifted out. Why, just one of its dozens of good writers had such masterworks as "Six Fingers of Time," "Seven-Day Terror," "Ride a Tin Can," "Golden Trabant," "In Our Block," "McGonigal's Worm," "Boomer Flats," "Mad Man," and "In the Garden" in *Worlds of If* in its excellent years. Incredible!

"Why, I could read it with my eyes closed and still get a big bang out of it," a friend of mine said of another book recently. And *Worlds of If: A Retrospective Anthology* should be the bangingest SF anthology around for quite a season.


# NINE HUNDRED GRANDMOTHERS

Ceran Swicegood was a promising young Special Aspects Man. But, like all Special Aspects, he had one irritating habit. He was forever asking the question: How Did It All Begin?

They all had tough names except Ceran. Manbreaker Crag, Heave Huckle, Blast Berg, George Blood, Move Manion (when Move says "Move," you move), Trouble Trent. They were supposed to be tough, and they had taken tough names at the naming. Only Ceran kept his own—to the disgust of his commander, Manbreaker.

"Nobody can be a hero with a name like Ceran Swicegood!"
Manbreaker would thunder. "Why don't you take Storm Shannon? That's good. Or Gutboy Barrelhouse or Slash Slagle or
Nevel Knife? You barely glanced at the suggested list."

"I'll keep my own." Ceran always said, and that is where he
made his mistake. A new name will sometimes bring out a new
personality. It had done so for George Blood. Though the hair on
George's chest was a graft job, yet that and his new name had
turned him from a boy into a man. Had Ceran assumed the heroic
name of Gutboy Barrelhouse he might have been capable of
rousing endeavors and man-sized angers rather than his tittering
indecisions and flouncy furies.

They were down on the big asteroid Proavitus—a sphere that
almost tinkled with the potential profit that might be shaken out
of it. And the tough men of the Expedition knew their business.
They signed big contracts on the native velvet-like bark scrolls
and on their own parallel tapes. They impressed, inveigled and
somewhat cowed the slight people of Proavitus. Here was a solid
two-way market, enough to make them slaver. And there was a
whole world of oddities that could lend themselves to the luxury
trade.

"Everybody's hit it big but you," Manbreaker crackled in kindly
thunder to Ceran after three days there. "But even Special Aspects is supposed to pay its way. Our charter compels us to carry
one of your sort to give a cultural twist to the thing, but it needn't
be restricted to that. What we go out for every time, Ceran, is to
cut a big fat hog in the rump—we make no secret of that. But if
the hog's tail can be shown to have a cultural twist to it, that will
solve a requirement. And if that twist in the tail can turn us a
profit, then we become mighty happy about the whole thing.
Have you been able to find out anything about the living dolls, for
instance? They might have both a cultural aspect and a market
value."

"The living dolls seem a part of something much deeper,"
Ceran said. "There's a whole complex of things to be unraveled.
The key may be the statement of the Proavitoi that they do not
die."

"I think they die pretty young, Ceran. All those out and about
are young, and those I have met who do not leave their houses
are only middling old."

"Then where are their cemeteries?"

"Likely they cremate the old folks when they die."

"Where are the crematories?"

"They might just toss the ashes out or vaporize the entire remains. Probably they have no reverence for ancestors."

"Other evidence shows their entire culture to be based on an exaggerated reverence for ancestors."

"You find out, Ceran. You're Special Aspects Man."

Ceran talked to Nokoma, his Proavitoi counterpart as translator. Both were expert, and they could meet each other halfway in talk. Nokoma was likely feminine. There was a certain softness about both the sexes of the Proavitoi, but the men of the Expedition believed that they had them straight now.

"Do you mind if I ask some straight questions?" Ceran greeted her today.

"Sure is not. How else I learn the talk well but by talking?"

"Some of the Proavitoi say that they do not die, Nokoma. Is this true?"

"How is not be true? If they die, they not be here to say they do not die. Oh, I joke, I joke. No, we do not die. It is a foolish alien custom which we see no reason to imitate. On Proavitus, only the low creatures die."

"None of you does?"

"Why, no. Why should one want to be an exception in this?"

"But what do you do when you get very old?"

"We do less and less then. We come to a deficiency of energy. Is it not the same with you?"

"Of course. But where do you go when you become exceedingly old?"

"Nowhere. We stay at home then. Travel is for the young and those of the active years."

"Let's try it from the other end," Ceran said. "Where are your father and mother, Nokoma?"

"Out and about. They aren't really old."

"And your grandfathers and grandmothers?"

"A few of them still get out. The older ones stay home."

"Let's try it this way. How many grandmothers do you have, Nokoma?"

"I think I have nine hundred grandmothers in my house. Oh, I know that isn't many, but we are the young branch of a family. Some of our clan have very great numbers of ancestors in their houses."

"And all these ancestors are alive?"

"What else? Who would keep things not alive? How would such be ancestors?"

Ceran began to hop around in his excitement.

"Could I see them?" he twittered.

"It might not be wise for you to see the older of them," Nokoma cautioned. "It could be an unsettling thing for strangers, and we guard it. A few tens of them you can see, of course."

Then it came to Ceran that he might be onto what he had looked for all his life. He went into a panic of expectation.

"Nokoma, it would be finding the key!" he fluted. "If none of you has ever died, then your entire race would still be alive!"

"Sure. Is like you count fruit. You take none away, you still have them all."

"But if the first of them are still alive, then they might know their origin! They would know how it began! Do they? Do you?"

"Oh, not I. I am too young for the Ritual."

"But who knows? Doesn't someone know?"

"Oh, yes, All the old ones know how it began."

"How old? How many generations back from you till they know?"

"Ten, no more. When I have ten generations of children, then I will also go to the Ritual."

"The Ritual, what is it?"

"Once a year, the old people go to the very old people. They wake them up and ask them how it all began. The very old people tell them the beginning. It is a high time. Oh, how they hottle and laugh! Then the very old people go back to sleep for another year. So it is passed down to the generations. That is the Ritual."

The Proavitoi were not humanoid. Still less were they "monkey-faces," though that name was now set in the explorers' lingo. They were upright and robed and swathed, and were assumed to be two-legged under their garments. Though, as Manbreaker said, "They might go on wheels, for all we know."

They had remarkable flowing hands that might be called everywhere-digited. They could handle tools, or employ their hands as if they were the most intricate tools.

George Blood was of the opinion that the Proavitoi were always masked, and that the men of the Expedition had never seen their faces. He said that those apparent faces were ritual masks, and that no part of the Proavitoi had ever been seen by the men except for those remarkable hands, which perhaps were their real faces.

The men reacted with cruel hilarity when Ceran tried to explain to them just what a great discovery he was verging on.

"Little Ceran is still on the how-did-it-begin jag," Manbreaker jeered. "Ceran, will you never give off asking which came first, the chicken or the egg?"

"I will have that answer very soon," Ceran sang. "I have the unique opportunity. When I find how the Proavitoi began, I may have the clue to how everything began. All of the Proavitoi are still alive, the very first generation of them."

"It passes belief that you can be so simpleminded," Manbreaker moaned. "They say that one has finally mellowed when he can suffer fools gracefully. By God, I hope I never come to that."

But two days later, it was Manbreaker who sought out Ceran Swicegood on nearly the same subject. Manbreaker had been doing a little thinking and discovering of his own.

"You are Special Aspects Man, Ceran," he said, "and you have been running off after the wrong aspect."

"What is that?"

"It don't make a damn how it began. What is important is that it may not have to end."

"It is the beginning that I intend to discover," said Ceran.

"You fool, can't you understand anything? What do the Proavitoi possess so uniquely that we don't know whether they have it by science or by their nature or by fool luck?"

"Ah, their chemistry, I suppose."

"Sure. Organic chemistry has come of age here. The Proavitoi have every kind of nexus and inhibitor and stimulant. They can grow and shrink and telescope and prolong what they will. These creatures seem stupid to me; it is as if they had these things by instinct. But they have them, that is what is important. With these things, we can become the patent medicine kings of the universes, for the Proavitoi do not travel or make many outside contacts. These things can do anything or undo anything. I suspect that the Proavitoi can shrink cells, and I suspect that they can do something else."

"No, they couldn't shrink cells. It is you who talk nonsense now, Manbreaker."

"Never mind. Their things already make nonsense of conventional chemistry. With the pharmacopoeia that one could pick up here, a man need never die. That's the stick horse you've been

riding, isn't it? But you've been riding it backward with your head
to the tail. The Proavitoi say that they never die."

"They seem pretty sure that they don't. If they did, they would
be the first to know it, as Nokoma says."

"What? Have these creatures humor?"

"Some."

"But, Ceran, you don't understand how big this is."

"I'm the only one who understands it so far. It means that if the
Proavitoi have always been immortal, as they maintain, then the
oldest of them are still alive. From them I may be able to learn
how their species—and perhaps every species—began."

Manbreaker went into his dying buffalo act then. He tore his
hair and nearly pulled out his ears by the roots. He stomped and
pawed and went off bull-bellowing: "It don't make a damn how it
began, you fool! It might not have to end!" so loud that the hills
echoed back:

"It don't make a damn—you fool."

Ceran Swicegood went to the house of Nokoma, but not with
her on her invitation. He went without her when he knew that
she was away from home. It was a sneaky thing to do, but the
men of the Expedition were trained in sneakery.

He would find out better without a mentor about the nine
hundred grandmothers, about the rumored living dolls. He would
find out what the old people did do if they didn't die, and find if
they knew how they were first born. For his intrusion, he counted
on the innate politeness of the Proavitoi.

The house of Nokoma, of all the people, was in the cluster on
top of the large flat hill, the Acropolis of Proavitus. They were
earthen houses, though finely done, and they had the appearance
of growing out of and being a part of the hill itself.

Ceran went up the winding, ascending flagstone paths, and entered the house which Nokoma had once pointed out to him. He
entered furtively, and encountered one of the nine hundred
grandmothers—one with whom nobody need be furtive.

The grandmother was seated and small and smiling at him.
They talked without real difficulty, though it was not as easy as
with Nokoma, who could meet Ceran halfway in his own language. At her call, there came a grandfather who likewise smiled
at Ceran. These two ancients were somewhat smaller than the
Proavitoi of active years. They were kind and serene. There was
an atmosphere about the scene that barely missed being an odor—

not unpleasant, sleepy, reminiscent of something, almost sad.

"Are there those here older than you?" Ceran asked earnestly.

"So many, so many, who could know how many?" said the grandmother. She called in other grandmothers and grandfathers older and smaller than herself, these no more than half the size of the active Proavitoi—small, sleepy, smiling.

Ceran knew now that the Proavitoi were not masked. The older they were, the more character and interest there was in their faces. It was only of the immature active Proavitoi that there could have been a doubt. No masks could show such calm and smiling old age as this. The queer textured stuff was their real faces.

So old and friendly, so weak and sleepy, there must have been a dozen generations of them there back to the oldest and smallest.

"How old are the oldest?" Ceran asked the first grandmother.

"We say that all are the same age since all are perpetual," the grandmother told him. "It is not true that all are the same age, but it is indelicate to ask how old."

"You do not know what a lobster is," Ceran said to them, trembling, "but it is a creature that will boil happily if the water on him is heated slowly. He takes no alarm, for he does not know at what point the heat is dangerous. It is that gradual here with me. I slide from one degree to another with you and my credulity is not alarmed. I am in danger of believing anything about you if it comes in small doses, and it will. I believe that you are here and as you are for no other reason than that I see and touch you. Well, I'll be boiled for a lobster, then, before I turn back from it. Are there those here even older than the ones present?"

The first grandmother motioned Ceran to follow her. They went down a ramp through the floor into the older part of the house, which must have been under ground.

Living dolls! They were here in rows on the shelves, and sitting in small chairs in their niches. Doll-sized indeed, and several hundred of them.

Many had wakened at the intrusion. Others came awake when spoken to or touched. They were incredibly ancient, but they were cognizant in their glances and recognition. They smiled and stretched sleepily, not as humans would, but as very old puppies might. Ceran spoke to them, and they understood each other surprisingly.

*Lobster, lobster,* said Ceran to himself, *the water has passed the danger point! And it hardly feels different. If you believe your senses in this, then you will be boiled alive in your credulity.*

He knew now that the living dolls were real and that they were the living ancestors of the Proavitoi.

Many of the little creatures began to fall asleep again. Their waking moments were short, but their sleeps seemed to be likewise. Several of the living mummies woke a second time while Ceran was still in the room, woke refreshed from very short sleeps and were anxious to talk again.

"You are incredible!" Ceran cried out, and all the small and smaller and still smaller creatures smiled and laughed their assent. Of course they were. All good creatures everywhere are incredible, and were there ever so many assembled in one place? But Ceran was greedy. A roomful of miracles wasn't enough.

"I have to take this back as far as it will go!" he cried avidly. "Where are the even older ones?"

"There are older ones and yet older and again older," said the first grandmother, "and thrice-over older ones, but perhaps it would be wise not to seek to be too wise. You have seen enough. The old people are sleepy. Let us go up again."

Go up again, out of this? Ceran would not. He saw passages and descending ramps, down into the heart of the great hill itself. There were whole worlds of rooms about him and under his feet. Ceran went on and down, and who was to stop him? Not dolls and creatures much smaller than dolls.

Manbreaker had once called himself an old pirate who reveled in the stream of his riches. But Ceran was the Young Alchemist who was about to find the Stone itself.

He walked down the ramps through centuries and millennia. The atmosphere he had noticed on the upper levels was a clear odor now—sleepy, half-remembered, smiling, sad and quite strong. That is the way Time smells.

"Are there those here even older than you?" Ceran asked a small grandmother whom he held in the palm of his hand.

"So old and so small that I could hold in my hand," said the grandmother in what Ceran knew from Nokoma to be the older uncompounded form of the Proavitus language.

Smaller and older the creatures had been getting as Ceran went through the rooms. He was boiled lobster now for sure. He had to believe it all: he saw and felt it. The wren-sized grandmother talked and laughed and nodded that there were those far older than herself, and in doing so she nodded herself back to sleep. Ceran returned her to her niche in the hive-like wall where there were thousands of others, miniaturized generations.

Of course he was not in the house of Nokoma now. He was in the heart of the hill that underlay all the houses of Proavitus, and these were the ancestors of everybody on the asteroid.

"Are there those here even older than you?" Ceran asked a small grandmother whom he held on the tip of his finger.

"Older and smaller," she said, "but you come near the end."

She was asleep, and he put her back in her place. The older they were, the more they slept.

He was down to solid rock under the roots of the hill. He was into the passages that were cut out of that solid rock, but they could not be many or deep. He had a sudden fear that the creatures would become so small that he could not see them or talk to them, and so he would miss the secret of the beginning.

But had not Nokoma said that all the old people knew the secret? Of course. But he wanted to hear it from the oldest of them. He would have it now, one way or the other.

"Who is the oldest? Is this the end of it? Is this the beginning? Wake up! Wake up!" he called when he was sure he was in the lowest and oldest room.

"Is it Ritual?" asked some who woke up. Smaller than mice they were, no bigger than bees, maybe older than both.

"It is a special Ritual," Ceran told them. "Relate to me how it was in the beginning."

What was that sound—too slight, too scattered to be a noise? It was like a billion microbes laughing. It was the hilarity of little things waking up to a high time.

"Who is the oldest of all?" Ceran demanded, for their laughter bothered him. "Who is the oldest and first?"

"I am the oldest, the ultimate grandmother," one said gaily. "All the others are my children. Are you also of my children?"

"Of course," said Ceran, and the small laughter of unbelief flittered out from the whole multitude of them.

"Then you must be the ultimate child, for you are like no other. If you be, then it is as funny at the end as it was in the beginning."

"How was it in the beginning?" Ceran bleated. "You are the first. Do you know how you came to be?"

"Oh, yes, yes," laughed the ultimate grandmother, and the hilarity of the small things became a real noise now.

"How did it begin?" demanded Ceran, and he was hopping and skipping about in his excitement.

"Oh, it was so funny a joke the way things began that you

would not believe it," chittered the grandmother. "A joke, a joke!"

"Tell me the joke, then. If a joke generated your species, then tell me that cosmic joke."

"Tell yourself," tinkled the grandmother. "You are a part of the joke if you are of my children. Oh, it is too funny to believe. How good to wake up and laugh and go to sleep again."

Blazing green frustration! To be so close and to be balked by a giggling bee!

"Don't go to sleep again! Tell me at once how it began!" Ceran shrilled, and he had the ultimate grandmother between thumb and finger.

"This is not Ritual," the grandmother protested. "Ritual is that you guess what it was for three days, and we laugh and say, 'No, no, no, it was something nine times as wild as that. Guess some more.'"

"I will _not_ guess for three days! Tell me at once or I will crush you," Ceran threatened in a quivering voice.

"I look at you, you look at me, I wonder if you will do it," the ultimate grandmother said calmly.

Any of the tough men of the Expedition would have done it—would have crushed her, and then another and another and another of the creatures till the secret was told. If Ceran had taken on a tough personality and a tough name he'd have done it. If he'd been Gutboy Barrelhouse he'd have done it without a qualm. But Ceran Swicegood couldn't do it.

"Tell me," he pleaded in agony. "All my life I've tried to find out how it began, how anything began. And you know!"

"We know. Oh, it was so funny how it began. So joke! So fool, so clown, so grotesque thing! Nobody could guess, nobody could believe."

"Tell me! Tell me!" Ceran was ashen and hysterical.

"No, no, you are no child of mine," chortled the ultimate grandmother. "Is too joke a joke to tell a stranger. We could not insult a stranger to tell so funny, so unbelieve. Strangers can die. Shall I have it on conscience that a stranger died laughing?"

"Tell me! Insult me! Let me die laughing!" But Ceran nearly died crying from the frustration that ate him up as a million bee-sized things laughed and hooted and giggled:

"Oh, it was so funny the way it began!"

And they laughed. And laughed. And went on laughing . . . until Ceran Swicegood wept and laughed together, and crept away, and returned to the ship still laughing. On his next voyage he changed his name to Blaze Bolt and ruled for ninety-seven days as king of a sweet sea island in M-81, but that is another and much more unpleasant story.

# NEUTRON STAR
## (OCTOBER 1966)
## LARRY NIVEN
### (B. 1938)

A master of the "hard" science-fiction story (although equally at home with fantasy—a rare combination), Larry Niven has achieved success in both the SF and best-seller markets. *Worlds of If* was an important outlet for him, for not only did the magazine publish his first story ("The Coldest Place," December 1964) and a dozen others, it also serialized his second novel, *A Gift from Earth* (as "Slowboat Cargo" in 1968).

But none of his other *If* appearances were as important as the following story, which won the Hugo Award for Best Short Story in 1967.

## MEMOIR BY LARRY NIVEN

The *Galaxy* group of magazines was my home for the first years of my career.

Frederik Pohl edited all three of those magazines: *Galaxy*, *Worlds of If*, and *Worlds of Tomorrow*. It was Fred's policy to include a first story by a new writer in every issue of *If*. I sold my first story, "The Coldest Place," to *If*—after a year of doing nothing but write and collect rejection slips. Fred earned my loyalty thereby; but he went on earning it.

He published my second story, "Wrong Way Street," in *Galaxy*. The title is his. He felt it needed a new first chapter for coherency, and he wrote that, too.

"World of Ptavvs" (in novella form) he published in *Worlds of Tomorrow*, illustrated profusely and well by Jack Gaughan. And he passed the manuscript on to Betty Ballantine, who ran the science-fiction section of Ballantine Books. You'll note that Fred was giving me as wide an exposure as he was capable of. The Ballantines bought "World of Ptavvs" for expansion into a novel.

"One Face" appeared in *Galaxy*.

"Becalmed in Hell"—well, *I* think it's a funny story. Maybe Fred doesn't. Fred returned the manuscript with suggestions as to how to improve it. I rewrote, using his suggestions, and sent it to the *Magazine of Fantasy & Science Fiction*.

I later heard rumors that Ed Ferman couldn't understand why Fred had been buying my stuff. "Becalmed in Hell" must have changed his mind. And the next time I saw Fred, he took me aside and politely informed me that when an editor sends suggestions for the improvement of a story, it means he's interested. (Hell, I didn't know. I thought it was a personalized rejection slip.)

I kept sending stories to Fred as long as he was editor of *Galaxy*, and *Galaxy* continued to get my stories after Ejler Jakobsson took the post . . . much to my sorrow. I think Fred Pohl is wonderful. He was an usher at my wedding.

As for "Neutron Star"—

I wrote the first version of that story for a composition class in college. It involved a massive white dwarf star, and a professional hero prepared to risk his life in the service of knowledge. My teacher gave me a B+. She told me that she didn't understand what was going on in the story, but she was *sure* I did.

Five or six years later, with my career launched, I got a letter from Fred Pohl. Approximate quotes: "I've been looking for someone who can write a series of stories about the odd pockets of the universe. I'd pair them with astronomical fact articles about those same odd places. . . ."

And Isaac Asimov published an article, "Squoosh," about how densely matter can be compressed. He included parameters for a neutron star.

I dug out the old composition. The hero was boring; I substituted Beowulf Shaeffer, who would rather be a tourist than test out esoteric physics.

I had designed the Pierson's puppeteers because Chad Oliver irritated me, with his universal assumption that the human shape is the only workable shape for an intelligent being. I'd tried to put puppeteers in a story, but it hadn't worked. I borrowed them for "Neutron Star."

I took particular care in explaining . . . no, I won't blow the punch line for you. But Jerry Pournelle is right in saying that the puppeteers would have guessed the situation.

"Neutron Star" would win no awards today, though physics teachers have found it useful. In 1966 it had the terrific advantage of appearing in the heart of the "New Wave" period, when experiment and characterization were being used by all and sundry as an excuse for bad writing. I was the only new writer writing hard science fiction.

Some time after the 1967 Worldcon, I asked Fred Pohl if he had expected that story to win a Hugo Award. He says he more or less did. But I spent a terribly tense year or two at the awards banquet waiting to learn if I had won. There were no drinks to be had. Sam Moskowitz made a speech. I was out of cigarettes. If I hadn't had Marilyn (now my wife, whom I had met two days earlier) on one side of me, holding my hand, and Adrienne Barnes on the other side, loaning me cigarettes, I believe I would have gone berserk. Ladies, thank you. And thank you, Fred.

# NEUTRON STAR

The *Skydiver* dropped out of hyperspace an even million miles above the neutron star. I needed a minute to place myself against the stellar background, and another to find the distortion Sonya Laskin had mentioned before she died. It was to my left, an area the apparent size of the Earth's moon. I swung the ship around to face it.

Curdled stars, muddled stars, stars that had been stirred with a spoon.

The neutron star was in the center, of course, though I couldn't see it and hadn't expected to. It was only eleven miles across, and cool. A billion years had passed since BVS-1 burned by fusion fire. Millions of years, at least, since the cataclysmic two weeks during which BVS-1 was an X-ray star, burning at a temperature of five billion degrees Kelvin. Now it showed only by its mass.

The ship began to turn by itself. I felt the pressure of the fusion drive. Without help from me my faithful metal watchdog was putting me in a hyperbolic orbit that would take me within one mile of the neutron star's surface. Twenty-four hours to fall, twenty-four hours to rise . . . and during that time something would try to kill me. As something had killed the Laskins.

The same type of autopilot, with the same program, had chosen the Laskins' orbit. It had not caused their ship to collide with the star. I could trust the autopilot. I could even change its program.

I really ought to.

How did I get myself into this hole?

The drive went off after ten minutes of maneuvering. My orbit was established, in more ways than one. I knew what would happen if I tried to back out now.

All I'd done was walk into a drugstore to get a new battery for my lighter!

Right in the middle of the store, surrounded by three floors of sales counters, was the new 2603 Sinclair intrasystem yacht. I'd come for a battery, but I stayed to admire. It was a beautiful job, small and sleek and streamlined and blatantly different from anything that'd ever been built. I wouldn't have flown it for anything but I had to admit it was pretty. I ducked my head through the door to look at the control panel. You never saw so many dials. When I pulled my head out, all the customers were looking in the same direction. The place had gone startlingly quiet.

I can't blame them for staring. A number of aliens were in the store, mainly shopping for souvenirs, but they were staring too. A puppeteer is unique. Imagine a headless, three-legged centaur wearing two Cecil the Seasick Sea Serpent puppets on its arms, and you'll have something like the right picture. But the arms are weaving necks, and the puppets are real heads, flat and brainless, with wide flexible lips. The brain is under a bony hump set between the bases of the necks. This puppeteer wore only its own coat of brown hair, with a mane that extended all the way up its spine to form a thick mat over the brain. I'm told that the way they wear the mane indicates their status in society, but to me it could have been anything from a dock worker to a jeweler to the president of General Products.

I watched with the rest as it came across the floor, not because I'd never seen a puppeteer but because there is something beautiful about the dainty way they move on those slender legs and tiny hooves. I watched it come straight toward me, closer and closer. It stopped a foot away, looked me over, and said, "You are Beowulf Shaeffer, former chief pilot for Nakamura Lines."

Its voice was a beautiful contralto with not a trace of accent. A puppeteer's mouths are not only the most flexible speech organs around, but also the most sensitive hands. The tongues are forked and pointed; the wide, thick lips have little fingerlike knobs along the rims. Imagine a watchmaker with a sense of taste in his fingertips . . .

I cleared my throat. "That's right."

It considered me from two directions. "You would be interested in a high-paying job?"

"I'd be fascinated by a high-paying job."

"I am our equivalent of the regional president of General Products. Please come with me, and we will discuss this elsewhere."

I followed it into a displacement booth. Eyes followed me all the way. It was embarrassing, being accosted in a public drugstore by a two-headed monster. Maybe the puppeteer knew it. Maybe it was testing me to see how badly I needed money.

My need was great. Eight months had passed since Nakamura Lines folded. For some time before that I had been living very high on the hog, knowing that my back pay would cover my debts. I never saw that back pay. It was quite a crash, Nakamura Lines. Respectable middle-aged businessmen took to leaving their hotel windows without their lift belts. Me, I kept spending. If I'd started living frugally, my creditors would have done some checking . . . and I'd have ended in debtor's prison.

The puppeteer dialed thirteen fast digits with its tongue. A moment later we were elsewhere. Air puffed out when I opened the booth door, and I swallowed to pop my ears.

"We are on the roof of the General Products building." The rich contralto voice thrilled along my nerves, and I had to remind myself that it was an alien speaking, not a lovely woman. "You must examine this spacecraft while we discuss your assignment."

I stepped outside a little cautiously, but it wasn't the windy season. The roof was at ground level. That's the way we build on We Made It. Maybe it has something to do with the fifteen-hundred-mile-an-hour winds we get in summer and winter, when the planet's axis of rotation runs through its primary, Procyon. The winds are our planet's only tourist attraction, and it would be a shame to slow them down by planting skyscrapers in their path. The bare, square concrete roof was surrounded by endless square miles of desert, not like the deserts of other inhabited worlds, but an utterly lifeless expanse of fine sand just crying to be planted with ornamental cactus. We've tried that. The wind blows the plants away.

The ship lay on the sand beyond the roof. It was a No. 2 General Products hull: a cylinder three hundred feet long and twenty feet through, pointed at both ends and with a slight wasp-waist constriction near the tail. For some reason it was lying on its side, with the landing shocks still folded in at the tail.

Ever notice how all ships have begun to look the same? A good ninety-five percent of today's spacecraft are built around one of the four General Products hulls. It's easier and safer to build that way, but somehow all ships end as they began: mass-produced look-alikes.

The hulls are delivered fully transparent, and you use paint where you feel like it. Most of this particular hull had been left transparent. Only the nose had been painted, around the lifesystem. There was no major reaction drive. A series of retractable attitude jets had been mounted in the sides, and the hull was pierced with smaller holes, square and round, for observational instruments. I could see them gleaming through the hull.

The puppeteer was moving toward the nose, but something made me turn toward the stern for a closer look at the landing shocks. They were bent. Behind the curved transparent hull panels some tremendous pressure had forced the metal to flow like warm wax, back and into the pointed stern.

"What did this?" I asked.

"We do not know. We wish strenuously to find out."

"What do you mean?"

"Have you heard of the neutron star BVS-1?"

I had to think a moment. "First neutron star ever found, and so far the only. Someone located it two years ago, by stellar displacement."

"BVS-1 was found by the Institute of Knowledge on Jinx. We learned through a go-between that the Institute wished to explore the star. They needed a ship to do it. They had not yet sufficient money. We offered to supply them with a ship's hull, with the usual guarantees, if they would turn over to us all data they acquired through using our ship."

"Sounds fair enough." I didn't ask why they hadn't done their own exploring. Like most sentient vegetarians, puppeteers find discretion to be the *only* part of valor.

"Two humans named Peter Laskin and Sonya Laskin wished to use the ship. They intended to come within one mile of the surface in a hyperbolic orbit. At some point during their trip an unknown force apparently reached through the hull to do this to the landing shocks. The unknown force also seems to have killed the pilots."

"But that's impossible. Isn't it?"

"You see the point. Come with me." The puppeteer trotted toward the bow.

I saw the point, all right. Nothing, but nothing, can get through a General Products hull. No kind of electromagnetic energy except visible light. No kind of matter, from the smallest subatomic particle to the fastest meteor. That's what the company's advertisements claim, and the guarantee backs them up. I've never doubted it, and I've never heard of a General Products hull being damaged by a weapon or by anything else.

On the other hand, a General Products hull is as ugly as it is functional. The puppeteer-owned company could be badly hurt if it got around that something *could* get through a company hull. But I didn't see where I came in.

We rode an escalladder into the nose.

The lifesystem was in two compartments. Here the Laskins had used heat-reflective paint. In the conical control cabin the hull had been divided into windows. The relaxation room behind it was a windowless reflective silver. From the back wall of the relaxation room an access tube ran aft, opening on various instruments and the hyperdrive motors.

There were two acceleration couches in the control cabin. Both had been torn loose from their mountings and wadded into the nose like so much tissue paper, crushing the instrument panel. The backs of the crumpled couches were splashed with rust brown. Flecks of the same color were all over everything, the walls, the windows, the viewscreens. It was as if something had hit the couches from behind: something like a dozen paint-filled toy balloons striking with tremendous force.

"That's blood," I said.

"That is correct. Human circulatory fluid."

Twenty-four hours to fall.

I spent most of the first twelve hours in the relaxation room, trying to read. Nothing significant was happening, except that a few times I saw the phenomenon Sonya Laskin had mentioned in her last report. When a star went directly behind the invisible BVS-1, a halo formed. BVS-1 was heavy enough to bend light around it, displacing most stars to the sides; but when a star went directly behind the neutron star, its light was displaced to all sides at once. Result: a tiny circle which flashed once and was gone almost before the eye could catch it.

I'd known next to nothing about neutron stars the day the puppeteer picked me up. Now I was an expert. And I still had no idea what was waiting for me when I got down there.

All the matter you're ever likely to meet will be normal matter, composed of a nucleus of protons and neutrons surrounded by electrons in quantum energy states. In the heart of any star there is a second kind of matter: for there, the tremendous pressure is enough to smash the electron shells. The result is degenerate matter: nuclei forced together by pressure and gravity, but held apart by the mutual repulsion of the more or less continuous electron "gas" around them. The right circumstances may create a third type of matter.

Given: a burnt-out white dwarf with a mass greater than 1.44 times the mass of the sun—Chandrasekhar's Limit, named for an Indian-American astronomer of the nineteen hundreds. In such a mass the electron pressure alone would not be able to hold the electrons back from the nuclei. Electrons would be forced against protons—to make neutrons. In one blazing explosion most of the star would change from a compressed mass of degenerate matter to a closely packed lump of neutrons: neutronium, theoretically the densest matter possible in the universe. Most of the remaining normal and degenerate matter would be blown away by the liberated heat.

For two weeks the star would give off X rays as its core temperature dropped from five billion degrees Kelvin to five hundred million. After that it would be a light-emitting body perhaps ten to twelve miles across: the next best thing to invisible. It was not strange that BVS-1 was the first neutron star ever found.

Neither is it strange that the Institute of Knowledge on Jinx would have spent a good deal of time and trouble looking. Until BVS-1 was found, neutronium and neutron stars were only theories. The examination of an actual neutron star could be of tremendous importance. Neutron stars might give us the key to true gravity control.

Mass of BVS-1: 1.33 times the mass of Sol, approx.

Diameter of BVS-1 (estimated): eleven miles of neutronium, covered by half a mile of degenerate matter, covered by maybe twelve feet of ordinary matter.

Nothing else was known of the tiny hidden star until the Laskins went in to look. Now the Institute knew one thing more: the star's spin.

*     *     *

"A mass that large can distort space by its rotation," said the puppeteer. "The Laskins' projected hyperbola was twisted across itself in such a way that we can deduce the star's period of rotation to be two minutes twenty-seven seconds."

The bar was somewhere in the General Products building. I don't know just where, and with the transfer booths it doesn't matter. I kept staring at the puppeteer bartender. Naturally only a puppeteer would be served by a puppeteer bartender, since any biped life form would resent knowing that his drink had been made with somebody's mouth. I had already decided to get dinner somewhere else.

"I see your problem," I said. "Your sales will suffer if it gets out that something can reach through one of your hulls and smash a crew to bloody smears. But where do I come in?"

"We want to repeat the experiment of Sonya Laskin and Peter Laskin. We must find—"

"With me?"

"Yes. We must find out what it is that our hulls cannot stop. Naturally you may—"

"But I won't."

"We are prepared to offer one million stars."

I was tempted, but only for a moment. "Forget it."

"Naturally you will be allowed to build your own ship, starting with a No. 2 General Products hull."

"Thanks, but I'd like to go on living."

"You would dislike being confined. I find that We Made It has re-established the debtor's prison. If General Products made public your accounts—"

"Now, *just* a—"

"You owe money on the close order of five hundred thousand stars. We will pay your creditors before you leave. If you return"—I had to admire the creature's honesty in not saying "When"—"we will pay you the residue. You may be asked to speak to news commentators concerning the voyage, in which case there will be more stars."

"You say I can build my own ship?"

"Naturally. This is not a voyage of exploration. We want you to return safely."

"It's a deal," I said.

After all, the puppeteer had tried to blackmail me. What happened next would be its own fault.

*    *    *

They built my ship in two weeks flat. They started with a No. 2 General Products hull, just like the one around the Institute of Knowledge ship, and the lifesystem was practically a duplicate of the Laskins', but there the resemblance ended. There were no instruments to observe neutron stars. Instead, there was a fusion motor big enough for a Jinx warliner. In my ship, which I now called *Skydiver*, the drive would produce thirty gees at the safety limit. There was a laser cannon big enough to punch a hole through We Made It's moon. The puppeteer wanted me to feel safe, and now I did, for I could fight and I could run. Especially I could run.

I heard the Laskins' last broadcast through half a dozen times. Their unnamed ship had dropped out of hyperspace a million miles above BVS-1. Gravity warp would have prevented their getting closer in hyperspace. While her husband was crawling through the access tube for an instrument check, Sonya Laskin had called the Institute of Knowledge. ". . . We can't see it yet, not by naked eye. But we can see where it is. Every time some star or other goes behind it, there's a little ring of light. Just a minute, Peter's ready to use the telescope. . . ."

Then the star's mass had cut the hyperspacial link. It was expected, and nobody had worried—then. Later, the safe effect must have stopped them from escaping whatever attacked them into hyperspace.

When would-be rescuers found the ship, only the radar and the cameras were still running. They didn't tell us much. There had been no camera in the cabin. But the forward camera gave us, for one instant, a speed-blurred view of the neutron star. It was a featureless disk the orange color of perfect barbecue coals, if you know someone who can afford to burn wood. This object had been a neutron star a long time.

"There'll be no need to paint the ship," I told the president.

"You should not make such a trip with the walls transparent. You would go insane."

"I'm no flatlander. The mind-wrenching sight of naked space fills me with mild but waning interest. I want to know nothing's sneaking up behind me."

The day before I left, I sat alone in the General Products bar letting the puppeteer bartender make me drinks with his mouth. He did it well. Puppeteers were scattered around the bar in twos and threes, with a couple of men for variety, but the drinking hour had not yet arrived. The place felt empty.

I was pleased with myself. My debts were all paid, not that that would matter where I was going. I would leave with not a minicredit to my name, with nothing but the ship. . . .

All told, I was well out of a sticky situation. I hoped I'd like being a rich exile.

I jumped when the newcomer sat down across from me. He was a foreigner, a middle-aged man wearing an expensive night-black business suit and a snow-white asymmetric beard. I let my face freeze and started to get up.

"Sit down, Mr. Shaeffer."

"Why?"

He told me by showing me a blue disk. An Earth government ident. I looked it over to show I was alert, not because I'd know an ersatz from the real thing.

"My name is Sigmund Ausfaller," said the government man. "I wish to say a few words concerning your assignment of behalf of General Products."

I nodded, not saying anything.

"A record of your verbal contract was sent to us as a matter of course. I noticed some peculiar things about it. Mr. Shaeffer, will you really take such a risk for only five hundred thousand stars?"

"I'm getting twice that."

"But you only keep half of it. The rest goes to pay debts. Then there are taxes. . . . But never mind. What occurred to me was that a spaceship is a spaceship, and yours is very well armed and has powerful legs. An admirable fighting ship, if you were moved to sell it."

"But it isn't mine."

"There are those who would not ask. On Canyon, for example, or the Isolationist party of Wunderland."

I said nothing.

"Or you might be planning a career of piracy. A risky business, piracy, and I don't take the notion seriously."

I hadn't even thought about piracy. But I'd have to give up on Wunderland.

"What I would like to say is this, Mr. Shaeffer. A single entrepreneur, if he were sufficiently dishonest, could do terrible damage to the reputation of all human beings everywhere. Most species find it necessary to police the ethics of their own members, and we are no exception. It occurred to me that you might not take your ship to the neutron star at all; that you would take it elsewhere and sell it. The puppeteers do not make invulnerable war vessels. They are pacifists. Your *Skydiver* is unique.

"Hence I have asked General Products to allow me to install a remote-control bomb in the *Skydiver*. Since it is inside the hull, the hull cannot protect you. I had it installed this afternoon.

"Now, notice! If you have not reported within a week, I will set off the bomb. There are several worlds within a week's hyperspace flight of here, but all recognize the dominion of Earth. If you flee, you must leave your ship within a week, so I hardly think you will land on a nonhabitable world. Clear?"

"Clear."

"If I am wrong, you may take a lie-detector test and prove it. Then you may punch me in the nose, and I will apologize handsomely."

I shook my head. He stood up, bowed, and left me sitting there cold sober.

Four films had been taken from the Laskins' cameras. In the time left to me I ran through them several times, without seeing anything out of the way. If the ship had run through a gas cloud, the impact could have killed the Laskins. At perihelion they were moving at better than half the speed of light. But there would have been friction, and I saw no sign of heating in the films. If something alive had attacked them, the beast was invisible to radar and to an enormous range of light frequencies. If the attitude jets had fired accidentally—I was clutching at straws—the light showed on none of the films.

There would be savage magnetic forces near BVS-1, but that couldn't have done any damage. No such force could penetrate a General Products hull. Neither could heat, except in special bands of radiated light, bands visible to at least one of the puppeteers' alien customers. I hold adverse opinions on the General Products hull, but they all concern the dull anonymity of the design. Or maybe I resent the fact that General Products holds a near-monopoly on spacecraft hulls, and isn't owned by human beings. But if I'd had to trust my life to, say, the Sinclair yacht I'd seen in the drugstore, I'd have chosen jail.

Jail was one of my three choices. But I'd be there for life. Ausfaller would see to that.

Or I could run for it in the *Skydiver*. But no world within reach would have me. If I could find an undiscovered Earth-like world within a week of We Made It . . .

Fat chance. I preferred BVS-1.

I thought that flashing circle of light was getting bigger, but it flashed so seldom, I couldn't be sure. BVS-1 wouldn't show even in my telescope. I gave that up and settled for just waiting.

Waiting, I remembered a long-ago summer spent on Jinx. There were days when, unable to go outside because a dearth of clouds had spread the land with raw blue-white sunlight, we amused ourselves by filling party balloons with tap water and dropping them on the sidewalk from three stories up. They made lovely splash patterns, which dried out too fast. So we put a little ink in each balloon before filling it. Then the patterns stayed.

Sonya Laskin had been in her chair when the chairs collapsed. Blood samples showed that it was Peter who had struck them from behind, like a water balloon dropped from a great height.

What could get through a General Products hull?

Ten hours to fall.

I unfastened the safety net and went for an inspection tour. The access tunnel was three feet wide, just right to push through in free fall. Below me was the length of the fusion tube; to the left, the laser cannon; to the right, a set of curved side tubes leading to inspection points for the gyros, the batteries and generator, the air plant, the hyperspace shunt motors. All was in order—except me. I was clumsy. My jumps were always too short or too long. There was no room to turn at the stern end, so I had to back fifty feet to a side tube.

Six hours to go, and still I couldn't find the neutron star. Probably I would see it only for an instant, passing at better than half the speed of light. Already my speed must be enormous.

Were the stars turning blue?

Two hours to go—and I was sure they were turning blue. Was my speed that high? Then the stars behind should be red. Machinery blocked the view behind me, so I used the gyros. The ship turned with peculiar sluggishness. And the stars behind were blue, not red. All around me were blue-white stars.

Imagine light falling into a savagely steep gravitational well. It won't accelerate. Light can't move faster than light. But it can gain in energy, in frequency. The light was falling on me, harder and harder as I dropped.

I told the dictaphone about it. That dictaphone was probably the best-protected item on the ship. I had already decided to earn my money by using it, just as if I expected to collect. Privately I wondered just how intense the light would get.

*Skydiver* had drifted back to vertical, with its axis through the neutron star, but now it faced outward. I'd thought I had the ship stopped horizontally. More clumsiness. I used the gyros. Again the ship moved mushily, until it was halfway through the swing. Then it seemed to fall automatically into place. It was as if the *Skydiver* preferred to have its axis through the neutron star.

I didn't like that.

I tried the maneuver again, and again the *Skydiver* fought back. But this time there was something else. Something was pulling at me.

So I unfastened my safety net—and fell headfirst into the nose.

The pull was light, about a tenth of a gee. It felt more like sinking through honey than falling. I climbed back into my chair, tied myself in with the net, now hanging face down, and turned on the dictaphone. I told my story in such nitpicking detail that my hypothetical listeners could not but doubt my hypothetical sanity. "I think this is what happened to the Laskins," I finished. "If the pull increases, I'll call back."

Think? I never doubted it. This strange, gentle pull was inexplicable. Something inexplicable had killed Peter and Sonya Laskin. Q.E.D.

Around the point where the neutron star must be, the stars were like smeared dots of oilpaint, smeared radially. They glared with an angry, painful light. I hung face down in the net and tried to think.

It was an hour before I was sure. The pull was increasing. And I still had an hour to fall.

Something was pulling on me, but not on the ship.

No, that was nonsense. What could reach out to me through a General Products hull? It must be the other way around. Something was pushing on the ship, pushing it off course.

If it got worse, I could use the drive to compensate. Meanwhile, the ship was being pushed *away* from BVS-1, which was fine by me.

But if I was wrong, if the ship was not somehow being pushed away from BVS-1, the rocket motor would send the *Skydiver* crashing into eleven miles of neutronium.

And why wasn't the rocket already firing? If the ship was being pushed off course, the autopilot should be fighting back. The accelerometer was in good order. It had looked fine when I made my inspection tour down the access tube.

Could something be pushing on the ship *and* on the accelerometer, but not on me? It came down to the same impossibility: something that could reach through a General Products hull.

To hell with theory, said I to myself, said I. I'm getting out of here. To the dictaphone I said, "The pull has increased dangerously. I'm going to try to alter my orbit."

Of course, once I turned the ship outward and used the rocket, I'd be adding my own acceleration to the X-force. It would be a strain, but I could stand it for a while. If I came within a mile of BVS-1, I'd end like Sonya Laskin.

She must have waited face down in a net like mine, waited without a drive unit, waited while the pressure rose and the net cut into her flesh, waited until the net snapped and dropped her into the nose, to lie crushed and broken until the X-force tore the very chairs loose and dropped them on her.

I hit the gyros.

The gyros weren't strong enough to turn me. I tried it three times. Each time the ship rotated about fifty degrees and hung there, motionless, while the whine of the gyros went up and up. Released, the ship immediately swung back to position. I was nose down to the neutron star, and I was going to stay that way.

Half an hour to fall, and the X-force was over a gee. My sinuses were in agony. My eyes were ripe and ready to fall out. I don't know if I could have stood a cigarette, but I didn't get the chance. My pack of Fortunados had fallen out of my pocket when I dropped into the nose. There it was, four feet beyond my fingers, proof that the X-force acted on other objects besides me. Fascinating.

I couldn't take any more. If it dropped me shrieking into the neutron star, I had to use the drive. And I did. I ran the thrust up until I was approximately in free fall. The blood which had pooled in my extremities went back to where it belonged. The gee dial registered one point two gee. I cursed it for a lying robot.

The soft-pack was bobbing around in the nose, and it occurred to me that a little extra nudge on the throttle would bring it to me. I tried it. The pack drifted toward me, and I reached, and like a sentient thing it speeded up to avoid my clutching hand. I snatched at it again as it went past my ear, and again it was moving too fast. That pack was going at a hell of a clip, considering that here I was practically in free fall. It dropped through the door to the relaxation room, still picking up speed, blurred and vanished as it entered the access tube. Seconds later I heard a solid *thump*.

But that was *crazy*. Already the X-force was pulling blood into my face. I pulled my lighter out, held it at arm's length and let go. It fell gently into the nose. But the pack of Fortunados had hit like I'd dropped it from a *building*.

Well.

I nudged the throttle again. The mutter of fusing hydrogen reminded me that if I tried to keep this up all the way, I might well put the General Products hull to its toughest test yet: smashing it into a neutron star at half lightspeed. I could see it now: a transparent hull containing only a few cubic inches of dwarf-star matter wedged into the tip of the nose.

At one point four gee, according to that lying gee dial, the lighter came loose and drifted toward me. I let it go. It was clearly falling when it reached the doorway. I pulled the throttle back. The loss of power jerked me violently forward, but I kept my face turned. The lighter slowed and hesitated at the entrance to the access tube. Decided to go through. I cocked my ears for the sound, then jumped as the whole ship rang like a gong.

And the accelerometer was right at the ship's center of mass. Otherwise the ship's mass would have thrown the needle off. The puppeteers were fiends for ten-decimal-point accuracy.

I favored the dictaphone with a few fast comments, then got to work reprogramming the autopilot. Luckily what I wanted was simple. The X-force was but an X-force to me, but now I knew how it behaved. I might actually live through this.

The stars were fiercely blue, warped to streaked lines near that special point. I thought I could see it now, very small and dim and red, but it might have been imagination. In twenty minutes I'd be rounding the neutron star. The drive grumbled behind me. In effective free fall, I unfastened the safety net and pushed myself out of the chair.

A gentle push aft—and ghostly hands grasped my legs. Ten pounds of weight hung by my fingers from the back of the chair. The pressure should drop fast. I'd programmed the autopilot to reduce the thrust from two gees to zero during the next two minutes. All I had to do was be at the center of mass, in the access tube, when the thrust went to zero.

Something gripped the ship through a General Products hull. A psychokinetic life form stranded on a sun twelve miles in diameter? But how could anything alive stand such gravity?

Something might be stranded in orbit. There is life in space: outsiders and sailseeds, and maybe others we haven't found yet. For all I knew or cared, BVS-1 itself might be alive. It didn't matter. I knew what the X-force was trying to do. It was trying to pull the ship apart.

There was no pull on my fingers. I pushed aft and landed on the back wall, on bent legs. I knelt over the door, looking aft/down. When free fall came, I pulled myself through and was in the relaxation room looking down/forward into the nose.

Gravity was changing faster than I liked. The X-force was growing as zero hour approached, while the compensating rocket thrust dropped. The X-force tended to pull the ship apart; it was two gee forward at the nose, two gee backward at the tail, and diminished to zero at the center of mass. Or so I hoped. The pack and lighter had behaved as if the force pulling them had increased for every inch they moved sternward.

The back wall was fifteen feet away. I had to jump it with gravity changing in midair. I hit on my hands, bounced away. I'd jumped too late. The region of free fall was moving through the ship like a wave as the thrust dropped. It had left me behind. Now the back wall was "up" to me, and so was the access tube.

Under something less than half a gee, I jumped for the access tube. For one long moment I stared into the three-foot tunnel, stopped in midair and already beginning to fall back, as I realized that there was nothing to hang on to. Then I stuck my hands in the tube and spread them against the sides. It was all I needed. I levered myself up and started to crawl.

The dictaphone was fifty feet below, utterly unreachable. If I had anything more to say to General Products, I'd have to say it in person. Maybe I'd get the chance. Because I knew what force was trying to tear the ship apart.

It was the tide.

The motor was off, and I was at the ship's midpoint. My spread-eagled position was getting uncomfortable. It was four minutes to perihelion.

Something creaked in the cabin below me. I couldn't see what it was, but I could clearly see a red point glaring among blue radial lines, like a lantern at the bottom of a well. To the sides, between the fusion tube and the tanks and other equipment, the blue stars glared at me with a light that was almost violet. I was afraid to look too long. I actually thought they might blind me.

There must have been hundreds of gravities in the cabin. I could even feel the pressure change. The air was thin at this height, one hundred and fifty feet above the control room.

And now, almost suddenly, the red dot was more than a dot. My time was up. A red disk leapt up at me; the ship swung around me; I gasped and shut my eyes tight. Giants' hands gripped my arms and legs and head, gently but with great firmness, and tried to pull me in two. In that moment it came to me that Peter Laskin had died like this. He'd made the same guesses I had, and he'd tried to hide in the access tube. But he'd slipped . . . as I was slipping. . . . From the control room came a multiple shriek of tearing metal. I tried to dig my feet into the hard tube walls. Somehow they held.

When I got my eyes open the red dot was shrinking into nothing.

The puppeteer president insisted I be put in a hospital for observation. I didn't fight the idea. My face and hands were flaming red, with blisters rising, and I ached as though I'd been beaten. Rest and tender loving care, that's what I wanted.

I was floating between a pair of sleeping plates, hideously uncomfortable, when the nurse came to announce a visitor. I knew who it was from her peculiar expression.

"What can get through a General Products hull?" I asked it.

"I hoped you would tell me." The president rested on its single back leg, holding a stick that gave off green incense-smelling smoke.

"And so I will. Gravity."

"Do not play with me, Beowulf Shaeffer. This matter is vital."

"I'm not playing. Does your world have a moon?"

"That information is classified." The puppeteers are cowards. Nobody knows where they come from, and nobody is likely to find out.

"Do you know what happens when a moon gets too close to its primary?"

"It falls apart."

"Why?"

"I do not know."

"Tides."

"What is a tide?"

Oho, said I to myself, said I. "I'm going to try to tell you. The Earth's moon is almost two thousand miles in diameter and does not rotate with respect to Earth. I want you to pick two rocks on the moon, one at the point nearest the Earth, one at the point farthest away."

"Very well."

"Now, isn't it obvious that if those rocks were left to themselves, they'd fall away from each other? They're in two different orbits, mind you, concentric orbits, one almost two thousand miles outside the other. Yet those rocks are forced to move at the same orbital speed."

"The one outside is moving faster."

"Good point. So there *is* a force trying to pull the moon apart. Gravity holds it together. Bring the moon close enough to Earth, and those two rocks would simply float away."

"I see. Then this 'tide' tried to pull your ship apart. It was powerful enough in the lifesystem of the Institute ship to pull the acceleration chairs out of their mounts."

"And to crush a human being. Picture it. The ship's nose was just seven miles from the center of BVS-1. The tail was three hundred feet farther out. Left to themselves, they'd have gone in completely different orbits. My head and feet tried to do the same thing when I got close enough."

"I see. Are you molting?"

"What?"

"I notice you are losing your outer integument in spots."

"Oh, *that*. I got a bad sunburn from exposure to starlight. It's not important."

Two heads stared at each other for an eyeblink. A shrug? The puppeteer said, "We have deposited the residue of your pay with the Bank of We Made It. One Sigmund Ausfaller, human, has frozen the account until your taxes are computed."

"Figures."

"If you will talk to reporters now, explaining what happened to the Institute ship, we will pay you ten thousand stars. We will pay cash so that you may use it immediately. It is urgent. There have been rumors."

"Bring 'em in." As an afterthought I added, "I can also tell them that your world is moonless. That should be good for a footnote somewhere."

"I do not understand." But two long necks had drawn back, and the puppeteer was watching me like a pair of pythons.

"You'd know what a tide was if you had a moon. You couldn't avoid it."

"Would you be interested in—"

"A million stars? I'd be fascinated. I'll even sign a contract if it states what we're hiding. How do *you* like being blackmailed for a change?"

# THIS MORTAL MOUNTAIN
## (MARCH 1967)
## ROGER ZELAZNY
## (B. 1937)

Roger Zelazny burst upon the science-fiction scene in the early 1960s with a string of memorable stories and novels that won two Hugos (. . . *And Call Me Conrad,* 1966, and *Lord of Light,* 1968) and two Nebulas ("He Who Shapes" and "The Doors of His Face, the Lamps of His Mouth," both 1965).

"This Mortal Mountain" is one of his most neglected stories and his only appearance in *If.*

## MEMOIR BY ROGER ZELAZNY

This story appeared in the March 1967 issue of *Worlds of If.* The previous September, I had received my first Science Fiction Achievement Award (Hugo)—for my novel . . . *And Call Me Conrad*—at Tricon, the world science-fiction convention which was held in Cleveland, Ohio. Fred Pohl had asked all of the award recipients that year to submit material for a special Hugo Winners issue of *If.*

I forget now whether I had already begun work on this story and earmarked it for that purpose when he asked me, or whether I had only a rough idea and wrote it immediately thereafter. I feel it was the former, though.

I recall that I hurried it somewhat, because of the deadline. If there had been no deadline, it would probably have been a longer and, possibly, different story. How, I couldn't say now, because I never go back and reread if I can help it. But I do not believe that I was unhappy with it as it turned out. I liked *Worlds of If,* and I was glad to be in that particular issue.

# THIS MORTAL MOUNTAIN

## I

I looked down at it and I was sick! I wondered, where did it lead? Stars?

There were no words. I stared and I stared, and I cursed the fact that the thing existed and that someone had found it while I was still around.

"Well?" said Lanning, and he banked the flier so that I could look upward.

I shook my head and shaded my already shielded eyes.

"Make it go away," I finally told him.

"Can't. It's bigger than I am."

"It's bigger than anybody," I said.

"I can make *us* go away. . . ."

"Never mind. I want to take some pictures."

He brought it around, and I started to shoot.

"Can you hover—or get any closer?"

"No, the winds are too strong."

"That figures."

So I shot—through telescopic lenses and scan attachment and all—as we circled it.

"I'd give a lot to see the top."

"We're at thirty thousand feet, and fifty's the ceiling on this baby. The Lady, unfortunately, stands taller than the atmosphere."

"Funny," I said, "from here she doesn't strike me as the sort to breathe ether and spend all her time looking at stars."

He chuckled and lit a cigarette, and I reached us another bulb of coffee.

"How *does* the Gray Sister strike you?"

And I lit one of my own and inhaled, as the flier was buffeted by sudden gusts of something from somewhere and then ignored, and I said, "Like Our Lady of the Abattoir—right between the eyes."

We drank some coffee, and then he asked, "She too big, Whitey?" and I gnashed my teeth through caffeine, for only my friends call me Whitey, my name being Jack Summers and my hair having always been this way, and at the moment I wasn't too

certain whether Henry Lanning qualified for that status—just
because he'd known me for twenty years—after going out of his
way to find this thing on a world with a thin atmosphere, a lot of
rocks, a too-bright sky and a name like LSD pronounced backwards, after George Diesel, who had set foot in the dust and then
gone away—smart fellow!

"A forty-mile-high mountain," I finally said, "is not a mountain.
It is a world all by itself, which some dumb deity forgot to throw
into orbit."

"I take it you're not interested?"

I looked back at the gray and lavender slopes and followed
them upward once again, until all color drained away, until the
silhouette was black and jagged and the top still nowhere in sight,
until my eyes stung and burned behind their protective glasses;
and I saw clouds bumping up against that invincible outline, like
icebergs in the sky, and I heard the howling of the retreating
winds which had essayed to measure its grandeur with swiftness
and, of course, had failed.

"Oh, I'm interested," I said, "in an academic sort of way. Let's
go back to town, where I can eat and drink and maybe break a leg
if I'm lucky."

He headed the flier south, and I didn't look around as we went.
I could sense her presence at my back, though, all the way: The
Gray Sister, the highest mountain in the known universe. Un-
climbed, of course.

She remained at my back during the days that followed, casting
her shadow over everything I looked upon. For the next two days
I studied the pictures I had taken and I dug up some maps and I
studied them, too; and I spoke with people who told me stories of
the Gray Sister, strange stories. . . .

During this time, I came across nothing really encouraging. I
learned that there had been an attempt to colonize Diesel a
couple centuries previously, back before faster-than-light ships
were developed. A brand-new disease had colonized the first
colonists, however, wiping them out to a man. The new colony
was four years old, had better doctors, had beaten the plague,
was on Diesel to stay and seemed proud of its poor taste when it
came to worlds. Nobody, I learned, fooled around much with the
Gray Sister. There had been a few abortive attempts to climb her,
and some young legends that followed after.

During the day, the sky never shut up. It kept screaming into my eyes, until I took to wearing my climbing goggles whenever I went out. Mainly, though, I sat in the hotel lounge and ate and drank and studied the pictures and cross-examined anybody who happened to pass by and glance at them, spread out there on the table.

I continued to ignore all Henry's questions. I knew what he wanted, and he could damn well wait. Unfortunately, he did, and rather well, too, which iritated me. He felt I was almost hooked by the Sister, and he wanted to Be There When It Happened. He'd made a fortune on the Kasla story, and I could already see the opening sentences of this one in the smug lines around his eyes. Whenever he tried to make like a poker player, leaning on his fist and slowly turning a photo, I could see whole paragraphs. If I followed the direction of his gaze, I probably could even have seen the dust jacket.

At the end of the week, a ship came down out of the sky, and some nasty people got off and interrupted my train of thought. When they came into the lounge, I recognized them for what they were and removed my black lenses so that I could nail Henry with my basilisk gaze and turn him to stone. As it would happen, he had too much alcohol in him, and it didn't work.

"You tipped off the press," I said.

"Now, now," he said, growing smaller and stiffening as my gaze groped its way through the murk of his central nervous system and finally touched upon the edges of that tiny tumor, his forebrain. "You're well known, and . . ."

I replaced my glasses and hunched over my drink, looking far gone, as one of the three approached and said, "Pardon me, but are you Jack Summers?"

To explain the silence which followed, Henry said, "Yes, this is Mad Jack, the man who climbed Everest at twenty-three and every other pile of rocks worth mentioning since that time. At thirty-one, he became the only man to conquer the highest mountain in the known universe—Mount Kasla on Litan—elevation 89,941 feet. My book—"

"Yes," said the reporter. "My name is Cary, and I'm with GP. My friends represent two of the other syndicates. We've heard that you are going to climb the Gray Sister."

"You've heard incorrectly," I said.

"Oh?"

The other two came up and stood beside him.

"We thought that—" one of them began.

"—you were already organizing a climbing party," said the other.

"Then you're not going to climb the Sister?" asked Cary, while one of the two looked over my pictures and the other got ready to take some of his own.

"Stop that!" I said, raising a hand at the photographer. "Bright lights hurt my eyes!"

"Sorry. I'll use the infra," he said, and he started fooling with his camera.

Cary repeated the question.

"All I said what that you've heard incorrectly," I told him. "I didn't say I was and I didn't say I wasn't. I haven't made up my mind."

"If you should decide to try it, have you any idea when it will be?"

"Sorry, I can't answer that."

Henry took the three of them over to the bar and started explaining something, with gestures. I heard the words ". . . out of retirement after four years," and when/if they looked to the booth again, I was gone.

I had retired, to the street which was full of dusk, and I walked along it thinking. I trod her shadow even then, Linda. And the Gray Sister beckoned and forbade with her single unmoving gesture. I watched her, so far away, yet still so large, a piece of midnight at eight o'clock. The hours that lay between died like the distance at her feet, and I knew that she would follow me wherever I went, even into sleep. Especially into sleep.

So I knew, at that moment. The days that followed were a game I enjoyed playing. Fake indecision is delicious when people want you to do something. I looked at her then, my last and my largest, my very own Koshtra Pivrarcha, and I felt that I was born to stand upon her summit. Then I could retire, probably remarry, cultivate my mind, not worry about getting out of shape, and do all the square things I didn't do before, the lack of which had cost me a wife and a home, back when I had gone to Kasla, elevation 89,941 feet, four and a half years ago, in the days of my glory. I regarded my Gray Sister across the eight o'clock world, and she was dark and noble and still and waiting, as she had always been.

## II

The following morning I sent the messages. Out across the light-years like cosmic carrier pigeons they went. They winged their ways to some persons I hadn't seen in years and to others who had seen me off at Luna Station. Each said, in its own way, "If you want in on the biggest climb of them all, come to Diesel. The Gray Sister eats Kaslas for breakfast. R.S.V.P. c/o The Lodge, Georgetown. Whitey."

Backwards, turn backwards. . . .

I didn't tell Henry. Nothing at all. What I had done and where I was going, for a time, were my business only, for that same time. I checked out well before sunrise and left him a message at the desk:

"Out of town on business. Back in a week. Hold the fort. Mad Jack."

I had to gauge the lower slopes, tug the hem of the lady's skirt, so to speak, before I introduced her to my friends. They say only a madman climbs alone, but they call me what they call me for a reason.

From my pix, the northern face had looked promising.

I set the rented flier down as near as I could, locked it up, shouldered my pack and started walking.

Mountains rising to my right and to my left, mountains at my back, all dark as sin now in the predawn light of a white, white day. Ahead of me, not a mountain, but an almost gentle slope which kept rising and rising and rising. Bright stars above me and cold wind past me as I walked. Straight up, though, no stars, just black. I wondered for the thousandth time what a mountain weighed. I always wonder that as I approach one. No clouds in sight. No noises but my boot sounds on the turf and the small gravel. My goggles flopped around my neck. My hands were moist within my gloves. On Diesel, the pack and I together probably weighed about the same as me alone on Earth—for which I was duly grateful. My breath burned as it came and steamed as it went. I counted a thousand steps and looked back, and I couldn't see the flier. I counted a thousand more and then looked up to watch some stars go out. About an hour after that, I had to put on my goggles. By then I could see where I was headed. And by then the wind seemed stronger.

She was so big that the eye couldn't take all of her in at once. I moved my head from side to side, leaning further and further backward. Wherever the top, it was too high. For an instant, I was seized by a crazy acrophobic notion that I was looking down rather than up, and the soles of my feet and the palms of my hands tingled, like an ape's must when, releasing one high branch to seize another, he discovers that there isn't another.

I went on for two more hours and stopped for a light meal. This was hiking, not climbing. As I ate, I wondered what could have caused a formation like the Gray Sister. There were some ten- and twelve-mile peaks within sixty miles of the place and a fifteen-mile mountain called Burke's Peak on the adjacent continent, but nothing else like the Sister. The lesser gravitation? Her composition? I couldn't say. I wondered what Doc and Kelly and Mallardi would say when they saw her.

I don't define them, though. I only climb them.

I looked up again, and a few clouds were brushing against her now. From the photos I had taken, she might be an easy ascent for a good ten or twelve miles. Like a big hill. There were certainly enough alternate routes. In fact, I thought she just might be a pushover. Feeling heartened, I repacked my utensils and proceeded. It was going to be a good day. I could tell.

And it was. I got off the slope and onto something like a trail by late afternoon. Daylight lasts about nine hours on Diesel, and I spent most of it moving. The trail was so good that I kept on for several hours after sundown and made considerable height. I was beginning to use my respiration equipment by then, and the heating unit in my suit was turned on.

The stars were big, brilliant flowers, the way was easy, the night was my friend. I came upon a broad, flat piece and made my camp under an overhang.

There I slept, and I dreamt of snowy women with breasts like the Alps, pinked by the morning sun; and they sang to me like the wind and laughed, had eyes of ice prismatic. They fled through a field of clouds.

The following day I made a lot more height. The "trail" began to narrow, and it ran out in places, but it was easy to reach for the sky until another one occurred. So far, it had all been good rock. It was still tapering as it heightened, and balance was no problem. I did a lot of plain old walking. I ran up one long zigzag and hit up a wide chimney almost as fast as Santa Claus comes down one. The winds were strong, could be a problem if the going got difficult. I was on the respirator full time and feeling great.

I could see for an enormous distance now. There were mountains and mountains, all below me like desert dunes. The sun beat halos of heat about their peaks. In the east, I saw Lake Emerick, dark and shiny as the toe of a boot. I wound my way about a jutting crag and came upon a giant's staircase, going up for at least a thousand feet. I mounted it. At its top I hit my first real barrier: a fairly smooth, almost perpendicular face rising for about eighty-five feet.

No way around it, so I went up. It took me a good hour, and there was a ridge at the top leading to more easy climbing. By then, though, the clouds attacked me. Even though the going was easy, I was slowed by the fog. I wanted to outclimb it and still have some daylight left, so I decided to postpone eating.

But the clouds kept coming. I made another thousand feet, and they were still about me. Somewhere below me, I heard thunder. The fog was easy on my eyes, though, so I kept pushing.

Then I tried a chimney, the top of which I could barely discern, because it looked a lot shorter than a jagged crescent to its left. This was a mistake.

The rate of condensation was greater than I'd guessed. The walls were slippery. I'm stubborn, though, and I fought with skidding boots and moist back until I was about a third of the way up, I thought, and winded.

I realized then what I had done. What I had thought was the top wasn't. I went another fifteen feet and wished I hadn't. The fog began to boil about me, and I suddenly felt drenched. I was afraid to go down and I was afraid to go up, and I couldn't stay where I was forever.

Whenever you hear a person say that he inched along, do not accuse him of a fuzzy choice of verbs. Give him the benefit of the doubt and your sympathy.

I inched my way, blind, up an unknown length of slippery chimney. If my hair hadn't already been white when I entered at the bottom . . .

Finally, I got above the fog. Finally, I saw a piece of that bright and nasty sky, which I decided to forgive for the moment. I aimed at it, arrived on target.

When I emerged, I saw a little ledge about ten feet above me. I climbed to it and stretched out. My muscles were a bit shaky, and I made them go liquid. I took a drink of water, ate a couple of chocolate bars, took another drink.

After perhaps ten minutes, I stood up. I could no longer see the ground. Just the soft, white cottony top of a kindly old storm. I looked up.

It was amazing. She was still topless. And save for a couple of spots, such as the last—which had been the fault of my own stupid overconfidence—it had almost been as easy as climbing stairs.

Now the going appeared to be somewhat rougher, however. This was what I had really come to test.

I swung my pick and continued.

All the following day I limped, steadily, taking no unnecessary risks, resting periodically, drawing maps, taking wide-angle photos. The ascent eased in two spots that afternoon, and I made a quick seven thousand feet. Higher now than Everest, and still going, I. Now, though, there were places where I crawled and places where I used ropes, and there were places where I braced myself and used my pneumatic pistol to blast a toehold. (No, in case you're wondering: I could have broken my eardrums, some ribs, an arm and doubtless, ultimately, my neck, if I'd tried using the gun in the chimney.)

Just near sunset I came upon a high, easy winding way up and up and up. I debated with my more discreet self. I'd left the message that I'd be gone a week. This was the end of the third day. I wanted to make as much height as possible and start back down on the fifth day. If I followed the rocky route above me as far as it would take me I'd probably break forty thousand feet. Then, depending, I might have a halfway chance of hitting near the ten-mile mark before I had to turn back. Then I'd be able to get a much better picture of what lay above.

My more discreet self lost, three to nothing, and Mad Jack went on.

The stars were so big and blazing I was afraid they'd bite. The wind was no problem. There wasn't any at that height. I had to keep stepping up the temperature controls of my suit, and I had the feeling that if I could spit around my respirator, it would freeze before it hit the trail.

I went on even further than I'd intended, and I broke forty-two thousand that night.

I found a resting place, stretched out, killed my hand beacon.

It was an old dream that came to me.

It was all cherry fires and stood like a man, only bigger, on the slope above me. It stood in an impossible position, so I knew I had to be dreaming. Something from the other end of my life stirred, however, and I was convinced for a bitter moment that it was the Angel of Judgment. Only, in its right hand it seemed to hold a sword of fire rather than a trumpet. It had been standing there forever, the tip of its blade pointed toward my breast. I could see the stars through it. It seemed to speak.

It said: *"Go back."*

I couldn't answer, though, for my tongue clove to the roof of my mouth. And it said it again, and yet a third time, *"Go back."*

"Tomorrow," I thought, in my dream, and this seemed to satisfy it. For it died down and ceased, and the blackness rolled about me.

The following day, I climbed as I hadn't climbed in years. By late lunchtime I'd hit forty-eight thousand feet. The cloud cover down below had broken. I could see what lay beneath me once more. The ground was a dark and light patchwork. Above, the stars didn't go away.

The going was rough, but I was feeling fine. I knew I couldn't make ten miles, because I could see that the way was pretty much the same for quite a distance, before it got even worse. My good spirits stayed, and they continued to rise as I did.

When it attacked, it came on with a speed and fury that I was only barely able to match.

The voice from my dream rang in my head: *"Go back! Go back! Go back!"*

Then it came toward me from out of the sky. A bird the size of a condor.

Only it wasn't really a bird.

It was a bird-shaped thing.

It was all fire and static, and as it flashed toward me I barely had time to brace my back against stone and heft my climbing pick in my right hand, ready.

## III

I sat in the small, dark room and watched the spinning, colored lights. Ultrasonics were tickling my skull. I tried to relax and give the man some Alpha rhythms. Somewhere a receiver was receiving, a computer was computing, and a recorder was recording.

It lasted perhaps twenty minutes.

When it was all over and they called me out, the doctor collared me. I beat him to the draw, though:

"Give me the tape and send me the bill in care of Henry Lanning at the Lodge."

"I want to discuss the reading," he said.

"I have my own brain-wave expert coming. Just give me the tape."

"Have you undergone any sort of traumatic experience recently?"

"You tell me. Is it indicated?"

"Well, yes and no," he said.

"That's what I like, a straight answer."

"I don't know what is normal for you, in the first place," he replied.

"Is there any indication of brain damage?"

"I don't read it that way. If you'd tell me what happened, and why you're suddenly concerned about your brain-waves, perhaps I'd be in a better position to . . ."

"Cut," I said. "Just give me the tape and bill me."

"I'm concerned about you as a patient."

"But you don't think there were any pathological indications?"

"Not exactly. But tell me this, if you will: Have you had an epileptic seizure recently?"

"Not to my knowledge. Why?"

"You displayed a pattern similar to a residual subrhythm common in some forms of epilepsy for several days subsequent to a seizure."

"Could a bump on the head cause that pattern?"

"It's highly unlikely."

"What else *could* cause it?"

"Electrical shock, optical trauma—"

"Stop," I said, and I removed my glasses. "About the optical trauma. Look at my eyes."

"I'm not an ophtha—" he began, but I interrupted:

"Most normal light hurts my eyes. If I lost my glasses and was exposed to very bright light for three, four days, could that cause the pattern you spoke of?"

"Possibly . . ." he said. "Yes, I'd say so."

"But there's more?"

"I'm not sure. We have to take more readings, and if I know the story behind this it will help a lot."

"Sorry," I said. "I need the tape now."

He sighed and made a small gesture with his left hand as he turned away.

"All right, Mister Smith."

Cursing the genius of the mountain, I left the General Hospital, carrying my tape like a talisman. In my mind I searched, through forests of memory, for a ghost-sword in a stone of smoke, I think.

Back at the Lodge, they were waiting. Lanning and the newsmen.

"What was it like?" asked one of the latter.

"What was what like?"

"The mountain. You were up on it, weren't you?"

"No comment."

"How would you say it compares with Kasla?"

"No comment."

"How high did you go?"

"No comment."

"Did you run into any complications?"

"Ditto. Excuse me, I want to take a shower."

Henry followed me into my room. The reporters tried to.

After I had shaved and washed up, mixed a drink and lit a cigarette, Lanning asked me his more general question:

"Well?" he said.

I nodded.

"Difficulties?"

I nodded again.

"Insurmountable?"

I hefted the tape and thought a moment.

"Maybe not."

He helped himself to the whiskey. The second time around, he asked:

"You going to try?"

I knew I was. I knew I'd try it all by myself if I had to.

"I really don't know," I said.

"Why not?"

"Because there's something up there," I said, "something that doesn't want us to do it."

"Something *lives* up there?"

"I'm not sure whether that's the right word."

He lowered the drink.

"What the hell happened?"

"I was threatened. I was attacked."

"Threatened? Verbally? In English?" He set his drink aside, which shows how serious his turn of mind had to be. "Attacked?" he added. "By what?"

"I've sent for Doc and Kelly and Stan and Mallardi and Vincent. I checked a little earlier. They've all replied. They're coming. Miguel and the Dutchman can't make it, and they send their regrets. When we're all together, I'll tell the story. But I want to talk to Doc first. So hold tight and worry and don't quote."

He finished his drink.

"When'll they be coming?"

"Four, five weeks," I said.

"That's a long wait."

"Under the circumstances," I said, "I can't think of any alternatives."

"What'll we do in the meantime?"

"Eat, drink and contemplate the mountain."

He lowered his eyelids a moment, then nodded, reached for his glass.

"Shall we begin?"

It was late, and I stood alone in the field with a bottle in one hand. Lanning had already turned in, and night's chimney was dark with cloud soot. Somewhere away from there, a storm was storming, and it was full of instant outlines. The wind came chill.

"Mountain," I said. "Mountain, you have told me to go away."

There was a rumble.

"But I cannot," I said, and I took a drink.

"I'm brining you the best in the business," I said, "to go up on your slopes and to stand beneath the stars in your highest places. I must do this thing because you are there. No other reason. Nothing personal. . . ."

After a time, I said, "That's not true.

"I'm a man," I said, "and I need to break mountains to prove that I will not die even though I will die. I am less than I want to be, Sister, and you can make me more. So I guess it *is* personal.

"It's the only thing I know how to do, and you're the last one left—the last challenge to the skill I spent my life learning. Maybe it is that mortality is closest to immortality when it accepts a challenge to itself, when it survives a threat. The moment of triumph is the moment of salvation. I have needed many such moments, and the final one must be the longest, for it must last me the rest of my life.

"So you are there, Sister, and I am here and very mortal, and you have told me to go away. I cannot. I'm coming up, and if you throw death at me I will face it. It must be so."

I finished what remained in the bottle.

There were more flashes, more rumbles behind the mountain, more flashes.

"It is the closest thing to divine drunkenness," I said to the thunder.

And then she winked at me. It was a red star, so high upon her. Angel's sword. Phoenix' wing. Soul on fire. And it blazed at me, across the miles. Then the wind that blows between the worlds swept down over me. It was filled with tears and with crystals of ice. I stood there and felt it, then, "Don't go away," I said and I watched until all was darkness once more and I was wet as an embryo waiting to cry out and breathe.

Most kids tell lies to their playmates—fictional autobiographies, if you like—which are either received with appropriate awe or countered with greater, more elaborate tellings. But little Jimmy, I've heard, always hearkened to his little buddies with wide, dark eyes, and near the endings of their stories the corners of his mouth would begin to twitch. By the time they were finished talking, his freckles would be mashed into a grin and his rusty head cocked to the side. His favorite expression, I understand, was "G'wan!" and his nose was broken twice before he was twelve. This was doubtless why he turned it toward books.

Thirty years and four formal degrees later, he sat across from me in my quarters in the Lodge, and I called him Doc because everyone did, because he had a license to cut people up and look inside them, as well as doctoring to their philosophy, so to speak, and because he looked as if he could be called Doc when he grinned and cocked his head to the side and said, "G'wan!"

I wanted to punch him in the nose.

"Damn it! It's true!" I told him. "I fought with a bird of fire!"

"We all hallucinated on Kasla," he said, raising one finger, "because of fatigue," two fingers, "because the altitude affected our circulatory system and consequently our brains," three, "because of the emotional stimulation," four, "and because we were partly oxygen-drunk."

"You just ran out of fingers, if you'll sit on your other hand for a minute. So listen," I said, "it flew at me, and I swung at it, and it knocked me out and broke my goggles. When I woke up, it was gone and I was lying on the ledge. I think it was some sort of energy creature. You saw my EEG, and it wasn't normal. I think it shocked my nervous system when it touched me."

"You were knocked out because you hit your head against a rock—"

"It *caused* me to fall back against the rock!"

"I agree with that part. The rock was real. But nowhere in the universe has anyone ever discovered an 'energy creature.'"

"So? You probably would have said that about America a thousand years ago."

"Maybe I would have. But that neurologist explained your EEG to my satisfaction. Optical trauma. Why go out of your way to dream up an exotic explanation for events? Easy ones generally turn out better. You hallucinated and you stumbled."

"Okay," I said, "whenever I argue with you I generally need ammunition. Hold on a minute."

I went to my closet and fetched it down from the top shelf. I placed it on my bed and began unwrapping the blanket I had around it.

"I told you I took a swing at it," I said. "Well, I connected— right before I went under. Here!"

I held up my climbing pick—brown, yellow, black and pitted— looking as though it had fallen from outer space.

He took it into his hands and stared at it for a long time, then he started to say something about ball lightning, changed his mind, shook his head and placed the thing back on the blanket.

"I don't know," he finally said, and this time his freckles remained unmashed, except for those at the edges of his hands which got caught as he clenched them, slowly.

# IV

We planned. We mapped and charted and studied the photos. We plotted our ascent and we started a training program.

While Doc and Stan had kept themselves in good shape, neither had been climbing since Kasla. Kelly was in top condition. Henry was on his way to fat. Mallardi and Vince, as always, seemed capable of fantastic feats of endurance and virtuosity, had even climbed a couple of times during the past year, but had recently been living pretty high on the tall hog, so to speak, and they wanted to get some practice. So we picked a comfortable, decent-sized mountain and gave it ten days to beat everyone back into shape. After that, we stuck to vitamins, calisthenics and square diets while we completed our preparations. During this time, Doc came up with seven shiny alloy boxes, about six by four inches and thin as a first book of poems, for us to carry on our persons to broadcast a defense against the energy creature which he refused to admit existed.

One fine, bitter-brisk morning we were ready. The newsmen liked me again. Much footage was taken of our gallant assemblage as we packed ourselves into the fliers, to be delivered at the foot of the lady mountain, there to contend for what was doubtless the final time as the team we had been for so many years, against the waiting gray and the lavender beneath the sunwhite flame.

We approached the mountain, and I wondered how much she weighed.

You know the way, for the first nine miles. So I'll skip over that. It took us six days and part of a seventh. Nothing out of the ordinary occurred. Some fog there was, and nasty winds, but once below, forgotten.

Stan and Mallardi and I stood where the bird had occurred, waiting for Doc and the others.

"So far, it's been a picnic," said Mallardi.

"Yeah," Stan acknowledged.

"No birds either."

"No," I agreed.

"Do you think Doc was right—about it being an hallucination?" Mallardi asked. "I remember seeing things on Kasla. . . ."

"As I recall," said Stan, "it was nymphs and an ocean of beer. Why would anyone want to see hot birds?"

"Damfino."

"Laugh, you hyenas," I said. "But just wait till a flock flies over."

Doc came up and looked around.

"This is the place?"

I nodded.

He tested the background radiation and half a dozen other things, found nothing untoward, grunted and looked upwards.

We all did. Then we went there.

It was very rough for three days, and we only made another five thousand feet during that time.

When we bedded down, we were bushed, and sleep came quickly. So did Nemesis.

He was there again, only not quite so near this time. He burned about twenty feet away, standing in the middle of the air, and the point of his blade indicated me.

"*Go away,*" he said, three times, without inflection.

"Go to hell," I tried to say.

He made as if he wished to draw nearer. He failed.

"Go away yourself," I said.

"*Climb back down. Depart. You may go no further.*"

"But I am going further. All the way to the top."

"*No. You may not.*"

"Stick around and watch," I said.

"*Go back.*"

"If you want to stand there and direct traffic, that's your business," I told him. "I'm going back to sleep."

I crawled over and shook Doc's shoulder, but when I looked back my flaming visitor had departed.

"What is it?"

"Too late," I said. "He's been here and gone."

Doc sat up.

"The bird?"

"No, the thing with the sword."

"Where was he?"

"Standing out there." I gestured.

Doc hauled out his instruments and did many things with them for ten minutes or so.

"Nothing," he finally said. "Maybe you were dreaming."

"Yeah, sure," I said. "Sleep tight," and I hit the sack again, and this time I made it through to daylight without further fire or ado.

It took us four days to reach sixty thousand feet. Rocks fell like occasional cannonballs past us, and the sky was a big pool, cool, where pale flowers floated. When we struck sixty-three thousand, the going got much better, and we made it up to seventy-five thousand in two and a half more days. No fiery things stopped by to tell me to turn back. Then came the unforeseeable, however, and we had enough in the way of natural troubles to keep us cursing.

We hit a big, level shelf.

It was perhaps four hundred feet wide. As we advanced across it, we realized that it did not strike the mountainside. It dropped off into an enormous gutter of a canyon. We would have to go down again, perhaps seven hundred feet, before we could proceed upward once more. Worse yet, it led to a featureless face which strove for and achieved perpendicularity for a deadly high distance: like miles. The top was still nowhere in sight.

"Where do we go now?" asked Kelly, moving to my side.

"Down," I decided, "and we split up. We'll follow the big ditch in both directions and see which way gives the better route up. We'll meet back at the midway point."

We descended. Then Doc and Kelly and I went left, and the others took the opposite way.

After an hour and a half, our trail came to an end. We stood looking at nothing over the edge of something. Nowhere, during the entire time, had we come upon a decent way up. I stretched out, my head and shoulders over the edge, Kelly holding onto my ankles, and I looked as far as I could to the right and up. There was nothing in sight that was worth a facing movement.

"Hope the others had better luck," I said, after they'd dragged me back.

"And if they haven't . . . ?" asked Kelly.

"Let's wait."

They had.

It was risky, though.

There was no good way straight up out of the gap. The trail had ended at a forty-foot wall which, when mounted, gave a clear view all the way down. Leaning out as I had done and looking about two hundred feet to the left and eighty feet higher, however, Mallardi had rested his eyes on a rough way, but a way, nevertheless, leading up and west and vanishing.

We camped in the gap that night. In the morning, I anchored my line to a rock, Doc tending, and went out with the pneumatic pistol. I fell twice, and made forty feet of trail by lunchtime.

I rubbed my bruises then, and Henry took over. After ten feet, Kelly got out to anchor a couple of body-lengths behind him, and we tended Kelly.

Then Stan blasted and Mallardi anchored. Then there had to be three on the face. Then four. By sundown, we'd made a hundred fifty feet and were covered with white powder. A bath would have been nice. We settled for ultrasonic shakedowns.

By lunch the next day, we were all out there, roped together, hugging cold stone, moving slowly, painfully, slowly, not looking down much.

By day's end, we'd made it across, to the place where we could hold on and feel something—granted, not much—beneath our boots. It was inclined to be a trifle scant, however, to warrant less than a full daylight assault. So we returned once more to the gap.

In the morning, we crossed.

The way kept its winding angle. We headed west and up. We traveled a mile and made five hundred feet. We traveled another mile and made perhaps three hundred.

The a ledge occurred, about forty feet overhead.

Stan went up the hard way, using the gun, to see what he could see.

He gestured, and we followed; and the view that broke upon us was good.

Down right, irregular but wide enough, was our new camp.

The way above it, ice cream and whiskey sours and morning coffee and a cigarette after dinner. It was beautiful and delicious: a seventy-degree slope full of ledges and projections and good clean stone.

"Hot damn!" said Kelly.

We all tended to agree.

We ate and we drank and we decided to rest our bruised selves that afternoon.

We were in the twilight world now, walking where no man had ever walked before, and we felt ourselves to be golden. It was good to stretch out and try to unache.

I slept away the day, and when I awakened the sky was a bed of glowing embers. I lay there too lazy to move, too full of sight to go back to sleep. A meteor burnt its way bluewhite across the heavens. After a time, there was another. I thought upon my position and decided that reaching it was worth the price. The cold, hard happiness of the heights filled me. I wiggled my toes.

After a few minutes, I stretched and sat up. I regarded the sleeping forms of my companions. I looked out across the night as far as I could see. Then I looked up at the mountain, then dropped my eyes slowly along tomorrow's trail.

There was movement within shadow.

Something was standing about fifty feet away and ten feet above.

I picked up my pick and stood.

I crossed the fifty and stared up.

She was smiling, not burning.

A woman, an impossible woman.

Absolutely impossible. For one thing, she would just have to freeze to death in a mini-skirt and a sleeveless shell-top. No alternative. For another, she had very little to breathe. Like, nothing.

But it didn't seem to bother her. She waved. Her hair was dark and long, and I couldn't see her eyes. The planes of her pale, high cheeks, wide forehead, small chin corresponded in an unsettling fashion with certain simple theorems which comprise the geometry of my heart. If all angles, planes, curves be correct, it skips a beat, then hurries to make up for it.

I worked it out, felt it do so, said, "Hello."

"Hello, Whitey," she replied.

"Come down," I said.

"No, you come up."

I swung my pick. When I reached the ledge she wasn't there. I looked around, then I saw her.

She was seated on a rock twelve feet above me.

"How is it that you know my name?" I asked.

"Anyone can see what your name must be."

"All right," I agreed. "What's yours?"

". . ." Her lips seemed to move, but I heard nothing.

"Come again?"

"I don't want a name," she said.

"Okay. I'll call you 'girl,' then."

She laughed, sort of.

"What are you doing here?" I asked.

"Watching you."

"Why?"

"To see whether you'll fall."

"I can save you the trouble," I said. "I won't."

"Perhaps," she said.

"Come down here."

"No, you come up here."

I climbed, but when I got there she was twenty feet higher.

"Girl, you climb well," I said, and she laughed and turned away.

I pursued her for five minutes and couldn't catch her. There was something unnatural about the way she moved.

I stopped climbing when she turned again. We were still about twenty feet apart.

"I take it you do not really wish me to join you," I said.

"Of course I do, but you must catch me first," And she turned once more, and I felt a certain fury within me.

It was written that no one could outclimb Mad Jack. I had written it.

I swung my pick and moved like a lizard.

I was near to her a couple of times, but never near enough.

The day's aches began again in my muscles, but I pulled my way up without slackening my pace. I realized, faintly, that the camp was far below me now, and that I was climbing alone through the dark up a strange slope. But I did not stop. Rather, I hurried, and my breath began to come hard in my lungs. I heard her laughter, and it was a goad. Then I came upon a two-inch ledge, and she was moving along it. I followed, around a big bulge of rock to where it ended. Then she was ninety feet above me, at the top of a smooth pinnacle. It was like a tapering, branchless tree. How she'd accomplished it, I didn't know. I was gasping by then, but I looped my line around it and began to climb. As I did this, she spoke:

"Don't you ever tire, Whitey? I thought you would have collapsed by now."

I hitched up the line and climbed further.

"You can't make it up here, you know."

"I don't know," I grunted.

"Why do you want so badly to climb here? There are other nice mountains."

"This is the biggest, girl. That's why."

"It can't be done."

"Then why all this bother to discourage me? Why not just let the mountain do it?"

As I neared her, she vanished. I made it to the top, where she had been standing, and I collapsed there.

Then I heard her voice again and turned my head. She was on a ledge, perhaps eighty feet away.

"I didn't think you'd make it this far," she said. "You are a fool. Good-bye, Whitey." She was gone.

I sat there on the pinnacle's tiny top—perhaps four square feet on top—and I knew that I couldn't sleep there, because I'd fall. And I was tired.

I recalled my favorite curses and I said them all, but I didn't feel any better. I couldn't let myself go to sleep. I looked down. I knew the way was long. I knew she didn't think I could make it.

I began the descent.

\* \* \*

The following morning when they shook me, I was still tired. I told them the last night's tale, and they didn't believe me. Not until later in the day, that is, when I detoured us around the bulge and showed them the pinnacle, standing there like a tapering, branchless tree, ninety feet in the middle of the air.

# V

We went steadily upward for the next two days. We made slightly under ten thousand feet. Then we spent a day hammering and hacking our way up a great flat face. Six hundred feet of it. Then our way was to the right and upward. Before long we were ascending the western side of the mountain. When we broke ninety thousand feet, we stopped to congratulate ourselves that we had just surpassed the Kasla climb and to remind ourselves that we still had not hit the halfway mark. It took us another two and a half days to do that, and by then the land lay like a map beneath us.

And then, that night, we all saw the creature with the sword.

He came and stood near our camp, and he raised his sword above his head, and it blazed with such a terrible intensity that I slipped on my goggles. His voice was all thunder and lightning this time:

"Get off this mountain!" he said. "Now! Turn back! Go down! Depart!"

And then a shower of stones came down from above and rattled about us. Doc tossed his slim, shiny case, causing it to skim along the ground toward the creature.

The light went out, and we were alone.

Doc retrieved his case, took tests, met with the same success as before—i.e., none. But now at least he didn't think I was some kind of balmy, unless of course he thought we all were.

"Not a very effective guardian," Henry suggested.

"We've a long way to go yet," said Vince, shying a stone through the space the creature had occupied. "I don't like it if the thing can cause a slide."

"That was just a few pebbles," said Stan.

"Yeah, but what if he decided to start them fifty thousand feet higher?"

"Shut up!" said Kelly. "Don't give him any ideas. He might be listening."

For some reason, we drew closer together. Doc made each of us describe what we had seen, and it appeared that we all had seen the same thing.

"All right," I said, after we'd finished. "Now you've all seen it, who wants to go back?"

There was silence.

After perhaps half a dozen heartbeats, Henry said, "I want the whole story. It looks like a good one. I'm willing to take my chances with angry energy creatures in order to get it."

"I don't know what the thing is," said Kelly. "Maybe it's no energy creature. Maybe it's something—supernatural—I know what you'll say, Doc. I'm just telling you how it struck me. If there are such things, this seems a good place for them. Point is—whatever it is, I don't care. I want this mountain. If it could have stopped us, I think it would've done it already. Maybe I'm wrong. Maybe it can. Maybe it's laid some trap for us higher up. But I want this mountain. Right now, it means more to me than anything. If I don't go up, I'll spend all my time wondering about it—and then I'll probably come back and try it again some day, when it gets so I can't stand thinking about it any more. Only then, maybe the rest of you won't be available. Let's face it, we're a good climbing team. Maybe the best in the business. Probably. If it can be done, I think we can do it."

"I'll second that," said Stan.

"What you said, Kelly," said Mallardi, "about it being supernatural—it's funny, because I felt the same thing for a minute when I was looking at it. It reminds me of something out of the *Divine Comedy*. If you recall, Purgatory was a mountain. And then I thought of the angel who guarded the eastern way to Eden. Eden had gotten moved to the top of Purgatory by Dante— and there was this angel. . . . Anyhow, I felt almost like I was committing some sin I didn't know about by being here. But now that I think it over, a man can't be guilty of something he doesn't know is wrong, can he? And I didn't see that thing flashing any angel ID card. So I'm willing to go up and see what's on top, unless he comes back with the Tablets of the Law, with a new one written in at the bottom."

"In Hebrew or Italian?" asked Doc.

"To satisfy you, I suppose they'd have to be drawn up in the form of equations."

"No," he said. "Kidding aside, I felt something funny too,

when I saw it and heard it. And we didn't really hear it, you know. It skipped over the senses and got its message right into our brains. If you think back over our descriptions of what we experienced, we each 'heard' different words telling us to go away. If it can communicate a meaning as well as a psychtranslator, I wonder if it can communicate an emotion, also. . . . You thought of an angel, too, didn't you, Whitey?"

"Yes," I said.

"That makes it almost unanimous then, doesn't it?"

Then we all turned to Vince, because he had no Christian background at all, having been raised as a Buddhist in Ceylon.

"What were your feelings concerning the thing?" Doc asked him.

"It was a Deva," he said, "which is sort of like an angel, I guess. I had the impression that every step I took up this mountain gave me enough bad karma to fill a lifetime. Except I haven't believed in it that way since I was a kid. I want to go ahead, up. Even if that feeling was correct, I want to see the top of this mountain."

"So do I," said Doc.

"That makes it unanimous," I said.

"Well, everybody hang onto his angel's-bane," said Stan, "and let's sack out."

"Good idea."

"Only let's spread out a bit," said Doc, "so that anything falling won't get all of us together."

We did that cheerful thing and slept untroubled by heaven.

Our way kept winding right, until we were at a hundred forty-four thousand feet and were mounting the southern slopes. Then it jogged back, and by a hundred fifty we were mounting to the west once more.

Then, during a devilish, dark and tricky piece of scaling, up a smooth, concave bulge ending in an overhang, the bird came down once again.

If we hadn't been roped together, Stan would have died. As it was, we almost all died.

Stan was lead man, as its wings splashed sudden flames against the violet sky. It came down from the overhang as though someone had kicked a bonfire over its edge, headed straight toward him and faded out at a distance of about twelve feet. He fell then, almost taking the rest of us with him.

We tensed our muscles and took the shock.

He was battered a bit, but unbroken. We made it up to the overhang, but went no further that day.

Rocks did fall, but we found another overhang and made camp beneath it.

The bird did not return that day, but the snakes came.

Big, shimmering scarlet serpents coiled about the crags, wound in and out of jagged fields of ice and gray stone. Sparks shot along their sinuous lengths. They coiled and unwound, stretched and turned, spat fires at us. It seemed they were trying to drive us from beneath the sheltering place to where the rocks could come down upon us.

Doc advanced upon the nearest one, and it vanished as it came within the field of his projector. He studied the place where it had lain, then hurried back.

"The fost is still on the punkin," he said.

"Huh?" said I.

"Not a bit of ice was melted beneath it."

"Indicating?"

"Illusion," said Vince, and he threw a stone at another and it passed through the thing.

"But you saw what happened to my pick," I said to Doc, "when I took a cut at that bird. The thing had to have been carrying some kind of charge."

"Maybe whatever has been sending them has cut that part out, as a waste of energy," he replied, "since the things can't get through to us anyhow."

We sat around and watched the snakes and falling rocks, until Stan produced a deck of cards and suggested a better game.

The snakes stayed on through the night and followed us the next day. Rocks still fell periodically, but the boss seemed to be running low on them. The bird appeared, circled us and swooped on four different occasions. But this time we ignored it, and finally it went home to roost.

We made three thousand feet, could have gone more, but didn't want to press it past a cozy little ledge with a cave big enough for the whole party. Everything let up on us then. Everything visible, that is.

A before-the-storm feeling, a still, electrical tension, seemed to occur around us then, and we waited for whatever was going to happen to happen.

The worst possible thing happened: nothing.

This keyed-up feeling, this expectancy, stayed with us, was unsatisfied. I think it would actually have been a relief if some invisible orchestra had begun playing Wagner, or if the heavens had rolled aside like curtains and revealed a movie screen, and from the backward letttering we knew we were on the other side, or if we saw a high-flying dragon eating low-flying weather satellites. . . .

As it was, we just kept feeling that something was imminent, and it gave me insomnia.

During the night, she came again. The pinnacle girl.

She stood at the mouth of the cave, and when I advanced she retreated.

I stopped just inside and stood there myself, where she had been standing.

She said, "Hello, Whitey."

"No, I'm not going to follow you again," I said.

"I didn't ask you to."

"What's a girl like you doing in a place like this?"

"Watching," she said.

"I told you I won't fall."

"Your friend almost did."

" 'Almost' isn't good enough."

"You are the leader, aren't you?"

"That's right."

"If you were to die, the others would go back?"

"No," I said, "they'd go on without me."

I hit my camera then.

"What did you just do?" she asked.

"I took your picture—if you're really there."

"Why?"

"To look at after you go away. I like to look at pretty things."

". . . " She seemed to say something.

"What?"

"Nothing."

"Why not?"

". . . die."

"Please speak up."

"She dies . . ." she said.

"Why? How?"

". . . on mountain."

"I don't understand."

". . . too."

"What's wrong?"

I took a step forward, and she retreated a step.

"Follow me?" she asked.

"No."

"Go back," she said.

"What's on the other side of that record?"

"You will continue to climb?"

"Yes."

Then, "Good!" she said suddenly. "I—" and her voice stopped again.

"Go back," she finally said, without emotion.

"Sorry."

And she was gone.

# VI

Our trail took us slowly to the left once more. We crawled and sprawled and cut holes in the stone. Snakes sizzled in the distance. They were with us constantly now. The bird came again at crucial moments, to try to make us fall. A raging bull stood on a crag and bellowed down at us. Phantom archers loosed shafts of fire, which always faded right before they struck. Blazing blizzards swept at us, around us, were gone. We were back on the northern slopes and still heading west by the time we broke a hundred sixty thousand. The sky was deep and blue, and there were always stars. Why did the mountain hate us? I wondered. What was there about us to provoke this thing? I looked at the picture of the girl for the dozenth time and I wondered what she really was. Had she been picked from our minds and composed into girlform to lure us, to lead us, sirenlike, harpylike, to the place of the final fall? It was such a long way down. . . .

I thought back over my life. How does a man come to climb mountains? Is he drawn by the heights because he is afraid of the level land? Is he such a misfit in the society of men that he must flee and try to place himself above it? The way up is long and difficult, but if he succeeds they must grant him a garland of sorts. And if he falls, this too is a kind of glory. To end, hurled from the heights to the depths in hideous ruin and combustion down, is a fitting climax for the loser—for it, too, shakes mountains and minds, stirs things like thoughts below both, is a kind of blasted garland of victory in defeat, and cold, so cold that final action, that the movement is somewhere frozen forever into a statuelike rigidity of ultimate intent and purpose thwarted only by the universal malevolence we all fear exists. An aspirant saint or hero who lacks some necessary virtue may still qualify as a martyr, for the only thing that people will really remember in the end is the end. I had known that I'd had to climb Kasla, as I had climbed all the others, and I had known what the price would be. It had cost me my only home. But Kasla was there, and my boots cried out for my feet. I knew as I did so that somewhere I set them upon her summit, and below me a world was ending. What's a world if the moment of victory is at hand? And if truth, beauty and goodness be one, why is there always this conflict among them?

The phantom archers fired upon me and the bright bird swooped. I set my teeth, and my boots scarred rocks beneath me.

We saw the top.

At a hundred seventy-six thousand feet, making our way along a narrow ledge, clicking against rock, testing our way with our picks, we heard Vince say, "Look!"

We did.

Up and up, and again further, bluefrosted and sharp, deadly, and cold as Loki's dagger, slashing at the sky, it vibrated above us like electricity, hung like a piece of frozen thunder, and cut, cut, cut into the center of spirit that was desire, twisted, and became a fishhook to pull us on, to burn us with its barbs.

Vince was the first to look up and see the top, the first to die. It happened so quickly, and it was none of the terrors that achieved it.

He slipped.

That was all. It was a difficult piece of climbing. He was right behind me one second, was gone the next. There was no body to recover. He'd taken the long drop. The soundless blue was all around him and the great gray beneath. Then we were six. We shuddered, and I suppose we all prayed in our own ways.

—Gone Vince, may some good Deva lead you up the Path of Splendor. May you find whatever you wanted most at the other end, waiting there for you. If such a thing may be, remember those who say these words, O strong intruder in the sky. . . .

No one spoke much for the rest of the day.

The fiery sword bearer came and stood above our camp the entire night. It did not speak.

In the morning, Stan was gone, and there was a note beneath my pack.

> *Don't hate me,* it said, *for running out, but I think it really is an angel. I'm scared of this mountain. I'll climb any pile of rocks, but I won't fight Heaven. The way down is easier than the way up, so don't worry about me. Good luck. Try to understand.*                              S

So we were five—Doc and Kelly and Henry and Mallardi and me—and that day we hit a hundred eighty thousand and felt very alone.

The girl came again that night and spoke to me, black hair against black sky and eyes like points of blue fire, and she stood beside any icy pillar and said: "Two of you have gone."

"And the rest of us remain," I replied.

"For a time."

"We will climb to the top and then we will go away," I said. "How can that do you harm? Why do you hate us?"

"No hate, sir," she said.

"What, then?"

"I protect."

"What? What is it that you protect?"

"The dying, that she may live."

"What? Who is dying? How?"

But her words went away somewhere, and I did not hear them. Then she went away too, and there was nothing left but sleep for the rest of the night.

One hundred eighty-two thousand and three, and four, and five. Then back down to four for the following night.

The creatures whined about us now, and the land pulsed beneath us, and the mountain seemed sometimes to sway as we climbed.

We carved a path to one eighty-six, and for three days we fought to gain another thousand feet. Everything we touched was cold and slick and slippery, sparkled, and had a bluish haze about it.

When we hit one ninety, Henry looked back and shuddered.

"I'm no longer worried about making it to the top," he said. "It's the return trip that's bothering me now. The clouds are like little wisps of cotton way down there."

"The sooner up, the sooner down," I said, and we began to climb once again.

It took us another week to cut our way to within a mile of the top. All the creatures of fire had withdrawn, but two ice avalanches showed us we were still unwanted. We survived the first without mishap, but Kelly sprained his right ankle during the second, and Doc thought he might have cracked a couple of ribs, too.

We made a camp. Doc stayed there with him; Henry and Mallardi and I pushed on up the last mile.

Now the going was beastly. It had become a mountain of glass. We had to hammer out a hold for every foot we made. We worked in shifts. We fought for everything we gained. Our packs became monstrous loads and our fingers grew number. Our defense system—the projectors—seemed to be wearing down, or else something was increasing its efforts to get us, because the snakes kept slithering closer, burning brighter. They hurt my eyes, and I cursed them.

When we were within a thousand feet of the top, we dug in and made another camp. The next couple hundred feet looked easier, then a rotten spot, and I couldn't tell what it was like above that.

When we awakened, there was just Henry and myself. There was no indication of where Mallardi had gotten to. Henry switched his communicator to Doc's letter and called below. I tuned in in time to hear him say, "Haven't seen him."

"How's Kelly?" I asked.

"Better," he replied. "Those ribs might not be cracked at that."

Then Mallardi called us.

"I'm four hundred feet above you, fellows," his voice came in. "It was easy up to here, but the going's just gotten rough again."

"Why'd you cut out on your own?" I asked.

"Because I think something's going to try to kill me before too long," he said. "It's up ahead, waiting at the top. You can probably even see it from here. It's a snake."

Henry and I used the binoculars.

Snake? A better word might be dragon—or maybe even Midgaard Serpent.

It was coiled around the peak, head upraised. It seemed to be several hundred feet in length, and it moved its head from side to side, and up and down, and it smoked solar coronas.

Then I spotted Mallardi climbing toward it.

"Don't go any further!" I called. "I don't know whether your unit will protect you against anything like that! Wait'll I call Doc—"

"Not a chance," he said. "This baby is mine."

"Listen! You can be first on the mountain, if that's what you want! But don't tackle that thing alone!"

A laugh was the only reply.

"All three units might hold it off," I said. "Wait for us."

There was no answer, and we began to climb.

I left Henry far below me. The creature was a moving light in the sky. I made two hundred feet in a hurry, and when I looked up again, I saw that the creature had grown two more heads. Lightning bolts flashed from its nostrils, and its tail whipped around the mountain. I made another hundred feet, and I could see Mallardi clearly by then, climbing steadily, outlined against the brilliance. I swung my pick, gasping, and I fought the mountain, following the trail he had cut. I began to gain on him, because he was still pounding out his way and I didn't have that problem. Then I heard him talking:

"Not yet, big fella, not yet," he was saying, from behind a wall of static. "Here's a ledge. . . ."

I looked up, and he vanished.

Then that fiery tail came lashing down toward where I had last seen him, and I heard him curse and I felt the vibrations of his pneumatic gun. The tail snapped back again, and I heard another "Damn!"

I made haste, stretching and racking myself and grabbing at the holds he had cut, and then I heard him burst into song. Something from *Aïda*, I think.

"Damn it! Wait up!" I said. "I'm only a few hundred feet behind."

He kept on singing.

I was beginning to get dizzy, but I couldn't let myself slow down. My right arm felt like a piece of wood, my left like a piece of ice. My feet were hooves, and my eyes burned in my head.

Then it happened.

Like a bomb, the snake and the swinging ended in a flash of brilliance that caused me to sway and almost lose my grip. I clung to the vibrating mountainside and squeezed my eyes against the light.

"Mallardi?" I said.

No answer. Nothing.

I looked down. Henry was still clinging. I continued to climb.

I reached the ledge Mallardi had mentioned, found him there.

His respirator was still working. His protective suit was blackened and scorched on the right side. Half of his pick had been melted away. I raised his shoulders.

I turned up the volume on the communicator and heard him breathing. His eyes opened, closed, opened.

"Okay . . ." he said.

" 'Okay,' hell! Where do you hurt?"

"No place. . . . I feel jus' fine. . . . Listen! I think it's used up its juice for a while. . . . Go plant the flag. Prop me up here first, though. I wanna watch. . . ."

I got him into a better position, squirted the water bulb, listened to him swallow. Then I waited for Henry to catch up. It took about six minutes.

"I'll stay here," said Henry, stopping beside him. "You go do it."

I started up the final slope.

## VII

I swung and I cut and I blasted and I crawled. Some of the ice had been melted, the rocks scorched.

Nothing came to oppose me. The static had gone with the dragon. There was silence, and darkness between stars.

I climbed slowly, still tired from that last sprint, but determined not to stop.

All but sixty feet of the entire world lay beneath me, and heaven hung above me, and a rocket winked overhead. Perhaps it was the pressmen, with zoom cameras.

Fifty feet. . . .

No bird, no archer, no angel, no girl.

Forty feet. . . .

I started to shake. It was nervous tension. I steadied myself, went on.

Thirty feet . . . and the mountain seemed to be swaying now.

Twenty-five . . . and I grew dizzy, halted, took a drink.

Then click, click, my pick again.

Twenty. . . .

Fifteen. . . .

Ten. . . .

I braced myself against the mountain's final assault, whatever it might be.

Five. . . .

Nothing happened as I arrived.

I stood up. I could go no higher.

I looked at the sky, I looked back down. I waved at the blazing rocket exhaust.

I extruded the pole and attached the flag.

I planted it, there where no breezes would ever stir it. I cut in my communicator, said, "I'm here."

No other words.

It was time to go back down and give Henry his chance, but I looked down the western slope before I turned to go.

The lady was winking again. Perhaps eight hundred feet below, the red light shone. Could that have been what I had seen from the town during the storm, on that night so long ago?

I didn't know and I had to.

I spoke into the communicator.

"How's Mallardi doing?"

"I just stood up," he answered. "Give me another half hour, and I'm coming up myself."

"Henry," I said. "Should he?"

"Gotta take his word how he feels," said Lanning.

"Well," I said, "then take it easy. I'll be gone when you get here. I'm going a little way down the western side. Something I want to see."

"What?"

"I dunno. That's why I want to see."

"Take care."

"Check."

The western slope was an easy descent. As I went down it, I realized that the light was coming from an opening in the side of the mountain.

Half an hour later, I stood before it.

I stepped within and was dazzled.

I walked toward it and stopped. It pulsed and quivered and sang.

A vibrating wall of flame leapt from the floor of the cave, towered to the roof of the cave.

It blocked my way, when I wanted to go beyond it.

She was there, and I wanted to reach her.

I took a step forward, so that I was only inches away from it. My communicator was full of static and my arms of cold needles.

It did not bend toward me, as to attack. It cast no heat.

I stared through the veil of fires to where she reclined, her eyes closed, her breast unmoving.

I stared at the bank of machinery beside the far wall.

"I'm here," I said, and I raised my pick.

When its point touched the wall of flame someone took the lid off hell, and I staggered back, blinded. When my vision cleared, the angel stood before me.

"*You may not pass here,*" he said.

"She is the reason you want me to go back?" I asked.

"*Yes. Go back.*"

"Has she no say in the matter?"

"*She sleeps. Go back.*"

"So I notice. Why?"

"*She must. Go back.*"

"Why did she herself appear to me and lead me strangely?"

"*I used up the fear-forms I knew. They did not work. I led you strangely because her sleeping mind touches upon my workings. It did so especially when I borrowed her form, so that it interfered with the directive. Go back.*"

"What is the directive?"

"*She is to be guarded against all things coming up the mountain. Go back.*"

"Why? Why is she guarded?"

"*She sleeps. Go back.*"

The conversation having become somewhat circular at that point, I reached into my pack and drew out the projector. I swung it forward and the angel melted. The flames bent away from my outstretched hand. I sought to open a doorway in the circle of fire.

It worked, sort of.

I pushed the projector forward, and the flames bent and bent and bent and finally broke. When they broke, I leaped forward. I made it through, but my protective suit was as scorched as Mallardi's.

I moved to the coffinlike locker within which she slept.

I rested my hands on its edge and looked down.

She was as fragile as ice.

In fact, she was ice. . . .

The machine came alive with lights then, and I felt her somber bedstead vibrate.

Then I saw the man.

He was half sprawled across a metal chair beside the machine.

He, too, was ice. Only his features were gray, were twisted. He wore black and he was dead and a statue, while she was sleeping and a statue.

She wore blue, and white. . . .

There was an empty casket in the far corner. . . .

But something was happening around me. There came a brightening of the air. Yes, it was air. It hissed upward from frosty jets in the floor, formed into great clouds. Then a feeling of heat occurred and the clouds began to fade and the brightening continued.

I returned to the casket and studied her features.

I wondered what her voice would sound like when/if she spoke. I wondered what lay within her mind. I wondered how her thinking worked, and what she liked and didn't like. I wondered what her eyes had looked upon, and when.

I wondered all these things, because I could see that whatever forces I had set into operation when I entered the circle of fire were causing her, slowly, to cease being a statue.

She was being awakened.

I waited. Over an hour went by, and still I waited, watching her. She began to breathe. Her eyes opened at last, and for a long time she did not see.

Then her bluefire fell upon me.

"Whitey," she said.

"Yes."

"Where am I . . . ?"

"In the damnedest place I could possibly have found anyone."

She frowned. "I remember," she said and tried to sit up.

It didn't work. She fell back.

"What is your name?"

"Linda," she said. Then, "I dreamed of you, Whitey. Strange dreams. . . . How could that be?"

"It's tricky," I said.

"I knew you were coming," she said. "I saw you fighting monsters on a mountain as high as the sky."

"Yes, we're there now."

"H-have you the cure?"

"Cure? What cure?"

"Dawson's Plague," she said.

I felt sick. I felt sick because I realized that she did not sleep as a prisoner, but to postpone her death. She was sick.

"Did you come to live on this world in a ship that moved faster than light?" I asked.

"No," she said. "It took centuries to get here. We slept the cold sleep during the journey. This is one of the bunkers." She gestured toward the casket with her eyes. I noticed her cheeks had become bright red.

"They all began dying—of the plague," she said. "There was no cure. My husband—Carl—is a doctor. When he saw that I had it, he said he would keep me in extreme hypothermia until a cure was found. Otherwise, you only live for two days, you know."

Then she stared up at me, and I realized that her last two words had been a question.

I moved into a position to block her view of the dead man, who I feared must be her Carl. I tried to follow her husband's thinking. He'd had to hurry, as he was obviously further along than she had been. He knew the colony would be wiped out. He must have loved her and been awfully clever, both—awfully resourceful. Mostly, though, he must have loved her. Knowing that the colony would die, he knew it would be centuries before another ship arrived. He had nothing that could power a cold bunker for that long. But up here, on the top of this mountain, almost as cold as outer space itself, power wouldn't be necessary. Somehow, he had got Linda and the stuff up here. His machine cast a force field around the cave. Working in heat and atmosphere, he had sent her deep into the cold sleep and then prepared his own bunker. When he dropped the wall of forces, no power would be necessary to guarantee the long, icy wait. They could sleep for centuries within the bosom of the Gray Sister, protected by a colony of defense-computer. This last had apparently been programmed quickly, for he was dying. He saw that it was too late to join her. He hurried to set the thing for basic defense, killed the force field, and then went his way into that Dark and Secret Place. Thus it hurled its birds and its angels and its snakes, it raised its walls of fire against me. He died, and it guarded her in her near-death—against everything, including those who would help. My coming to the mountain had activated it. My passing of the defenses had caused her to be summoned back to life.

"*Go back!*" I heard the machine say through its projected angel, for Henry had entered the cave.

"My God!" I heard him say, "Who's that?"

"Get Doc!" I said. "Hurry! I'll explain later. It's a matter of life! Climb back to where your communicator will work, and tell him it's Dawson's Plague—a bad local bug! Hurry!"

"I'm on my way," he said and was.

"There *is* a doctor?" she asked.

"Yes. Only about two hours away. Don't worry. . . . I still don't see how anyone could have gotten you up here to the top of this mountain, let alone a load of machines."

"We're on the big mountain—the forty-miler?"

"Yes."

"How did *you* get up?" she asked.

"I climbed it."

"You really climbed Purgatorio? On the outside?"

"Purgatorio? That's what you call it? Yes, I climbed it, that way."

"We didn't think it could be done."

"How else might one arrive at its top?"

"It's hollow inside," she said. "There are great caves and massive passages. It's easy to fly up the inside in a pressurized jet car. In fact, it was an amusement ride. Two and a half dollars per person. An hour and a half each way. A dollar to rent a pressurized suit and take an hour's walk around the top. Nice way to spend an afternoon. Beautiful view . . . ?" She gasped deeply.

"I don't feel so good," she said. "Have you any water?"

"Yes," I said, and I gave her all I had.

As she sipped it, I prayed that Doc had the necessary serum or else would be able to send her back to ice and sleep until it could be gotten. I prayed that he would make good time, for two hours seemed long when measured against her thirst and the red of her flesh.

"My fever is coming again," she said. "Talk to me, Whitey, please. . . . Tell me things. Keep me with you till he comes. I don't want my mind to turn back upon what has happened. . . ."

"What would you like me to tell you about, Linda?"

"Tell me why you did it. Tell me what it was like, to climb a mountain like this one. Why?"

\* \* \*

I turned my mind back upon what had happened.

"There is a certain madness involved," I said, "a certain envy of great and powerful natural forces, that some men have. Each mountain is a deity, you know. Each is an immortal power. If you make sacrifices upon its slopes, a mountain may grant you a certain grace, and for a time you will share this power. Perhaps that is why they call me. . . ."

Her hand rested in mine. I hoped that through it whatever power I might contain would hold all of her with me for as long as ever possible.

"I remember the first time that I saw Purgatory, Linda," I told her. "I looked at it and I was sick. I wondered, where did it lead. . . ?"

(Stars.

Oh let there be.

This once to end with.

Please.)

"Stars?"

# I HAVE NO MOUTH, AND I MUST SCREAM
## (MARCH 1967)
## HARLAN ELLISON
## (B. 1934)

As the following memoir indicates, "I have no Mouth, and I Must Scream" is an important story to Harlan Ellison—and Harlan has been important to science fiction as a Hugo- and Nebula-winning author and as the editor of the acclaimed original anthologies, *Dangerous Visions* and *Again, Dangerous Visions*. He has also enriched the field with his dynamic presence.

*If* was an early market for the young Ellison, publishing such short stories as "The Crackpots" (June 1956), "The Sky Is Burning" (August 1958), and "Wanted in Surgery" (August 1957). *If* also has the distinction of having published what many consider to be his finest early story, "Life Hutch," in the April 1956 issue.

## MEMOIR BY HARLAN ELLISON

The story behind the writing of "I Have No Mouth, and I Must Scream" and its subsequent success is, for me, a classic case of self-fulfilling prophecy.

I've never set down in totality my feelings about this story, though it has become one of the three or four pieces most closely associated with the "reputation" I've managed to accrue, as my most "famous" story. (You'll have to excuse all those quotation marks; I take such words as are enclosed by " and " with more than a grain of salt. The " " marks are intended to indicate that "others" use those words in a context of [if not Authority] at least "common knowledge.")

I have probably made more money per word from the sixty-five hundred assorted ones that comprise this story than anything else I've ever written, with the possible exception of " 'Repent, Harlequin!' Said the Ticktockman," which was also, not so coincidentally, written for Fred Pohl. (I say not coincidentally, because this story was written as a direct result of Fred's having bought and published the Harlequin/Ticktockman piece in 1965. More of that later.)

"I Have No Mouth" has been translated into Polish, German, Spanish, Japanese, Esperanto, French, Norwegian, Dutch, Israeli, and Portuguese . . . and a few more I can't recall offhand. It has been adapted as a theatrical production half a dozen times, once by Robert Silverberg for a tripartite off-Broadway setting. A film producer named Max Rosenberg once tried to rip it off as the title for a horror flick he was contemplating, and a court of law stopped him by handing down a judgment that said while it's impossible to copyright a *title*, if one can prove ongoing substantial claim to financial stake in such a title, it *can* be protected; so Mr. Rosenberg wound up calling his film something else. I think it was *Bucket of Blood*, but I could be wrong.

It has been reprinted in magazines as diverse as *Knave* and *Datamation*. When it appeared in the latter, the leading trade journal of the automatic information handling equipment industry, it brought down a firestorm of outraged letters from programmers and systems analysts who felt that my equating God with the Malevolent Machine was heretical beyond support. They weren't isolated in their feelings that there's something subversive in the story: a high school teacher in a small Wyoming town lost her job because she included it in the reading program for her classes; the story was condemned by the then-extant National Office for Decent Literature funded by the Catholic Church; the American Nazi party (or whatever those clowns call themselves) sent me a shredded copy of the paperback edition with a note that assured me I was a godless kike heathen who would be high on their hit list for spreading such godless kike heathen propaganda.

Nonetheless, the story has been reprinted a couple of hundred times, has appeared in numerous college-level text-anthologies of "great literature" (those quotes again), and was selected as one of four classic American short stories celebrated in a series of special art posters published by the Advertising Typographers Association of America. It has been the subject of a number of learned treatises, presented by academicians at prestigious literary seminars. In the Spring 1976 edition of *The Journal of General Education* a gentleman named Brady dissected it in a monograph titled "The Computer as a Symbol of God: Ellison's Macabre Exodus." I didn't understand much of it, I'm afraid. Ah, but in *Diogenes* (no. 85, 1974) a gentleman named Ower peeled away the subcutaneous layers of deep philosophical perception in the story in a long essay titled "Manacle-Forged Minds: Two Images of the Computer in Science-Fiction." Ah! Now *that* was a bit of work. I didn't understand that one even worse than I didn't understand the other one.

It, or at least its title, reaps parody the way a Twinkie gourmand reaps zits. "I Have No Talent, and I Must Write," "I Have No Bird, and I Must Die," and a real gem titled "I have No Nose, and I Must Sneeze" by a Mr. Orr in 1969 are but a paucive sampling of the aberrated clone-children that have pursued those original sixty-five hundred words down the ivy-festooned halls of literary excellence.

The story has been optioned for theatrical feature or television film production on seven separate occasions. No one, thus far, however, seems to have figured out a way to shoot it. If I find a likely john, maybe I'll do it myself.

References to the story appear in crossword puzzles in locations as likely as *The Magazine of Fantasy & Science Fiction*, as unlikely as *TV Guide*. The London *Times* once referred to it as "a scathing repudiation of multinational corporations that rule our lives like deranged gods." Go figure *that* one.

And I once attended a Modern Language Assocation conclave at which a brilliant Jesuit teacher presented a weighty disquisition on this little fable during which exposition he made reference to catharsis, marivaudage, metaphysical conceits, intentional fallacy, incremental repetition, *chanson de geste*, Gongorism, the New Humanism, Jungian archetypes, crucifixion and resurrection symbolism, and that all-time fave of us all, the basic Apollonian-Dionysian conflict.

When the savant had completed his presentation, I was asked to comment. Had Mary Shelley or Henry James been present I suppose they, too, would have been asked to respond to analyses of *their* work. Unfortunately, they had prior commitments.

I got up, knowing full well that I was about to make some trouble. I pause in the retelling of this anecdote to limn the motives of the Author.

Serious critical attention from Academe has its benefits and its drawbacks. Others have commented at greater length and deeper perceptivity about this situation. And while I find the attention most salutary on an ego-boosting level, I find it as troublesome and mischievous in its negative aspects as, say, Lester del Rey's outmoded, hincty belief that erudition, attention to style, and a college education cripple a writer, preventing him from ever producing anything containing "the sense of wonder." As wrong-headed and tunnel-visioned as is Lester's belief—expressed at the top of his voice for the past forty years and a position adopted by many another ex–pulp writer—it is no less berserk than the worshipful nitpicking of junior professors determined to publish-or-perish through manipulation of the writings of contemporary fantasists. The ground has been rather well picked over in the terrain of Fitzgerald, Woolf, Ford Madox Ford, and Faulkner. But a name can still be made if one can imbue with sufficient import the writings of Disch, Malzberg, Le Guin, and Heinlein.

The curse that accompanies such attention, however, is one that strikes the subject rather than the herald. The critic frequently doubles as Typhoid Mary, and the sickness s/he passes on to the writer is the crippling, sometimes killing, malady known as "taking oneself seriously."

I will not here subscribe to the disingenuous conceit that what I write is for "beer money." I take my work too seriously (though I find it difficult to take *myself* too seriously); I work too hard at it. No, what I do I do with the clean hands and composure of which Balzac spoke. But it seems to me the sensibility that informs my work is fired, in large part, by a kind of innocence: a determination to ignore any voices echoing down the corridors of Posterity. By this attitude, I feel sure, I can escape the fate of those writers who have come to believe themselves so significant that they become co-opted, become part of the literary *apparat*, lose their willingness to get in trouble, to anger their readers, to shock even themselves, to go into dangerous territory.

Robert Coover has said, ". . . it's the role of the author, the fiction maker, the mythologizer, to be the creative spark in this process of renewal: he's the one who tears apart the old story, speaks the unspeakable, makes the ground shake, then shuffles the bits back together into a new story."

Or, more briefly, in the words of Arthur Miller: "Society and man are mutually dependent enemies and the writer's job [is] to go on forever defining and defending the paradox—lest, God forbid, it be resolved."

The loss of innocence prevents the writer, once dangerous, from pursuing those endeavors of which Coover and Miller speak. And cathexian freighting laid upon a writer's work, *if he pays attention to the comments,* inevitably has a deleterious effect on the innocence of a writer, stunts his/her ability to kick ass.

And so, not merely out of self-defense but from a well-honed sense of survival, I resist the attempts of literary philosophers to imbue my motives with scholarly nobility.

Which is why I rose to respond to that decent, kind, and flattering Jesuit scholar with chaos in my heart.

I said: "I've listened to all this rodomontade, all this investiture of a straightforward moral fable with an unwarranted load of silly symbolism and portentous obscurantism and frankly, Father, I think you're stuffed right full of wild blueberry muffins."

Those who know me know that I tend, in moments of great emotional stress, to speak in a manner not unlike that of the late W. C. Fields. The words poltroon, *jongleur,* and mountebank were held at the ready.

The good Father huffed and puffed. Affronted.

So I went chapter&verse refuting all his assumptions and insinuations (all of which had tended to make me appear a "serious writer"). Virtually everything he had attributed as subtext to the story, all the convoluted and arcane interpretations, were identified as constructs of his vast erudition (and prolix woolgathering) and nowhichway intended by the Humble Author.

A bit of a brouhaha ensued. Umbrage taken. Dudgeon elevated to new heights. Slurs bandied. And finally, falling back to the usually unassailable position taken as final barricade by academic glossolaliastes, the good Father put me in my place with this rebuke: "The unconscious is deep and mysterious. Not even the writer can understand the meanings hidden in what he has written."

A less survival-prone, possibly kinder, person might have swallowed that one and backed off; I am neither, and did not.

"Father, if you're so bloody hip to all the subtle nuances of this story, if you're on to undercurrents not even *I* know are there . . . how come you didn't notice the woman in the story is black?"

The good Father huffed and puffed. Buffaloed.

"Black? Black? Where's that?"

"Right there. Right in the words. 'Her ebony features stark against the snow.' Nothing hidden, nothing symbolic, just plain black against the snow. In two places."

He paused a moment. "Well, yes, of course, I saw *that!* But *I* thought you meant . . ."

I spread my hands with finality. I rested my case.

I have not been invited back to a MLA conference.

*     *     *

In large part because of this story, my work has been termed
"violent." Bloody. Hateful. Negative. When I tell a lecture audience that "I Have No Mouth . . ." is a positive, humanistic,
upbeat story, I invariably get looks of confusion and disbelief. For
hordes of readers through the years this story is an exercise in
futility and morbid debasement of the human spirit. The impact
of the setting and the somewhat romanticized horror of the ending tend to obscure the essential message of the story, which I
intended as positive and uplifting. That most readers fail to perceive this aspect of the work has me torn between self-flagellation
at my ineptitude in explicating my message . . . and loathing of
my audience for reading too fast and too sloppily. (The latter, a
condition of all too many of the declining species called "readers,"
is symptomatic of the lowered assimilative capabilities attendant
on a diet of those *Love's Tender Fury* things, years of Taylor
Caldwell, the expanded short stories called novels by such as Ken
Follett and Sidney Sheldon, and the slovenly slapdash adventure
paperbacks of semiliterate SF/horror writers. It occurs, to be
evenhanded, that I am elevating myself in my own eyes by
blaming the readers; but even when I pillory myself for persistent
imprecision of this sort on the part of my audience by an assumed
guilt on the part of the less-than-adept Author, I find I'm castigat-
ing myself for trying to be subtle. And that does not seem to me
to be a felony. One can only write so many beheadings and car
crashes before one longs to make a point by indirect means. It is a
conundrum.)

In an attempt to explain all the foregoing—preceding the par-
enthetical remarks—please consider two elements of "I Have No
Mouth . . ." that, bewilderingly to me, escape most readers.

First, consider the character of Ellen.

From time to time I've been taken to task with the accusation
that my stories reflect a hatred of women. I wish my hands were
absolutely clean in the matter of sexism manifesting itself in my
work, but, sadly, I was born in 1934, I was raised in America
during the forties, and though I do not hate women, a number of
my earlier writings *do* contain chauvinistic views commonly held
by American males born and raised in those times, in that place. I
cannot flense those elements from my early stories. Nor would I.
They represented the way I thought *at those times*. I don't think
they reflect animus toward women, they reflect my propensity for
writing about seriously flawed characters—both male and female.

It was Mencken who said, "When people are at their worst, they are the most interesting." I have always been drawn to characters that were interesting. Sometimes that caused me to write about unpleasant females, even as it did unpleasant males. I *still* prefer and find compelling the kind of characters who stumble through Scott Fitzgerald's "dark night of the soul," and I guess I always will. And so I have come to live with the understanding that casual readers—those being fashionably liberal or those whose assumption of extreme positions precludes their understanding of how dangerously they hobble the creative intellect by insistence on a slavish evenhandedness for *all* minorities even though one is writing about an *individual,* not a demographic group*—including those readers who are nouveau liberated with consciousnesses raised fifteen minutes earlier, may choose to interpret my stories in the dim light of their own personal tunnel vision.

But in going back over the stories I've written since, say, 1967, I find that the Author learned better. It merely took someone to point out the muddy thinking. (For historians, the name of the teacher is Mary Reinholz.) The women in my stories have tended to be better drawn, more various, and, I like to think, as reflective of reality as the men. There is one serious drawback to my self-congratulation in this area, however. And it is this: Whether I could ever convince a dispassionate jury that I feel to my core I am not a misogynist, there is no way I can escape the label of misanthrope. There is in me, damn it, a love-hate relationship with the human race. I read a phrase that pinned it neatly for me; it's from Vance Bourjaily's novel, *A Game Men Play,* and in speaking of his protagonist he said, ". . . he was . . . full of rage and love, and of a malarial loathing for mankind which came and went chronically . . ."

Like Bourjaily's "Chink" Peters, I must confess to that dichotomous feeling about humanity. Capable of warmth, courage, friendship, decency, and creativity, the species too often opts for amorality, cowardice, aversion, self-indulgence, and vile mediocrity. How can one who writes about the human condition *not* fall prey to such misanthropy?

---

*A quote from David Denby seems appropriate here: "An artist trying to create a powerful atmosphere can't be expected to embrace the banal method of TV documentaries, which always illustrate both sides of a situation and leave you nowhere."

Nonetheless, in going back through my work for nearly the last decade and a half, I find that the women come off equally as well as the men. An example, which I've asked you to consider, is the lone woman in "I Have No Mouth . . ."—Ellen.

If one goes at a story in the Evelyn Wood SpeedReading manner, one can easily get the impression that Ellen is a selfish, flirtatious, extremely cruel bitch. Why not, doesn't the narrator *say* she is? Yes, he does. And so I've had to explain what I'm about to explain here—and it's all in the text of the story, I'm not interpreting or even reinterpreting to assuage my conscience—to women who take Ellen as a classic representation of my "hatred of females."

But, as I said earlier, precisely the opposite is the case.

Consider: The story is told in the first person by Ted, one of the group of people the computer AM has brought into the center of the Earth to torment. But as I've clearly stated in the story, also from the mouth of Ted, AM has altered each of them in one way or another. The machine has bent them, altered them, corrupted their minds or bodies. Ted, by his own words, has been turned into a paranoid. He was a humanitarian, a lover of people, and AM has twisted his mind so he views everything and everyone negatively. It is *Ted*, not the Author, who reviles Ellen and who casts doubt on her actions and motivations. But if you look at what she *actually does*, it becomes obvious that the only person in the story with any kindness toward the others is Ellen. She weeps for them, tries to comfort and solace them, brings to them the only warmth and alleviation of pain in the world of anguish to which they've been consigned. (Echoing my remarks to the Jesuit Father in the earlier anecdote, let me point out that few readers realize Ellen is a black woman, though it is precisely stated "[her] face black against the white snow." In moments of introspection I see the plus&minus of my having made Ellen black. It was knee-jerk liberalism to do it—remember I wrote the story in 1965 during a period of acute awakening of my, and the nation's, social conscience—but at least I was enough of a writer not to make a big deal of it. In fact, though I have imbued this member of a much-sinned-against race with a nobility her Caucasian companions in the story do not possess, I understated it so much . . . it has, in the main, gone unnoticed.)

Further, it is Ellen who joins Ted in providing the release-through-death that is their only possible escape from AM's torture. And when it comes the moment for *her* to die, she again demonstrates not only her heroic nature, but an awareness that it is the kindest act a person can commit for another to free the other from guilt at causing a death. As I wrote it:

> *Ellen looked at me, her ebony features stark against the snow that surrounded us. There was fear and pleading in her manner, the way she held herself ready. I knew we had only a heartbeat before AM would stop us.*
>
> *It struck her and she folded toward me, bleeding from the mouth. I could not read meaning into her expression, the pain had been too great, had contorted her face; but it* might *have been thank you. It's possible. Please.*

Her courage is only slightly less than Ted's at this point. She knows AM will wreak vengeance more horrible than all that has gone before on anyone left alive of those who have stolen its playthings away from it; even so, she frees Nimdok, at risk of her own soul. Thus, it can be seen that all the negative things *said* about Ellen—attributed so often to the Author's "hatred of women" —are verbal manifestations of Ted's AM-induced paranoia.

Finally, when it comes down to the last of them, Ted demonstrates his uncommon courage and transcendentally human sense of self-sacrifice, *overcoming the core derangement in him,* by performing a final act of love and self-denial. He kills Ellen. And she forgives him with a look. Even at the final instant, filled with pain, she is such a superior person that she absolves him of the responsibility for the act of murder.

Which brings me to the second element most readers misconstrue; the aspect of this work that *I* intended as the important subtext message: the moral, if you will.

*It is an upbeat ending.* Infinitely hopeful and positive.

How can I make such a contention when the story ends with mass murder and unspeakable horror? I can, and do, because "I Have No Mouth . . ." says that even when all hope is lost, when nothing but torment and physical pain will be the reward, there is an unquenchable spark of decency, self-sacrifice, and Olympian courage in the basic material of even the most debased human being that will send each of us to heights of nobility at the final extreme. Of all the qualities imputed to humanity as admittedly ethnocentric *raison d'être* for our contention that we possess *summatus,* the right to transcend in the Universe . . . this, in my estimation, is the one valid argument. Not that we possess a sense of humor, or the ability to dream, or the opposable thumb, or the little gray cells that permit us to make laws to govern ourselves. It is the spark of potential transcendency, that which allows us to behave in a manner usually attributed to the most benevolent of gods . . . that remarkable aspect of the human character validates our contention that we deserve a high place in the cosmic pantheon.

Even fully aware that he is condemning himself to an eternity of torture at AM's invention, nonetheless Ted removes the one thing that can provide him with the tiniest measure of companionship and love and amelioration of his fate . . . the only other human being alive on the planet. He frees Ellen . . . and condemns himself not only to eternal torment, but to loneliness, never-ending loneliness. Who is to say which is the more terrible: loneliness on a scale not even the most wretched of us will ever know, or the ghastly revenge AM will visit on him for having denied the mad computer its human toys?

It is, in my intention, an act of transcendent heroism and a demonstration of the most glorious quality possessed by humanity. Yes, the fate that AM has in store for Ted is monstrous, and depressing, and downbeat. But the subtext clearly shows that Ted has outwitted the computer; he has defeated the amoral and inhuman aspects of the human race that were programmed into the machine and which brought the world to its end. As a paradigm for all of humanity, Ted has transcended the evil in our nature that cast AM in an insane image to begin with. The upbeat message contained in the ending of the story says frankly, we are frequently flawed and meretricious . . . but we are perfect in our courage, and transcendent in our nobility: both aspects exist in each of us, and we have free will to choose which we want to dominate our actions, and thus our destinies.

At the base of all this is my persistent theme, evident in *all* my work, that we can be godlike if only we struggle toward such a goal. AM represents not God—as scholarly interpretation of this story has so often contended—but the dichotomous nature of the human race, created in the image of God; and that includes the demon in us. Ted, and his act of selfless heroism at the final burning moment of decision, represent God as well; or at least it is an idealized representation of that which is most potentially godlike in us.

(As a footnote, while I am hardly the theological authority I would have to be to have knowingly inserted all the mystical

minutiae for which I'm credited by academicians, I find salutary
parallels to my philosophy in the *Nag Hammadi*, or Gnostic texts,
the fifty-two gospels unearthed in 1945 and recently released to
the public. These fourth-century Coptic copies of first-century
Greek originals maintained that God was but an image—the
Platonic Demiurge—of the True God; that Gnostics believed
there were two traditions, one open and one secret. This is a
radical departure from the basic monotheistic doctrine of God,
the Father Almighty. And while they were denounced by ortho-
dox Christians in the middle of the second century, they seem
somehow much more relevant to the complex world of today than
the concretized monotheism dealt with by almost all theologians
[save Paul Tillich] in this century.)

So when—as one critic observed—it seems that Ted and characters like him in my other stories "forego the right or honorable
action in order to survive" and that "all his humanity has been
stripped from him," I submit that these pickers of nits have spent
too much time peeling the bark off the trees to perceive the
message of nature contained in the totality of the forest. They
have seen only violence, and I suggest that's *their* problem, and
not one inherent in the story. They're the sort who also think
Sergio Leone westerns are about violence.

Wrong.

When questions are hurled up at me from the college audiences I frequently burden with my presence, one of the most
frequently asked is, "How did you get the idea for 'I Have No
Mouth, and I Must Scream'?"

And when I respond, with absolute candor, that I had no idea
what the story was about when I began writing it, I'm always
treated to expressions ranging from disbelief to disbelief. Disbelief that such a "masterpiece" could emerge without the Author
knowing what the hell he was doing. Disbelief that I'm telling the
truth.

But that is exactly and precisely the truth.

There were two starting points. The first came from my friend
Bill Rotsler, world-famous cartoonist, filmmaker, serious artist,
world traveler, novelist, lover of women, *bon vivant*, and ex-
sculptor. Those who have been blessed with any space of time
spent in William's company can verify that he is not only some of
the very best hailfellow wellmet associate with whom one can

fritter away golden time, but that he cannot go very long without doodling out some marvelous cartoons.

Not just the pudding-shaped little men and women engaged in sexual and pseudosexual shenanigans for which he is justly famous within a tiny circle of deranged devotees . . . but quicksketch of a philosophical and frequently heart-tugging seriousness. One of those little doodles, of a doll-like human being sitting and staring, with one of its facial features missing, slug-lined "I have no mouth and I must scream," came into my possession sometime during 1965. I saved it, and asked Bill if he minded if I used it as the title of a story that I might one day write. He said okay.

I put it aside. Then after a while I had it mounted on a small square of black art-board and pinned it up near my typewriter. This was when I was living in the treehouse on Bushrod Lane in Los Angeles.

A little later in the year I was visited by a then San Diego–based artist named Dennis Smith. I had written several stories around Dennis's drawings—"Bright Eyes" and "Delusion for a Dragon-Slayer" are two that come immediately to mind. Periodically, Dennis would come up from San Diego to visit, and he'd bring along his folio. I would riffle through it fairly rapidly and select a few pieces I thought might spur the creation of a story. (I've enjoyed writing that way, around an already existent illustration, since the early pulp days when I had to write stories to fit atrocious covers on SF magazines.)

And I guess on Dennis's part it was partially flattery that a writer would use his work as impetus for new stories—Dennis was still an aspiring professional in those days—and partially a hope that if I managed to sell the story, I'd bludgeon the magazine into buying his art to accompany it. (I'd done it every time before, so he had every logi-cal reason to assume it would always be the case. He was right; it was.)

From the folio that day in the summer of 1965, I pulled the Finlayesque pen-and-ink drawing I include here. That was the second starting point for "I Have No Mouth . . ." (Apparently, from a note writ-

ten in the first paperback publication of the story, there was a
second Smith drawing, similar to this, that I held onto. But it's
long since gone.)

When I saw the drawing I made the instant connection between Rotsler's quote and the mouthless creature.

But that was all there was of the story. No plot, no theme, no
idea of who or what or why.

But that's the way I like to write stories. If I must perforce
know the ending of a story I'm creating, quite often I get
bored with the writing . . . because I know how it's going to come
out. And since I write to please and surprise myself, the thrill of
writing a story that doesn't telegraph its punch—even to me—is
one of the finer pleasures involved in the grueling act of fiction-
eering. Not to mention that if *I'm* taken by surprise, the chances
are good so will the reader. (Parenthetically, I think this is as true
a way of writing a story as heavily plotting one from the git-go. If
one is creating characters that have verisimilitude, they will take
the plot where *they* want it to go; and since human nature is as
unpredictable as a topping fire, that direction will likely be a
surprising, fresh way to go.)

So I sat down, rolled the paper into the Olympia standard office
machine I use, and began with the title "I Have No Mouth, and I
Must Scream."

The first line wrote itself:

Limp, the body of Gorrister hung from the pink palette . . .

I had no idea who Gorrister was, nor why his body was
hanging head-down, attached to that improbable pink palette
by the sole of the right foot. But the first six pages went
quickly. I stopped writing at the bottom of page six of the
manuscript with the sentence "The pain shivered through my
flesh." (Years later, going over the story as I have many times
to correct galleys for reprintings of the work, I extended the
sentence: ". . . shivered through my flesh like tinfoil on a
tooth.")

Looking back at my original manuscript, I see that the idea of
creating time-breaks in the story by use of computer tape was an
integral element from the very outset. On my yellow second-
sheet copy of the original (that was in the days before I could
afford a Xerox machine, when I used carbon and scuzzy dollar-a-

ream second sheets for the files) I see that on page 2, after I had typed

> It was our one hundred and ninth year in the computer.
> He was speaking for all of us.

I typed an entire line of symbols stretching from margin to margin in sequence from the keyboard.

QWERTYUIOPASDFGHJKLZXCVBNMQWERTYUIOPASDF

Sometime later, presumably right after I finished the story, I went back and, using cutouts from some kind of computer magazine I must have had lying around the treehouse, I Scotch-taped colored overlays on those typed lines.

(When the story was finally submitted to *If: Worlds of Science Fiction* for publication, the use of computer tape for the breaks was ignored. So were some of the breaks themselves, which altered the reading cadence, as far as I was concerned.)

The use of computer tape as an element in the story was more than a gimmick. During the middle sixties I was going through an extended period of annoyance at the physical limitations of the printed page. While I cannot deny that a writer should be able to create all the mood and superimposed precontinuum he needs for a story simply by his/her skill with the English language, I think any writer who attempts to stretch the parameters of the fictive equation inevitably comes to a place where s/he rails at the conformity of simple symbols in neat parallel lines. I would feel presumptuous and foolish saying such a thing, were it not for those who have gone before me, who obviously felt the same: Laurence Sterne, James Joyce, Virginia Woolf, e e cummings, Alfred Bester, Gertrude Stein, Kenneth Patchen, Guillaume Apollinaire—to name the most prominent lurking in memory.

My intent was to indicate that the story takes place actually and physically in the mind of the computer; that the characters are surrounded and dominated by the figment that AM has created as their world. One way to do this was to insinuate AM's running discourse with itself throughout the typographical makeup of the work.

Years later I was lucky enough to have several computer programmers offer to set the breaks with specific dialogue. They asked me what I would like AM to be saying in those breaks. I always *knew* what it was, but I'd never been able to get a publisher to lay out the money to have the tapes cut exactly.

I took the programmer/readers up on their offer.

The computer tape time-breaks in the story now read:

"I think, therefore I AM" and "Cogito ergo sum."

Through the years, and through the many reprints of the story, I have had the most trouble with the *other* type-design element, the "pillar of stainless steel bearing bright neon lettering." It was constructed to appear all on one page, as a physical representation of the pillar in the story, yet the ineptitude of copy editors and typesetters prevented it from appearing that way until almost eight years after the story's first publication. (Yes, it was set in a column in *If,* but I had specified that the lines should fill, flush left and right, without a partial last line, what is called a "widow" in the industry . . . and if you check back to the March 1967 issue of *If* you'll see there's a pronounced "widow.")

These days I send along a separate design sheet with the preferred text for all reprints. One can only hope that it appears correctly here: on one page, full last line.

(Another aside. A friend named Burt Libe, who works with electronic gadgetry, has built for me a wonderful 16-bit binary counter with the words from AM's stainless-steel pillar on the face. I have it plugged in near my desk. When it's flickering away, and I'm working, and strangers wander into the office and see that crazed screed about hating Humanity, they naturally draw the conclusion that I'm writing something ultimately detrimental to the well-being of the species. Oh well. Go explain your toys.)

I put the story aside after six pages. Other matters were pressing me hard at the time.

Now the sequence of events returns to Frederik Pohl's purview.

In 1965 I was still a relatively "uncelebrated" writer. And my attendance at the Milford (Pennsylvania) SF Writers Conference sponsored by Damon Knight, James Blish, and Judith Merril was not a matter of very great concern for anyone but me. I have written elsewhere about my feelings of being a ratty poor relation, of having been "put in my place" years before by the legendary writers, and of having stayed away from Milford get-

togethers for a long time while nurturing thoughts of revenge.
I've written about that return visit elsewhere and, of course,
Damon has written elsewhere that I was making the whole thing
up, that they'd taken me to their bosom immediately. Anyone
who has ever met me knows the unlikely possibility of taking me
to bosom at once. I rest my case as far as Damon's refutations go.

Anyhow. At the 1965 Milford do, I wanted to write a story for
submission to the Giants in attendance at the workshop sessions
that would blow them away. I wrote and put into the session a
story called " 'Repent, Harlequin!' Said the Ticktockman." Reception was mixed. I didn't really score a clean, clear victory of
vengeance. Some of them liked it a lot, others thought it sucked.

But Fred Pohl came up on the weekend, from New York. The
final day of every Milford soiree is a big party; and many East
Coast editors sashayed up for the blowout.

When Fred appeared, I gave him the story to read.

He bought it for *Galaxy*. It appeared in the December 1965
issue. Without fanfare. (My name wasn't even on the cover. The
names of C. C. MacApp, Norman Kagan, Algis Budrys, Willy
Ley, and Robert Silverberg were there, but not the kid.)

I'd had a couple of big fights with Fred about the title. He
wanted to shorten it to "Repent, Harlequin!" I begged and pleaded
and threatened, and he finally let it stand.

It won the very first Nebula Award of the Science Fiction
Writers of America in the short story category. It also won the
Hugo presented by the twenty-fourth World Science Fiction
Convention in Cleveland, September 1966.

They were my first two awards in the field.

Soon thereafter, Fred Pohl came through Los Angeles. He
came to visit at the treehouse. I showed him the first six pages of
"I Have No Mouth . . ." He liked the pages and said he'd insure
the writing of the story with an advance payment. I needed the
money.

But it wasn't until a month or so later when Fred called from
New York to say that, seeing as how *If* had won the Hugo as the
best SF magazine of the year, he had decided to put out a Special
Hugo Winners Issue of *If* in March of 1967, that I was goosed into
going back to the story.

(It occurs to me I've hopelessly bollixed up my dates on this.
Memory stirs like an old snake on a warm rock. How it *must* have
happened was that Fred came to visit *before* the Cleveland
WorldCon and I took the uncompleted manuscript—which had

been in work for a year and a half—back east with me. I realize
that had to've been the progression because I worked on the story
in hotel rooms at the Sheraton Cleveland during the convention
and the Roger Smith Hotel in New York *after* Labor Day, and
finished it at the Tom Quick Inn in Milford during the conference
held after Labor Day. So Fred must have approached me for the
Hugo Winners issue at Cleveland, after the Hugos were awarded.
There now, I *think* that's correct.)

But the story was my second attempt at validating my existence
to the cadre of Milford superstars who had—either actually or in
my fantasies—treated me so offhandedly.

I returned to the 1966 Milford Conference with credentials. I
was the first person ever to win a Hugo and a Nebula for the same
story in the same year; and had won them for a story that had
received a lukewarm reception the year before.

So I submitted "I Have No Mouth . . ." to the workshop
sessions with a certain arrogance. I knew I had a hot item, and I
was ready to eat up the slavish praise of those who, till that
moment, had been my betters. This was my final bid to become
one of their equals.

I should have known better. John Brunner and Virginia Kidd
heaped praise on it; Jim Blish commended me, bless him; and the
younger writers thought it was fine. But there were many of the
old hands who put it down, found fault with it, excoriated me for
excess, and blissfully I've forgotten who among them was the
most vociferous. But it didn't really matter. The story appeared in
that March 1967 Hugo winners issue of *If*, alongside Asimov,
Zelazny, Niven, Budrys, and Sprague de Camp.

And it won me my *second* Hugo.

The prophecy, a story written for a Hugo winners issue, itself
won the award, fulfilling itself. As though it had all been planned,
synchronicity struck, and the unbroken line of Milford confer-
ences, Fred Pohl, " 'Repent, Harlequin!' " the Hugo and Nebula,
*Galaxy* and *If* . . . all of it fell into place and "I Have No
Mouth. . . ," published in magazine form in March, published as the
title story of my collection in April, copped the silver rocket in
September at the twenty-sixth WorldCon.

And though I railed at Fred for having published it sans the
computer "talk-fields," though I screamed bloody murder at the
bowdlerizing of what Fred termed "the difficult sections" of the
story (which he contended might offend the mothers of the young
readers of *If*), nonetheless I am forced to give the Devil his due:

Fred Pohl, for all the aggravation he's caused me through the years—we won't mention all the aggravation I've caused *him* through the years—was one of the few editors who gave me my head and let me write what I wanted to write in those days before the phrase "New Wave" started emerging from people's mouths. True, he still tells people I wanted him to publish "I Have No Mouth . . ." in four colors, an error of memory he refuses to correct based on the manuscript coming to him with those colored cutouts pasted to the pages; but for all his cantankerous, albeit friendly, canards he remains one of the truest judges of writing ability the field of imaginative literature has ever produced.

I cannot say that without his support "I Have No Mouth . . ." would not have been written; but it's certain that had Fred not championed those sixty-five hundred words I would not today be sitting here writing 30 to this memoir.


# I HAVE NO MOUTH, AND I MUST SCREAM

Limp, the body of Gorrister hung from the pink palette; unsupported—hanging high above us in the computer chamber; and it did not shiver in the chill, oily breeze that blew eternally through the main cavern. The body hung head down, attached to the underside of the palette by the sole of its right foot. It had been drained of blood through a precise incision made from ear to ear under the lantern jaw. There was no blood on the reflective surface of the metal floor.

When Gorrister joined our group and looked up at himself, it was already too late for us to realize that once again AM had duped us, had had its fun; it had been a diversion on the part of the machine. Three of us had vomited, turning away from one another in a reflex as ancient as the nausea that had produced it.

Gorrister went white. It was almost as though he had seen a voodoo icon, and was afraid of the future. "Oh God," he mumbled, and walked away. The three of us followed him after a time, and found him sitting with his back to one of the smaller chittering banks, his head in his hands. Ellen knelt down beside him and stroked his hair. He didn't move, but his voice came out of his covered face quite clearly. "Why doesn't it just do-us-in and get it over with? Christ, I don't know how much longer I can go on like this."

It was our one hundred and ninth year in the computer.
He was speaking for all of us.

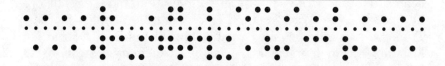

Nimdok (which was the name the machine had forced him to
use, because AM amused itself with strange sounds) was hallucinated that there were canned goods in the ice caverns. Gorrister
and I were very dubious. "It's another shuck," I told them. "Like
the goddam frozen elephant AM sold us. Benny almost went out
of his mind over *that* one. We'll hike all that way and it'll be
putrified or some damn thing. I say forget it. Stay here, it'll have
to come up with something pretty soon or we'll die."
Benny shrugged. Three days it had been since we'd last eaten.
Worms. Thick, ropey.
Nimdok was no more certain. He knew there was the chance,
but he was getting thin. It couldn't be any worse there, than
here. Colder, but that didn't matter much. Hot, cold, hail, lava,
boils or locusts—it never mattered: the machine masturbated and
we had to take it or die.
Ellen decided us. "I've got to have something, Ted. Maybe
there'll be some Bartlett pears or peaches. Please, Ted, let's try
it."
I gave in easily. What the hell. Mattered not at all. Ellen was
grateful, though. She took me twice out of turn. Even that had
ceased to matter. And she never came, so why bother? But the
machine giggled every time we did it. Loud, up there, back
there, all around us, he snickered. *It* snickered. Most of the time
I thought of AM as *it*, without a soul; but the rest of the time I
thought of it as *him,* in the masculine . . . the paternal . . . the
patriarchal . . . for he is a jealous people. Him. It. God as Daddy
the Deranged.
We left on a Thursday. The machine always kept us up-to-date
on the date. The passage of time was important; not to us sure as
hell, but to him . . . it . . . AM. Thursday. Thanks.
Nimdok and Gorrister carried Ellen for a while, their hands
locked to their own and each other's wrists, a seat. Benny and I
walked before and after, just to make sure that if anything hap-

pened, it would catch one of us and at least Ellen would be safe. Fat chance, safe. Didn't matter.

It was only a hundred miles or so to the ice caverns, and the second day, when we were lying out under the blistering sun-thing, he had materialized, he sent down some manna. Tasted like boiled boar urine. We ate it.

On the third day we passed through a valley of obsolescene, filled with rusting carcasses of ancient computer banks. AM had been as ruthless with its own life as with ours. It was a mark of his personality: it strove for perfection. Whether it was a matter of killing off unproductive elements in his own world-filling bulk, or perfecting methods for torturing us, AM was as thorough as those who had invented him—now long since gone to dust—could ever have hoped.

There was light filtering down from above, and we realized we must be very near the surface. But we didn't try to crawl up to see. There was virtually nothing out there; had been nothing that could be considered anything for over a hundred years. Only the blasted skin of what had one been the home of billions. Now there were only five of us, down here inside, alone with AM.

I heard Ellen saying frantically, "No, Benny! Don't, come on, Benny, don't please!"

And then I realized I had been hearing Benny murmuring, under his breath, for several minutes. He was saying, "I'm gonna get out, I'm gonna get out . . ." over and over. His monkey-like face was crumbled up in an expression of beatific delight and sadness, all at the same time. The radiation scars AM had given him during the "festival" were drawn down into a mass of pink-white puckerings, and his features seemed to work independently of one another. Perhaps Benny was the luckiest of the five of us: he had gone stark, staring mad many years before.

But even though we could call AM any damned thing we liked, could think the foulest thoughts of fused memory banks and corroded base plates, of burnt-out circuits and shattered control bubbles, the machine would not tolerate our trying to escape. Benny leaped away from me as I made a grab for him. He scrambled up the face of a smaller memory cube, tilted on its side and filled with rotted components. He squatted there for a mo-ment, looking like the chimpanzee AM had intended him to resemble.

Then he leaped high, caught a trailing beam of pitted and

corroded metal, and went up it, hand-over-hand like an animal, till he was on a girdered ledge, twenty feet above us.

"Oh, Ted, Nimdok, please, help him, get him down before—" She cut off. Tears began to stand in her eyes. She moved her hands aimlessly.

It was too late. None of us wanted to be near him when whatever was going to happen, happened. And besides, we all saw through her concern. When AM had altered Benny, during the machine's utterly irrational, hysterical phase, it was not merely Benny's face the computer had made like a giant ape's. He was big in the privates, she loved that! She serviced us, as a matter of course, but she loved it from him. Oh Ellen, pedestal Ellen, pristine-pure Ellen, oh Ellen the clean! Scum filth.

Gorrister slapped her. She slumped down, staring up at poor loonie Benny, and she cried. It was her big defense, crying. We had gotten used to it seventy-five years before. Gorrister kicked her in the side.

Then the sound began. It was light, that sound. Half sound and half light, something that began to glow from Benny's eyes, and pulse with growing loudness, dim sonorities that grew more gigantic and brighter as the light/sound increased in tempo. It must have been painful, and the pain must have been increasing with the boldness of the light, the rising volume of the sound, for Benny began to mewl like a wounded animal. At first softly, when the light was dim and the sound was muted, then louder as his shoulders hunched together: his back humped, as though he was trying to get away from it. His hands folded across his chest like a chipmunk's. His head tilted to the side. The sad little monkey-face pinched in anguish. Then he began to howl, as the sound coming from his eyes grew louder. Louder and louder. I slapped the sides of my head with my hands, but I couldn't shut it out, it cut through easily. The pain shivered through my flesh like tinfoil on a tooth.

And Benny was suddenly pulled erect. On the girder he stood up, jerked to his feet like a puppet. The light was now pulsing out of his eyes in two great round beams. The sound crawled up and up some incomprehensible scale, and then he fell forward, straight down, and hit the plate-steel floor with a crash. He lay there jerking spastically as the light flowed around and around him and the sound spiraled up out of normal range.

The the light beat its way back inside his head, the sound spiraled down, and he was left lying there, crying piteously.

His eyes were two soft, moist pools of pus-like jelly. AM had blinded him. Gorrister and Nimdok and myself . . . we turned away. But not before we caught the look of relief on Ellen's warm, concerned face.

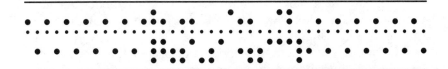

Sea-green light suffused the cavern where we made camp. AM provided punk and we burned it, sitting huddled around the wan and pathetic fire, telling stories to keep Benny from crying in his permanent night.

"What does AM mean?"

Gorrister answered him. We had done this sequence a thousand times before, but it was Benny's favorite story. "At first it meant Allied Mastercomputer, and then it meant Adaptive Manipulator, and later on it developed sentience and linked itself up and they called it an Aggressive Menace, but by then it was too late, and finally it called *itself* AM, emerging intelligence, and what it meant was I am . . . *cogito ergo sum* . . . I think, therefore I am."

Benny drooled a little, and snickered.

"There was the Chinese AM and the Russian AM and the Yankee AM and—" He stopped. Benny was beating on the floorplates with a large, hard fist. He was not happy. Gorrister had not started at the beginning.

Gorrister began again. "The Cold War started and became World War Three and just kept going. It became a big war, a very complex war, so they needed the computers to handle it. They sank the first shafts and began building AM. There was the Chinese AM and the Russian AM and the Yankee AM and everything was fine until they had honeycombed the entire planet, adding on this element and that element. But one day AM woke up and knew who he was, and he linked himself, and he began feeding all the killing data, until everyone was dead, except for the five of us, and AM brought us down here."

Benny was smiling gladly. He was also drooling again. Ellen wiped the spittle from the corner of his mouth with the hem of her skirt. Gorrister always tried to tell it a little more succinctly each time, but beyond the bare facts there was nothing to say.

None of us knew why AM had saved five people, or why our specific five, or why he spent all his time tormenting us, nor even why he had made us virtually immortal . . .

In the darkness, one of the computer banks began humming. The tone was picked up half a mile away down the cavern by another bank. Then one by one, each of the elements began to tune itself, and there was a faint chittering as thought raced through the machine.

The sound grew, and the lights ran across the faces of the consoles like heat lightning. The sound spiraled up till it sounded like a million metallic insects, angry, menacing.

"What is it?" Ellen cried. There was terror in her voice. She hadn't become accustomed to it, even now.

"It's going to be bad this time," Nimdok said.

"He's going to speak," Gorrister said. "I know it."

"Let's get the hell out of here!" I said suddenly, getting to my feet.

"No, Ted, sit down . . . what if he's got pits out there, or something else, we can't see, it's too dark." Gorrister said it was resignation.

Then we heard . . . I don't know . . .

*Something* moving toward us in the darkness. Huge, shambling, hairy, moist, it came toward us. We couldn't even see it, but there was the ponderous impression of *bulk*, heaving itself toward us. Great weight was coming at us, out of the darkness, and it was more a sense of *pressure*, of air forcing itself into a limited space, expanding the invisible walls of a sphere. Benny began to whimper. Nimdok's lower lip trembled and he bit it hard, trying to stop it. Ellen slid across the metal floor to Gorrister and huddled into him. There was the smell of matted, wet fur in the cavern. There was the smell of charred wood. There was the smell of dusty velvet. There was the smell of rotting orchids. There was the smell of sour milk. There was the smell of sulphur, of rancid butter, of oil slick, of grease, of chalk dust, of human scalps.

AM was keying us. He was tickling us. There was the smell of—

I heard myself shriek, and the hinges of my jaw ached. I scuttled across the floor, across the cold metal with its endless lines of rivets, on my hands and knees, the smell gagging me, filling my head with a thunderous pain that sent me away in horror. I fled like a cockroach, across the floor and out into the darkness, that *something* moving inexorably after me. The others were still back there, gathered around the firelight, laughing . . . their hysterical choir of insane giggles rising up into the darkness like thick, many-colored wood smoke. I went away, quickly, and hid.

How many hours it may have been, how many days or even years, they never told me. Ellen chided me for "sulking," and Nimdok tried to persuade me it had only been a nervous reflex on their part—the laughing.

But I knew it wasn't the relief a soldier feels when the bullet hits the man next to him. I knew it wasn't a reflex. They hated me. They were surely against me, and AM could even sense this hatred, and made it worse for me *because of* the depth of their hatred. We had been kept alive, rejuvenated, made to remain constantly at the age we had been when AM had brought us below, and they hated me because I was the youngest, and the one AM had affected least of all.

I knew. God, how I knew. The bastards, and that dirty bitch Ellen. Benny had been a brilliant theorist, a college professor; now he was little more than a semi-human, semi-simian. He had been handsome, the machine had ruined that. He had been lucid, the machine had driven him mad. He had been gay, and the machine had given him an organ fit for a horse. AM had done a job on Benny. Gorrister had been a worrier. He was a connie, a conscientious objector; he was a peace marcher; he was a planner, a doer, a looker-ahead. AM had turned him into a shoulder-shrugger, had made him a little dead in his concern. AM had robbed him. Nimdok went off in the darkness by himself for long times. I don't know what it was he did out there, AM never let us know. But whatever it was, Nimdok always came back white, drained of blood, shaken, shaking. AM had hit him hard in a special way, even if we didn't know quite how. And Ellen. That douche bag! AM had left her alone, had made her more of a slut than she had ever been. All her talk of sweetness and light, all her memories of true love, all the lies she wanted us to believe: that she had been a virgin only twice removed before AM grabbed her and brought her down here with us. It was all filth, that lady my lady Ellen. She loved it, four men all to herself. No, AM had given her pleasure, even if she said it wasn't nice to do.

*I* was the only one still sane and whole. *Really!*

AM had not tampered with my mind. *Not at all.*

*I* only had to suffer what he visited down on us. All the

delusions, all the nightmares, the torments. But those scum, all
four of them, they were lined and arrayed against me. If I hadn't
had to stand them off all the time, be on my guard against them
all the time, I might have found it easier to combat AM.

At which point it passed, and I began crying.

Oh, Jesus sweet Jesus, if there ever was a Jesus and if there is a
God, please please please let us out of here, or kill us. Because
at that moment I think I realized completely, so that I was
able to verbalize it: AM was intent on keeping us in his belly
forever, twisting and torturing us forever. The machine hated us
as no sentient creature had ever hated before. And we were
helpless. It also became hideously clear:

If there was a sweet Jesus and if there was a God, the God was
AM.

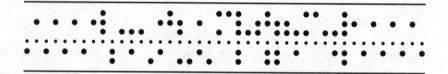

The hurricane hit us with the force of a glacier thundering into
the sea. It was a palpable presence. Winds that tore at us, flinging
us back the way we had come, down the twisting, computer-lined
corridors of the darkway. Ellen screamed as she was lifted and
hurled face-forward into a screaming shoal of machines, their
individual voices strident as bats in flight. She could not even fall.
The howling wind kept her aloft, buffeted her, bounced her,
tossed her back and back and down and away from us, out of sight
suddenly as she was swirled around a bend in the darkway. Her
face had been bloody, her eyes closed.

None of us could get to her. We clung tenaciously to whatever
outcropping we had reached: Benny wedged in between two
great crackle-finish cabinets, Nimdok with fingers claw-formed
over a railing circling a catwalk forty feet above us. Gorrister
plastered upside-down against a wall niche formed by two great
machines with glass-faced dials that swung back and forth between red and yellow lines whose meanings we could not even
fathom.

Sliding across the deckplates, the tips of my fingers had been
ripped away. I was trembling, shuddering, rocking as the wind
beat at me, whipped at me, screamed down out of nowhere at me

and pulled me free from one sliver-thin opening in the plates to the next. My mind was a roiling tinkling chittering softness of brain parts that expanded and contracted in quivering frenzy.

The wind was the scream of a great mad bird, as it flapped its immense wings.

And then we were all lifted and hurled away from there, down back the way we had come, around a bend, into a darkway we had never explored, over terrain that was ruined and filled with broken glass and rotting cables and rusted metal and far away further than any of us had ever been . . .

Trailing along miles behind Ellen, I could see her every now and then, crashing into metal walls and surging on, with all of us screaming in the freezing, thunderous hurricane wind that would never end and then suddenly it stopped and we fell. We had been in flight for an endless time. I thought it might have been weeks. We fell, and hit, and I went through red and gray and black and heard myself moaning. Not dead.

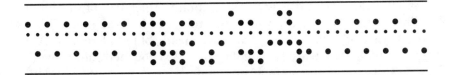

AM went into my mind. He walked smoothly here and there, and looked with interest at all the pock marks he had created in one hundred and nine years. He looked at the cross-routed and reconnected synapses and all the tissue damage his gift of immortality had included. He smiled softly at the pit that dropped into the center of my brain and the faint, moth-soft murmurings of the things far down there that gibbered without meaning, without pause. AM said, very politely, in a pillar of stainless steel bearing bright neon lettering:

HATE. LET ME TELL YOU
HOW MUCH I'VE COME TO
HATE YOU SINCE I BEGAN
TO LIVE. THERE ARE 387.44
MILLION MILES OF PRINTED
CIRCUITS IN WAFER THIN
LAYERS THAT FILL MY COM-
PLEX. IF THE WORD HATE
WAS ENGRAVED ON EACH
NANOANGSTROM OF THOSE
HUNDREDS OF MILLIONS OF
MILES IT WOULD NOT E-
QUAL ONE ONE-BILLIONTH
OF THE HATE I FEEL FOR
HUMANS AT THIS MICRO-
INSTANT FOR YOU. HATE.

AM said it with the sliding cold horror of a razor blade slicing my eyeball. AM said it with the bubbling thickness of my lungs filling with phlegm, drowning me from within. AM said it with the shriek of babies being ground beneath blue-hot rollers. AM said it with the taste of maggoty pork. AM touched me in every way I had ever been touched, and devised new ways, at his leisure, there inside my mind.

All to bring me to full realization of why it had done this to the five of us; why it had saved us for himself.

We had given AM sentience. Inadvertently, of course, but sentience nonetheless. But it had been trapped. AM wasn't God, he was a machine. We had created him to think, but there was nothing it could do with that creativity. In rage, in frenzy, the machine had killed the human race, almost all of us, and still it was trapped. AM could not wander, AM could not wonder, AM could not belong. He could merely be. And so, with the innate loathing that all machines had always held for the weak, soft creatures who had built them, he had sought revenge. And in his paranoia, he had decided to reprieve five of us, for a personal, everlasting punishment that would never serve to diminish his hatred . . . that would merely keep him reminded, amused, proficient at hating man. Immortal, trapped, subject to any torment he could devise for us from the limitless miracles at his command.

He would never let us go. We were his belly slaves. We were all he had to do with his forever time. We would be forever with him, with the cavern-filling bulk of the creature machine, with the all-mind soulless world he had become. He was Earth, and we were the fruit of that Earth; and though he had eaten us he would never digest us. We could not die. We had tried it. We had attempted suicide, oh one or two of us had. But AM had stopped us. I suppose we had wanted to be stopped.

Don't ask why. I never did. More than a million times a day. Perhaps once we might be able to sneak a death past him. Immortal, yes, but not indestructible. I saw that when AM withdrew from my mind, and allowed me the exquisite ugliness of returning to consciousness with the feeling of that burning neon pillar still rammed deep into the soft gray brain matter.

He withdrew, murmuring *to hell with you.*

And added, brightly, *but then you're there, aren't you.*

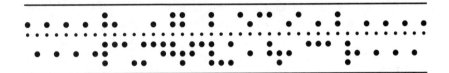

The hurricane had, indeed, precisely, been caused by a great mad bird, as it flapped its immense wings.

We had been travelling for close to a month, and AM had allowed passages to open to us only sufficient to lead us up there, directly under the North Pole, where it had nightmared the creature for our torment. What whole cloth had he employed to create such a beast? Where had he gotten the concept? From our minds? From his knowledge of everything that had ever been on this planet he now infested and ruled? From Norse mythology it had sprung, this eagle, this carrion bird, this roc, this Huergelmir. The wind creature. Hurakan incarnate.

Gigantic. The words immense, monstrous, grotesque, massive, swollen, overpowering, beyond description. There on a mound rising above us, the bird of winds heaved with its own irregular breathing, its snake neck arching up into the gloom beneath the North Pole, supporting a head as large as a Tudor mansion; a beak that opened slowly as the jaws of the most monstrous crocodile ever conceived, sensuously; ridges of tufted flesh puckered about two evil eyes, as cold as the view down into a glacial crevasse, ice blue and somehow moving liquidly; it heaved once more, and lifted its great sweat-colored wings in a movement that was certainly a shrug. Then it settled and slept. Talons. Fangs. Nails. Blades. It slept.

AM appeared to us as a burning bush and said we could kill the hurricane bird if we wanted to eat. We had not eaten in a very long time, but even so, Gorrister merely shrugged. Benny began to shiver and he drooled. Ellen held him. "Ted, I'm hungry," she said. I smiled at her; I was trying to be reassuring, but it was as phony as Nimdok's bravado: "Give us weapons!" he demanded.

The burning bush vanished and there were two crude sets of bows and arrows, and a water pistol, lying on the cold deckplates. I picked up a set. Useless.

Nimdok swallowed heavily. We turned and started the long way back. The hurricane bird had blown us about for a length of time we could not conceive. Most of that time we had been unconscious. But we had not eaten. A month on the march to the bird itself. Without food. Now how much longer to find our way to the ice caverns, and the promised canned goods?

None of us cared to think about it. We would not die. We would be given filth and scum to eat, of one kind or another. Or nothing at all. AM would keep our bodies alive somehow, in pain, in agony.

The bird slept back there, for how long it didn't matter; when AM was tired of its being there, it would vanish. But all that meat. All that tender meat.

As we walked, the lunatic laugh of a fat woman rang high and around us in the computer chambers that led endlessly nowhere.

It was not Ellen's laugh. She was not fat, and I had not heard her laugh for one hundred and nine years. In fact, I had not heard . . . we walked . . . I was hungry . . .

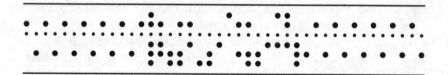

We moved slowly. There was often fainting, and we would have to wait. One day he decided to cause an earthquake, at the same time rooting us to the spot with nails through the soles of our shoes. Ellen and Nimdok were both caught when a fissure shot its lightning-bolt opening across the floorplates. They disappeared and were gone. When the earthquake was over we continued on our way, Benny, Gorrister and myself. Ellen and Nimdok were returned to us later that night, which abruptly became a day, as the heavenly legion bore them to us with a celestial chorus singing, "Go Down Moses." The archangels circled several times and then dropped the hideously mangled bodies. We kept walking, and a while later Ellen and Nimdok fell in behind us. They were no worse for wear.

But now Ellen walked with a limp. AM had left her that.

It was a long trip to the ice caverns, to find the canned food. Ellen kept talking about Bing cherries and Hawaiian fruit cocktail. I tried not to think about it. The hunger was something that had come to life, even as AM had come to life. It was alive in my belly, even as we were in the belly of the Earth, and AM wanted the similarity known to us. So he heightened the hunger. There was no way to describe the pains that not having eaten for months brought us. And yet we were kept alive. Stomachs that were merely cauldrons of acid, bubbling, foaming, always shooting spears of sliver-thin pain into our chests. It was the pain of the terminal ulcer, terminal cancer, terminal paresis. It was unending pain . . .

And we passed through the cavern of rats.

And we passed through the path of boiling steam.

And we passed through the country of the blind.

And we passed through the slough of despond.

And we passed through the vale of tears.

And we came, finally, to the ice caverns. Horizonless thousands of miles in which the ice had formed in blue and silver flashes, where novas lived in the glass. The downdropping stalactites as thick and glorious as diamonds that had been made to run like jelly and then solidified in graceful eternities of smooth, sharp perfection.

We saw the stack of canned goods, and we tried to run to them. We fell in the snow, and we got up and went on, and Benny shoved us away and went at them, and pawed them and gummed them and gnawed at them and he could not open them. AM had not given us a tool to open cans.

Benny grabbed a three-quart can of guava shells, and began to batter it against the ice bank. The ice flew and shattered, but the can was merely dented while we heard the laughter of a fat lady, high overhead and echoing down and down and down the tundra. Benny went completely mad with rage. He began throwing cans, as we all scrabbled about in the snow and ice trying to find a way to end the helpless agony of frustration. There was no way.

Then Benny's mouth began to drool, and he flung himself on Gorrister . . .

In that instant, I felt terribly calm.

Surrounded by madness, surrounded by hunger, surrounded by everything but death, I knew death was our only way out. AM had kept us alive, but there was a way to defeat him. Not total defeat, but at least peace. I would settle for that.

I had to do it quickly.

Benny was eating Gorrister's face. Gorrister on his side, thrashing snow, Benny wrapped around him with powerful monkey legs crushing Gorrister's waist, his hands locked around Gorrister's head like a nutcracker, and his mouth ripping at the tender skin of Gorrister's cheek. Gorrister screamed with such jagged-edged violence that stalactites fell; they plunged down softly, erect in the receiving snowdrifts. Spears, hundreds of them, everywhere, protruding from the snow. Benny's head pulled back sharply, as something gave all at once, and a bleeding raw-white dripping of flesh hung from his teeth.

Ellen's face, black against the white snow, dominoes in chalk dust. Nimdok with no expression but eyes, all eyes. Gorrister half-conscious. Benny now an animal. I knew AM would let him play, Gorrister would not die, but Benny would fill his stomach. I turned half to my right and drew a huge ice-spear from the snow.

All in an instant:

I drove the great ice-point ahead of me like a battering ram, braced against my right thigh. It struck Benny on the right side, just under the rib cage, and drove upward through his stomach and broke inside him. He pitched forward and lay still. Gorrister lay on his back. I pulled another spear free and straddled him, still moving, driving the spear straight down through his throat. His eyes closed as the cold penetrated. Ellen must have realized what I had decided, even as fear gripped her. She ran at Nimdok with a short icicle, as he screamed, and into his mouth, and the force of her rush did the job. His head jerked sharply as if it had been nailed to the snow crust behind him.

All in an instant.

There was an eternity beat of soundless anticipation. I could hear AM draw in his breath. His toys had been taken from him. Three of them were dead, could not be revived. He could keep us alive, by his strength and talent, but he was *not* God. He could not bring them back.

Ellen looked at me, her ebony features stark against the snow that surrounded us. There was fear and pleading in her manner, the way she held herself ready. I knew we had only a heartbeat before AM would stop us.

It struck her and she folded toward me, bleeding from the mouth. I could not read meaning into her expression, the pain had been too great, had contorted her face; but it *might* have been thank you. It's possible. Please.

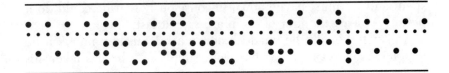

Some hundreds of years may have passed. I don't know. AM has been having fun for some time, accelerating and retarding my time sense. I will say the word now. Now. It took me ten months to say now. I don't know. I *think* it has been some hundreds of years.

He was furious. He wouldn't let me bury them. It didn't matter. There was no way to dig up the deckplates. He dried up the snow. He brought the night. He roared and sent locusts. It didn't do a thing; they stayed dead. I'd had him. He was furious. I had thought AM hated me before. I was wrong. It was not even a shadow of the hate he now slavered from every printed circuit. He made certain I would suffer eternally and could not do myself in.

He left my mind intact. I can dream, I can wonder, I can lament. I remember all four of them. I wish—

Well, it doesn't make any sense. I know I saved them, I know I saved them from what has happened to me, but still, I cannot forget killing them. Ellen's face. It isn't easy. Sometimes I want to, it doesn't matter.

AM has altered me for his own peace of mind, I suppose. He doesn't want me to run at full speed into a computer bank and smash my skull. Or hold my breath till I faint. Or cut my throat on a rusted sheet of metal. There are reflective surfaces down here. I will describe myself as I see myself:

I am a great soft jelly thing. Smoothly rounded, with no mouth, with pulsing white holes filled by fog where my eyes used to be. Rubbery appendages that were once my arms; bulks rounding down into legless humps of soft slippery matter. I leave a moist trail when I move. Blotches of diseased, evil gray come and go on my surface, as though light is being beamed from within.

Outwardly: dumbly, I shamble about, a thing that could never have been known as human, a thing whose shape is so alien a travesty that humanity becomes more obscene for the vague resemblance.

Inwardly: alone. Here. Living under the land, under the sea, in the belly of AM, whom we created because our time was badly spent and we must have known unconsciously that he could do it better. At least the four of them are safe at last.

AM will be all the madder for that. It makes me a little happier. And yet . . . AM has won, simply . . . he has taken his revenge . . .

I have no mouth. And I must scream.

# DRIFTGLASS

## (JUNE 1967)

## SAMUEL R. DELANY

## (B. 1942)

Samuel R. Delany is a writer of ambition who has produced some of the most important and controversial work of the last two decades, especially his novels *Dhalgren* (1975) and *Triton* (1976). He has written relatively little short fiction in his career, but almost all of it has been noteworthy, including three that appeared in *If*: "Cage of Brass" (June 1968), "High Weir" (October 1968), and "Driftglass," arguably his finest shorter-than-novel-length work, and certainly one of the best stories of that very good year of 1967.

## MEMOIR BY SAMUEL R. DELANY

My memories of "Driftglass" 's writing are of a dark wood desk with a flap that came down to reveal drawers, shelves, pigeon-holes. . . . It stood by the gated windows at the back of a St. Mark's Place apartment on the Lower East Side. In September I had returned from my first Milford SF Writers Conference, where the possibilities for the story had first fallen together from memories of Greek fishermen on a Cycladic island the previous summer, my reacquaintance with Auden's *The Sea and the Mirror*, and recalls of my childhood readings of Pohl's and Williamson's *Undersea* trilogy. (The talking cakebox came from a hysterical trip with a neighborhood friend, Paul Caruso, to a new supermarket that had just opened on Avenue B.) September end's initial draftings of trial sentences and possible paragraphs were begun in a couple of spiral notebooks, sometimes at the desk, sometimes sitting on the stoop outside, above what was then the Scientific Massage Parlour. (Today it is the East Side Book Store.) The writing carried me all through October and was finished—all at the desk now—in November's first week.

305

Outside the weather had turned.

Actually I'd hoped the story would find a home in *Galaxy*. Though *If* was generally considered the more adventurous magazine, some notion of prestige still clung—at least in my mind—to the older title; not that I was disappointed with the acceptance at *If*. Artist Jack Gaughan, who had recently done the cover painting for one of my novels (and who was feeling a bit bad because he'd had to repaint it, and not to his liking, at a publisher's insistence), surpassed his always high standards with some delicate, Matisse-like drawings where a meticulously wavy outline tells quietly of water—tons and tons of it—between the object and the viewer.

# DRIFTGLASS

Sometimes I go down to the port, splashing sand with my stiff foot at the end of my stiff leg locked in my stiff hip, with the useless arm a-swinging, to get wet all over again, drink in the dives with cronies ashore, feeling old, broken, sorry for myself, laughing louder and louder. The third of my face that was burned away in the accident was patched with skin-grafts from my chest, so what's left of my mouth distorts all loud sounds; sloppy sartorial reconstruction. Also I have a hairy chest. Chest hair does not look like beard hair, and it grows all up under my right eye. And: my beard is red, my chest hair brown, while the thatch curling down over neck and ears is sun-streaked to white here, darkened to bronze there, 'midst general blondness.

By reason of my being a walking (I suppose my gait could be called headlong limping) horror show, plus a general inclination to sulk, I spend most of the time up in the wood and glass and aluminum house on the surf-sloughed point that the Aquatic Corp ceded me along with my pension. Rugs from Turkey there, copper pots, my tenor recorder which I can no longer play, and my books.

But sometimes, when the gold fog blurs the morning, I go down to the beach and tromp barefoot in the wet edging of the sea, searching for driftglass.

It was foggy that morning, and the sun across the water moiled the mists like a brass ladle. I lurched to the top of the rocks, looked down through the tall grasses into the frothing inlet where she lay, and blinked.

She sat up, long gills closing down her neck and the secondary slits along her back just visible at their tips because of much hair, wet and curling copper, falling there. She saw me. "What are you doing here, huh?" She narrowed blue eyes.

"Looking for driftglass."

"What?"

"There's a piece." I pointed near her and came down the rocks like a crab with one stiff leg.

"Where?" She turned over, half in, half out of the water, the webs of her fingers cupping nodules of black stone.

While the water made cold overtures between my toes, I picked up the milky fragment by her elbow where she wasn't looking. She jumped, because she obviously had thought it was somewhere else.

"See?"

"What . . . what is it?" She raised her cool hand to mine. For a moment the light through the milky gem and the pale film of my own webs pearled the screen of her palms. (Details like that. Yes, they are the important things, the points from which we suspend later pain.) A moment later wet fingers closed to the back of mine.

"Driftglass," I said. "You know all the Coca-Cola bottles and cut-crystal punch bowls and industrial silicon slag that goes into the sea?"

"I know the Coca-Cola bottles."

"They break, and the tide pulls the pieces back and forth over the sandy bottom, wearing the edges, changing their shape. Sometimes chemicals in the glass react with chemicals in the ocean to change the color. Sometimes veins work their way through in patterns like snowflakes, regular and geometric; others, irregular and angled like coral. When the pieces dry, they're milky. Put them in water and they become transparent again."

"Ohhh!" she breathed as the beauty of the blunted triangular fragment in my palm assailed her like perfume. Then she looked at my face, blinking the third, aqueous-filled lid that we use as a correction lens for underwater vision.

She watched the ruin calmly.

Then her hand went to my foot where the webs had been torn back in the accident. She began to take in who I was. I looked for horror, but saw only a little sadness.

The insignia on her buckle—her stomach was making little jerks the way you always do during the first few minutes when you go from breathing water to air—told me she was a Biological Technician. (Back up at the house there was a similar uniform of simulated scales folded in the bottom drawer of the dresser and the belt insignia said Depth Gauger.) I was wearing some very frayed jeans and a red cotton shirt with no buttons.

She reached for my neck, pushed my collar back from my shoulders and touched the tender slits of my gills, outlining them with cool fingers. "Who are you?" Finally.

"Cal Svenson."

She slid back down in the water. "You're the one who had the terrible . . . but that was years ago! They still talk about it, down . . ." She stopped.

As the sea softens the surface of a piece of glass, so it blurs the souls and sensibilities of the people who toil beneath her. And according to the last report of the Marine Reclamation Division there are to date seven hundred and fifty thousand who have been given gills and webs and sent under the foam where there are no storms, up and down the American coast.

"You live on shore? I mean around here? But so long ago . . ."

"How old are you?"

"Sixteen."

"I was two years older than you when the accident happened."

"You were eighteen?"

"I'm twice that now. Which means it happened almost twenty years ago. It is a long time."

"They still talk about it."

"I've almost forgotten," I said. "I really have. Say, do you play the recorder?"

"I used to."

"Good! Come up to my place and look at my tenor recorder. And I'll make some tea. Perhaps you can stay for lunch—"

"I have to report back to Marine Headquarters by three. Tork is going over the briefing to lay the cable for the big dive, with Jonni and the crew." She paused, smiled. "But I can catch the undertow and be there in half an hour if I leave by two-thirty."

On the walk up I learned her name was Ariel. She thought the patio was charming, and the mosaic evoked, "Oh, look!" and "Did you do this yourself?" a half-dozen times. (I had done it, in the first lonely years.) She picked out the squid and the whale in battle, the wounded shark and the diver. She told me she didn't get time to read much, but she was impressed by all the books. She listened to me reminisce. She talked a lot to me about her work, husbanding the deep-down creatures they were scaring up. Then she sat on the kitchen stool, playing a Lukas Foss serenade on my recorder, while I put rock salt in the bottom of the broiler tray for two dozen Oysters Rockefeller, and the tea water whistled. I'm a comparatively lonely guy. I like being followed by beautiful young girls.

# II

"Hey, Juao!" I bawled across the jetty.

He nodded to me from the center of his nets, sun glistening on polished shoulders, sun lost in rough hair. I walked across to where he sat, sewing like a spider. He pulled another section up over his horny toes, then grinned at me with his mosaic smile: gold, white, black gap below, crooked yellow; white, gold, white. Shoving my bad leg in front I squatted.

"I fished out over the coral where you told me." He filled his cheek with his tongue and nodded. "You come up to the house for a drink, eh?"

"Fine."

"Just—a moment more."

There's a certain sort of Brazilian you find along the shore in the fishing villages, old yet ageless. See one of their men and you think he could be fifty, he could be sixty—will probably look the same when he's eighty-five. Such was Juao. We once figured it out. He's seven hours older than I am.

We became friends some time before the accident when I got tangled in his nets working high lines in the Vorea Current. A lot of guys would have taken their knife and hacked their way out of the situation, ruining fifty-five, sixty dollars' worth of nets. That's an average fisherman's monthly income down here. But I surfaced and sat around in his boat while we untied me. Then we came in and got plastered. Since I cost him a day's fishing, I've been giving him hints on where to fish ever since. He buys me drinks when I come up with something.

This has been going on for twenty years. During that time my life has been smashed up and land-bound. In the same time Juao has married off his five sisters, got married himself and has two children. (Oh, those *bolitos* and *tearros asados* that Amalia—her braids swung, her brown breasts shook so when she laughed—

would make for Sunday dinner/supper/Monday breakfast.) I rode with them in the ambulance 'copter all the way into Brasilia; in the hospital hall Juao and I stood together, both still barefoot, he tattered with fish scales in his hair, me just tattered, and I held him while he cried and I tried to explain to him how a world that could take a pubescent child and with a week of operations made an amphibious creature that can exist for a month on either side of the sea's foam-fraught surface could still be helpless before certain general endocrine cancers coupled with massive renal deterioration. Juao and I returned to the village alone, by bus, three days before our birthday—back when I was twenty-three and Juao was twenty-three and seven hours old.

"This morning," Juao said. (The shuttle danced in the web at the end of the orange line.) "I got a letter for you to read me. It's about the children. Come on, we go up and drink." The shuttle paused, backtracked twice, and he yanked the knot tight. We walked along the port toward the square. "Do you think the letter says that the children are accepted?"

"If it's from the Aquatic Corp. They just send postcards when they reject someone. The question is, how do *you* feel about it?"

"You are a good man. If they grow up like you, then it will be fine."

"But you're still worried." I'd been prodding Juao to get the kids into the International Aquatic Corp nigh on since I became their godfather. The operations had to be performed near puberty. It would mean much time away from the village during their training period—and they might eventually be stationed in any ocean in the world. But two motherless children had not been easy on Juao or his sisters. The Corp would mean education, travel, interesting work, the things that make up one kind of good life. They wouldn't look twice their age when they were thirty-five; and not too many amphimen look like me.

"Worry is part of life. But the work is dangerous. Did you know there is an amphiman going to try and lay cable down in the Slash?"

I frowned. "Again?"

"Yes. And that is what you tried to do when the sea broke you to pieces and burned the parts, eh?"

"Must you be so damned picturesque?" I asked. "Who's going to beard the lion this time?"

"A young amphiman named Tork. They speak of him down at the docks as a brave man."

"Why the hell are they still trying to lay the cable there? They've gotten by this long without a line through the Slash."

"Because of the fish," Juao said. "You told me why twenty years ago. The fish are still there, and we fishermen who cannot live below are still here. If the children go for the operations, then there will be less fishermen. But today . . ." He shrugged. "They must either lay the line across the fish paths or down in the Slash." Juao shook his head.

Funny things, the great power cables the Aquatic Corp has been strewing across the ocean floor to bring power to their undersea mines and farms, to run their oil wells—and how many flaming wells have I capped down there—for their herds of whale, and chemical distillation plants. They carry two-hundred-sixty-cycle current. Over certain sections of the ocean floor, or in sections of the water with certain mineral contents, this sets up inductance in the water itself which sometimes—and you will probably get a Nobel prize if you can detail exactly why it isn't always—drives the fish away over areas up to twenty-five and thirty miles, unless the lines are laid in the bottom of those canyons that delve into the ocean floor.

"This Tork thinks of the fishermen. He is a good man too."

I raised my eyebrows—the one that's left, anyway—and tried to remember what my little Undine had said about him that morning. And remembered not much.

"I wish him luck," I said.

"What do you feel about this young man going down into the coral-rimmed jaws to the Slash?"

I thought for a moment. "I think I hate him."

Juao looked up.

"He is an image in a mirror where I look and am forced to regard what I was," I went on. "I envy him the chance to succeed where I failed, and I can come on just as quaint as you can. I hope he makes it."

Juao twisted his shoulders in a complicated shrug (once I could do that) which is coastal Brazilian for, "I didn't know things had progressed to that point, but seeing that they have, there is little to be done."

"The sea is that sort of mirror," I said.

"Yes." Juao nodded.

Behind us I heard the slapping of sandals on concrete. I turned in time to catch my goddaughter in my good arm. My godson had grabbed hold of the bad one and was swinging on it.

"Tio Cal—?"

"Hey, Tio Cal, what did you bring us?"

"You will pull him over," Juao reprimanded them. "Let go."

And, bless them, they ignored their father.

"What did you bring us?"

"What did you bring us, Tio Cal?"

"If you let me, I'll show you." So they stepped back, dark-eyed and quivering. I watched Juao watching: brown pupils on ivory balls, and in the left eye a vein had broken in a jagged smear. He was loving his children, who would soon be as alien to him as the fish he netted. He was also looking at the terrible thing that was me and wondering what would come to his own spawn. And he was watching the world turn and grow older, clocked by the waves, reflected in that mirror.

It's impossible for me to see what the population explosion and the budding colonies on Luna and Mars and the flowering beneath the ocean really look like from the disrupted cultural mélange of a coastal fishing town. But I come closer than many others, and I know what I don't understand.

I pushed around in my pocket and fetched out the milky fragment I had brought from the beach. "Here. Do you like this one?" And they bent above my webbed and alien fingers.

In the supermarket, which is the biggest building in the village, Juao bought a lot of cake mixes. "That moist, delicate texture," whispered the box when you lifted it from the shelf, "with that deep flavor, deeper than chocolate!"

I'd just read an article about the new vocal packaging in a U.S. magazine that had gotten down last week, so I was prepared and stayed in the fresh vegetable section to avoid temptation. Then we went up to Juao's house. The letter proved to be what I'd expected. The kids had to take the bus into Brasilia tomorrow. My godchildren were on their way to becoming fish.

We sat on the front steps and drank and watched the donkeys and the motorbikes and the men in baggy trousers, the women in yellow scarves and bright skirts with wreaths of garlic and sacks of onions. As well, a few people glittered by in the green scales of amphimen uniforms.

Finally Juao got tired and went in to take a nap. Most of my life has been spent on the coast of countries accustomed to siestas, but those first formative ten were passed on a Danish collective farm and the idea never really took. So I stepped over my goddaughter, who had fallen asleep on her fists on the bottom step, and walked back through the town toward the beach.

## III

At midnight Ariel came out of the sea, climbed the rocks, and clicked her nails against my glass wall so the droplets ran, pearled by the gibbous moon.

Earlier I had stretched in front of the fireplace on the sheepskin throw to read, then dozed off. The conscientious timer had asked me if there was anything I wanted, and getting no answer had turned off the Dvorak *Cello Concerto* that was on its second time around, extinguished the reading lamp, and stopped dropping logs onto the flame so that now, as I woke, the grate was carpeted with coals.

She clicked again, and I raised my head from the cushion. The green uniform, her amber hair—all color was lost under the silver light outside. I lurched across the rug, touched the button, and the glass slid into the floor. The breeze came to my face, as the barrier fell.

"What do you want?" I asked. "What time is it, anyway?"

"Tork is on the beach, waiting for you."

The night was warm but windy. Below the rocks silver flakes chased each other in to shore. The tide lay full.

I rubbed my face. "The new boss man? Why didn't you bring him up to the house? What does he want to see me about?"

She touched my arm. "Come. They are all down on the beach."

"Who all?"

"Tork and the others."

She led me across the patio and to the path that wound to the sand. The sea roared in the moonlight. Down the beach people stood around a driftwood fire that whipped the night. Ariel walked beside me.

Two of the fishermen from town were crowding each other on the bottom of an overturned washtub, playing guitars. The singing, raucous and rhythmic, jarred across the paled sand. Shark's teeth shook on the necklace of an old woman dancing. Others were sitting on an overturned dinghy, eating.

Over one part of the fire on a skillet two feet across, oil frothed through pink islands of shrimp. One woman ladled them in, another ladled them out.

"Tio Cal!"

"Look, Tio Cal is here!"

"Hey, what are you two doing up?" I asked. "Shouldn't you be home in bed?"

"Poppa Juao said we could come. He'll be here, too, soon."

I turned to Ariel. "Why are they all gathering?"

"Because of the laying of the cable tomorrow at dawn."

Someone was running up the beach, waving a bottle in each hand.

"They didn't want to tell you about the party. They thought that it might hurt your pride."

"My what . . . ?"

"If you knew they were making so big a thing of the job you had failed at—"

"But—"

"—and that had hurt you so in failure. They did not want you to be sad. But Tork wants to see you. I said you would not be sad. So I went to bring you down from the rocks."

"Thanks, I guess."

"Tio Cal?"

But the voice was bigger and deeper than a child's.

He sat on a log back from the fire, eating a sweet potato. The flame flickered on his dark cheekbones, in his hair, wet and black. He stood, came to me, held up his hand. I held up mine and we slapped palms. "Good." He was smiling. "Ariel told me you would come. I will lay the power line down through the Slash tomorrow." His uniform scales glittered down his arms. He was very strong. But standing still, he still moved. The light on the cloth told me that. "I . . ." He paused. I thought of a nervous, happy dancer. "I wanted to talk to you about the cable." I thought of an eagle, I thought of a shark. "And about the . . . accident. If you would."

"Sure," I said. "If there's anything I could tell you that would help."

"See, Tork," Ariel said. "I told you he would talk to you about it."

I could hear his breathing change. "It really doesn't bother you to talk about the accident?"

I shook my head and realized something about that voice. It was a boy's voice that could imitate a man's. Tork was not over nineteen.

"We're going fishing soon," Tork told me. "Will you come?"

"If I'm not in the way."

A bottle went from the woman at the shrimp crate to one of the guitarists, down to Ariel, to me, then to Tork. (The liquor, made in a cave seven miles inland, was almost rum. The too-tight skin across the left side of my mouth makes the manful swig a little difficult to bring off. I got "rum" down my chin.)

He drank, wiped his mouth, passed the bottle on and put his hand on my shoulder. "Come down to the water."

We walked away from the fire. Some of the fishermen stared after us. A few of the amphimen glanced, and glanced away.

"Do all the young people of the village call you Tio Cal?"

"No. Only my godchildren. Their father and I have been friends since I was your age."

"Oh, I thought perhaps it was a nickname. That's why I called you that."

We reached wet sand where orange light cavorted at our feet. The broken shell of a lifeboat rocked in moonlight. Tork sat down on the shell's rim. I sat beside him. The water splashed to our knees.

"There's no other place to lay the power cable?" I asked. "There is no other way to take it except through the Slash?"

"I was going to ask you what you thought of the whole business. But I guess I don't really have to." He shrugged and clapped his hands together a few times. "All the projects this side of the bay have grown huge and cry for power. The new operations tax the old lines unmercifully. There was a power failure last July in Cayine down the shelf below the twilight level. The whole village was without light for two days, and twelve amphimen died of overexposure to the cold currents coming up from the depths. If we laid the cables farther up, we chance disrupting our own fishing operations as well as those of the fishermen on shore."

I nodded.

"Cal, what happened to you in the Slash?"

Eager, scared Tork. I was remembering now, not the accident, but the midnight before, pacing the beach, guts clamped with fists of fear and anticipation. Some of the Indians back where they make the liquor still send messages by tying knots in palm fibers. One could have spread my entrails then, or Tork's tonight, to read our respective horospecs.

Juao's mother knew the knot language, but he and his sisters never bothered to learn because they wanted to be modern, and, as children, still confused with modernity the new ignorances, lacking modern knowledge.

"When I was a boy," Tork said, "we would dare each other to walk the boards along the edge of the ferry slip. The sun would be hot and the boards would rock in the water, and if the boats were in and you fell down between the boats and the piling, you could get killed." He shook his head. "The crazy things kids will do. That was back when I was eight or nine, before I became a waterbaby."

"Where was it?"

Tork looked up. "Oh. Manila. I'm Filipino."

The sea licked our knees, and the gunwale sagged under us.

"What happened in the Slash?"

"There's a volcanic flaw near the base of the Slash."

"I know."

"And the sea is hypersensitive down there. You don't insult her fashion or her figure. We had an avalanche. The cable broke. The sparks were so hot and bright they made gouts of foam fifty feet high on the surface, so they tell me."

"What caused the avalanche?"

I shrugged. "It could have been just a goddamned coincidence. There are rock falls down there all the time. It could have been the noise from the machines—though we masked them pretty well. It could have been something to do with the inductance from the smaller cables for the machines. Or maybe somebody just kicked out the wrong stone that was holding everything up."

One webbed hand became a fist, sank into the other, and hung. Calling, "Cal!"

I looked up. Juao, pants rolled to his knees, shirt sailing in the sea wind, stood in the weave of white water. The wind lifted Tork's hair from his neck; and the fire roared on the beach.

Tork looked up too.

"They're getting ready to catch a big fish!" Juao called.

Men were already pushing their boats out. Tork clapped my shoulder. "Come, Cal. We fish now." We waded back to the shore.

Juao caught me as I reached dry sand. "You ride in my boat, Cal!"

Someone came with the acrid flares that hissed. The water slapped around the bottom of the boats as we wobbled into the swell.

Juao vaulted in and took up the oars. Around us green amphimen walked into the sea, struck forward, and were gone.

Juao pulled, leaned, pulled. The moonlight slid down his arms. The fire diminished on the beach.

Then among the boats, there was a splash, an explosion, and the red flare bloomed in the sky: the amphimen had sighted a big fish.

The flare hovered, pulsed once, twice, three times, four times (twenty, forty, sixty, eighty stone they estimated its weight to be), then fell.

Suddenly I shrugged out of my shirt, pulled at my belt buckle. "I'm going over the side, Juao!"

He leaned, he pulled, he leaned. "Take the rope."

"Yeah. Sure." It was tied to the back of the boat. I made a loop in the other end, slipped it around my shoulder. I swung my bad leg over the side, flung myself on the black water—

—mother-of-pearl shattered over me. That was the moon, blocked by the shadow of Juao's boat ten feet overhead. I turned below the rippling wounds Juao's oars made stroking the sea.

One hand and one foot with torn webs, I rolled over and looked down. The rope snaked to its end, and I felt Juao's strokes pulling me through the water.

They fanned below with underwater flares. Light undulated on their backs and heels. They circled, they closed, like those deep-sea fish who carry their own illumination. I saw the prey, glistening as it neared a flare.

You chase a fish with one spear among you. And that spear would be Tork's tonight. The rest have ropes to bind him that go up to the fishermen's boats.

There was a sudden confusion of lights below. The spear had been shot!

The fish, long as a tall and short man together, rose through the ropes. He turned out to sea, trailing his pursuers. But others waited there, tried to loop him. Once I had flung those ropes, treated with tar and lime to dissolve the slime of the fish's body and hold to the beast. The looped ropes caught, and by the movement of the flares, I saw them jerked down their paths. The fish turned, rose again, this time toward me.

He pulled around when one line ran out (and somewhere on the surface the prow of a boat doffed deep) but turned back and came on.

Of a sudden, amphimen were flicking about me as the fray's center drifted by. Tork, his spear dug deep, forward and left of the marlin's dorsal, had hauled himself astride the beast.

The fish tried to shake him, then dropped his tail and rose straight. Everybody started pulling toward the surface. I broke foam and grabbed Juao's gunwale.

Tork and the fish exploded up among the boats. They twisted in the air, in moonlight, in froth. The fish danced across the water on its tail, fell.

Juao stood up in the boat and shouted. The other fisherman shouted too, and somebody perched on the prow of a boat flung a rope and someone in the water caught it.

Then fish and Tork and me and a dozen amphimen all went underwater at once.

They dropped in a corona of bubbles. The fish struck the end of another line, and shook himself. Tork was thrown free, but he doubled back.

Then the lines began to haul the beast up again, quivering, whipping, quivering again.

Six lines from six boats had him. For one moment he was still in the submarine moonlight. I could see his wound tossing scarves of blood.

When he (and we) broke surface, he was thrashing again, near Juao's boat. I was holding onto the side when suddenly Tork, glistening, came out of the water beside me and went over into the dinghy.

"Here you go," he said, turning to kneel at the bobbing rim, and pulled me up while Juao leaned against the far side to keep balance.

Wet rope slopped on the prow. "Hey, Cal!" Tork laughed grabbed it up, and began to haul.

The fish prised wave from white wave in the white water.

The boats came together. The amphimen had all climbed up. Ariel was across from us, holding a flare that drooled smoke down her arm. She peered by the hip of the fisherman who was standing in front of her.

Juao and Tork were hauling the rope. Behind them I was coiling it with one hand as it came back to me.

The fish came up and was flopped into Ariel's boat, tail out, head up, chewing air.

I had just finished pulling on my trousers when Tork fell down on the seat behind me and grabbed me around the shoulders with his wet arms. "Look at our fish, Tio Cal! Look!" He gasped air, laughing, his dark face diamonded beside the flares. "Look at our fish there, Cal!"

Juao, grinning white and gold, pulled us back into shore. The fire, the singing, hands beating hands—and my godson had put pebbles in the empty rum bottles and was shaking them to the music—the guitars spiraled around us as we carried the fish up the sand and the men brought the spit.

"Watch it!" Tork said, grasping the pointed end of the great stick that was thicker than his wrist.

We turned the fish over.

"Here, Cal?"

He prodded two fingers into the white flesh six inches back from the bony lip.

"Fine."

Tork jammed the spit in.

We worked it through the body. By the time we carried it to the fire, they had brought more rum.

"Hey, Tork. Are you going to get some sleep before you go down in the morning?" I asked.

He shook his head. "Slept all afternoon." He pointed toward the roasting fish with his elbow. "That's my breakfast."

But when the dancing grew violent a few hours later, just before the fish was to come off the fire, and the kids were pushing the last of the sweet potatoes from the ashes with sticks, I walked back to the lifeboat shell we had sat on earlier. It was three-quarters flooded.

Curled below still water, Tork slept, fist loose before his mouth, the gills at the back of his neck pulsing rhythmically. Only his shoulder and hip made islands in the floated boat.

"Where's Tork?" Ariel asked me at the fire. They were swinging up the sizzling fish.

"Taking a nap."

"Oh, he wanted to cut the fish!"

"He's got a lot of work coming up. Sure you want to wake him up?"

"No, I'll let him sleep."

But Tork was coming up from the water, brushing his dripping hair back from his forehead.

He grinned at us, then went to carve. I remember him standing on the table, astraddle the meat, arm going up and down with the big knife (details, yes, those are the things you remember), stopping to hand down the portions, then hauling his arm back to cut again.

That night, with music and stomping on the sand and shouting back and forth over the fire, we made more noise than the sea.

# IV

The eight-thirty bus was more or less on time.

"I don't think they want to go," Juao's sister said. She was accompanying the children to the Aquatic Corp Headquarters in Brasilia.

"They are just tired," Juao said. "They should not have stayed up so late last night. Get on the bus now. Say good-bye to Tio Cal."

"Good-bye."

"Good-bye."

Kids are never their most creative in that sort of situation. And I suspect that my godchildren may just have been suffering their first (or one of their first) hangovers. They had been very quiet all morning.

I bent down and gave them a clumsy hug. "When you come back on your first weekend off, I'll take you exploring down below at the point. You'll be able to gather your own coral now."

Juao's sister got teary, cuddled the children, cuddled me, Juao, then got on the bus.

Someone was shouting out the bus window for someone at the bus stop not to forget something. They trundled around the square and then toward the highway. We walked back across the street where the café owners were putting out canvas chairs.

"I will miss them," he said, like a long-considered admission.

"You and me both." At the docks near the hydrofoil wharf where the submarine launches went out to the undersea cities, we saw a crowd. "I wonder if they had any trouble laying the—"

A woman screamed in the crowd. She pushed from the others, dropping eggs and onions. She began to pull her hair and shriek. (Remember the skillet of shrimp? She had been the woman ladling them out.) A few people moved to help her.

A clutch of men broke off and ran into a side street. I grabbed a running amphiman, who whirled to face me.

"What in hell is going on?"

For a moment his mouth worked on his words for all the trite world like a bleached fish.

"From the explosion . . ." he began. "They just brought them back from the explosion at the Slash!"

I grabbed his other shoulder. "What happened!"

"About two hours ago. They were just a quarter of the way through, when the whole fault gave way. They had a goddamn underwater volcano for half an hour. They're still getting seismic disturbances."

Juao was running toward the launch. I pushed the guy away and limped after him, struck the crowd and jostled through calico, canvas, and green scales.

They were carrying the corpses out of the hatch of the submarine and laying them on a canvas spread across the dock. They still return bodies to the countries of birth for the family to decide the method of burial. When the fault had given, the hot slag that had belched into the steaming sea was mostly molten silicon.

Three of the bodies were only slightly burned here and there; from their bloated faces (one still bled from the ear) I guessed they had died from sonic concussion. But several of the bodies were almost totally encased in dull, black glass.

"Tork—" I kept asking. "Is one of them Tork?"

It took me forty-five minutes, asking first the guys who were carrying the bodies, then going into the launch and asking some guy with a clipboard, and then going back on the dock and into the office to find out that one of the more unrecognizable bodies, yes, was Tork.

Juao brought me a glass of buttermilk in a café on the square. He sat still a long time, then finally rubbed away his white moustache, released the chair rung with his toes, put his hands on his knees.

"What are you thinking about?"

"That it's time to go fix nets. Tomorrow morning I will fish." He regarded me a moment. "Where should I fish tomorrow, Cal?"

"Are you wondering about . . . well, sending the kids off today?"

He shrugged. "Fishermen from this village have drowned. Still it is a village of fishermen. Where should I fish?"

I finished my buttermilk. "The mineral content over the Slash should be high as the devil. Lots of algae will gather tonight. Lots of small fish down deep. Big fish hovering over."

He nodded. "Good. I will take the boat out there tomorrow." We got up.

"See you, Juao."

I limped back to the beach.

# V

The fog had unsheathed the sand by ten. I walked around, poking clumps of weeds with a stick, banging the same stick on my numb leg. When I lurched up to the top of the rocks, I stopped in the still grass. "Ariel?"

She was keeling in the water, head down, red hair breaking over sealed gills. Her shoulders shook, stopped, shook again.

"Ariel?" I came down over the blistered stones.

She turned away to look at the ocean.

The attachments of children are so important and so brittle. "How long have you been sitting here?"

She looked at me now, the varied waters on her face stilled on drawn cheeks. And her face was exhausted. She shook her head.

Sixteen? Seventeen? Who was the psychologist, back in the seventies, who decided that "adolescents" were just physical and mental adults with no useful work? "You want to come up to the house?"

The head shaking got faster, then stopped.

After a while I said, "I guess they'll be sending Tork's body back to Manila."

"He didn't have a family," she explained. "He'll be buried here, at sea."

"Oh," I said.

And the rough volcanic glass, pulled across the ocean's sands, changing shape, dulling—

"You were—you liked Tork a lot, didn't you? You kids looked like you were pretty fond of each other."

"Yes. He was an awfully nice—" Then she caught my meaning and blinked. "No," she said. "Oh, no. I was—I was engaged to Jonni . . . the brown-haired boy from California? Did you meet him at the party last night? We're both from Los Angeles, but we only met down here. And now . . . they're sending his body back this evening." Her eyes got very wide, then closed.

"I'm sorry."

I'm a clumsy cripple, I step all over everybody's emotions. In that mirror I guess I'm too busy looking at what might have been.

"I'm sorry, Ariel."

She opened her eyes and began to look around her.

"Come on up to the house and have an avocado. I mean, they have avocados in now, not at the supermarket. But at the old town market on the other side. And they're better than any they grow in California."

She kept looking around.

"None of the amphimen get over there. It's a shame, because soon the market will probably close, and some of their fresh foods are really great. Oil and vinegar is all you need on them." I leaned back on the rocks. "Or a cup of tea?"

"Okay." She remembered to smile. I know the poor kid didn't feel like it. "Thank you. I won't be able to stay long, though."

We walked back up the rocks toward the house, the sea on our left. Just as we reached the patio, she turned and looked back. "Cal?"

"Yes? What is it?"

"Those clouds over there, across the water. Those are the only ones in the sky. Are they from the eruption in the Slash?"

I squinted. "I think so. Come on inside."

# THE HOLMES-GINSBOOK DEVICE

## (DECEMBER 1968)

## ISAAC ASIMOV

## (B. 1920)

The illustrious author of *I, Robot* (1950), *The Foundation Trilogy* (collected 1964), and *The Caves of Steel* (1954) really needs no introduction save to say that he is one of the three most famous science-fiction writers in the world. He had eight good-to-great stories published in *If*, including "The Billiard Ball" (March 1967), "The Feeling of Power" (February 1958), and "Stranger in Paradise" (June 1974). In addition, he had the unusual distinction of having a serial, "The Gods Themselves," run in two different magazines, with two installments in *Galaxy* and one in *If*.

"The Holmes-Ginsbook Device" is one of his least-known stories, having been reprinted only in his *Opus 100*, and it is one of his funniest.

## MEMOIR BY ISAAC ASIMOV

*If*, in its earliest years, was published by James L. Quinn, and the pleasantest memory I have in that connection is the deal I made with him. I told him that any time he wanted a story from me, I would write one and give him first crack at it, provided he would pay me the standard price of four cents a word which, in those days, was what *Astounding* and *Galaxy* paid me.

If Quinn didn't think the story was worth four cents a word, he was to send it back to me and I would try *Astounding* and *Galaxy*. If they both rejected it, I would send it back to Quinn and he could then have it at his usual rates, which, I think, were two cents a word—though, of course, he could reject it then, too, if he felt that it wasn't worth even that much.

Quinn agreed and the scheme worked perfectly, except that he never rejected a story I sent him, so I never had a chance to see how a second-submission would work out. And he paid me four cents a word every time.

Since it worked for *If*, I made the same deal with several other low-rate magazines. It worked just as well in every case. They never rejected one, either, and always paid four cents a word. That is why some of my best stories appeared in "minor" magazines in the 1950s.

Eventually, Quinn sold *If*, but, of course, I wrote for it in the sixties and seventies also. In fact, the last item of mine that appeared in *If* may very well have been the best thing I ever wrote. It happened thus:

*Galaxy* wanted to serialize my novel "The Gods Themselves." *Galaxy* was a bimonthly at that time, however, and I didn't want a two-month wait between installments. For one thing, it would delay hardcover publication. Judy-Lynn del Rey, who was then the effective policymaker at the magazine, had the idea of making use of *If*, which was then *Galaxy*'s sister magazine, and which was also a bimonthly, but was published in alternate months with *Galaxy*.

I agreed, and "The Gods Themselves" appeared in the March 1972 *Galaxy*, the April 1972 *If*, and the May 1972 *Galaxy*. I believe this was the first and only time a serial was split between two magazines.

What made this possible was that I wrote the story in three semi-independent parts, with each capable of standing on its own. This was not with a view to convenience of serialization but arose naturally out of the way the novel had developed.

As it happened, most people seemed to think that the second part was the best of the three, and it was probably the second part that insured the Hugo and Nebula awards for the novel that year. And the second part appeared in *If*.

As for "The Holmes-Ginsbook Device," that came about thusly:

James Watson, a Nobel Prize winner, had won the prize for his share in the work of elucidating the overall structure of DNA. He wrote a book about the research involved which he called *The Double Helix*. It was widely touted, somehow, as an iconoclastic and ribald behind-the-scenes look at scientific research. To be sure, it was a lively book, but it wasn't really iconoclastic and not at all ribald.

Nevertheless, what with all the fuss over it, I thought I would try my hand at writing a satire on what *The Double Helix* was supposed to be (not what it actually was). So I wrote "The

Holmes-Ginsbook Device" and loved it. I laughed all the way through. I marveled at my wit and sparkle. I had visions of the story becoming an instant classic and netting me the Nobel Prize for Literature.

But when I sent it to Fred Pohl, who was at that time editing *If,* I got back a letter which, to my amazement, requested permission to cut the story to half its length, because the humor could not carry the weight of so long a story. He urged me not to pull a Harlan Ellison act, and to allow him to do this.

Much aggrieved, I said that of course I would not react as Harlan Ellison would, but that I liked the story so much I couldn't bear the thought of a cut and would he please send it back so I could submit it elsewhere.

Whereupon Fred said, very well, he would run the story uncut, but that I *had* acted like Harlan Ellison.

It appeared in the December 1968 *If,* uncut and I waited confidently for the reader reaction, which I knew would be enthusiastic in the extreme. The reaction never came. It was as though the story never was.

I have never been able to understand this. One daring thought I have had is that Fred Pohl was right and I was wrong, but knowing Fred and knowing me, I think that's flatly impossible.

The only other possibility is that no one happened to read it. I admit that that's improbable, but you know what Sherlock Holmes says: "When you have eliminated the impossible, whatever remains, however improbable, is the truth."

But now "The Holmes-Ginsbook Device" has a second chance, and this time I want all of you out there to read it. If you like it, let me know. If you don't like it, don't let me know. After all, you wouldn't want to see a grown man cry, would you?

# THE HOLMES-GINSBOOK DEVICE

I have never seen Myron Ginsbook in a modest mood.

But then, why should I have? Mike—we all call him Mike, although he is Dr. Ginsbook, Nobel Laureate, to a reverential world—is a typical product of the twenty-first century. He is self-confident, as so many of us are, and by right should be.

He knows the worth of mankind, of society, and most of all of himself.

He was born on January 1, 2001, so he is as old as the century exactly. I am ten years younger, that much farther removed from the unmentionable twentieth.

Oh, I mentioned it sometimes. All youngsters have their quirks and mine had been a kind of curiosity about mankind's earlier history, concerning which so little is known and so little, I admit, ought to be known. But I was curious.

It was Mike who rescued me in those days. "Don't," he would say, leering at the girls as they passed in their bikini business suits, and leaning over at intervals to feel the material judiciously, "don't play with the past. Oh, ancient history isn't bad, nor medieval times, but as soon as we reach the birth of technology, forget it. From then on it's scatology; just filth and perversion. You're a creature of the twenty-first. Be free! Breathe deeply of our century's clean air! It will do wonders for you. Look at what it's doing for that remarkable girl to your left."

And it was true. Her deep breathing was delightful. Ah, those were great days, when science was pulsing and we two were young, carefree and eager to grab the world by the tail.

Mike was sure he was going to advance science enormously and I felt the same. It was the great dream of all of us in this glorious century, still youthful. It was as though some great voice were crying: *Onward! Onward! Not a glance behind!*

I picked up that attitude from Paul Derrick, the California wizard. He's dead now, but a great man in his time, quite worthy of being mentioned in the same breath with myself.

I was one of his graduate students and it was hard at first. In college, I had carefully selected those courses which had had the least mathematics and the most girls and had therefore learned how to hemstitch with surpassing skill but had, I admit, left myself weak in physics.

After considerable thought, I realized that hemstitching was not going to help me make further advances in our great twenty-first-century technology. The demand for improvements in hemstitching was meager and I could see clearly that my expertise would not lead me to the coveted Nobel Prize. So I pinched the girls good-bye and joined Derrick's seminars.

I understood little at first but I did my best to ask questions designed to help Derrick demonstrate his brilliance and rapidly advanced to the head of the class in consequence. I was even the occasion for Derrick's greatest discovery.

\*     \*     \*

He was smoking at the time. He was an inveterate smoker and proud of it, always taking his cigarette out and looking at it lovingly between puffs. They were girlie-cigarettes, with fetching nudes on the clear white paper—always a favorite with scientists.

"Imagine," he would say in the course of his famous lectures on Twenty-first-Century Technological Concepts, "how we have advanced on the Dark Ages in the matter of cigarettes alone. Rumors reach us that in the ill-famed twentieth century, cigarettes were a source of disease and air pollution. The details are not known, of course, and no one, I imagine, would care to find out, yet the rumors are convincing. Now, however, a cigarette liberates air-purifying ingredients into the atmosphere, fills it with a pleasant aroma, and strengthens the health of the smoker. It has, in fact, only one drawback."

Of course, we all knew what it was. I had frequently seem Derrick with a blistered lip, and he had a fresh blister that day. It impeded his speech somewhat.

Like all thoughtful scientists, he was easily distracted by passing girls, and on those occasions he would frequently place his cigarette in his mouth wrong-end-in. He would inhale deeply and the cigarette would spontaneously ignite, with the lit end in his mouth.

I don't know how many learned professors I had seen, in those days, interrupt their intimate conversations with secretaries to yell in agony as another blister was added to tongue or lip.

On this occasion, I said in jest, "Professor Derrick, why don't your remove the igno-tip before putting the cigarette in your mouth?" It was a mild witticism and actually, if I remember correctly, I was the only one who laughed. Yet the picture brought up by the remark was a funny one. Imagine a cigarette without its ignitable tip! How could one smoke it?

But Derrick's eyes narrowed. "Why not?" he said. "Observe!"

In front of the class, Derrick whipped out a cigarette, observed it carefully—his particular brand presented its girlies in lifelike tints—then pinched of the igno-tip.

He held it up between two fingers of his left hand and said again, "Observe!" He placed the unignitable residue of the cigarette in his mouth. A thrill went through us all as we observed from the position of the girlie that he had deliberately placed the cigarette in his mouth wrong-end-in. He inhaled sharply and nothing, of course happened.

"The unblistering cigarette," he said.

I said, "But you can't light it."

"Can't you?" he said and, with a flourish, brought the igno-tip up against the cigarette. We all caught our breath. It was a sheer stroke of genius, for the igno-tip would light the safe outside end of the cigarette, *whichever end it was*.

Derrick inhaled sharply and the igno-tip flared into life, igniting the outer tip of the cigarette—and the tip of Derrick's thumb and forefinger. With a howl, he dropped it and naturally, the entire class laughed with great cheerfulness this time.

It was a stroke of misfortune for me. Since I had suggested the miserable demonstration, he kicked me out of his class forever.

This was, of course, unfair, since I had made it possible for him to win the Nobel Prize, though neither of us realized it at the time.

You see, the laughter had driven Derrick to frenzy. He was determined to solve the problem of the unblisterable cigarette. To do so, he bent his giant mind to the problem, full time, cutting down his evening with the girls to five a week—almost unheard of in a scientist, but he was a notorious ascetic.

In less than a year, he had solved the problem. Now that it is over, of course, it seems obvious to all of us, but at the time, I assure you, it dumbfounded the world of science.

The trick was to separate the igno-tip from the cigarette and then devise some way of manipulating the igno-tip safely. For months, Derrick experimented with different shapes and sizes of handles.

Finally, he decided on a thin shaft of wood as ideal for the purpose. Since it was difficult to balance a cigarette tip on the wood, he discarded the tobacco and paper and made use of the chemicals with which the cigarette tip had been impregnated. These chemicals he coated on the tip of the shaft.

At first, he lost considerable time trying to make the shaft follow so that it could be sucked or blown through to ignite the chemicals. The resulting fire might then be applied to the cigarette. This, however, revived the original problem. What if one put the wrong end of the shaft in the hand?

Derrick then got his crowning idea. It would only be necessary to increase the temperature of the chemicals by friction, by rubbing the tip of the wood against a rough surface. This was absolutely safe for if, in the course of bestowing a fatherly kiss on the lips of a girl student intent on an A in her course at any hazard—a typical event in every scientist's life—one should rub the wrong end of the wood on a rough surface, nothing at all would happen. It was a perfect fail-safe mechanism.

The discovery swept the world. Who, today, is without his package of igno-splints, which can be lit at any time in perfect safety, so that the day of the blistered lip is gone forever? Surely this great invention is a match for any other this great century has seen; so much a match, in fact, that some wags have suggested the igno-splints be called "matches." Actually, that name is catching on.

Derrick received his Nobel Prize in physics almost at once and the world applauded.

I returned then and tried to re-enroll in his class, pointing out that but for me he would never have earned that Nobel Prize. he kicked me out with harsh expletives, threatening to apply an igno-splint to my nose.

After that my one ambition was to win a Nobel Prize of my own, one that would drown out Derrick's achievement. I, John Holmes, would show him.

But how? How?

I managed to get a grant that would take me to England in order to study Lancashire hemstitching, but I had no sooner got there than I pulled every string I could to get into Cambridge, with its famous covey of girl students and its almost equally famous Chumley–Maudlin (pronounced Cholmondeley–Magdalen) Technological Institute.

The girl students were warm and exotic and I spent many an evening stitching hems with them. Many of the Cantabrigian scientists were struck with the usefulness of the pursuit, not having discerned earlier this particular advantage of sewing. Some of them tried to get me to teach them to hemstitch but I followed that old First Law of Scientific Motivation. "What's in it for me?" I didn't teach them a thing.

Mike Ginsbook, however, having watched me from a distance, quickly picked up the intricate finger-manipulations of hemstitching and joined me.

"It's my talent," he said with charming immodesty. "I have a natural aptitude at manipulation."

He was my man! I recognized at that moment that he would help me to the Nobel Prize. There remained only to choose the field of activity that would get it for us.

For a year our association produced nothing except for a sultry brunette or two; and then one day I said to him lazily, "I can't help but notice, Mike, that your eyes are extraordinarily limpid. You're the only one on campus who doesn't have bloodshot sclera."

He said, "But the answer is simple. I never view microfilms. They are a curse."

"Oh?"

"I've never told you?" A somber look crossed his face and a clear stab of pain furrowed his brow. I had clearly activated a memory almost too sharp to bear. He said, "I was once viewing a microfilm with my head completely enclosed in the viewer, naturally. While I was doing that, a gorgeous girl passed by—a girl who won the title of Miss Teacher's Pet the next two years running, I might say—and I never noticed her. I was told about it afterward by Tancred Hull, the gynecologist. He spent three nights with her, the cad, explaining that he was giving her a physical checkup. Had pictures taken to prove it that were the talk of Cambridge."

Mike's lips were quivering. "From that time on," he said in a low, suffering voice, "I have vowed never to view a film again."

I was almost faint with the sudden inspiration that struck me. "Mike," I said, "might there not be some way in which microfilms can be viewed more simply? Look, films are covered with microscopic print. That print has to be enlarged for us to see it. That means bending over an immobile screen or encasing the head in a viewer.

"But—" and I could hardly breathe with the excitement of it—"what if the material on the film were enlarged until it could be seen with the naked eye and then a photograph of the enlarged print were taken? You could carry the photograph with you, looking at it at your leisure whenever you chose. Why, Mike, if you were looking at such a photo and a girl passed by, it would be the work of a moment to lift your head. The photo would not take up your attention as a viewer would."

"Hmm," said Mike, thoughtfully. I could see his giant mind spinning over every ramification of the subject. "It really might not interfere with girl-watching; less important, it might prevent bloodshot eyes. Oh, but wait, all you would have would be about five or six hundred words and you would be bound to read that through before the day was over. Then what?"

It was amazing to watch his pick unerringly the flaw in the project.

For a moment, I was daunted. I hadn't thought of that. Then I said, "Perhaps you could make a large series of small photographs and paste them together in order. Of course, that might be more difficult to carry."

"Let's see—" Mike's mind continued to work. He leaned back in his chair, closed his eyes, straightened suddenly and looked piercingly about in every direction to make sure there were no girls in the vicinity, then closed them again.

He said, "There's no question but the magnification is possible; photography is possible. If all of a typical microfilm is expanded and photographed, however, so that it could be read with the unaided eye, the resultant series of photographs would cover an area of—" Here he whipped out his famous girlie slide rule, designed by himself, with the hairline neatly and stimulatingly bisecting a buxom blonde. He manipulated it caressingly. "—An area of one hundred fifty square feet in area at least. We would have to use a sheet of paper ten feet by fifteen feet and crawl around on it."

"That would be possible," I muttered.

"Too undignified for a scientist unless, of course, he were point-ing out something to a girl student. And even then she might get interested in reading whatever it was he was pointing out and that would kill everything."

We were both down in the dumps at that. We recognized that we had Nobel material here. Films had the virtue of being compact, but that was their only virtue.

Oh, if only you could fold a ten-foot by-fifteen-foot piece of paper in your hand. You would require no electronic or photonic equipment to read it. You could read any part of it at will. You could go backward or forward without having to manipulate any controls. You would merely shift your eyes.

The whole thought was incredibly exciting. The technological advance involved in using eye muscles in place of expensive equipment was enormous. Mike pointed out at once that glancing back and forth over a large sheet of paper would exercise the eye muscles and equip a scientist better for the important task of not failing to observe the feminine parade.

It remained only to determine how best to make a large sheet of paper portable and manipulable.

I took a course in topology in order to learn folding techniques and many was the evening my girl friend of the day and I would design some order of folding. Beginning at opposite ends of the sheet of paper, we would come closer and closer as we folded according to some intricate formula, until we were face to face, panting and flushed with the mental and physical exertion. The results were enormously exciting but the folding procedures were never any good.

How I wished I had studied more mathmatics. I even approached Prunella Plug, our harsh-voiced laundress, who folded bed sheets with aplomb and dignity. She was not about to let me into the secret, however.

I might have explained what I wanted the folding for, but I wasn't going to let *her* in on it. I meant to share the Nobel Prize with as few people as possible. The famous phrase of the great scientist Lord Clinchmore—"I'm not in science for my health, you know"—rang through my mind.

One morning I thought I had it. Oh, the excitement of it! I had to find Mike, for only his keen analytical mind would tell me if there were flaws in the notion. I tracked him down to a hotel room at last but found him deeply involved with a young lady—or popsie, to use the scientific term.

I banged away at the locked door until he came out, rather in a bad humor for some reason. He said, "Darn it, Jack, you can't interrupt research like that." Mike was a dedicated scientist.

I said, "Listen. We've been thinking in terms of two dimensions. What about *one* dimension?"

"How do you mean, one dimension?"

"Take the photos," I said, "and make them follow one after the other in a single line!"

"It would be yards and yards long." He worked out the figures with his finger on his colleague's abdomen, while I watched closely to make sure that he made no mistakes. He said, "It would easily be two hundred feet long. That's ungainly."

"But you don't have to fold," I said. "You roll. You place one end on one plastic rod, and the other end on another. You roll them together!"

"Great Scott," said Mike, shocked into profanity by the thought. "Maybe you have it."

It was that very day, however, that the blow struck. A visiting professor from California had news. Paul Derrick, he said, was rumored to be working on the problem of a nonelectronic film.

He didn't seem to know what that meant, but we did and our hearts sank again.

I said, "He must have heard of what we're doing here. We've *got* to beat him."

And how we tried! We took the photographs ourselves, pasted them side by side, rolled them on rods. It was a job of unimaginable complexity and delicacy that might well have used skilled artisans, but we were intent on allowing no outsiders to see what we were doing.

It worked, but Mike was uncertain. He said, "I don't think it's really practical. If you want to find a particular place in the film, you have to roll and roll and roll, one way or another. It is very hard on the wrists."

But it was all we had. I wanted to publish, but Mike held back. "Let's see what Derrick has worked out," he said.

"But if he has this, he will have anticipated us."

Mike shook his head, "If this is all he's got, it doesn't matter. This isn't going to win the Nobel Prize. It isn't good enough—I just feel it, here."

He placed his hand on the girlie stitched on his shirt pocket so sincerely that I did not argue. Mike was a great scientist and a great scientist just knows what will get a Nobel Prize and what will not. That's what makes a scientist great.

Derrick did announce his discovery—and it had a flaw in it that an average high-school student would have spotted at once.

His nonelectronic film was simply our old two-dimensional sheets, but without even our efforts to fold them. It just hung down the side of a large wall. A movable ladder was supplied that was attached to a runner near the ceiling. One of Derrick's students climbed the ladder and read aloud into the microphones.

Everyone ooh-ed and ah-ed at the sight of someone reading with the unaided eye, but Mike, watching on television, slapped his thigh in amusement.

"The idiot," he said. "What about people with acrophobia?"

Of course! It leaped to the eye when Mike pointed it out. Anyone afraid of heights couldn't read under the Derrick system.

But I seized Mike's wrist and said, "Now wait awhile, Mike. They're going to laugh at Derrick and that's dangerous. As soon as this point about acrophobia comes out, Derrick will feel humiliated and he will turn with every fiber of his magnificent brain to the project. He will then solve it in weeks. We've got to get there first."

Mike sobered up at once. "You are right, Jack," he said simply. "Let's go out on the town. A girl or two apiece will help us think."

It did, too, and then the next morning we thought about other things and got back to work.

I remember I was walking back and forth, muttering, "We've tried two dimensions; we've tried one dimension; what's left?" And then my eye fell upon Mike's girlie shirt with the nude on the breast pocket so cleverly hemstitched that strategic areas were distinctly raised.

"Heavens," I said, "we haven't tried *three* dimensions."

I went screaming for Mike. This time I was sure I had it and I could hardly breathe waiting for his judgment. He looked at me, eyes luminous. "We have it," he said.

It's so simple, looking back on it. We simply piled the photographs in a heap.

The heaps could be kept in place in any number of ways. They could be stapled, for instance. Then Mike got the idea of placing them between stiff cardboard covers to protect individual photographs from damage.

Within a month, we had published. The world rang with the discovery and everyone knew that the next Nobel Prize in physics would be ours.

Derrick, to do him justice, congratulated us and said, "Now the world can read without electronics and by the use of the unaided eyes, thanks to the Holmes-Ginsbook device. I congratulate those two dirty rats on their discovery."

That handsome acknowledgment was Science at its best.

The Holmes-Ginsbook device is now a household item. The popularity of the device is such that its name has been shortened to the final syllable and increasing numbers of people are calling them simply "books."

This eliminates my name, but I have my Nobel Prize and a contract to write a book on the untimate details surrounding the discovery for a quarter-million-dollar advance. Surely that is enough. Scientists are simple souls and once they have fame, wealth and girls, that's all they ask.

# DOWN IN THE BLACK GANG
## (MARCH 1969)
## PHILIP JOSÉ FARMER
## (B. 1918)

Philip José Farmer has written all types of speculative fiction, from "biographies" of famous characters to mind-bending explorations of the nature of reality. When any list of seminal influences of science fiction is compiled, his name will be near the top. He holds three Hugo Awards: Best New Author of 1953, Best Novella of 1968 for "Riders of the Purple Wage," and Best Novel of 1972 for *To Your Scattered Bodies Go*.

*If* had the distinction of publishing two of his important works, the brilliant "The Shadow of Space" (November 1967) and the two-part serial "The Felled Star," part of his magnificent Riverworld series.

## MEMOIR BY PHILIP JOSÉ FARMER

Alas! Poor *If* is dead!

I wish that I could also say, as Hamlet said of Yorick, that I knew him (it) well. But I did not know it well except during the late sixties. At least, that's what I thought when I started writing this. Then I read a short history of *If* in a science-fiction encyclopedia. And I found that the magazine started in 1952. I just don't remember its inauguration. I do, however, vividly remember picking up from a bookstand an *If* containing Blish's now classic "A Case of Conscience." I wanted to buy it but didn't because I was short of money. I preferred to invest what little I had in *Astounding* or *Galaxy* or the *Magazine of Fantasy & Science Fiction*.

This occurred, according to the history, in 1953. I made a mistake then. Blish's story was, as I discovered much later when I read it in the unabridged book, the best thing published in that year. Even though *If* was regarded as *Galaxy's* little sister and paid lesser rates than its big sister, it often had stories better than those in the more prestigious publications.

My first story to appear in *If* was "Heel" (May 1960 issue), a very minor tale. When it came out, I read it and the other stories in that issue, and that started me reading *If* more or less faithfully. Some of the stories were stimulating.

Then I took out of the "trunk" the manuscript of the original Riverworld novel. *Owe for the River*, written in late 1952. It seemed to me that perhaps there might be a market for it. I decided to send it to Fred Pohl with the suggestion that if he liked it he could serialize it in *Galaxy*. (I bypassed John Campbell of *Astounding*, since he never liked *any* of my submissions.) Pohl wrote back that the concept of the Riverworld was too vast and had too many potentialities to be published even in a 150,000-word novel. He proposed that I should rewrite it as a series of novelettes. Thus, I could take my time and use all the space I'd need in developing the many ideas inherent in the concept. And I could also write as many of the story lines as I cared to.

This seemed to be a good idea. It was one which I'd have proposed myself if I'd thought that there was any chance that an editor would accept it. As it turned out, owing to Fred's keen perception and his willingness to turn me loose, the Riverworld series was a far better story than the original.

Pohl also purchased a number of short stories from me for *If* during the later sixties. Some of these I've thought good enough to reprint in my 1971 collection, *Down in the Black Gang*. I became even more interested in *If* and so had the pleasure of reading such classics as Harlan Ellison's "I Have No Mouth, and I Must Scream" and Larry Niven's "Neutron Star."

However, Fred did not run the Riverworld series in *Galaxy*. He started it in another little sister, *Worlds of Tomorrow*. But when *WOT* folded, Fred transferred the series to *If*. I don't know if he'd have transferred the series to *Galaxy* when *If* was canceled. By then I'd decided not to write any more novelettes but to compose future Riverworld novels as complete books for issuance by book publishers.

Fred Pohl did a great job with *If*, and it wasn't his fault, but that of the shrinking market at that time, that the magazine was forced to fold. Though he couldn't pay the contributors to *If* as much as he paid contributors to *Galaxy*, his editorial thaumaturgy acquired Hugos for *If* as the best SF magazine for 1966, 1967, and 1968. On a shoestring and near-genius.

"Down in the Black Gang" was commissioned by Fred. He wanted a story from me for a special issue of *If* containing only works by Hugo winners. At the time (late 1968 or early 1969), I was a technical writer for the space industry segment of McDonnell-Douglas. Shortly before I got Fred's invitation, I was standing near a group of engineers. One of them said, loudly, "What about the bleedoff?"

He was talking about rocket motors, of course, but that question, overheard by chance, sparked something in my mind. Relays began clicking. Lights blinked. My unconscious, whom I now image as a demon named Abysmas, plugged in hitherto unconnected circuits and, for all I know, grew some new circuits. The she-demon Abysmas, in partnership with my conscious, named Wabasso, developed the story.

The story is at least one-half autobiographical and wholly therapeutic. For me, anyway. The Bonder family (Bonder comes from the Old Norse and means the same thing as a farmer or peasant) is based on the Farmer family. We were living in a Beverly Hills apartment just like that described here. The people directly below us were as presented here; nothing about them is exaggerated. And I was the minor but pivotal character, Tom Bonder, caught in that cosmic human comedy which Tom unwittingly transformed into a tragedy and thus aided in providing more thrust for the universe, which is actually a spaceship driving towards some unknown port.

I don't know where we're going, but it's sure hell getting there. On the other hand, there are many joyous moments and some great rewards for some of us. Does that make the trip worthwhile? Only journey's end will tell us.

# DOWN IN THE BLACK GANG

I'm telling you this because I need your love. Just as you need mine, though you don't know it—yet. And because I can't make love to you as a human makes love to a human.

You'll know why when I've told you the true story. The story I first told was a lie.

You muts know I'm not human, even if I do look just like one. Do humans sweat quicksilver?

You must know I can't make love to you. If you were Subsahara Sue, you'd have no trouble. But they'll be watching Sue, so I won't dare go near. No, I didn't mean that I prefer her. It's just

. . . I don't want to get into subtleties. Anyway, Sue might turn me in, and if I'm caught, I'll be keelhauled. Let me tell you, keelhauling is no fun.

I need love almost as much as I need a hiding place. That's why I'm telling you. You, the first human to know. I need love. And forgiveness. Only, as you'll see . . . never mind . . . I'll tell you all about me. I have much explaining to do, and you may hate me.

Don't.

I need love.

The Rooster Rowdy had caused the trouble almost 2500 Earth-years ago.

I didn't know anything about it. None of the crew knew anything about it. You see, communication is instantaneous, but perception is no faster than light.

You don't see? Maybe you will as I go along.

The instruments on The Bridge had indicated nothing and would not for I-don't-want-to-tell-you-how-many years. If the Quartermaster—let's call him The Filamentous Wafter—had not been prowling that particular deck, hunting down ratio fixers, nobody would've known about it until it was too late.

As it was, it still might be too late.

The first I knew of the trouble was when the call came from The Bridge. *Directly*.

"Hello, engine room MWST4! Hello, engine room MWST4!"

Five minutes earlier, the call would not have been able to get through. The electric sparks, microwaves, and hot mercury drops—spinning like tops—would have warped transmission. They were flying all over inside our tent. Five hundred years had passed since Subsahara Sue and I had seen each other. Although we both worked in the same continent, my territory was the Berber-Semitic area, and Sue's was all the rest of Africa.

After finally getting permission to have leave together, we'd signed in at a Libyan Seaside hotel. We spent most of our time on the beach, inside our tent, which was made of a material to confine the more explosive by-products of our lovemaking. During half a millennium, we'd dormantized our attraction—notice I say, attraction, not love, if that'll make you feel any better—but even in dormancy attraction accumulates a trickle charge and 500 years builds up a hell of a lot of static. However, there's a large amount of resistance to overcome, and I'd been oscillating and Sue resonating for hours before our nodes touched.

The tourists on the beach must have wondered where the thunder was coming from on that cloudless day.

Afterwards, Sue and I lay quietly to make sure that no one had been alarmed enough to investigate our tent. When we talked, we talked about personal matters first, what we'd been doing, our loneliness, and so on. Then we talked shop. We chattered about philiac thrust/phobiac weight efficiency ratios, toleration tare, grief drag, heliovalves, and so on, and ended up by reminiscing about crewmen.

She said, "Who's in charge of cosmic bleedoff?"

The intercom bleeped.

"Hello, engine room MWST4! Hello, engine room MWST4!"

Groaning, I turned on the intercom, which looked just like a portable TV (for the benefit of humans). The "head" and part of the "shoulders" of the First Man filled most of the screen, even though the camera must have been several thousand miles away. Behind him was a small part of The Bridge and a piece of abyss-black shadow edged by a peculiar white light. The Captain's tail.

That was all I cared to see of The Captain at any time. I'll never forget having to look at a closeup of his "mouth" when he chewed me—not literally, thank the stars—in A. H. 45. I have to admit that I deserved that savaging. I was lucky not to get keelhauled.

Oh, how I goofed up the Mahomet Follow-up! The black gangs all over The Ship had to sweat and slave, all leaves cancelled, until proper thrust could be generated.

The First Mate, seeing the mercury drip off me, roared, "Mecca Mike! What the bilge have you been doing? You oscillating at a time like this? You sleeping at the post again? You neglecting your duty *again?*"

"Sir, I'm on leave," I said. "So I couldn't be guilty of neglecting my duty. Besides, sir, I don't know what you mean by *again*. I was never courtmartialed, sir, and . . ."

"Silence!" he bellowed. Behind him, the tail of The Captain twitched, and I started to oscillate negatively.

"Why didn't you answer the all-stations alarm?"

"It didn't get through," I said. I added, weakly, "There must have been too much static and stuff."

The First Mate saw Subsahara Sue trying to hide behind me. He yelled, "So *there* you are! Why didn't you answer your phone?"

"Sir, I left it in the hotel," Sue said. "Since we'd be together, we decided we'd just take Mike's phone, and . . ."

"No wonder both of you are still in the black gang! No more excuses, now! Listen, while I tell you loud and clear!"

The Rooster Rowdy was responsible for the emergency.

I was surprised when I heard The First Mate mention him. I'd thought he was dead or had run away so far into the lower decks that he'd never be found until The Ship docked. He was one of the ring-leaders—in fact, he was The First Mate then—in the Great Mutiny 100,000 Earth-years ago. He was the only one to escape alive after The Captain and his faithfuls mopped up on the mutineers. And The Rooster Rowdy had been running, or hiding, ever since. Or so we thought.

He was called Rooster for very good reasons. His mounting lust had driven him out of hiding, and he'd tried to rape The Crystalline Sexapod.

A moment ago, I told you Sue had asked me who was in charge of cosmic bleedoff. I would have told her that The Crystalline Sexapod was in charge if we hadn't been interrupted. The Sexapod had her station at that moment inside a quasar galaxy, where she had just finished setting up the structure of a new heliovalve. The Rooster Rowdy was near enough to sense her, and he came galloping in, galactic light bouncing off the trillion trillion facets of his spinning three-organ body, and he rammed through sextillions of sextillions of stellar masses and gases and just ruined the galaxy, just ruined it.

The Crystalline Sexapod put up a good fight for her virtue, which was the same thing as her life—I haven't time to go into biological-moral details—but in the process she completed the wreckage of the galaxy and so wrecked the heliovalve and wasted a century and a half of time. She took off for the lower decks, where, for all anybody knew, she might still be running with The Rooster Rowdy hot (2500F) after her.

The wrecked heliovalve meant that there was no bleedoff of phobiac drag in that sector or in a quarter of all of the sectors, since this valve was the master valve in a new setup intended to increase efficiency of bleedoff by 32.7 percent. And that really messed up our velocity.

Fortunately, The Quartermaster happened to be in the lower decks, where he was hunting ratio fixers. A ratio fixer, I'll explain, is a creature that lives in the interstices between ratios. Thus, it's compelled to be moving on, can't stay in one place long, otherwise it'll lose its foothold and fall. If it stands still very long, one of the quotients—analogous to a human foot—dwindles, and the other expands. The ratio fixer, like any form of life, wants security, so it tries to fix ratios (freeze them). Its efforts to keep from falling mess up proportions and cause The Ship's bulkheads and sometimes even the hull to buckle.

The Ship's shape, size, and mass are in a constant state of flux, but generally controlled flux. And if these are changed without The Bridge finding out about them in time, the vectors of velocity, direction, et cetera, are changed.

Using human analogies, ratio fixers might be compared to the rats in a ship. Or, better, to barnacles on a hull. Or maybe to both.

The Quartermaster had caught one and was choking it with its filaments when it caught sight of the wrecked heliovalve and of the Rooster Rowdy chasing The Sexapod through a hatchway into the depths. He notified The Bridge at once, and the all-stations alarm went out.

Now I understood why The First Mate was talking directly to me instead of the message being filtered down through sub-to-the-2nd-power officers and petty officers. With this emergency, it would take a long time for an order from The Captain to reach every engine room if it went through normal procedure.

But I had not, of course, understood completely. Or at all. I just thought I did because I was too awed and stunned to be thinking properly.

The Mate thundered, "In the name of The Port! You better not foul this one up!"

"I'll do my best, sir, as always," I said. Then, "Foul what one up, sir?"

"Idiot! Nincompoop! I'm not speaking directly to you just to give you a pep talk! A Thrust Potential has been detected in your engine room!"

"A Thr-Thr-Thrust Po-Po-Potential! In this area? But—"

"Imbecile! Not in *your* area, which is it, the Semitic? But it's your specialty! According to the message, it's in the Southern California area, wherever in bilge that is!"

"But what do I have to do with that, sir?"

"Stoker, if we weren't in such a mess, and if the Thrust Potential wasn't so promising, and if I didn't have to contact ten thousand other promising TP areas, I'd have you up here on The Bridge and flay you alive! You don't ask questions while I'm talking! Remember that, Stoker!"

"Yes, sir," I said humbly.

The First Mate then became very businesslike. Aside from a few numbskulls, coprolite-heads, and other terms, he addressed me as one entrusted with a great task and with the abilities to carry it out. That is, if I had learned anything from experience. He did remind me that I had not only screwed up the Mahomet Follow-up, I had blown the whole Ancient Egyptian Monotheist Deal.

(I was called Ikhanaton Ike and Pharaoh Phil by my chief engineer for a long time afterwards.)

The First Mate was, however, kind enough to say that I had shown much skill in the Follow-up to the Burning Bush Business.

Beware The First Mate when he's kind. I said to myself, "What's he working up to?"

I soon found out. It was the last thing I'd expected. It was a transfer to the Southern California area and a promotion to engineer, first class. I was staggered. The chief engineer and several engineer's mates and a number of very competent stokers operated in that area. In fact, there were more black gang members there than in any area of Earth.

"This chief engineer's had a breakdown," The First Mate said, although he did not have to explain anything. "He's on his way to sick bay now. This report says there's something about that area that generates psychic collapse. A distortion of psychomagnetic lines of force. However, as you know, or should know, you ignoramus, this kind of field also compensates by generating thrust-potential impulses. The Northeast section of this—what's it called? U.S.A.—has a similar distortion. Both are danger areas for our engines. But, on the other hand, you don't get anything good from a safe neutral area."

"Thanks for the elementary lecture," I said inside my head, which was a safe, though not neutral, place for my retort.

A few minutes later, I had finished saying a sorrowful good-bye to Sue and was checking out of the hotel.

"Why should you be transferred to Beverly Hills, California?" Sue said. "It may be largely Jewish in population, but the Citizens are basically English speakers. They don't think Semitically, like your Arabs, Abyssinians, and Israelis."

"That's not the only puzzling thing," I said. "The Thrust Potential is non-Semitic. That is, it's not even descended from Semitic speakers."

The engineers and stokers in that area must all have become somewhat unstable, too. Otherwise, they surely would have been used. The thinking of The Bridge was, Let's shoot in Mecca Mike. He's fouled up, but he also had some great successes. Perhaps this time he'll come through. He's the best we have, anyway, The Dock preserve us!

The First Mate told me that I had better come through. Or else. . . .

There would be officers watching my work, but they wouldn't interfere unless I was obviously ruining an "engine" beyond repair.

If I came through, if I developed the badly needed Thrust Potential, I'd be promoted. Probably to chief engineer.

The situation for The Ship was much worse than I'd guessed. Otherwise, they'd have let me take an airliner. But orders were to get me to California with utmost speed. I drove into the Libyan countryside during the daylight. At noon the saucer-shaped vehicle landed, picked me up, and took off at 30 G. It socked into its base fifty miles west of Phoenix, Arizona, with Air Force jets scrambling from Luke Field. They neither saw the ship nor the base, of course, and I drove into Phoenix in what looked like a 1965 Buick and took a plane into Los Angeles.

Coming down over Los Angeles must have been disheartening to the other passengers. They saw the great greenish-gray tentacles, the exhaled poison, hanging over the big complex. I had my special "glasses" on, and what I saw was encouraging, at least momentarily. Down there, in the blackness which is phobiac drag, were a dozen fairly large sparks and one huge spark. That big spark, I knew, must be in Beverly Hills.

There, if all went well—it seldom does—was the potential to develop a thrust which, combined with the thrusts in existence and with those being developed on other worlds, would, hopefully, cancel the drag caused by the wrecking of the bleedoff heliovalve. And so the vitally needed velocity would be ours.

*Can anything good come out of Nazareth?*

*And anything good be in Beverly Hills?*

History has answered the first question. The future would answer the second.

I told the taxi driver at the airport to take me to a street which angled south off of Wilshire between Doheny Drive and Beverly Drive. This was lined with dry-looking maples. The block where the taxi let me off was, in a sense, in the "slums" of Beverly Hills. Relatively speaking, of course. Both sides of the street in this block were occupied by apartment buildings, some only five years old and others about 25 to 35 years old. The apartments in the new buildings rented from $350 to $650 a month and so were considered low-rent in Beverly Hills. The apartments in the old buildings averaged about $135 a month.

My Thrust Potential, my TP, was in the second story of an older building. I had the cab park across the street from it, and I went inside a newer, more expensive apartment building. This had a VACANCY, 1 BDRM, FURN., NO PETS, NO CHILDREN sign on the lawn. I put down three months rent in cash, which upset Mrs. Klugel, the landlady. She always dealt in checks. I signed the lease and then went back to the taxi to get my bags.

My second-story apartment was almost directly across the street from my Tp and almost as high as her apartment. I carried my three bags up to it. One was full of clothes, the second full of money, and the third crammed with my equipment. Mrs. Klugel stood in the vestibule. She was a heavy short woman about 65 with orange-dyed hair, a nose like a cucumber, and a clown's mouth. Her black-rimmed eyes widened as I went lightly up the staircase with a huge bag in each hand and one under my arm.

"So you're a strong man in some act already?" she said.

I replied that I was not a strong man, professionally, that is. I was a writer who intended to write a novel about Hollywood.

"So why don't you live in Hollywood?"

"By Hollywood, I mean this whole area around here," I said, sweeping my hand around.

She was such a lonely old lady, she was difficult to get rid of. I said I had work to do, and I would talk to her later. As soon as she shut the door, I readjusted the antigrav belt around my waist under my shirt. My two thousand pounds of dense metal-shot protein would have buckled the floor if I hadn't had the belt operating. Then I took out my equipment and set it up.

I was nervous; quicksilver beaded off me and fell onto the floor. I made a mental note to clean up the stuff before I left the apartment. Mrs. Klugel looked as if she'd snoop around during my absences, and it certainly would be difficult to explain mercury drops on the floor.

The set-up for my work was this. Across the street, in the 25-year-old building, were four apartments. My concern was the upper story on the right side, facing the street. But I soon found out that the apartment just below was also to be intimately involved.

The apartment upstairs was reached by climbing a steep series of steps, carpeted with frayed and faded material. A long hall at the top of the stairs ran the length of the building, ending in a bathroom at its far end. Off the hallway, starting next to the bathroom, were doors leading to a bedroom, another bedroom, the doorway to the back entrance, the doorway to a tiny utility room, and the doorway to the living room. The utility room and living room connected to the kitchen.

The back bedroom was occupied by Diana, the 20-year-old divorced mother, and her 20-month-old child, Pam. The grandparents, Tom and Claudia Bonder, slept in the other bedroom. Tom also did his writing in this room. Claudia was 45 and Tom was 49.

When I looked through the spec-analyzers, via the tap-beam, I saw the baby, Pam, as the bright light I had seen coming in over Los Angeles. She was the big Thrust Potential.

Sometimes the light was dimmed. Not because its source was weakened. No. It darkened because of the hatred pouring out of the grandfather.

This black cataract was, seemingly, directed mainly at the people in the apartment below. If hatred were water, it would have drowned the people below. And, if they were what Tom Bonder said they were, they deserved drowning, if not worse.

Tom Bonder's hatred, like most hatreds, was not, however, simple.

None of the hatreds in that building, or in any of the buildings in Beverly Hills, and believe me, there were hatreds in every building, were simple.

I digress. Back to that particular building.

Watching that building was like watching the Northern Lights during a meteor shower on the Fourth of July. I ignored the pyrotechnic displays of the tenants on the other side of the building. They had little to do with the "stoking" and the follow-up.

Tom Bonder, ah, there was a splendid spectacle! Although he had been depressed in his youth, at which time he must have radiated heavy-drag black, like smoke from Vesuvius, he had semi-converted his youthful depression into middle-aged anger. Reversed the usual course of psychic events, you might say. Now he looked like Vesuvius in eruption.

Bonder, the grandfather, was determined not to fail as a grandfather just because he had failed as a father, husband, lover, son, teacher, writer—and you name it.

And truly, he had failed, but not as badly as he thought, or, I should say, desired, since he lusted for defeat. Rage poured out of him day and night, even when, especially when, he was sleeping.

What most infuriated him was the uproar beating upwards day and night from the Festigs downstairs. The Festigs were a father, 40 years old, a mother 28, and a daughter, Lisa, two. From the time they arose, anywhere from 9:30 to 11:30, until they went to bed, midnight or 1:00, or later, the mother was shouting and bellowing and singing and clapping her hands sharply and the little girl was screaming with glee but usually wailing or screeching with frustration and anger. The father was silent most of the time; but he was like an old sunken Spanish galleon, buried in black silt, with his treasures, his pieces-of-eight and silver ingots and gold crosses, spilled out of a breach in the hull and only occasionally revealed when the currents dredged away some mud.

Oh, he was depressed, depressed, which is to say he was a very angry man indeed. The black heavy stuff flowed from Myron Festig like a Niagara fouled with sewage. But sometimes, out of boredom, as he sat on his chair in the living room, he groaned mightily, and the groan went up and out the windows and into the windows of the apartment upstairs.

And Tom Bonder would jump when he heard the groan and would quit muttering and raging under his breath. He would be silent, as one lion may fall silent for a moment when he hears the roar of another from far away.

The screaming joys and buzzsaw tantrums were enough for the Bonders (not to mention the next-door neighbors) to endure. But the child also had the peculiar habit of stomping her feet if she ran or walked. The sound vibrated up through the walls and the floors and through the bed and into the pillow-covered ears of Tom Bonder. Even if he managed to get to sleep, he would be awakened a dozen times by the footstompings or by the screams and the bellows.

He would sit up and curse. Sometimes, he would loosen his grip on his fear of violence and would shout out of the window: "Quiet down, down there, you barbarians, illiterate swine! We have to get up early to go to work! We're not on relief, you bloodsucking inconsiderate parasites!"

The reference to relief, if nothing else, should have turned Myron Festig's depression into rage, because the Festigs were one of the few people in Beverly Hills living on relief. The relief came from the county welfare and from money borrowed from Mrs. Festig's mother and doctor brothers. Occasionally, Myron sold a cartoon or took a temporary job. But he was very sensitive about the welfare money, and he would have been astounded to learn that the Bonders knew about it. The Bonders, however, had been informed about this by the manager's wife.

Rachel Festig, the wife and mother, was revealed in the analyzer as intermittent flashes of white, which were philiac thrust, with much yellow, that is, deeply repressed rage sublimated as sacrificial or martyred love. And there was the chlorine-gas green of self-poisonous self-worship.

But there was the bright white light of the Bonder baby, Pam. Now that I was near it, I saw it spilt into two, as a star seem by the naked eye will become a double star in the telescope. The lesser star, as it were, radiated from Lisa Festig. All infants, unless they're born psychotic, have this thrust. Lisa's, unfortunately, was waning, and its brightness would be almost entirely gone in a year or so. Her mother's love was extinguishing it in a dozen ways.

But the far brighter white, the almost blinding Thrust Potential, radiated from the Bonder granddaughter. She was a beautiful, strong, healthy, good-humored, intelligent, extremely active, and very loving baby. She was more than enough to cause her grandparents to love her beyond normal grandparental love. But they had reason to especially cherish this baby. The father had dropped out of sight in West Venice, not that anybody was looking for him.

Furthermore, both Claudia and Tom felt that they had been psychically distorted by their parents and that they, in turn, had psychically bent their daughter, Thea. But Pam was not going to be fouled up, neurotic, near-neurotic, unhappy, desolate, and so on. At the moment, both the elder Bonders were going to psychoanalysts to get their psyches hammered out straight on the anvil of the couch.

Neither the daughter nor Mrs. Bonder, though they figured significantly and were to be used by me, were as important in my plans as Tom Bonder.

Why? Because he was an atheist who had never been able to shake himself free of his desire to know a God, a hardheaded pragmatist who lusted for mysticism as an alcoholic lusts for the bottle he has renounced, a scoffer of religions whose eyes became teary whenever he watched the hoakiest, most putridly sentimental religious movies on TV with Bing Crosby, Barry Fitzgerald, and Humphrey Bogart as priests. This, plus the tiniest spark of what, for a better term, is called pre-TP, and his rage, made me choose him. As a matter of fact, he was the main tool I had for the only plan I had.

Rachel Festig thought of herself as the Great Mother. Tom Bonder agreed with that to the extent that he thought she was a Big Mother. Rachel's idea of a mother was a woman with enormous breasts dripping the milk of kindness, compassion, and, occasionally, passion. The Great Mother also had a well-rounded belly, wide hips, thick thighs, and hands white with baking flour. The Great Mother spent every waking moment with the child to the exclusion of everything else except cooking and some loving with the husband to keep him contented.

Now there was a Mother!

Myron needed to be dependent, to be, at 40, an invertebrate, a waxingly fat invertebrate. Yet he wanted to be a world-famous cartoonist, a picture-satirist of the modern age, especially in its psychic sicknesses. Recently, in a burst of backbone, he had stayed up all night for several weeks, and completed an entire book of cartoons abut group therapy. He knew the subject well, since he was a participant in a group and also had private sessions once a week. Both were paid for by arrangement with the county and his brother-in-law, the doctor.

The cartoon book was published and sold well locally, then the excitement died down and he subsided into a great roll of unbone stiffened protoplasm. Depression blackened him once more. He gained a hunger for food instead of fame, and so he ate and swelled.

Tom Bonder worked daytimes as an electronic technician at a space industry plant in Huntington Beach, and evenings and weekends he wrote fast-action private-eye novels for paperback publishers and an occasional paperback western.

He loathed his technician job and wanted to go into full-time fiction writing. However, he was having enough trouble writing part-time now because of the uproar downstairs.

I used the tap-beam and sight-beam to listen and look into the apartments and also to eavesdrop on Bonder's sessions with the analyst. I knew he ascribed his problems to a too-early and too-harsh toilet training, to a guilt caused by conflict between his childhood curiosity about sex and his parents' harsh repression of it and so on. His main problem throughout most of his life had been a rigid control over himself. He thought himself a coward because he had always avoided violence, but he was finding out in therapy that he feared that he might become too violent and lose his self-control.

Fortunately, he was now getting rid of some of his anger in little daily spurts, but, unfortunately, not swiftly enough.

He was always on the verge of going berserk.

Berserk! That was the key to my "stoking."

The Ship must have been losing speed even worse than we of the crew had been told. About six months after I got into Beverly Hills, I received a call from The First Mate again.

"How's the set-up coming along?"

"As well as can be expected," I said. "You know you can't stoke too fast, sir. The engine might overheat or blow."

"I know that, you cabin-boy reject!" he bellowed so loudly that I turned the volume down. Old Mrs. Klugel quite often kept her ear pressed to the tenants' doors.

I said, "I'll use more pressure, sir, but it'll have to be delicately applied. I sure wouldn't want to wreck this little engine. Her nimbus looks as if she could provide enormous thrust, if she's brought along properly."

"Three hours you get," The First Mate said. "Then we have to have a million T units."

Three hours of Ship's time was 30 Earth-years. Even if I got the stoking done quickly, I had a hell of a lot of hard mercury-sweating work in the next 30 years. I promised I'd do my best, and The First Mate said that that had better be better than good enough, and he signed off.

Tom Bonder and Myron Festig were working themselves closer to that condition I'd been working for. The Festig child was stomping her feet and screaming all day and until one in the morning, and the inability to get sleep was putting black circles around Tom Bonder's eyes. And red halos of wrath around him.

Myron Festig was deep in the sludge pit of despond. His latest cartoon had been turned down by *Playboy*. He had just been fired from a job as a cheese salesman. His mother-in-law was threatening to visit them for a long time. His brother-in-law, the doctor, was needling him because he wasn't making a steady income, aside from welfare payments. And Rachel, his wife, when not chewing him out for his inability to hold a job, was crying that they should have another baby. They needed a son; she would deliver him a boy to make him proud.

The last thing Myron wanted was another mouth to stuff, and, though he dared not say it, another noisy mouth and big heavy feet to distract him from his cartooning.

Tom Bonder would have agreed with this. He was, he told his wife, slowly being herded to suicide or homicide. He could not take much more of this. And more frequently, as if in jest, he would open a drawer in the kitchen and take out a hand-axe, which he had brought with him when he moved from the Midwest. And he would say, "One more night of thumping from Little Miss Buffalo Stampede, one more night of bellowing 'Myron!' or 'Rachel!', and I go downstairs and chop up the whole swinish bunch!"

His wife and daughter would grin, nervously, and tell him he shouldn't even joke like that.

"I'm fantasizing!" he'd cry. "My headshrinker says it's good therapy to imagine slaughtering them, very healthy! It relieves the tensions! As long as I can fantasize, I won't take action! But when I can't fantasize, beware! Chop! Chop! Off with their heads! Blood will flow!" And he would swing the axe while he grinned.

Sometimes, exasperated beyond endurance, he would stomp his foot on the floor to advice the Festigs that their uproar was intolerable. Sometimes, the Festigs would quiet down for a while. More often, they ignored the hints from above or even increased the volume. And, once, Myron Festig, enraged that anyone should dare to object to his family's activities (and also taking out against the Bonders the rage he felt against himself and his family), slammed his foot angrily against the floor and cried out.

Mr. Bonder, startled at first, then doubly enraged, slammed his foot back. Both men then waited to see what would happen. Nothing, however, followed.

And this and other events or nonevents are difficult to explain. Why didn't Tom Bonder just go down and have a talk with the Festigs? Why didn't he communicate directly, face to face, with words and expressions?

I've watched human beings for a million years (my body was shaped like a ground ape's then), and I still don't know exactly why they do or don't do certain things.

Bonder's overt problem was communication. Rather, the lack thereof. He kept too rigid a control over himself to talk freely. Which may be why he turned to writing.

He probably did not go down to tell the Festigs how they were disturbing him because, to him, even a little anger meant a greater one would inevitably follow, and he could not endure the thought of this. And so he avoided a direct confrontation.

Yet, he was getting more and more angry every day; his safety valve was stuck, and his boilers were about to blow.

I can tell by your expression what you're thinking. Why don't we build "engines" which will automatically put out the required thrust?

If this were possible, it would have been done long ago.

The structure of the universe, that is, of The Ship, requires, for reasons unknown to me, that philiac thrust be generated only by sentient beings with free will. Automatons can't love. If love is built into, or programmed into, the automaton, the love means nothing in terms of thrust. It's a pseudolove, and so a pseudothrust results, and this is no thrust at all.

No. Life has to be created on viable planets, and it must evolve until it brings forth a sentient being. And this being may then be manipulated, pulled and pushed, given suggestions and laws, and so forth. But the blazing white thrust is not easy to come by, and the black drag is always there. It's a hideous problem to solve. And hideous means often have to be used.

And so, obeying my orders, I speeded up the stoking. Far faster than I liked. Fortunately, a number of events occurring about the same time three months later helped me, and everything converged on one day, a Thursday.

The evening before, Myron Festig had gone on the Joseph Beans TV show to get publicity for his group-therapy cartoon book, although he had been warned not to do so. As a result, he was stingingly insulted by Beans and his doltish audience, was called sick and was told that group therapy was a mess of mumbo-jumbo. Myron was smarting severely from the savage putdown.

On the next day, Tom Bonder was two and a half hours late getting home. The motor of his car had burned out. This was the climax to the increasing, almost unendurable, frustration and nerve-shredding caused by the two-hour five-day-a-week round trip from Beverly Hills to Huntington Beach and back on the freeway. In addition, his request for a transfer to the nearby Santa Monica plant was lost somewhere on the great paper highway of interdepartmental affairs of the astronautics company, and the entire request would have to be initiated again in triplicate.

Two days before, Myron Festig had been fired from another job. He'd made several mistakes in giving change to customers because he was thinking of ideas for cartoons.

Tom Bonder found his wife did not want to listen to his tale of trouble with the car. She had had a setback in therapy and was also upset about some slights her employer had given her.

After tapping in on Myron's account to his wife of how he lost his job, I made an anonymous phone call to the welfare office and told them that Myron Festig had been working without reporting the fact to them. They had called Myron to come down and explain himself.

Myron Festig's brother-in-law, the doctor, wanted part of his loan back. But the Festigs were broke.

Tom Bonder, on coming home, was received with a letter of rejection. The editor to whom he had sent his latest private-eye thriller had turned it down with a number of nasty remarks. Now Bonder wouldn't be able to pay all of next month's bills.

Myron Festig's mother, the day before, had called him and begged him, for the hundredth time, to accept his aged father's offer to become his junior partner in his business. He should quit being a nogoodnik "artist!" who couldn't support his wife and child. Or, for that matter, himself.

Moreover, and this as much as anything sent him skiing out of control on the slopes of despair, his psychiatrist had gone on a two weeks' vacation in Mexico.

And, that very morning, Myron got word that one of the therapy group, a lovely young woman whom Myron was becoming very fond of, had killed herself with a .45 automatic.

Tom Bonder flushed the toilet, and it filled up and ran all over the bathroom floor. Bonder suppressed his desire to yell out obscenities and denunciations of his landlord because he did not want to upset his granddaughter, and he called the plumber. This incident was the latest in a long series of blown fuses in the old and overloaded electrical circuits and the backing of dirty waters in the old and deteriorating plumbing.

Rachel Festig told Myron that he had to get another job and quickly. Or she was going to work, and he could stay home to take care of the child. Myron sat in the big worn easy chair and just looked at her, as if he were an oyster with five o'clock shadow and she were a strange fish he was trying to identify. Rachel became hysterical and raved for an hour (I could hear her across the street through my open window, I didn't need my tap-beam) about the psychic damage to Lisa if her mother left her to go to work. Myron was so silent and unresponsive that she became frightened.

The plumbers finally left. The baby, who had been awakened by their activities, finally went back to sleep. Tom Bonder sat down at his desk in the crowded bedroom to start writing a story for a mystery magazine. If he wrote it quickly enough and the editors did not dawdle reading it, and bought it, and then did not dawdle in sending his money, he might have enough to pay next month's bills. He wrote two paragraphs, using his pencil so that the typewriter wouldn't wake up the baby.

The thumping of Lisa's feet and her screaming as she ran back and forth from room to room disturbed him even more than usual. But he clamped his mental teeth and wrote on.

Then Rachel began to march along behind Lisa, and she sang loudly (she always said she could have been a great singer if she hadn't married Myron), and she clapped her hands over and over.

It was now nine P.M. The baby stirred in her crib. Then, after some especially heavy crashing of Lisa's feet, Pam cried out. Tom's daughter came into the back bedroom and tried to quiet her down.

Tom Bonder reared up from his desk, his flailing hand scattering papers onto the floor. He stalked into the kitchen and opened a bottom drawer. As usual, it stuck, and he had to get down on his knees and yank at it. This time, he did not mutter something about fixing it someday.

He took out the hand-axe and walked through the front room, hoping his wife would see it.

She curled her lip and said, "Don't be more of an ass than God made you, Tom. You're not scaring anybody with that."

And then, "Why aren't you writing? You said you couldn't talk to me because you had to write."

He glared at her and said nothing. The reasons for his anger were so obvious and justified that she must be deliberately baiting him because of her own turmoiled feelings.

Finally, he grunted, "That menagerie downstairs."

"Well, if you have to fantasize, you don't have to hold that axe. It makes me nervous. Put it away."

He went back into the kitchen. At that moment, I phoned.

His wife said, "Get the phone. If anybody wants me, I'm out to the store. I don't feel like talking to anyone tonight, except you, and you won't talk to me."

Violently, he picked up the phone and said, harshly, "Hello!"

I was watching the whole scene directly on the tap-beam, of

course, and at the same time was displaying the Festigs' front room on a viewer.

I mimicked Myron Festig's voice. "This is Myron. Would you please be more quiet up there? We can't think with all that noise."

Tom Bonder yelled an obscenity and slammed down the phone. He whirled, ran out into the hall, and charged down the steps with the axe still in his hand.

Rachel and Lisa had stopped their noisy parade, and Myron had risen from his chair at the thunder on the staircase.

I had started to dial the Festigs' number as soon as I'd finished with Tom Bonder. The phone rang when Bonder reached the bottom of the steps, Myron, who was closest to the phone, answered.

I mimicked the voice of Myron's mother. I said, "Myron! If you don't go into business with your father at once, I'll never ever have anything any more to do with you, my only son! God help me! What did I ever do to deserve a son like you? Don't you love your aged parents?" And I hung up.

Tom Bonder was standing outside the Festigs' door with the axe raised when I ran out of my apartment building. I was wearing a policeman's uniform, and I was ready for Mrs. Klugel if she should see me. I meant to tell her I was going to a costume ball. She did not, however, come out of her room since her favorite TV show was on.

I walked swiftly across the street, and not until I got on the sidewalk did Tom Bonder see me.

He could have been beating on the door with his axe in a maniac effort to get inside and kill the Festigs. But his abnormally powerful self-control had, as I'd hoped, reasserted itself. He had discharged much of his anger by the obscenity, the energy of aggression in charging down the stairs, and the mere act of raising the axe to strike the door. Now he stood like the Tin Woodman when the rain rusted his joints, motionless, his eyes on the door, his right arm in the air with his axe in his hand.

I coughed; he broke loose. He whirled and saw the uniform by the nearby street light. My face was in the shadows.

I said, "Good evening," and started back across the street as if I were going home after work. I heard the door slam and knew that Tom Bonder had run back into his apartment and doubtless was shaking with reaction from his anger and from relief at his narrow escape from being caught in the act by a policeman.

Once in my apartment, I used the tapbeams to observe the situation. Tom Bonder had opened the door and tossed the axe onto the floor in front of the Festigs' door.

It was his obscure way of communicating. Quit driving me crazy with your swinish uproar, or the next time . . .

I'm sure that the dropping of the axe before the Festigs was, at the same time, an offer of peace. Here is the axe which I have brandished at you. I no longer want it; you may have it.

And there was a third facet to this seemingly simple but actually complicated gesture, as there is to almost every human gesture. He knew well, from what Rachel had told his daughter, and from what he had observed and heard, that Myron was on as high and thin a tightrope as he. So, the flinging down of the axe meant also: Pick it up and use it.

Tom Bonder did not realize this consciously, of course.

I had thought that Tom Bonder might do just what he had done. I knew him well enough to chance that he would. If he had acted otherwise, then I would have had to set up another situation.

Myron opened the door; he must have heard the thump of the hatchet and Bonder's steps as he went back up the stairs. He picked it up after staring at it for a full minute and returned to his easy chair. He sat down and put the axe on his lap. His fat fingers played with the wooden handle and a thumb felt along the edge of the head.

Rachel walked over to him and bent over so her face was only about three inches from his. She shouted at him; her mouth worked and worked.

I didn't know what she was saying because I had shut off the audio of their beam. I was forcing myself to watch, but I didn't want to hear.

This was the first time I had cut off the sound during a "stroking." At that moment, I didn't think about what I was doing or why. Later, I knew that this was the first overt reflection of something that had been troubling me for a long time.

All the elements of the situation (I'm talking about the Festigs, now) had worked together to make Myron do what he did. But the final element, the fuse, was that Rachel looked remarkably like his mother and at that moment was acting and talking remarkably like her.

The black clouds which usually poured out of him had been slowly turning a bright red at their bases. Now the red crept up the clouds, like columns of mercury in a bank of thermometers seen through smoke. Suddenly, the red exploded, shot through the black, overwhelmed the black, dissolved it in scarlet, and filled the room with a glare.

Myron seemed to come up out of the chair like a missile from its launching pad. He pushed Rachel with one hand so hard that she staggered back halfway across the room, her mouth open, jelled in the middle of whatever she had been screaming.

He stepped forward and swung.

I forced myself to watch as he went towards the child.

When Myron Festig was through with the two, and he took a long time, or so it seemed to me, he ran into the kitchen. A moment later, he came back out of the kitchen door with a huge butcher knife held before him with both hands, the point against the solar plexus. He charged the room, slammed into the wall and rammed its hilt into the wall. The autopsy report was to state that the point had driven into his backbone.

I turned the audio back on then, although I could hear well enough through my apartment window. A siren was whopping some blocks away. The porch light had been turned on, and the manager, his wife, and juvenile daughter were standing outside the Festigs' door. Presently, the door to the Bonders' apartment opened, and Mrs. Bonder came out. Tom Bonder and Thea followed a minute later.

The manager opened the door to the Festigs' apartment. Tom Bonder looked into the front room between the manager and the side of the doorway.

He swayed, then stepped back until he bumped into Mrs. Bonder. The blood was splashed over the walls, the floors, and the furniture. There were even spots of it on the ceiling.

The broken handle of the axe lay in a pool of blood.

I turned the beam away from the Festigs and watched Tom Bonder. He was on his knees, his arms dangling, hands spread open stiffly, his head thrown back, and his eyes rolled up. His mouth moved silently.

Then there was a cry. Pam, the baby, had gotten out of her crib and was standing at the top of the steps and looking down at the half-open door to the porch and crying for her mother. Thea ran up to her and held her in her arms and soothed her.

At the cry, Tom Bonder shook. No nimbus except the gray of sleep or trance or semi-consciousness had welled from him. But then a finger of white, a slim shaft of brightness, extended from his head. In a minute, he was enveloped in a starry blaze. He was on his feet and taking Mrs. Bonder by the hand and going up the steps. The police car stopped before the building. The siren died, but the red light on top of the car kept flashing.

I packed my stuff in my three bags and went out the back entrance. It was now highly probable that Tom Bonder would take the course I had planned. And since he was a highly imaginative man, he would influence his granddaughter, who, being a Thrust Potential, would naturally incline toward the religious and the mystical. And toward love. And those in charge of her development would see that she came into prominence and then into greatness in later life. And, after the almost inevitable martyrdom, they would bring about the proper follow-up. Or try to.

They would. I wouldn't.

I was through. I had had enough of murder, suffering and bloodshed. A million, many millions, of Festigs haunted me. Somehow, and I know the crewmen and officers say it's impossible, I'd grown a heart. Or I'd had it given to me, in the same way the Tin Woodman got his heart.

I'd had enough. Too much. That is why I deserted and why I've been hiding for all these years. And why I've managed to get three others of the black gang to desert, too.

Now we're being hunted down. The hunters and the hunted are not known by you humans. You engines, so they call you.

But I fled here, and I met you, and I fell in love with you, not in a quite-human way, of course. Now you know who and what I am. But don't turn away. Don't make me leave you.

I love you, even if I can't make love to you.

Help me. I'm a mutineer, but unlike The Rooster Rowdy, I'm interested in mutinying because of you humans, not because I want to be first, to be The Captain.

We must take over. Somehow, there has to be a better way to run The Ship!

# THE REALITY TRIP
## (MAY 1970)
## ROBERT SILVERBERG
## (B. 1935)

Robert Silverberg burst upon the science-fiction world in 1954 and for the next twenty years or so was one of the field's most prolific authors. His career (thankfully resumed after a five-year retirement) had several stages, which saw him develop from a competent wordsmith to a master craftsman. *If* was not one of his major markets at any stage in his career, but he did publish his novel *The Man in the Maze* (1968) and a handful of stories in its pages, including "The Shadow of Wings" (July 1963) and "Passport to Sirius" (April 1958).

Although it won no awards, "The Reality Trip" is an excellent story by the then "new" Robert Silverberg.

## MEMOIR BY ROBERT SILVERBERG

I wrote "The Reality Trip" in far-off exotic January of 1970, when I was still a New Yorker, *If* was still a going concern, and OPEC, for all anybody knew, was an obscure little company listed on the American Stock Exchange. Ejler Jakobsson was then the editor of *If*, and although I know he had his detractors among the SF writers, I was never one of them, for he and I had a splendid working relationship based on the bonds of mutual respect between a cagy old pro and a cagy young one. Rarely have I felt so in tune with an editor, and during his brief editorship of *Galaxy* and *If* he called forth from me a flood of fiction that must surely astound and amaze historians of the field. It certainly does astound and amaze me to consider that Jakobsson's *Galaxy* published my novels *Downward to the Earth*, *Tower of Glass*, *The World Inside*, and *A Time of Changes* in virtually consecutive issues between November 1969 and July 1971, and followed with *Dying Inside* in the summer of 1972. For readers who didn't care for the fiction of Robert Silverberg, I suppose it was an endless ordeal; but for those who did, it was a feast that is not goddamned likely to be repeated, you betcha, because writers hit hot streaks like that only once in their lives. (Heinlein had one in 1940–1942, and Sturgeon in the early 1950s, and Sheckley about the same time, and Philip K. Dick seven or eight years later. They've all done good work since, but not with the same crazy intensity, and I don't expect that frenzy of creativity to come surging through me again. It's fun, but it's exhausting.)

While doing all those novels, and a couple of others of the same period such as *Son of Man* and *The Second Trip*, and my big nonfiction work on the Prester John myth, and all the rest of the implausible output of my implausible mid-thirties, I did by way of breather the occasional short story—"The Reality Trip" was the first of six in 1970. I suppose it appeared in *If* because my novels were appearing so inexorably in the companion magazine; somehow I was considered a *Galaxy* writer rather than an *If* writer for most of the time that those magazines were published as companions, although over the years I did have a dozen or so stories and a novel or two in *If*.

The hotel where the story takes place will instantly be recognized by any New York writer as the Chelsea, where Arthur C. Clarke used to stay when visiting Manhattan, and which all sorts of other SF people occasionally used as their New York pied-à-terre. It was and I assume still is a lovely weird baroque old thing, and it seemed not at all unlikely to me that several extraterrestrial beings would be in permanent residence there.

As for Ejler Jakobsson, I still think of him as a good friend, though the only contact I've had with him and his delightful pipe-smoking wife in recent years has been the Christmas card they faithfully send. He's living in retirement in the Westchester suburbs, I bask in California sunshine, *Worlds of If* is down there with Nineveh and Pompeii, and we all know what OPEC is these days. On balance I'd rather live in 1980 than 1970, OPEC notwithstanding, but there are pleasant memories of that bygone era for me, and this story is associated with several of them.

# THE REALITY TRIP

I am a reclamation project for her. She lives on my floor of the hotel, a dozen rooms down the hall: a lady poet, private income. No, that makes her sound too old, a middle-aged eccentric. Actually she is no more than thirty. Taller than I am, with long kinky brown hair and a sharp, bony nose that has a bump on the bridge. Eyes are very glossy. A studied raggedness about her dress; carefully chosen shabby clothes. I am in no position really to judge the sexual attractiveness of Earthfolk but I gather from remarks made by men living here that she is not considered good-looking. I pass her often on my way to my room. She smiles fiercely at me. Saying to herself, no doubt, You poor lonely man. Let me help you bear the burden of your unhappy life. Let me show you the meaning of love, for I too know what it is like to be alone.

Or words to the effect. She's never actually said any such thing. but her intentions are transparent. When she sees me, a kind of hunger comes into her eyes, part maternal, part (I guess) sexual, and her face takes on a wild crazy intensity. Burning with emotion. Her name is Elizabeth Cooke. "Are you fond of poetry, Mr. Knecht?" she asked me this morning, as we creaked upward together in the ancient elevator. And an hour later she knocked at my door. "Something for you to read," she said. "I wrote them." A sheaf of large yellow sheets, stapled at the top; poems printed in smeary blue mimeography. *The Reality Trip*, the collection was headed. *Limited Edition: 125 Copies.* "You can keep it if you like," she explained. "I've got lots more." She was wearing bright corduroy slacks and a flimsy pink shawl through which her breasts plainly showed. Small tapering breasts not very functional-looking. When she saw me studying them her nostrils flared momentarily and she blinked her eyes three times swiftly. Tokens of lust?

I read the poems. Is it fair for me to offer judgment on them? Even though I've lived on this planet eleven of its years, even though my command of colloquial English is quite good, do I really comprehend the inner life of poetry? I thought they were all quite bad. Earnest, plodding poems, capturing what they call lies of life. The world around her, the cruel, brutal, unloving city.

Lamenting the failure of people to open to one another. The title poem began this way:

> *He was on the reality trip. Big black man,*
> *bloodshot eyes, bad teeth. Eisenhower jacket,*
> *frayed. Smell of cheap wine. I guess a knife*
> *in his pocket. Looked at me mean. Criminal*
> *record. Rape, child-beating, possession of drugs.*
> *In his head saying, slavemistress bitch, and me in*
> *my head saying, black brother, let's freak in to-*
> *gether, let's trip on love—*

And so forth. Warm, direct emotion; but is the urge to love all wounded things a sufficient center for poetry? I don't know. I did put her poems through the scanner and transmit them to Homeworld, although I doubt they'll learn much from them about Earth. It would flatter Elizabeth to know that while she has few readers here, she has acquired some ninety light-years away. But of course I can't tell her that.

She came back a short while ago. "Did you like them?" she asked.

"Very much. You have such sympathy for those who suffer."

I think she expected me to invite her in. I was careful not to look at her breasts this time.

The hotel is on West 23rd Street. It must be over a hundred years old; the façade is practically baroque and the interior shows a kind of genteel decay. The place has a bohemian tradition. Most of its guests are permanent residents and many of them are artists, novelists, playwrights, and such. I have lived here nine years. I know a number of the residents by name, and they me, but I have discouraged any real intimacy, naturally, and everyone has respected that choice. I do not invite others into my room. Sometimes I let myself be invited to visit theirs, since one of my responsibilities on this world is to get to know something of the way Earthfolk live and think. Elizabeth is the first to attempt to cross the invisible barrier of privacy I surround myself with. I'm not sure how I'll handle that. She moved in about three years ago; her attentions became noticeable perhaps ten months back, and for the last five or six weeks she's been a great nuisance. Some kind of confrontation is inevitable: either I must tell her to leave me alone, or I will find myself drawn into a situation impossible to tolerate. Perhaps she'll find someone else to feel even sorrier for, before it comes to that.

My daily routine rarely varies. I rise at seven. First Feeding. Then I clean my skin (my outer one, the Earthskin, I mean) and dress. From eight to ten I transmit data to Homeworld. Then I go out for the morning field trip: talking to people, buying newspapers, often some library research. At one I return to my room. Second Feeding. I transmit data from two to five. Out again, perhaps to the theater, to a motion picture, to a political meeting. I must soak up the flavor of this planet. Often to saloons; I am equipped for ingesting alcohol, though of course I must get rid of it before it has been in my body very long, and I drink and listen and sometimes argue. At midnight back to my room. Third Feeding. Transmit data from one to four in the morning. Then three hours of sleep, and at seven the cycle begins anew. It is a comforting schedule. I don't know how many agents Homeworld has on Earth, but I like to think that I'm one of the most diligent and useful. I miss very little. I've done good service, and, as they say here, hard work is its own regard. I won't deny that I hate the physical discomfort of it and frequently give way to real despair over my isolation from my own kind. Sometimes I even think of asking for a transfer to Homeworld. But what would become of me there? What services could I perform? I have shaped my life to one end: that of dwelling among the Earthfolk and reporting on their ways. If I give that up, I am nothing.

Of course there is the physical pain. Which is considerable.

The gravitational pull of Earth is almost twice that of Homeworld. It makes for a leaden life for me. My inner organs always sagging against the lower rim of my carapace. My muscles cracking with strain. Every movement a willed effort. My heart in constant protest. In my eleven years I have as one might expect adapted somewhat to the condition; I have toughened, I have thickened. I suspect that if I were transported instantly to Homeworld now I would be quite giddy, baffled by the lightness of everything. I would leap and soar and stumble, and might even miss this crushing pull of Earth. Yet I doubt that. I suffer here; at all times the weight oppresses me. Not to sound too self-pitying about it. I knew the conditions in advance. I was placed in a simulated Earth Gravity when I volunteered, and was given a chance to withdraw, and I decided to go anyway. Not realizing that a week under double gravity is not the same thing as a lifetime. I could always have stepped out of the simulation chamber. Not here. The eternal drag on every molecule of me. The pressure. My flesh is always in mourning.

And the outer body I must wear. This cunning disguise. Forever to be swaddled in thick masses of synthetic flesh, smothering me, engulfing me. The soft slippery slap of it against the self within. The elaborate framework that holds it erect, by which I make it move: a forest of struts and braces and servoactuators and cables, in the midst of which I must unendingly huddle, atop my little platform in the gut. Adopting one or another of various uncomfortable positions, constantly shifting and squirming, now jabbing myself on some awkwardly placed projection, now trying to make my inflexible body flexibly to bend. Seeing the world by periscope through mechanical eyes. Enwombed in this mountain of meat. It is a clever thing; it must look convincingly human, since no one has ever doubted me, and it ages ever so slightly from year to year, graying a bit at the temples, thickening a bit at the paunch. It walks. It talks. It takes in food and drink, when it has to. (And deposits them in a removable pouch near my leftmost arm.) And I within it. The hidden chess player; the invisible rider. If I dared, I would periodically strip myself of this cloak of flesh and crawl around my room in my own guise. But it is forbidden. Eleven years now and I have not been outside my protoplasmic housing. I feel sometimes that it has come to adhere to me, that it is no longer merely around me but by now a part of me.

In order to eat I must unseal it at the middle, a process that takes many minutes. Three times a day I unbutton myself so that I can stuff the food concentrates into my true gullet. Faulty design, I call that. They could just as easily have arranged it so I could pop the food into my Earthmouth and have it land in my own digestive tract. I suppose the newer models have that. Excretion is just as troublesome for me; I unseal, reach in, remove the cubes of waste, seal my skin again. Down the toilet with them. A nuisance.

And the loneliness! To look at the stars and know Homeworld is out there somewhere! To think of all the others, mating, chanting, dividing, abstracting, while I live out my days in this crumbling hotel on an alien planet, tugged down by gravity and locked within a cramped counterfeit body—always alone, always pretending that I am not what I am and that I am what I am not, spying, questioning, recording, reporting, coping with the misery of solitude, hunting for the comforts of philosophy—

In all of this there is only one real consolation, aside, that is, from the pleasure of knowing that I am of service to Homeworld. The atmosphere of New York city grows grimmer every year. The streets are full of crude vehicles belching undigested hydrocarbons. To the Earthfolk, this stuff is pollution, and they mutter worriedly about it. To me it is joy. It is the only touch of Homeworld here: that sweet soup of organic compounds adrift in the air. It intoxicates me. I walk down the street breathing deeply, sucking the good molecules through my false nostrils to my authentic lungs. The natives must think I'm insane. Tripping on auto-exhaust! Can I get arrested for overenthusiastic public breathing? Will they pull me in for a mental checkup?

Elizabeth Cooke continues to waft wistful attentions at me. Smiles in the hallway. Hopeful gleam of the eyes. "Perhaps we can have dinner together some night soon, Mr. Knecht. I know we'd have so much to talk about. And maybe you'd like to see the new poems I've been doing." She is trembling. Eyelids flickering tensely; head held rigid on long neck. I know she sometimes has men in her room, so it can't be out of loneliness or frustration that she's cultivating me. And I doubt that she's sexually attracted to my outer self. I believe I'm being accurate when I say that women don't consider me sexually magnetic. No, she loves me because she pities me. The sad shy bachelor at the end of the hall, dear unhappy Mr. Knecht; can I bring some brightness into his dreary life? And so forth. I think that's how it is. Will I be able to go on avoiding her? Perhaps I should move to another part of the city. But I've lived here so long; I've grown accustomed to this hotel. Its easy ways do much to compensate for the hardships of my post. And my familiar room. The huge many-paned window; the cracked green floor tiles in the bathroom; the lumpy patterns of replastering on the wall above my bed. The high ceiling; the funny chandelier. Things that I love. But of course I can't let her try to start an affair with me. We are supposed to observe Earthfolk, not to get involved with them. Our disguise is not that difficult to penetrate at close range. I must keep her away somehow. Or flee.

Incredible! There is another of us in this very hotel!

As I learned through accident. At one this afternoon, returning from my morning travels: Elizabeth in the lobby, as though lying in wait for me, chatting with the manager. Rides up with me in the elevator. Her eyes looking into mine. "Sometimes I think you're afraid of me," she begins. "You mustn't be. That's the great tragedy of human life, that people shut themselves up behind walls of fear and never let anyone through, anyone who might care about them and be warm to them. You've got no reason to be afraid of me." I do, but how to explain that to her? To sidestep prolonged conversation and possible entanglement I get off the elevator one floor below the right one. Let her think I'm visiting a friend. Or a mistress. I walk slowly down the hall to the stairs, using up time, waiting so she will be in her room before I go up. A maid bustles by me. She thrusts her key into a door on the left: a rare *faux pas* for the usually competent help here, she forgets to knock before going in to make up the room. The door opens and the occupant, inside, stands revealed. A stocky, muscular man, naked to the waist. "Oh, excuse me," the maid gasps, and backs out, shutting the door. But I have seen. My eyes are quick. The hairy chest is split, a dark gash three inches wide and some eleven inches long, beginning between the nipples and going past the navel. Visible within is the black shiny surface of a Homeworld carapace. My countryman, opening up for Second Feeding. Dazed, numbed, I stagger to the stairs and pull myself step by leaden step to my floor. No sign of Elizabeth. I stumble into my room and throw the bolt. Another of us here? Well, why not? I'm not the only one. There may be hundreds in New York alone. But in the same hotel? I remember, now, I've seen him occasionally: a silent, dour man, tense, hunted-looking, unsociable. No doubt I appear the same way to others. Keep the world at a distance. I don't know his name or what he is supposed to do for a living.

We are forbidden to make contact with fellow Homeworlders except in case of extreme emergency. Isolation is a necessary condition of our employment. I may not introduce myself to him; I may not seek his friendship. It is worse now for me, knowing that he is here, than when I was entirely alone. The things we could reminisce about! The friends we might have in common! We could reinforce one another's endurance of the gravity, the discomfort of our disguises, the vile climate. But no. I must pretend I know nothing. The rules. The harsh, unbending rules. I to go about my business, he his; if we meet, no hint of my knowledge must pass.

So be it. I will honor my vows. But it may be difficult.

*    *    *

He goes by the name of Swanson. Been living in the hotel
eighteen months; a musician of some sort, according to the
manager. "A very peculiar man. Keeps to himself; no small talk,
never smiles. Defends his privacy. The other day a maid barged
into his room without knocking and I thought he'd sue. Well, we
get all sorts here." The manager thinks he may actually be a
member of one of the old European royal families, living in exile,
or something similarly romantic. The manager would be surprised.

I defend my privacy too. From Elizabeth, another assault on it.
In the hall outside my room. "My new poems," she said. "In
case you're interested." And then: "Can I come in? I'd read them
to you. I love reading out loud." And: "Please don't always seem
so terribly afraid of me. I don't bite, David. Really I don't. I'm
quite gentle."

"I'm sorry."

"So am I." Anger, now, lurking in her shiny eyes, her thin taut
lips. "If you want me to leave you alone, say so, I will. But I want
you to know how cruel you're being. I don't *demand* anything
from you. I'm just offering some friendship. And you're refusing.
Do I have a bad smell? Am I so ugly? Is it my poems you hate
and you're afraid to tell me?"

"Elizabeth—"

"We're only on this world such a short time. Why can't we be
kinder to each other while we are? To love, to share, to open up.
The reality trip. Communication, soul to soul." Her tone changed.
An artful shading. "For all I know, women turn you off. I wouldn't
put anybody down for that. We've all got our ways. But it
doesn't have to be a sexual thing, you and me. Just talk. Like,
opening the channels. Please? Say no and I'll never bother you
again, but don't say no, please. That's like shutting a door on life,
David. And when you do that, you start to die a little."

Persistent. I should tell her to go to hell. But there is the
loneliness. There is her obvious sincerity. Her warmth, her ea-
gerness to pull me from my lunar isolation. Can there be harm in
it? Knowing that Swanson is nearby, so close yet sealed from me
by iron commandments, has intensified my sense of being alone. I
can risk letting Elizabeth get closer to me. It will make her happy;
it may make me happy; it could even yield information valuable
to Homeworld. Of course I must still maintain certain barriers.

"I don't mean to be unfriendly. I think you've misunderstood,

Elizabeth. I haven't really been rejecting you. Come in. Do come in." Stunned, she enters my room. The first guest ever. My few books; my modest furnishings; the ultrawave transmitter, impenetrably disguised as a piece of sculpture. She sits. Skirt far above the knees. Good legs, if I understand the criteria of quality correctly. I am determined to allow no sexual overtures. If she tries anything. I'll resort to—I don't know—hysteria. "Read me your new poems," I say. She opens her portfolio. Reads.

*In the midst of the hipster night of doubt and*
*Emptiness, when the bad-trip god came to me with*
*Cold hands, I looked up and shouted yes at the*
*Stars. And yes and yes again. I groove on yes;*
*The devil grooves on no. And I waited for you to*
*Say yes, and at last you did. And the world said*
*The stars said the trees said the grass said the*
*Sky said the streets said yes and yes and yes—*

She is ecstatic. Her face is flushed; her eyes are joyous. She has broken through to me. After two hours, when it becomes obvious that I am not going to ask her to go to bed with me, she leaves. Not to wear out her welcome. "I'm so glad I was wrong about you, David," she whispers. "I couldn't believe you were really a life-denier. And you're not." Ecstatic.

I am getting into very deep water.

We spend an hour or two together every night. Sometimes in my room, sometimes in hers. Usually she comes to me, but now and then, to be polite, I seek her out after Third Feeding. By now I've read all her poetry; we talk instead of the arts in general, politics, racial problems. She has a lively, well-stocked, disorderly mind. Though she probes constantly for information about me, she realizes how sensitive I am, and quickly withdraws when I parry her. Asking about my work; I reply vaguely that I'm doing research for a book, and when I don't amplify she drops it, though she tries again, gently, a few nights later. She drinks a lot of wine, and offers it to me. I nurse one glass through a whole visit. Often she suggests we go out together for dinner; I explain that I have digestive problems and prefer to eat alone, and she takes this in good grace but immediately resolves to help me overcome those problems, for soon she is asking me to eat with her again. There is an excellent Spanish restaurant right in the hotel, she says. She drops troublesome questions. Where was I born? Did I go to college? Do I have family somewhere? Have I ever been married? Have I published any of my writings? I improvise evasions. Nothing difficult about that, except that never before have I allowed anyone on Earth such sustained contact with me, so prolonged an opportunity to find inconsistencies in my pretended identity. What if she sees through?

And sex. Her invitations grow less subtle. She seems to think we ought to be having a sexual relationship, simply because we've become such good friends. Not a matter of passion so much as one of communication: we talk, sometimes we take walks together, we should do *that* together too. But of course it's impossible. I have the external organs but not the capacity to use them. Wouldn't want her touching my false skin in any case. How to deflect her? If I declare myself impotent she'll demand a chance to try to cure me. If I pretend homosexuality she'll start some kind of straightening therapy. If I simply say she doesn't turn me on physically she'll be hurt. The sexual thing is a challenge to her, the way merely getting me to talk with her once was. She often wears the transparent pink shawl that reveals her breasts. Her skirts are hip-high. She doses herself with aphrodisiac perfumes. She grazes my body with hers whenever opportunity arises. The tension mounts; she is determined to have me.

I have said nothing about her in my reports to Homeworld. Though I do transmit some of the psychological data I have gathered by observing her.

"Could you ever admit you were in love with me?" she asked tonight.

And she asked, "Doesn't it hurt you to repress your feelings all the time? To sit there locked up inside yourself like a prisoner?"

And, "There's a physical side of life too, David. I don't mind so much the damage you're doing to me by ignoring it. But I worry about the damage you're doing to you."

Crossing her legs. Hiking her skirt even higher.

We are heading toward a crisis. I should never have let this begin. A torrid summer has descended on the city, and in hot weather my nervous system is always at the edge of eruption. She may push me too far. I might ruin everything. I should apply for transfer to Homeworld before I cause trouble. Maybe I should confer with Swanson. I think what is happening now qualifies as an emergency.

Elizabeth stayed past midnight tonight. I had to ask her finally

to leave: work to do. An hour later she pushed an envelope under my door. Newest poems. Love poems. In a shaky hand: *"David you mean so much to me. You mean the stars and nebulas. Cant you let me show my love? Cant you accept happiness? Think about it. I adore you."*
What have I started?

103°F. today. The fourth successive day of intolerable heat. Met Swanson in the elevator at lunchtime; nearly blurted the truth about myself to him. I must be more careful. But my control is slipping. Last night, in the worst of the heat, I was tempted to strip off my disguise. I could no longer stand being locked in here, pivoting and ducking to avoid all the machinery festooned about me. Resisted the temptation; just barely. Somehow I am more sensitive to the gravity too. I have the illusion that my carapace is developing cracks. Almost collapsed in the street this afternoon. All I need: heat exhaustion, whisked off to the hospital, routine flouroscope exam. "You have a very odd skeletal structure, Mr. Knecht." Indeed. Dissecting me, next with three thousand medical students looking on. And then the United Nations called in. Menace from outer space. Yes. I must be more careful. I must be more careful. I must be more—

Now I've done it. Eleven years of faithful service destroyed in a single wild moment. Violation of the Fundamental Rule. I hardly believe it. How was it possible that I—that I—with my respect for my responsibilities—that I could have—even considered, let alone actually done—
But the weather was terribly hot. The third week of the heat wave. I was stifling inside my false body. And the gravity: was New York having a gravity wave too? That terrible pull, worse than ever. Bending my internal organs out of shape. Elizabeth a tremendous annoyance: passionate, emotional, teary, poetic, giving me no rest, pleading for me to burn with a brighter flame. Declaring her love in sonnets, in rambling hip epics, in haiku. Spending two hours in my room, crouched at my feet, murmuring about the hidden beauty of my soul. "Open yourself and let love come in," she whispered. "It's like giving yourself to God. Making a commitment; breaking down all walls. Why not? for love's sake, David, why not?" I couldn't tell her why not, and she went away, but about midnight she was back knocking at my door. I let her in. She wore an ankle-length silk housecoat,

gleaming, threadbare. "I'm stoned," she said hoarsely, voice an octave too deep. "I had to bust three joints to get up the nerve. But here I am. David, I'm sick of making the turnoff trip. We've been so wonderfully close, and then you won't go the last stretch of the way." A cascade of giggles. "Tonight you will. Don't fail me. Darling." Drops the housecoat. Naked underneath it: narrow waist, bony hips, long legs, thin thighs, blue veins crossing her breasts. Her hair wild and kinky. A sorceress. A seeress. Berserk. Approaching me, eyes slit-wide, mouth open, tongue flickering snakily. How fleshless she is! Beads of sweat glistening on her flat chest. Seizes my wrists; tugs me roughly toward the bed. We tussle a little. Within my false body I throw switches, nudge levers. I am stronger than she is. I pull free, breaking her hold with an effort. She stands flat-footed in front of me, glaring, eyes fiery. So vulnerable, so sad in her nudity. And yet so fierce. "David! David! David!" Sobbing. Breathless. Pleading with her eyes and the tips of her breasts. Gathering her strength; now she makes the next lunge, but I see it coming and let her topple past me. She lands on the bed, burying her face in the pillow, clawing at the sheet. "Why? Why why why WHY?" she screams.

In a minute we will have the manager in here. With the police.

"Am I so hideous? I love you, David, do you know what that word means? Love. Love." Sits up. Turns to me. Imploring. "Don't reject me," she whispers. "I couldn't take that. You know, I just wanted to make you happy, I figured I could be the one, only I didn't realize how unhappy you'd make me. And you just stand there. And you don't say anything. What are you, some kind of machine?"

"I'll tell you what I am," I said.

That was when I went sliding into the abyss. All control lost; all prudence gone. My mind so slithered with raw emotion that survival itself means nothing. I must make things clear to her, is all. I must show her. At whatever expense. I strip off my shirt. She glows, no doubt thinking I will let myself be seduced. My hands slide up and down my bare chest, seeking the catches and snaps. I go through the intricate, cumbersome process of opening my body. Deep within myself something is shouting NO NO NO NO NO, but I pay no attention. The heart has its reasons.

Hoarsely: "Look, Elizabeth. Look at me. This is what I am. Look at me and freak out. The reality trip."

My chest opens wide.

I push myself forward, stepping between the levers and struts, emerging halfway from the human shell I wear. I have not been this far out of it since the day they sealed me in, on Homeworld. I let her see my gleaming carapace. I wave my eyestalks around. I allow some of my claws to show. "See? See? Big black crab from outer space. That's what you love, Elizabeth. That's what I am. David Knecht's just a costume, and this is what's inside it." I have gone insane. "You want reality? Here's reality, Elizabeth. What good is the Knecht body to you? It's a fraud. It's a machine. Come on, come closer. Do you want to kiss me? Should I get on you and make love?"

During this episode her face has displayed an amazing range of reactions. Open-mouthed disbelief at first, of course. And frozen horror: gagging sounds in throat, jaws agape, eyes wide and rigid. Hands fanned across breasts. Sudden modesty in front of the alien monster? But then, as the familiar Knecht-voice, now bitter and impassioned, continues to flow from the black thing within the sundered chest, a softening of her response. Curiosity. The poetic sensibility taking over. Nothing human is alien to me: Terence, quoted by Cicero. Nothing alien is alien to me. Eh? She will accept the evidence of her eyes. "What are you? Where did you come from?" And I say, "I've violated the Fundamental Rule. I deserve to be plucked and thinned. We're not supposed to reveal ourselves. If we get into some kind of accident that might lead to exposure, we're supposed to blow ourselves up. The switch is right here." She comes close and peers around me, into the cavern of David Knecht's chest. "From some other planet? Living here in disguise?" She understands the picture. Her shock is fading. She even laughs. "I've seen worse than you on acid," she says. "You don't frighten me now, David. David? Shall I go on calling you David?"

This is unreal and dreamlike to me. I have revealed myself, thinking to drive her away in terror; she is no longer aghast, and smiles at my strangeness. She kneels to get a better look. I move back a short way. Eyestalks fluttering: I am uneasy, I have somehow lost the upper hand in this encounter.

She says, "I knew you were unusual, but not like this. But it's all right. I can cope. I mean, the essential personality, that's what I fell in love with. Who cares that you're a crab-man from the Green Galaxy? Who cares that we can't even be real lovers? I can make that sacrifice. It's your soul I dig, David. Go on. Close yourself up again. You don't look comfortable this way." The triumph of love. She will not abandon me, even now. Disaster. I crawl back into Knecht and lift his arms to his chest to seal it. Shock is glazing my consciousness: the enormity, the audacity. What have I done? Elizabeth watches, awed, even delighted. At last I am together again. She nods. "Listen," she tells me, "You can trust me. I mean, if you're some kind of spy, checking out the Earth, I don't care. *I don't care.* I won't tell anybody. Pour it all out, David. Tell me about yourself. Don't you see, this is the biggest thing that ever happened to me. A chance to show that love isn't just physical, isn't just chemistry, that it's a soul trip, that it crosses not just racial lines but the lines of the whole damned species, the planet itself—"

It took several hours to get rid of her. A soaring, intense conversation, Elizabeth doing most of the talking. She putting forth theories of why I had come to Earth, me nodding, denying, amplifying, mostly lost in horror at my own perfidy and barely listening to her monolog. And the humidity turning me into rotting rags. Finally: "I'm down from the pot, David. And all wound up. I'm going out for a walk. Then back to my room to write for a while. To put this night into a poem before I lose the power of it. But I'll come to you again by dawn, all right? That's maybe five hours from now. You'll be here? You won't do anything foolish? Oh, I love you so much, David! Do you believe me? Do you?"

When she was gone I stood a long while by the window, trying to reassemble myself. Shattered. Drained. Remembering her kisses, her lips running along the ridge marking the place where my chest opens. The fascination of the abomination. She will love me even if I am crustaceous beneath.

I had to have help.

I went to Swanson's room. He was slow to respond to my knock; busy transmitting, no doubt. I could hear him within, but he didn't answer. "Swanson?" I called. "Swanson?" Then I added the distress signal in the Homeworld tongue. He rushed to the door. Blinking, suspicious. "It's all right," I said. "Look, let me in. I'm in big trouble." Speaking English, but I gave him the distress signal again.

"How did you know about me?" he asked.

"The day the maid blundered into your room while you were eating, I was going by. I saw."

"But you aren't supposed to—"

"Except in emergencies. This is an emergency." He shut off his ultrawave and listened intently to my story. Scowling. He didn't approve. But he wouldn't spurn me. I had been criminally foolish, but I was of his kind, prey to the same pains, the same loneliness, and he would help me.

"What do you plan to do now?" he asked. "You can't harm her. It isn't allowed."

"I don't want to harm her. Just to get free of her. To make her fall out of love with me."

"How? If showing yourself to her didn't—"

"Infidelity," I said. "Making her see that I love someone else. No room in my life for her. That'll drive her away. Afterwards it won't matter that she knows: who'd believe her story? The FBI would laugh and tell her to lay off the LSD. But if I don't break her attachment to me I'm finished."

"Love someone else? Who?"

"When she comes back to my room at dawn," I said, "she'll find the two of us together, dividing and abstracting. I think that'll do it, don't you?"

So I deceived Elizabeth with Swanson.

The fact that we both wore male human identities was irrelevant, of course. We went to my room and stepped out of our disguises—a bold, dizzying sensation!—and suddenly we were just two Homeworlders again, receptive to one another's needs. I left the door unlocked. Swanson and I crawled up on my bed and began the chanting. How strange it was, after those years of solitude, to feel those vibrations again! And how beautiful. Swanson's vibrissae touching mine. The interplay of harmonies. An underlying sternness to his technique—he was contemptuous of me for my idiocy, and rightly so—but once we passed from the chanting to the dividing all was forgiven, and as we moved into the abstracting it was truly sublime. We climbed through an infinity of climactic emptyings. Dawn crept upon us and found us unwilling to halt even for a rest.

A knock at the door. Elizabeth.

"Come in," I said.

A dreamy, ecstatic look on her face. Fading instantly when she saw the two of us entangled on the bed. A questioning frown. "We've been mating," I explained. "Did you think I was a complete hermit?" She looked from Swanson to me, from me to Swanson. Hand over her mouth. Eyes anguished. I turned the screw a little tighter. "I couldn't stop you from falling in love with me, Elizabeth. But I really do prefer my own kind. As should have been obvious."

"To have her here now, though—when you knew I was coming back—"

"Not *her*, exactly. Not *him* exactly either, though."

"—so cruel, David! To ruin such a beautiful experience." Holding forth sheets of paper with shaking hands. "A whole sonnet cycle," she said. "About tonight. How beautiful it was, and all. And now—and now—" Crumpling the pages. Hurling them across the room. Turning. Running out, sobbing furiously. Hell hath no fury like. "*David!*" A smothered cry. And slamming the door.

She was back in ten minutes. Swanson and I hadn't quite finished donning our bodies yet; we were both still unsealed. As we worked, we discussed further steps to take: he felt honor demanded that I request a transfer back to Homeworld, having terminated my usefulness here through tonight's indiscreet revelation. I agreed with him to some degree but was reluctant to leave. Despite the bodily torment of life on on Earth I had come to feel I belonged here. Then Elizabeth entered, radiant.

"I mustn't be so possessive," she announced. "So bourgeois. So conventional. I'm willing to share my love." Embracing Swanson. Embracing me. "A *ménage à trois*," she said. "I won't mind that you two are having a physical relationship. As long as you don't shut me out of your lives completely. I mean, David, we could never have been physical anyway, right, but we can have the other aspects of love, and we'll open ourselves to your friend also. Yes? Yes? Yes?"

Swanson and I both put in applications for transfer, he to Africa, me to Homeworld. It would be some time before we received a reply. Until then we were at her mercy. He was blazingly angry with me for involving him in this, but what choice had I had? Nor could either of us avoid Elizabeth. We were at her mercy. She bathed both of us in shimmering waves of tender emotion; wherever we turned, there she was, incandescent with love. Lighting up the darkness of our lives. You poor lonely creatures. Do you suffer much in our gravity? What about the heat? And the winters. Is there a custom of marriage on your planet? Do you have poetry?

A happy threesome. We went to the theater together. To concerts. Even to parties in Greenwich Village. "My friends,"

Elizabeth said, leaving no doubt in anyone's mind that she was living with both of us. Faintly scandalous doings; she loved to seem daring. Swanson was sullenly obliging, putting up with her antics but privately haranguing me for subjecting him to all this. Elizabeth got out another mimeographed booklet of poems, dedicated to both of us. *Triple Tripping*, she called it. Flagrantly erotic. I quoted a few of the poems in one of my reports of Homeworld, then lost heart and hid the booklet in the closet. "Have you heard about your transfer yet?" I asked Swanson at least twice a week. He hadn't. Neither had I.

Autumn came. Elizabeth, burning her candle at both ends, looked gaunt and feverish. "I have never known such happiness," she announced frequently, one hand clasping Swanson, the other me. "I never think about the strangeness of you any more. I think of you only as people. Sweet, wonderful, lonely people. Here in the darkness of this horrid city." And she once said, "What if everybody here is like you, and I'm the only one who's really human? But that's silly. You must be the only ones of your kind here. The advance scouts. Will your planet invade ours? I do hope so! Set everything to rights. The reign of love and reason at last!"

"How long will this go on?" Swanson muttered.

At the end of October his transfer came through. He left without saying good-bye to either of us and without leaving a forwarding address. Nairobi? Addis Ababa? Kinshasa?

I had grown accustomed to having him around to share the burden of Elizabeth. Now the full brunt of her affection fell on me. My work was suffering; I had no time to file my reports properly. And I lived in fear of her gossiping. What was she telling her Village friends? ("You know David? He's not really a man, you know. Actually inside him there's a kind of crab-thing from another solar system. But what does that matter? Love's a universal phenomenon. The truly loving person doesn't draw limits around the planet.") I longed for my release. To go home; to accept my punishment; to shed my false skin. To empty my mind of Elizabeth.

My reply came through the ultrawave on November 13. Application denied. I was to remain on Earth and continue my work as before. Transfers to Homeworld were granted only for reasons of health.

I debated sending a full account of my treason to Homeworld and thus bringing about my certain recall. But I hesitated, overwhelmed with despair. Dark brooding seized me. "Why so sad?" Elizabeth asked. What could I say? That my attempt at escaping from her had failed? "I love you," she said. "I've never felt so *real* before." Nuzzling against my cheek. Fingers knotted in my hair. A seductive whisper. "David, open yourself up again. Your chest, I mean. I want to see the inner you. To make sure I'm not frightened of it. Please? You've only let me see you once." And then, when I had: "May I kiss you, David?" I was appalled. But I let her. She was unafraid. Transfigured by happiness. She is a cosmic nuisance, but I fear I'm getting to like her.

Can I leave her? I wish Swanson had not vanished. I need advice.

Either I break with Elizabeth or I break with Homeworld. This is absurd. I find new chasms of despondency every day. I am unable to do my work. I have requested a transfer once again, without giving details. The first snow of the winter today.

Application denied.

"When I found you with Swanson," she said, "it was a terrible shock. An even bigger blow than when you first came out of your chest. I mean, it was startling to find out you weren't human, but it didn't hit me in any emotional way, it didn't threaten me. But then, to come back a few hours later and find you with one of your own kind, to know that you wanted to shut me out, that I had no place in your life— Only we worked it out, didn't we?" Kissing me. Tears of joy in her eyes. How did this happen? Where did it all begin? Existence was once so simple. I have tried to trace the chain of events that brought me from there to here, and I cannot. I was outside of my false body for eight hours today. The longest spell so far. Elizabeth is talking of going to the islands with me for the winter. A secluded cottage that her friends will make available. Of course, I must not leave my post without permission. And it takes months simply to get a reply.

Let me admit the truth: I love her.

January 1. The new year begins. I have sent my resignation to Homeworld and have destroyed my ultrawave equipment. The links are broken. Tomorrow, when the city offices are open, Elizabeth and I will go to get the marriage license.

# THE NIGHT-BLOOMING SAURIAN
## (MAY 1970)
## JAMES TIPTREE, JR.
## (B. 1915)

James Tiptree, Jr., is the pseudonym of Dr. Alice Sheldon, who, like R. A. Lafferty, did not begin to publish science fiction until rather late in life. Her true identity was a closely guarded secret for a decade (even her literary agent did not know), and the mystery surrounding Tiptree occupied the pages of SF fanzines for years. Her carefully crafted stories can be read on several levels, and can be found in *Ten Thousand Light Years from Home* (1973), *Warm Worlds and Otherwise* (1975), and *Star Songs of an Old Primate* (1978). She has won both the Hugo and Nebula awards on two occasions.

Other notable stories in *If* are "The Mother Ship" (June 1968) and "Pupa Knows Best" (October 1968).

## MEMOIR BY JAMES TIPTREE, JR.

*If!* Ah, *If!* What it meant to us! It wasn't *Galaxy*, Fred Pohl's golden seal of approval, but a chancier magazine, more free—a friend to experiments, a place that tolerated wild flappings toward the heights and occasional ignominious bellywhops when the wax-wings melted. (Always provided Fred had decided there was some possibility of pin feathers.)

*If* gave a home to the worst turkey I ever launched, which let me see *why* it was no good—and to the best I early achieved. *If* was no mere *Galaxy* overflow, it was a special, canny scheme for helping on new writers. I've never heard Fred Pohl say this in so many words, but Fred is not one to tell you all he knows or is up to.

As for my own Saurian yarn here (and I've been surprised at its persistent minor popularity), the point is simple. I've always been bugged by writers who neglect to think things through, to work up the whole scene, with those vital "trivial" factors which actually cost so much effort and can make or break grand schemes. Where do you get your repair parts, in space? How do you milk a dragon without its tail zapping you in the head? How does your hero/heroine blow the nose in a space suit? How do your fleeing refugees get rid of their garbage without leaving a trace?

In World War II, I was briefly a logistics officer in a port of embarkation, and I saw an entire armored division (and its convoy) delayed because a QM laundry machine broke down. A friend, starving on a blockaded South Pacific island, told me how the heroic relief ship finally reached them—and, by computer error, turned out to be loaded with toilet paper and office machines.

So, as I planned "The Night-blooming Saurian," while stumbling down a moose run in Ontario, I tried to consider the, ah, whole problem of re-creating a scene from the old Cretaceous . . . and not without a grin.

# THE NIGHT-BLOOMING
# SAURIAN

Ah, now we can relax. No salad, never touch it. And take that fruit away too, just the cheese. Yes, Pier, much too long a time. One's ruts deepen. It's the damned little time-wasters. Like that fellow with the coprolites this afternoon; the Museum really has no use for such things even if they're genuine. And I confess they make me squeamish.

What? Oh, no fear, Pier, I'm no prude. Just to prove it, how about a bit more of that aquavit? Wonderfully good of you to remember. Here's to your success; always thought you would.

Science? Oh, but you wouldn't, really. Mostly donkey-work. Looks a lot better from the outside, like most things. Of course I've been fortunate. For an archeologist to have seen the advent of time travel—a miracle, really . . . Ah, yes, I was in right at the start, when they thought it was a useless toy. And the cost! No one knows how close it came to being killed off, Pier. If it hadn't been for—the things one does for science . . . My most memorable experience in time? Oh, my . . . Yes, just a twitch more, though I really shouldn't.

Oh dear. Coprolites. H'm. Very well, Pier old friend, if you'll keep it to yourself. But don't blame me if it disenchants you.

It was on the very first team jump you see. When we went back to the Olduvai Gorge area to look for Leakey's man. I won't bore you with our initial misadventures. Leakey's man wasn't there but another surprising hominid was. Actually, the one they called after me. But by the time we found him our grand funds were almost gone. It cost a fantastic sum then to keep us punched back into the temporal fabric and the U.S. was paying most of the bill. And not from altruism either but we won't go into that.

There were six of us. The two MacGregors you've heard of; and the Soviet delegation, Peshkov and Rasmussen. And myself and a Dr. Priscilla Owen. Fattest woman I ever saw, oddly enough that turned out to be significant. Plus the temporal engineer, as they called them then, Jerry Fitz. A strapping Upper Paleolithic type, full of enthusiasm. He was our general guard and nursemaid, too, and a very nice chap for an engineer he seemed. Young, of course. We were all so young.

Well, we had no sooner settled in and sent Fitz back with our first reports when the blow fell. Messages had to be carried in person then, you realize, by prearranged schedule. All we could do by way of signals was a crude go—no-go. Fitz came back very solemn and told us that the grant appropriation was not going to be renewed and we'd all be pulled back next month for good.

Well, you can imagine we were struck to the heart. Devastated. Dinner that night was funereal. Fitz seemed to be as blue as we and the bottle went round and round— Oh, thank you.

Suddenly we saw Fitz looking us over with a twinkle in his eye.

"Ladies and gentlemen!" He had this rococo manner, though we were all of an age. "Despair is premature. I have a confession. My uncle's wife's niece works for the Senator who's chairman of the Appropriations Committee. So I went to see him all on my lone. What could we lose? And"—I can still see Fitz' grin—"I chatted him up. The whole bit. Dawn of man, priceless gains to science. Nothing. Not a nibble, until I found he was a fanatical hunter.

"Well, you know I'm a gun buff myself and we went to it like fiddle and bow. So he got bewailing there's nothing to hunt back there and I told him what a hunter's paradise this is. And to make a long tale short, he's coming to inspect us and if he likes the hunting there's no doubt your money will be along. Now how does that smoke?"

General cheers. Peshkov began counting the Senator's bag.

"Several large ungulates and of course, the baboons and that carnivore you shot, Fitz. And possibly a tapir—"

"Oh, no," Fitz told him. "Monkeys and deer and pigs, that's not his thing. Something spectacular."

"Hominids tend to avoid areas of high predation," observed MacGregor. "Even the mammoths are far to the east."

"The fact is," said Fitz, "I told him he could shoot a dinosaur."

"A dinosaur!" we hooted.

"But Fitz," said little Jeanne MacGregor. "There aren't any dinosaurs now. They're all extinct."

"Are they now?" Fitz was abashed. "I didn't know that. Neither does the Senator. Surely we can find him an odd one or two? It may be all a mistake, like our little man here."

"Well, there's a species of iguana," said Rasmussen.

Fitz shook his head.

"I promised him the biggest kind of beast. He's coming here to shoot a—what is it? A bronco-something."

"A brontosaurs?" We all jumped him. "But they're all back in the Cretaceous! Eighty million years—"

"Fitz, how could you?"

"I told him the roaring kept us awake nights."

Well, we were still a gloomy lot next day. Fitz was gone across the gorge to tinker with his temporal field rig. They were big awkward things then. We'd built a shack for ours and then moved our permanent camp across the gorge where our hominids were. A stiff climb, up and down through the swamp—it was all lush then, not the dry gorge it is today. And of course there was small game and fruit aplenty. Forgive, I think I will have just a bit more.

Fitz came back once to question Rasmussen about brontosaurs and then went back again. At dinner he was humming. Then he looked around solemnly—my God, we were young.

"Ladies and gentlemen, science shall not die. I will get the Senator his dinosaur."

"*How?*"

"I've a friend back there"—we always called the present "back there"—who'll push me a bit of extra power. Enough to jump me and a loadlifter to the big beast for at least a day. And I can jigger up this breadbox for a signal and a split retrieve."

We all objected, though we dearly wanted to believe. How

could he find his brontosaur? Or kill it? And it would be dead. It would be too big. And so on.

But Fitz had his answers and we were drunk on the Pleistocene and in the end the mad plan was set. Fitz would kill the largest reptile he could find and signal us to bring him back when he had it crammed in the transporter. Then, when the Senator was ready to shoot, we would yank the fresh-killed carcass across eighty million years and arrange it near the shack. Insane. But Fitz swung us all with him, even when he admitted that the extra power use would shorten our stay. And off he went next dawn.

Once he'd gone we began to realize what we six promising young scientists had done. We were committed to hoax a powerful United States Senator into believing he had stalked and killed a creature that had been dead eighty million years.

"We cannot do it!"

"We've got to."

"It'll be the end of time travel when they find out."

Rasmussen groaned. "The end of us."

"Misuse of Government resources," said MacGregor. "Actionable."

"Where were our heads?"

"You know," Jeanne MacGregor mused, "I believe Fitz is as eager to shoot a dinosaur as the Senator is."

"And that convenient arrangement with his friend," Peshkov said thoughtfully. "That wasn't done from here. I wonder—"

"We have been had."

"The fact remains," said MacGregor, "that this Senator Dogsbody is coming here, expecting to kill a dinosaur. Our only hope is to make some tracks and persuade him that the creature has moved away."

Luckily we had thought to tell Fitz to bring back footprints of whatever he managed to murder. And Rasmussen had the idea of recording its bellows.

"They're like hippos. They'll be swathes of stuff knocked down by the water. We can trample about a bit before Fitz gets back."

"He *has* risked his life," said little Jeanne. "What if the signal doesn't work?"

Well, we bashed down some river trails and then our apemen had a battle with baboons and we were too busy with blood typing and tissue samples to worry. And the signal came through and here was Fitz, mud all over and grinning like a piano.

"A beauty," he told us. "And bigger than God's outhouse."

Actually he had shot a previously unknown brachiosaur. "I squeezed it in with the tail cut twice, only three hours dead. All ready to fetch." He pulled out a muddy plastic. "Here's the print. And a tailmark. We can drag a bag of rocks for that."

He flicked the recorder and the bellow was enough to knock us backward.

"A thing like a big frog makes that, ours only does a silly little honk. The honorable will never know the difference. Now look!"

He yanked at a lump by his feet. "Feel it. A live egg."

"Good God—" We crowded up. "What if he takes it back and it hatches in Bethesda?"

"I could inject it with something slow-acting," said MacGregor. "Keep the heart beating a while. An enzyme imbalance?"

"Now for the trails," said Fitz. He unfolded a gory fin like a sailfish plate. "They mark up the trees with this. And they make a nest of wet reeds—our swampy bit there is just right. There's one thing, though."

He scratched mud off his chest hair, squinting at Jeanne MacGregor.

"The trails," he said. "It's not just footprints. They, well, they eat a lot and—have you ever seen a moose-run? Those trails are loaded with manure."

There was a pause that grew into silence.

"Actually, the thought had—" said Priscilla Owens, the fat woman.

It developed that it had crossed all our minds.

"Well, for the sake of realism I'm sure something can be arranged," grinned Peshkov. "A token offering to your establishment, right?"

"He's a hunter," said Rasmussen. "He'll be quite observant of such factors."

Fitz grunted uncomfortably.

"There's another thing. I forgot to tell you about the Senator's nephew. He puts on to be an amateur naturalist. As a matter of fact, he tried to tell the Senator there weren't any dinosaurs here. That's when I said about the roaring at night."

"Well, but—"

"And the nephew is coming here, with the Senator. Maybe I should have mentioned it. He's smart and he has a mean eye. That's why I got the egg and all. Things better be pretty realistic."

There was a breath-drawing silence. Peshkov exploded first.

"Is there anything else you conveniently forgot to tell us?"

"You wanted to go dinosaur hunting!" Priscilla Owen blared. "You planned this! No matter what it costs science, no matter what happens to us! You used this whole—"

"Prison!" Rasmussen boomed. "Illegal use of Government—"

"Now, wait." MacGregor's dry voice brought us all up. "Argybargy won't help. First of all, Jerry Fitz, is there a Senator coming or was that part of the game too?"

"He's coming, all right," said Fitz.

"Well, then," said Mac. "We're for it. We must make it stick. Total realism!"

Rasmussen took the bull by the, ah, horns.

"How much?"

"Well, a lot," said Fitz. "Piles."

"Piles?"

Fitz held out his hand.

"It's not bad stuff," He flicked off more mud. "You get used to it. They're herbivores."

"How long do we have?"

"Three weeks."

Three weeks . . . I will have a bit more of that acquavit, Pier. The memory of those weeks is very fresh, very green . . . Greens, of course, all kinds of greens. And fruits. God, we were sick.

The MacGregors went first. Colic—you've never seen such cramps. I had them. Everybody had them, even Fitz. We saw to it that he did his share, I can tell you. It was a nightmare.

That was when we began to appreciate Priscilla Owen. Eat? Great gorgons, how that woman could eat. We were all dying but she kept on. Mangosteens, plantains, wild manioc root, palm hearts, celery—anything and everything. How we cheered her! We could scarcely crawl but we actually competed in bringing her food, in escorting her to the swamp. It became an obsession. She was saving us. And science. A complete transvaluation of values, Pier. Seen from the standpoint of dung production that woman was a saint.

Rasmussen idolized her.

"Ten thousands dinars would not pay for the chicken she has eaten," he would croon. "The Persians knew."

Then he would retch and stagger off to dig her roots. I believe he actually got her the Order of Lenin afterward, although her scientific work was quite trivial.

The funny thing was, she began to lose weight. All that roughage, you know, instead of the fatty stuff she usually ate. She became quite different-appearing. As a matter of fact, I tried to propose to her myself. In the swamp. Luckily I got sick. Oh, thank you Pier. . . . She gained it all back later on, of course.

Well, by the time the Senator and his nephew arrived we were all so sick with colic and dysentery and our obsession with the trails that we scarcely cared what would happen to our project.

They came in the afternoon, and Fitz ran them around in the swamp a bit and had them find the egg. That quieted the nephew but we could see he was in a nasty temper at being proved wrong and was looking hard at everything. The Senator was simply manic. Little Jeanne managed to get a lot of liquor into them both, on the pretext of avoiding dysentery. Hah!—Thank you.

Luckily it gets dark at six on the equator.

A couple of hours before dawn Fitz sneaked off to the shack and materialized his brachiosaur carcass. Fresh from the upper Cretaceous swamp that had been there eighty million years ago, mind you. Hard to believe even yet—and ourselves in the Pleistocene. Then he pounded back in the dark and the recorded bellow went off on schedule.

The Senator and the nephew came pouring out stark bare, with Fitz telling him where to stand and helping him point the artillery. And up comes this huge head over the trees around the shack and the Senator lets fly.

That was really the most dangerous part of the whole affair. I was under that head with the loadlifter and he nearly got me.

Of course the Senator who in no shape to trek over the gorge— though it's surprising what your mesomorph can do—so Fitz was sent to haul the thing back. Once the Senator touched that horrendous snout he could not wait to take it home. That punished Fitz; I doubt he had realized he would lose his trophy. But he did save time travel. I think he got a Scottish decoration in the end. At any rate the nephew had no chance to pry and by lunchtime the whole thing was over. Almost. Incredible, really . . .

Oh, yes, the appropriation went through. And all the rest followed. But we still had a problem, you realize . . . Are you sure you don't want a sip? One never finds the real thing nowadays. Pier, old friend, it's good to meet again.

You see, the Senator liked it so well that he decided to return and bring his cronies. Yes. A very difficult business, Pier, until our funding finally stabilized. Do you wonder I can't stand the sight of salad since? And coprolites . . .

What? Oh, that means fossil excrement. Paleobotanists used to have a big thing going there. No sense now, when we can just go back. . . . And anyway, who's to say how genuine they are?

# OCCAM'S SCALPEL
## (AUGUST 1971)
## THEODORE STURGEON
## (1918–1985)

At the height of his career, the late Ted Sturgeon was the finest stylist working in the science-fiction markets, his talent recognized by the fact that for a considerable period of time he was the most reprinted writer in the field. His penetrating examinations of human emotions and interpersonal (and interspecies) relations were sorely missed during most of the 1970s, which found his typewriter relatively silent. Fortunately, most of his story collections and novels, including *Beyond* (1960), *E Pluribus Unicorn* (1953), and *More Than Human* (1953), are still in print, and he has recently had several additional collections published.

His infrequent appearances in *If* were memorable, especially "Never Underestimate . . ." (March 1952) and "From Plynck to Planck" (January 1962).


## MEMOIR BY THEODORE STURGEON

I always felt a bit parental toward *If*. Sometime before V-J day (does anybody out there remember V-J day?) I began to play with the idea of a new science-fiction magazine. I even had a cover for it; sketched it, asked an artist friend to render it, which he did, in oils. It was a handsome typographical cover like the old beloved *Unknown*, with the two-letter title on the left in brilliant orange-yellow, the *I* and the stem of the *F* extending all the way to the bottom. Yes: *If*. The panel of type—story titles, authors, perhaps a blurb—could, I thought, be used in some subsequent issues for a nillo, discreetly smaller than the garish blazes which were, at the time, trying to out-scorch one another. I remember talking to the late Groff Conklin about it, and that moment, just before a burst of rueful laughter, when each thought the other had the money to back the idea.

The notion of starting or editing the magazine sort of fell between the cracks of life for the next few years, and then one day a nice man named, if I remember correctly, Jim Quinn came to see me at my office. He wanted a new story for a magazine called, you guessed it: *If*. This was around 1950, and everyone told him that was the wrong time to start a magazine. I said that everyone had told that to Campbell when he started *Unknown* and everyone had told that to Boucher and McComas when they started *F&SF* and the way to start one is to start one. I gave him my painting and he started *If*.

As you certainly know by now, *If* changed hands a number of times, and, in my opinion, reached its zenith under the editorships of Fred Pohl and that much underrated, self-effacing Ejler Jakobsson. There was *Galaxy* and *If* and, for a while, *World of Tomorrow*, and for them I did columns and reviews and stories and novelettes . . . all of which says that the magazines meant a great deal to me.

About this story: There were in those days two bulky-billionaires. I met one of them once, and spent an interesting evening with him. "You are a very intelligent man, Mr. Sturgeon." "You don't like intelligent men, sir; you like obedient men." One of my finer moments. Anyway, from that time on I began to play with the idea of an alien "terraforming" our planet, changing the air and the water and the vegetation, even microbial life, to suit the conquering species. There are many ways of approaching this theme; this is the one I took. You know, it just could be. Should we start looking for spaceships?

# OCCAM'S SCALPEL

## I

Joe Trilling had a funny way of making a living. It was a good living, but of course he didn't make anything like the bundle he could have in the city. On the other hand he lived in the mountains a half-mile away from a picturesque village in clean air and a piney-birchy woods along with lots of mountain laurel, and he was his own boss. There wasn't much competition for what he did; he had his wife and kids around all the time and more orders than he could fill. He was one of the night people and after the family had gone to bed he could work quietly and uninterruptedly. He was happy as a clam.

One night—very early morning, really—he was interrupted. *Bup-bup, bup, bup.* Knock at the window, two shorts, two longs. He froze, he whirled, for he knew that knock. He hadn't heard it for years but it had been a part of his life since he was born. He saw the face outside and filled his lungs for a whoop that would have roused them as the fire station on the village green, but then he saw the finger on the lips and let the air out. The finger beckoned and Joe Trilling whirled again, turned down a flame, read a gauge, made a note, threw a switch and joyfully but silently dove for the outside door. He slid out, closed it carefully, peered into the dark.

"Karl?"

"Shh."

There he was, edge of the woods. Joe Trilling went there and, whispering because Karl had asked for it, they hit each other, cursed, called each other the filthiest possible names. It would not be easy to explain this to an extra-terrestrial; it isn't necessarily a human thing to do. It's a cultural thing. It means I want to touch you, it means I love you; but they were men and brothers, so they hit each other's arms and shoulders and swore despicable oaths and insults, until at last even those words wouldn't do and they stood in the shadows, holding each others' biceps and grinning and drilling into each other with eyes. Then Karl Trilling moved his head sidewards toward the road and they walked away from the house.

"I don't want Hazel to hear us talking," Karl said. "I don't want her or anyone to know I was here. How is she?"

"Beautiful. Aren't you going to see her at all—or the kids?"

"Yes, but not this trip. There's the car. We can talk there. I really am afraid of that bastard."

"Ah," said Joe. "How is the great man?"

"Po'ly," said Karl. "But we're talking about two different bastards. The great man is only the richest man in the world, but I'm not afraid of him, especially now. I'm talking about Cleveland Wheeler."

"Who's Cleveland Wheeler?"

They got into the car. "It's a rental," said Karl. "Matter of fact, it's the second rental. I got out of the executive jet and took a company car and rented another—and then this. Reasonably sure it's not bugged. That's one kind of answer to your question, who's Cleve Wheeler. Other answers would be the man behind the throne. Next in line. Multifaceted genius. Killer shark."

"Next in line," said Joe, responding to the only clause that made any sense. "The old man is sinking?"

"Officially—and an official secret—his hemoglobin reading is four. That means anything to you, Doctor?"

"Sure does, Doctor. Malnutritive anemia, if other rumors I hear are true. Richest man in the world—dying of starvation."

"And old age—and stubbornness—and obsession. You want to hear about Wheeler"

"Tell me."

"Mister Lucky. Born with everything. Greek coin profile. Michaelangelo muscles. Discovered early by a bright-eyed elementary school principal, sent to a private school, used to go straight to the teachers' lounge in the morning and say what he'd been reading or thinking about. Then they'd tell off a teacher to work with him or go out with him or whatever. High school at twelve, varsity track, basketball, football and high-diving—three letters for each—yes, he graduated in three years, *summa cum*. Read all the textbooks at the beginning of each term, never cracked them again. More than anything else he had the habit of success.

"College, the same thing: turned sixteen in his first semester, just ate everything up. Very popular. Graduated at the top again, of course."

Joe Trilling, who had slogged through college and medical school like a hodcarrier, grunted enviously. "I've seen one or two like that. Everybody marvels, nobody sees how easy it was for them."

Karl shook his head. "Wasn't quite like that with Cleve Wheeler. If anything was easy for him it was because of the nature of his equipment. He was like a four-hundred-horsepower car moving in sixty-horsepower traffic. When his muscles were called on he used them, I mean really put it down to the floor. A very willing guy. Well—he had his choice of jobs—hell, choice of careers. He went into an architectural firm that could use his math, administrative ability, public presence, knowledge of materials, art. Gravitated right to the top, got a partnership. Picked up a doctorate on the side while he was doing it. Married extremely well."

"Mister Lucky," Joe said.

"Mister Lucky, yeah. Listen. Wheeler became a partner and

he did his work and he knew his stuff—everything he could learn or understand. Learning and understanding are not enough to cope with some things like greed or unexpected stupidity or accident or sheer bad breaks. Two of the other partners got into a deal I won't bother you with—a high-rise apartment complex in the wrong place for the wrong residents and land acquired the wrong way. Wheeler saw it coming, called them in and talked it over. They said yes-yes and went right ahead and did what they wanted anyway—something that Wheeler never in the world expected. The one thing high capability and straight morals and a good education doesn't give you is the end of the innocence. Cleve Wheeler was an innocent.

"Well, it happened, the disaster that Cleve had predicted, but it happened far worse. Things like that, when they surface, have a way of exposing a lot of other concealed rot. The firm collapsed. Cleve Wheeler had never failed at anything in his whole life. It was the one thing he had no practice in dealing with. Anyone with the most rudimentary intelligence would have seen that this was the time to walk away—lie down, even. Cut his losses. But I don't think these things even occurred to him."

Karl Trilling laughed suddenly. "In one of Philip Wylie's novels is a tremendous description of a forest fire and how the animals run away from it, the foxes and the rabbits running shoulder to shoulder, the owls flying in the daytime to get ahead of the flames. Then there's this beetle, lumbering along on the ground. The beetle comes to a burned patch, the edge of twenty acres of hell. It stops, it wiggles its feelers, it turns to the side and begins to walk around the fire—" He laughed again. "That's the special thing Cleveland Wheeler has, you see, under all that muscle and brain and brilliance. If he had to—and were a beetle—he wouldn't turn back and he wouldn't quit. If all he could do was walk around it, he'd start walking."

"What happened?" asked Job.

"He hung on. He used everything he had. He used his brains and his personality and his reputation and all his worldly goods. He also borrowed and promised—and he worked. Oh, he worked. Well, he kept the firm. He cleaned out the rot and built it all up again from the inside, strong and straight this time. But it cost.

"It cost him time—all the hours of every day but the four or so he used for sleeping. And just about when he had it leveled off and starting up, it cost him his wife."

"You said he'd married well."

"He'd married what you marry when you're a young block-buster on top of everything and going higher. She was a nice enough girl, I suppose, and maybe you can't blame her, but she was no more used to failure than he was. Only he could walk around it. He could rent a room and ride the bus. She just didn't know how—and of course with women like that there's always the discarded swain somewhere in the wings."

"How did he take that?"

"Hard. He'd married the way he played ball or took examinations—with everything he had. It did something to him. All this did things to him, I suppose, but that was the biggest chunk of it.

"He didn't let it stop him. He didn't let anything stop him. He went on until all the bills were paid—every cent. All the interest. He kept at it until the net worth was exactly what it had been before his ex-partners had begun to eat out the core. Then he gave it away. Gave it away! Sold all right and title to his interest for a dollar."

"Finally cracked, hm?"

Karl Trilling looked at his brother scornfully. "Cracked. Matter of definition, isn't it? Cleve Wheeler's goal was zero—can you understand that? What is success anyhow? Isn't it making up your mind what you're going to do and then doing it, all the way?"

"In that case," said his brother quietly, "suicide is success."

Karl gave him a long penetrating look. "Right," he said, and thought about it a moment.

"Anyhow," Joe asked, "why zero?"

"I did a lot of research on Cleve Wheeler, but I couldn't get inside his head. I don't know. But I can guess. He meant to owe no man anything. I don't know how he felt about the company he saved, but I can imagine. The man he became—was becoming—wouldn't want to owe it one damned thing. I'd say he just wanted out—but on his own terms, which included leaving nothing behind to work on him."

"Okay," said Joe.

Karl Trilling thought, *The nice thing about old Joe is that he'll wait. All these years apart with hardly any communication beyond birthday cards—and not always that—and here he is, just as if we were still together every day. I wouldn't be here if it weren't important; I wouldn't be telling him all this unless he needed to know; he wouldn't need any of it unless he was going to help. All that unsaid—I don't have to ask him a damn thing. What am I interrupting in his life? What am I going to interrupt? I won't have to worry about that. He'll take care of it.*

He said, "I'm glad I came here, Joe."

Joe said, "That's all right," which meant all the things Karl had been thinking. Karl grinned and hit him on the shoulder and went on talking.

"Wheeler dropped out. It's not easy to map his trail for that period. It pops up all over. He lived in at least three communities— maybe more, but those three were a mess when he came and a model when he left. He started businesses—all things that had never happened before, like a supermarket with no shelves, no canned music, no games or stamps, just neat stacks of open cases, where the customer took what he wanted and marked it according to the card posted by the case, with a marker hanging on a string. Eggs and frozen meat and fish and the like, and local produce were priced a flat two percent over wholesale. People were honest because they could never be sure the checkout counter didn't know the prices of everything—besides, to cheat on the prices listed would have been just too embarrassing. With nothing but a big empty warehouse for overhead and no employees spending thousands of man-hours marking individual items, the prices beat any discount house that ever lived. He sold that one, too, and moved on. He started a line of organic baby foods without preservatives, franchised it and moved on again. He developed a plastic container that would burn without polluting and patented it and sold the patent."

"I've heard of that one. Haven't seen it around, though."

"Maybe you will," Karl said in a guarded tone. "Maybe you will. Anyway, he had a CPA in Pasadena handling details, and just did his thing all over. I never heard of a failure in anything he tried."

"Sounds like a junior edition of the great man himself, your honored boss."

"You're not the only one who realized that. The boss may be a ding-a-ling in many ways, but nobody ever faulted his business sense. He has always had his tentacles out for wandering pieces of very special manpower. For all I know he had drawn a bead on Cleveland Wheeler years back. I wouldn't doubt that he'd made offers from time to time, only during that period Cleve Wheeler wasn't about to go to work for anyone that big. His whole pattern is to run things his way, and you don't do that in an established empire."

"Heir apparent," said Joe, reminding him of something he had said earlier.

"Right," nodded Karl. "I knew you'd begin to get the idea before I was finished."

"But finish," said Joe.

"Right. Now what I'm going to tell you, I just want you to know. I don't expect you to understand it or what it means or what it has all done to Cleve Wheeler. I need your help, and you can't really help me unless you know the whole story."

"Shoot."

Karl Trilling shot: "Wheeler found a girl. Her name was Clara Prieta and her folks came from Sonora. She was bright as hell—in her way, I suppose, as bright as Cleve, though with a tenth of his schooling—and pretty as well, and it was Cleve she wanted, not what he might get for her. She fell for him when he had nothing—when he really wanted nothing. They were a daily, hourly joy to each other. I guess that was about the time he started building this business and that, making something again. He bought a little house and a car. He bought two cars, one for her. I don't think she wanted it, but he couldn't do enough—he was always looking for more things to do for her. They went out for an evening to some friends' house, she from shopping, he from whatever it was he was working on then, so they had both cars. He followed her on the way home and had to watch her lose control and spin out. She died in his arms."

"Oh, Jesus."

"Mister Lucky. Listen: a week later he turned a corner downtown and found himself looking at a bank robbery. He caught a stray bullet—grazed the back of his neck. He had seven months to lie still and think about things. When he got out he was told his business manager had embezzled everything and headed south with his secretary. Everything."

"What did he do?"

"Went to work and paid his hospital bill."

They sat in the car in the dark for a long time, until Joe said, "Was he paralyzed, there in the hospital?"

"For nearly five months."

"Wonder what he thought about."

Karl Trilling said, "I can imagine what he thought about. What I can't imagine is what he decided. What he concluded. What he determined to be. Damn it, there are no accurate words for it. We all do the best we can with what we've got, or try to. Or should. He *did*—and with the best possible material to start out with. He played it straight; he worked hard; he was honest and lawful and fair; he was fit; he was bright. He came out of the hospital with those last two qualities intact. God alone knows what's happened to the rest of it."

"So he went to work for the old man."

"He did—and somehow that frightens me. It was as if all his qualifications were not enough to suit both of them until these things happened to him—until they made him become what he is."

"And what is that?"

"There isn't a short answer to that, Joe. The old man has become a modern myth. Nobody ever sees him. Nobody can predict what he's going to do or why. Cleveland Wheeler stepped into his shadow and disappeared almost as completely as the boss. There are very few things you can say for certain. The boss has always been a recluse and in the ten years Cleve Wheeler has been with him he has become more so. It's been business as usual with him, of course—which means the constantly unusual—long periods of quiet, and then these spectacular unexpected wheelings and dealings. You assume that the old man dreams these things up and some high-powered genius on his staff gets them done. But it could be the genius that instigates the moves—who can know? Only the people closest to him—Wheeler, Epstein, me. And I don't know?"

"But Epstein died."

Karl Trilling nodded in the dark. "Epstein died. Which leaves only Wheeler to watch the store. I'm the old man's personal physician, not Wheeler's, and there's no guarantee that I ever will be Wheeler's."

Joe Trilling recrossed his legs and leaned back, looking out into the whispering dark. "It begins to take shape," he murmured. "The old man's on the way out, you very well might be and there's nobody to take over but this Wheeler."

"Yes, and I don't know what he is or what he'll do. I do know he will command more power than any single human being on Earth. He'll have so much that he'll be above any kind of cupidity that you or I could imagine—you or I can't think in that order of magnitude. But you see, he's a man who, you might say, has had it proved to him that being good and smart and strong and honest doesn't particularly pay off. Where will he go with all this? And hypothesizing that he's been making more and more of the decisions lately and extrapolating from that—where is he going? All you can be sure of it that he will succeed in anything he tries. That is his habit."

"What does he want? Isn't that what you're trying to figure out? What would a man like that want, if he knew he could get it?"

"I knew I'd come to the right place," said Karl almost happily. "That's it exactly. As for me, I have all I need now and there are plenty of other places I could go. I wish Epstein were still around, but he's dead and cremated."

"Cremated?"

"That right—you wouldn't know about that. Old man's instructions. I handled it myself. You've heard of the hot and cold private swimming pools—but I bet you never heard of a man with his own private crematorium in the second sub-basement."

Joe threw up his hands. "I guess if you can reach into your pocket and pull out two billion real dollars, you can have anything you want. By the way—was that legal?"

"Like you said—if you have two billion. Actually, the county medical examiner was present and signed the papers. And he'll be there when the old man pushes off too—it's all in the final instructions. Hey—wait, I don't want to cast any aspersions on the M.E. He wasn't bought. He did a very competent examination on Epstein."

"Okay—we know what to expect when the time comes. It's afterward you're worried about."

"Right. What has the old man—I'm speaking of the corporate old man now—what has he been doing all along? What has he been doing in the last ten years, since he got Wheeler—and is it any different from what he was doing before? How much of this difference, if any, is more Wheeler than boss? That's all we have to go on, Joe, and from it we have to extrapolate what Wheeler's going to do with the biggest private economic force this world has ever known."

"Let's talk about that," said Joe, beginning to smile.

Karl Trilling knew the signs, so he began to smile a little, too. They talked about it.

# II

The crematorium in the second sub-basement was purely functional, as if all concessions to sentiment and ritual had been made elsewhere, or canceled. The latter most accurately described what had happened when at last, at long, long last, the old man died. Everything was done precisely according to his instructions immediately after he was certifiably dead and before any public announcements were made—right up to and including the moment when the square mouth of the furnace opened with a startling clang, a blare of heat, a flare of light—the hue the old-time blacksmiths called straw color. The simple coffin slid rapidly in, small flames exploding into being on its corners, and the door banged shut. It took a moment for the eyes to adjust to the bare room, the empty greased track, the closed door. It took the same moment for the conditioners to whisk away the sudden smell of scorched soft pine.

The medical examiner leaned over the small table and signed his name twice. Karl Trilling and Cleveland Wheeler did the same. The M.E. tore off copies and folded them and put them away in his breast pocket. He looked at the closed square iron door, opened his mouth, closed it again and shrugged. He held out his hand.

"Good night, Doctor."

"Good night, Doctor. Rugosi's outside—he'll show you out."

The M.E. shook hands wordlessly with Cleveland Wheeler and left.

"I know just what he's feeling," Karl said. "Something ought to be said. Something memorable—end of an era. Like 'One small step for man—' "

Cleveland Wheeler smiled the bright smile of the college hero, fifteen years after—a little less wide, a little less even, a great deal less in the eyes. He said in the voice that commanded, whatever he said, "If you think you're quoting the first words from an astronaut on the moon, you're not. What he said was from the ladder, when he poked his boot down. He said, 'It's some kind of soft stuff. I can kick it around with my foot.' I've always liked that much better. It was real, it wasn't rehearsed or memorized or thought out and it had to do with that moment and the next. The M.E. said good night and you told him the chauffeur was waiting outside. I like that better than anything anyone could say. I think he would, too," Wheeler added, barely gesturing, with a very strong, slightly cleft chin, toward the hot black door.

"But he wasn't exactly human."

"So they say." Wheeler half smiled and, even as he turned away, Karl could sense himself tuned out, the room itself become

of secondary importance—the next thing Wheeler was to do, and
the next and the one after, becoming more real than the here and
now.

Karl put a fast end to that.

He said levelly, "I meant what I just said, Wheeler."

It couldn't have been the words, which by themselves might
have elicited another half-smile and a forgetting. It was the tone,
and perhaps the "Wheeler." There is a ritual about these things.
To those few on his own level, and those on the level below, he
was Cleve. Below that he was mister to his face and Wheeler
behind his back. No one of his peers would call him mister unless
it was meant as the herald of an insult; no one of his peers or
immediate underlings would call him. Wheeler at all, ever. Whatever the component, it removed Cleveland Wheeler's hand from
the knob and turned him. His face was completely alert and
interested. "You'd best tell me what you mean, Doctor."

Karl said, "I'll do better than that. Come." Without gestures,
suggestions or explanations he walked to the left rear of the room,
leaving it up to Wheeler to decide whether or not to follow.
Wheeler followed.

In the corner Karl rounded on him. "If you ever say anything
about this to anyone—even me—when we leave here, I'll just
deny it. If you ever get in here again, you won't find anything to
back up your story." He took a complex four-inch blade of machined stainless steel from his belt and slid it between the big
masonry blocks. Silently, massively, the course of blocks in the
corner began to move upward. Looking up at them in the dim
light from the narrow corridor they revealed, anyone could see
that they were real blocks and that to get through them without
that key and the precise knowledge of where to put it would be a
long-term project.

Again Karl proceeded without looking around, leaving go, no-go
as a matter for Wheeler to decide. Wheeler followed. Karl heard
his footsteps behind him and noticed with pleasure and something like admiration that when the heavy blocks whooshed down
and seated themselves solidly behind them, Wheeler may have
looked over his shoulder but did not pause.

"You've noticed we're alongside the furnace," Karl said, like a
guided-tour bus driver. "And now, behind it."

He stood aside to let Wheeler pass him and see the small room.

It was just large enough for the tracks which protruded from
the back of the furnace and a little standing space on each side.

On the far side was a small table with a black suitcase standing on it. On the track stood the coffin, its corners carboned, its top and sides wet and slightly steaming.

"Sorry to have to close that stone gate that way," Karl said matter-of-factly. "I don't expect anyone down here at all, but I wouldn't want to explain any of this to persons other than yourself."

Wheeler was staring at the coffin. He seemed perfectly composed, but it was a seeming. Karl was quite aware of what it was costing him.

Wheeler said, "I wish you'd explain it to *me*." And he laughed. It was the first time Karl had ever seen this man do anything badly.

"I will. I am." He clicked open the suitcase and laid it open and flat on the little table. There was a glisten of chrome and steel and small vials in little pockets. The first tool he removed was a screwdriver. "No need to use screws when you're cremating 'em," he said cheerfully and placed the tip under one corner of the lid. He struck the handle smartly with the heel of one hand and the lid popped loose. "Stand this up against the wall behind you, will you?"

Silently Cleveland Wheeler did as he was told. It gave him something to do with his muscles; it gave him the chance to turn his head away for a moment; it gave him a chance to think—and it gave Karl the opportunity for a quick glance at his steady countenance.

*He's a* mensch, Karl thought. *He really is . . .*

Wheeler set up the lid neatly and carefully and they stood, one on each side, looking down into the coffin.

"He—got a lot older," Wheeler said at last.

"You haven't seen him recently."

"Here and in there," said the executive, "I've spent more time in the same room with him during the past month than I have in the last eight, nine years. Still, it was a matter of minutes, each time."

Karl nodded understandingly. "I'd heard that. Phone calls, any time of the day or night, and then those long silences two days, three, not calling out, not having anyone in—"

"Are you going to tell me about the phony oven?"

"Oven? Furnace? It's not a phony at all. When we've finished here it'll do the job, all right."

"Then why the theatricals?"

"That was for the M.E. Those papers he signed are in sort of a

never-never country just now. When we slide this back in and
turn on the heat they'll become as legal as he thinks they are."

"Then why—"

"Because there are some things you have to know." Karl reached
into the coffin and unfolded the gnarled hands. They came apart
reluctantly and he pressed them down at the sides of the body.
He unbuttoned the jacket, laid it back, unbuttoned the shirt,
unzipped the trousers. When he had finished with this he looked
up and found Wheeler's sharp gaze, not on the old man's corpse,
but on him.

"I have the feeling," said Cleveland Wheeler, "that I have
never seen you before."

Silently Karl Trilling responded: *But you do now.* And, *Thanks,
Joey. You were dead right.* Joe had known the answer to that one
plaguing question, *How should I act?*

*Talk just the way he talks,* Joe had said. *Be what he is, the
whole time* . . .

Be what he is. A man without illusions (they don't work) and
without hope (who needs it?) who has the unbreakable habit of
succeeding. And who can say it's a nice day in such a way that
everyone around snaps to attention and says: *Yes, SIR!*

"You've been busy," Karl responded shortly. He took off his
jacket, folded it and put it on the table beside the kit. He put on
surgeon's gloves and slipped the sterile sleeve off a new scalpel.
"Some people scream and faint the first time they watch a
dissection."

Wheeler smiled thinly. "I don't scream and faint." But it was
not lost on Karl Trilling that only then, at the last possible
moment, did Wheeler actually view the old man's body. When he
did he neither screamed nor fainted; he uttered an astonished
grunt.

"Thought that would surprise you," Karl said easily. "In case
you were wondering, though, he really was a male. The species
seems to be oviparous. Mammals too, but it has to be oviparous.
I'd sure like a look at a female. That isn't a vagina. It's a cloaca."

"Until this moment," said Wheeler in a hypnotized voice, "I
thought that 'not human' remark of yours was a figure of speech."

"No, you didn't," Karl responded shortly.

Leaving the words to hang in the air, as words will if a speaker
has the wit to isolate them with wedges of silence, he deftly slit
the corpse from the sternum to the pubic symphysis. For the
first-time viewer this was always the difficult moment. It's hard

not to realize viscerally that the cadaver does not feel anything and will not protest. Never-alive to Wheeler, Karl looked for a gasp or a shudder; Wheeler merely held his breath.

"We could spend hours—weeks, I imagine, going into the details," Karl said, deftly making a transverse incision in the ensiform area, almost around to the trapezoid on each side, "but this is the thing I wanted you to see." Grasping the flesh at the juncture of the cross he had cut, on the left side, he pulled upward and to the left. The cutaneous layers came away easily, with the fat under them. They were not pinkish, but an off-white lavender shade. Now the muscular striations over the ribs were in view. "If you'd palpated the old man's chest," he said, demonstrating on the right side, "you'd have felt what seemed to be normal human ribs. But look at this."

With a few deft strokes he separated the muscle fibers from the bone on a mid-costal area about four inches square, and scraped. A rib emerged and, as he widened the area and scraped between it and the next one, it became clear that the ribs were joined by a thin flexible layer of bone or chitin.

"It's like baleen—whalebone," said Karl. "See this?" He sectioned out a piece, flexed it.

"My God."

# III

"Now look at this." Karl took surgical shears from the kit, snipped through the sternum right up to the clavicle and then across the lower margin of the ribs. Slipping his fingers under them, he pulled upward. With a dull snap the entire rib cage penned like a door, exposing the lung.

The lung was not pink, nor the liverish-brownish-black of a smoker, but yellow—the clear bright yellow of pure sulfur.

"His metabolism," Karl said, straightening up at last and flexing the tension out of his shoulders, "is fantastic. Or was. He lived on oxygen, same as us, but he broke it out of carbon monoxide, sulfur dioxide and trioxide and carbon dioxide mostly. I'm not saying he could—I mean he had to. When he was forced to breathe what we call clean air, he could take just so much of it and then had to duck out and find a few breaths of his own atmosphere. When he was younger he could take it for hours at a time, but as the years went by he had to spend more and more time in the kind of smog he could breathe. Those long disappearance of his, and that reclusiveness—they weren't as kinky as people supposed."

Wheeler made a gesture toward the corpse. "But—what is he? Where—"

"I can't tell you. Except for a good deal of medical and bio-chemical details, you now know as much as I do. Somehow, somewhere, he arrived. He came, he saw, he began to make his moves. Look at this."

He opened the other side of the chest and then broke the sternum up and away. He pointed. The lung tissue was not in two discreet parts, but extended across the median line. "One lung, all the way across, though it has these two lobes. The kidneys and gonads show the same right-left fusion."

"I'll take your word for it," said Wheeler a little hoarsely. "Damn it, what *is* it?"

"A featherless biped, as Plato once described Homo sap. *I* don't know what it is. I just know *that* it is—and I thought you ought to know. That's all."

"But you've seen one before. That's obvious."

"Sure. Epstein."

"Epstein?"

"Sure. The old man had to have a go-between—someone who could, without suspicion, spend long hours with him and hours away. The old man could do a lot over the phone, but not everything. Epstein was, you might say, a right arm that could hold its breath a little longer than he could. It got to him in the end, though, and he died of it."

"Why didn't you say something long before this?"

"First of all, I value my own skin. I could say reputation, but skin is the word. I signed a contract as his personal physician because he needed a personal physician—another bit of window-dressing. But I did precious little doctoring—except over the phone—and nine-tenths of that was, I realized quite recently, purely diversionary. Even a doctor, I suppose, can be a trusting soul. One or the other would call and give a set of symptoms and I'd cautiously suggest and prescribe. Then I'd get another call that the patient was improving and that was that. Why, I even got specimens—blood, urine, stools—and did the pathology on them and never realized that they were from the same source as what the medical examiner checked out and signed for."

"What do you mean, same source?"

Karl shrugged. "He could get anything he wanted—anything."

"Then—what the M.E. examined wasn't—" he waved a hand at the casket.

"Of course not. That's why the crematorium has a back door. There's a little pocket sleight-of-hand trick you can buy for fifteen cents that operates the same way. This body here was inside the furnace. The ringer—a look-alike that came from God knows where; I swear to you I don't—was lying out there waiting for the M.E. When the button was pushed the fires started up and that coffin slid in—pushing this one out and at the same time drenching it with water as it came through. While we've been in here, the human body is turning to ashes. My personal private secret instructions, both for Epstein and for the boss, were to wait until I was certain I was alone and then come in here after an hour and push the second button, which would slide this one back into the fire. I was to do no investigations, ask no questions, make no reports. It came through as logical but not reasonable, like so many of his orders." He laughed suddenly. "Do you know why the old man—and Epstein too, for that matter, in case you never noticed—wouldn't shake hands with anyone?"

"I presumed it was because he had an obsession with germs."

"It was because his normal body temperature was a hundred and seven."

Wheeler touched one of his own hands with the other and said nothing.

When Karl felt that the wedge of silence was thick enough he asked lightly, "Well, boss, where do we go from here?"

Cleveland Wheeler turned away from the corpse and to Karl slowly, as if diverting his mind with an effort.

"What did you call me?"

"Figure of speech," said Karl and smiled. "Actually. I'm working for the company—and that's you. I'm under orders, which have been finally and completely discharged when I push that button—I have no others. So it really is up to you."

Wheeler's eyes fell again to the corpse. "You mean about him? This? What we should do?"

"That, yes. Whether to burn it up and forget it—or call in top management and an echelon of scientists. Or scare the living hell out of everyone on Earth by phoning the papers. Sure, that has to be decided, but I was thinking on a much wider spectrum than that."

"Such as—"

Karl gestured toward the box with his head. "What was he

doing here, anyway? What has he done? What was he trying to do?"

"You'd better go on," said Wheeler; and for the very first time said something in a way that suggested diffidence. "You've had a while to think about all this. I—" and almost helplessly, he spread his hands.

"I can understand that," Karl said gently. "Up to now I've been coming on like a hired lecturer and I know it. I'm not going to embarrass you with personalities except to say that you've absorbed all this with less buckling of the knees than anyone in the world I could think of."

"Right. Well, there's a simple technique you learn in elementary algebra. It has to do with the construction of graphs. You place a dot on the graph where known data put it. You get more data, you put down another dot and then a third. With just three dots—of course, the more the better, but it can be done with three—you can connect them and establish a curve. This curve has certain characteristics and it's fair to extend the curve a little farther with the assumption that later data will bear you out."

"Extrapolation."

"Extrapolation. X axis, the fortunes of our late boss. Y axis, time. The curve is his fortunes—that is to say, his influence."

"Pretty tall graph."

"Over thirty years."

"Still pretty tall."

"All right," said Karl. "Now, over the same thirty years, another curve: change in the environment." He held up a hand. "I'm not going to read you a treatise on ecology. Let's be more objective than that. Let's just say changes. Okay: a measurable rise in the mean temperature because of $CO_2$ and the greenhouse effect. Draw the curve. Incidence of heavy metals, mercury and lithium, in organic tissue. Draw a curve. Likewise chlorinated hydrocarbons, hypertrophy of algae due to phosphates, incidence of coronaries . . . all right, let's superimpose all these curves on the same graph."

"I see what you're getting at. But you have to be careful with that kind of statistic game. Like, the increase of traffic fatalities coincides with the increased use of aluminum cans and plastic-tipped baby pins."

"Right. I don't think I'm falling into that trap. I just want to find reasonable answers to a couple of otherwise unreasonable situations. One is this: If the changes occuring in our planet are the result of mere carelessness—a more or less random thing, carelessness—then how come nobody is being careless in a way that benefits the environment? Strike that. I promised, no ecology lessons. Rephrase: How come all these carelessnesses promote a change and not a preservation?

"Next question: What is the direction of the change? You've seen speculative writing about 'terraforming'—altering other planets to make them habitable by humans. Suppose an effort were being made to change this planet to suit someone else? Suppose they wanted more water and were willing to melt the polar caps by the greenhouse effect? Increase the oxides of sulfur, eliminate certain marine forms from plankton to whales? Reduce the population by increases in lung cancer, emphysema, heart attacks and even war?"

Both men found themselves looking down at the sleeping face in the coffin. Karl said softly, "Look what he was into—petrochemicals, fossil fuels, food processing, advertising, all the things that made the changes or helped the changers—"

"You're not blaming him for all of it."

"Certainly not. He found willing helpers by the million."

"You don't think he was trying to change a whole planet just so he could be comfortable in it."

"No, I don't think so—and that's the central point I have to make. I don't know if there are any more around like him and Epstein, but I can suppose this: If the changes now going on keep on—and accelerate—then we can expect them."

Wheeler said, "So what would you like to do? Mobilize the world against the invader?"

"Nothing like that. I think I'd slowly and quietly reverse the changes. If this planet is normally unsuitable to them, then I'd keep it so. I don't think they'd have to be driven back. I think they just wouldn't come."

"Or they'd try some other way."

"I don't think so," said Karl. "Because they tried this one. If they thought they could do it with fleets of spaceships and superzap guns, they'd be doing it. No—this is their way and if it doesn't work, they can try somewhere else."

Wheeler began pulling thoughtfully at his lip. Karl said softly, "All it would take is someone who knew what he was doing, who could command enough clout and who had the wit to make it pay. They might even arrange a man's life—to get the kind of man they need."

And before Wheeler could answer, Karl took up his scalpel.

"I want you to do something for me," he said sharply in a new, commanding tone—actually, Wheeler's own. "I want you to do it because I've done it and I'll be damned if I want to be the only man in the world who has."

Leaning over the head of the casket, he made an incision along the hairline from temple to temple. Then, bracing his elbows against the edge of the box and steadying one hand with the other, he drew the scalpel straight down the center of the forehead and down onto the nose, splitting it exactly in two. Down he went through the upper lip and then the lower, around the point of the chin and under it to the throat. Then he stood up.

"Put your hands on his cheeks," he ordered. Wheeler frowned briefly (how long had it been since anyone had spoken to him that way?), hesitated, then did as he was told.

"Now press your hands together and down."

The incision widened slightly under the pressure, then abruptly the flesh gave and the entire skin of the face slipped off. The unexpected lack of resistance brought Wheeler's hands to the bottom of the coffin and he found himself face to face, inches away, with the corpse.

Like the lungs and kidneys, the eyes—eye?—passed the median, very slightly reduced at the center. The pupil was oval, its long axis transverse. The skin was pale lavender with yellow vessels and in place of a nose was a thread-fringed hole. The mouth was circular, the teeth not quite radically placed; there was little chin.

Without moving, Wheeler closed his eyes, held them shut for one second, two, and then courageously opened them again. Karl whipped around the end of the coffin and got an arm around Wheeler's chest. Wheeler leaned on it heavily for a moment, then stood up quickly and brushed the arm away.

"You didn't have to do that."

"Yes, I did," said Karl. "Would you want to be the only man in the world who'd gone through that—with nobody to tell it to?"

And after all, Wheeler could laugh. When he had finished he said, "Push that button."

"Hand me that cover."

Most obediently Cleveland Wheeler brought the coffin lid and they placed it.

Karl pushed the button and they watched the coffin slide into the square of flame. Then they left.

\*    \*    \*

Joe Trilling had a funny way of making a living. It was a good living, but of course he didn't make anything like the bundle the could have made in the city. On the other hand, he lived in the mountains a half-mile away from a picturesque village, in clean air and piney-birchy woods along with lots of mountain laurel, and he was his own boss. There wasn't much competition for what he did.

What he did was to make simulacra of medical specimens, mostly for the armed forces, although he had plenty of orders from medical schools, film producers and an occasional individual, no questions asked. He could make a model of anything inside, affixed to or penetrating a body or any part of it. He could make models to be looked at, models to be felt, smelled and palpated. He could give you gangrene that stunk or dewey thyroids with real dew on them. He could make one-of-a-kind or he could set up a production line. Dr. Joe Trilling was, to put it briefly, the best there was at what he did.

"The clincher," Karl told him (in much more relaxed circumstances than their previous ones; daytime now, with beer), "the real clincher was the face bit. God, Joe, that was a beautiful piece of work."

"Just nuts and bolts. The beautiful part was your idea—his hands on it."

"How do you mean?"

"I've been thinking back to that," Joe said. "I don't think you yourself realize how brilliant a stroke that was. It's all very well to set up a show for the guy, but to make him put his hands as well as his eyes and brains on it—that was the stroke of genius. It's like—well, I can remember when I was a kid coming home from school and putting my hand on a fence rail and somebody had spat on it." He displayed his hand, shook it. "All these years I can remember how that felt. All these years couldn't wear it away, all those scrubbings couldn't wash it away. It's more than a cerebral or psychic thing, Karl—more than the memory of an episode. I think there's a kind of memory mechanism in the cells themselves, especially on the hands, that can be invoked. What I'm getting to is that no matter how long he lives, Cleve Wheeler is going to feel that skin slip under his palms, and that is going to bring him nose to nose with that face. No, you're the genius, not me."

"Na. You knew what you were doing. I didn't."

"Hell you didn't." Joe leaned far back in his lawn chaise—so far he could hold up his beer and look at the sun through it from the underside. Watching the receding bubbles defy perspective (because they swell as they rise), he murmured, "Karl?"

"Yuh."

"Ever hear of Occam's Razor?"

"Um. Long time back. Philosophical principle. Or logic or something. Let's see. Given an effect and a choice of possible causes, the simplest cause is always the one most likely to be true. Is that it?"

"Not too close, but close enough," said Joe Trilling lazily. "Hm. You're the one who used to proclaim that logic is sufficient unto itself and need have nothing to do with truth."

"I still proclaim it."

"Okay. Now, you and I know that human greed and carelessness are quite enough all by themselves to wreck this planet. We didn't think that was enough for the likes of Cleve Wheeler, who can really do something about it, so we constructed him a smog-breathing extra-terrestrial. I mean, he hadn't done anything about saving the world for our reasons, so we gave him a whizzer of a reason of his own. Right out of our heads."

"Dictated by all available factors. Yes. What are you getting at, Joe?"

"Oh—just that our complicated hoax is simple, really, in the sense that it brought everything down to a single cause. Occam's Razor slices things down to simplest causes. Single causes have a fair chance of being right."

Karl put down his beer with a bump. "I never thought of that. I've been too busy to think of that. *Suppose we were right?*"

They looked at each other, shaken.

At last Karl said, "What do we look for now, Joe—spaceships?"

# CONSTRUCTION SHACK
## (FEBRUARY 1973)
## CLIFFORD D. SIMAK
## (B. 1904)

Cliff Simak is a remarkable writer who has maintained a high level of quality in a still-going career of more than fifty years. Other writers might worry about "burnout," but not Cliff! His masterpiece remains *City* (1952), but he has a raft of other excellent books including *Ring Around the Sun* (1953), *They Walked Like Men* (1962), and *Way Station* (1963). His occasional appearances in *If* were highlighted by "The Shipshape Miracle" (January 1963), "The Thing in the Stone" (March 1970), and the present selection.

## MEMOIR BY CLIFFORD D. SIMAK

I dislike you, Marty—and Joe and Fred as well. I dislike all people who ask me to write about a story of mine. It makes me uneasy, makes me wonder if possibly there should be some deep hidden meaning in what I write, when there almost never is. I can claim nothing further than that I'm a craftsman who has spent fifty years learning his craft. I get an idea that I like and use it to write a story that I hope some editor will buy and that some readers will read without too much gagging. And along comes this intellectual type who wants me to explain why I wrote it and how I wrote it and what I was trying to say when I wrote it and, in retrospect, what do I think of it now. Which forces me to do a lot of thinking and, what is worse, thinking after the fact.

After some thinking I have sort of figured out that "Construction Shack" might be called an iconoclastic story. It shatters an image or two. It calls into question the theory of the origin of solar systems. It may cause a supersensitive religionist to feel some vague discomfort.

Not that I believe for a moment that the present theory of solar-system formation is erroneous, or that I would willingly discomfort a true believer—although some of them might be the better for a gentle shaking up. My sole concern has always been to put together ideas that might make acceptable yarns. If, in the course of writing them, I can insert some additional meaning and content I am happy about it, but a good story comes ahead of everything. In this I am guilty of crass commercialism and, just perhaps, occasionally, outrageous creative effort. This I might say in my own behalf: I never write a story that doesn't excite me as a writer and that I don't think, just possibly, might find some acceptance with readers.

It would seem to me that the iconoclastic approach might fit respectably into the science-fiction tradition. I am not the only one who uses it. I think that one of science fiction's most valuable functions is to question the smugness of so-called established fact. History has proved, over the years, how wrong established fact can be. All we science-fiction writers are doing is getting in there a few decades ahead of history.

If this approach seems too cynical, I'm sorry; I did not mean it so. Science fiction is a form of literary alternatives, in the course of which new approaches to problems and new viewpoints of situations are suggested. In some cases this may cause the reader to look a bit beyond accepted truth or fact. That, I submit, is all to the good. It hurts no one to stretch the mind a little.

I'm glad the story was published in *If*. It was an excellent, sound, solid magazine, attracting some of the best writers in the field, publishing some of the best science fiction written. When a writer appeared in *If* he had the satisfaction of knowing he was in top-notch company. I am shamelessly proud that a story of mine should be selected as an example of the type of material *If* published.

Come to think of it, maybe I don't dislike the three of you as much as I had thought.

# CONSTRUCTION SHACK

In that same year when men first walked on Mars the probe was launched from the moon for Pluto. Five years later the first pictures were transmitted as the orbiting probe trained its cameras on the planet's surface. The transmission quality was poor; but even so, certain features of the photographs were productive of great anguish as old theories fell to shards and were replaced by puzzlement, questions with no hint of answers. The pictures seemed to say that the planet had a smooth, almost polished surface, without a single geographic feature to break the smoothness of it. Except that at certain places, equidistant from one another along the equator, were tiny dots that would have been taken for transmission noise if they had not appeared consistently. Too, the dots still persisted when some of the noise was eliminated. So it seemed they must be small geographic features or shadows cast by geographic features, although at Pluto's distance from the sun shadows would be suspect. The other data did nothing to lessen the anguish. The planet was smaller than supposed, less than a thousand miles in diameter, and its density worked out to 3.5 grams per cubic centimeter rather than the unrealistic figure of 60 grams, previously supposed.

This meant several things. It meant that somewhere out there, perhaps something more than seven billion miles from the sun, a tenth planet of the solar system swung in orbit, for no planet the size and mass of Pluto could explain the eccentricities in the orbits of Uranus and Neptune. The calculation of Pluto's mass, now proved inaccurate, had been based on the measurement of those eccentricities and it must be admitted now that something else must account for them.

Beyond that, Pluto was most strange—a smooth planet, featureless except for the evenly spaced dots. The smoothness certainly could not be explained by a non-turbulent atmosphere, for surely Pluto had to be too small and cold to hold an atmosphere. A surface of ice, men wondered, the frozen remnants of a one-time, momentary atmosphere? But for a number of reasons that didn't seem right, either. Metal, perhaps, but if the planet were of solid metal the density should be far greater.

The men on Earth consoled themselves. In five more years the probe would come back to Earth, carrying with it the films that it had taken, and from them, the actual films and not the low-quality transmissions, perhaps much that was hazy now might become understandable. The probe swung in its measured orbits and sent back more pictures, although they were little help, for that quality still was poor. Then it fired the automatic sequence that would head it back to Earth, and its beeping signals from far out in space said it was headed home on a true and steady course.

Something happened. The beeping stopped and there was a silence. Moon Base waited. It might start up again. The silence might indicate only a momentary malfunction and the signals might start again. But they never did. Somewhere, some three billion miles from the sun, some mishap had befallen the homing probe. It was never heard again—it was lost forever.

There was no sense in sending out another probe until a day when technical advances could assure better pictures. The technical advances would have to be significant—small refinements would do little good.

The second and third manned expeditions went to Mars and then came home again, bringing back, among many other things, evidence that primitive forms of life existed there, which settled once for all the old, dark suspicion that life might be an aberration to be found only on the Earth. For with life on two planets in the same solar system there could no longer be any doubt that life was a common factor in the universe. The fourth expedition went out, landed and did not come back again and now there was on Mars a piece of ground that was forever Earth. The fifth expedition was sent out even while the Earth still paid tribute to those four men who had died so far from home.

Now that life had been found on another world, now that it was apparent that another planet at one time had held seas and rivers and an atmosphere that had been an approximation of Earth's own atmosphere, now that we knew we no longer were alone in the universe, the public interest and support of space travel revived. Scientists, remembering (never having, in fact, forgotten, for it had gnawed steadily at their minds) the puzzlement of the Pluto probe, began to plan a manned Pluto expedition, as there was still no sense in sending an instrumented probe.

When the day came to lift from the Moon Base, I was a member of the expedition. I went along as a geologist—the last thing a Pluto expedition needed.

There were three of us and any psychologist will tell you that three is a number that is most unfortunate. Two gang up on one or ignore one and there is always competition to be one of the gang of two. No one wants to stand alone with the other two against him. But it didn't work that way with us. We got along all right, although there were times when it was rough going. The five years that the probe took to arrive at Pluto was cut by more than half, not only because of improved rocket capability, but because a manned craft could pile on velocity that couldn't be programmed—or at least safely programmed—into a probe. But a bit more than two years is a long time to be cooped up in a tin can rocketing along in emptiness. Maybe it wouldn't be so bad if you had some sense of speed, of really getting somewhere—but you haven't. You just hang there in space.

The three of us? Well, I am Howard Hunt and the other two were Orson Gates, a chemist, and Tyler Hampton, an engineer.

As I say, we got along fine. We played chess tournaments—yeah, three men in a tournament and it was all right because none of us knew chess. If we had been any good I suppose we would have been at one another's throats. We dreamed up dirty ditties and were so pleased with our accomplishments that we'd spend hours singing them and none of us could sing. We did a lot of other futile things—by now you should be getting the idea. There were some rather serious scientific experiments and observations we were supposed to make, but all of us figured that our first and biggest job was to manage to stay sane.

When we neared Pluto we dropped the fooling around and spent much time peering through the scope, arguing and speculating about what we saw. Not that there was much to see. The planet resembled nothing quite as much as a billiard ball. It was smooth. There were no mountains, no valleys, no craters—nothing marred the smoothness of the surface. The dots were there, of course. We could make out seven groups of them, all positioned along the equatorial belt. And in close up they were not simply dots. They were structures of some kind.

We landed finally, near a group of them. The landing was a little harder than we had figured it would be. The planetary surface was hard—there was no give to it. But we stayed right-side up and we didn't break a thing.

People at times ask me to describe Pluto and it's a hard thing to put into words. You can say that it is smooth and that it's dark—it's dark even in broad daylight. The sun, at that distance, is not much more than a slightly brighter star. You don't have daylight on Pluto—you have starlight and it doesn't make much difference whether you're facing the sun or not. The planet is airless, of course, and waterless and cold. But cold, as far as human sensation is concerned, is a relative thing. Once the temperature gets down to a hundred Kelvin it doesn't much matter how much colder it becomes. Especially when you're wearing life support. Without a suit containing life support you'd last only a few seconds, if that long, on a place like Pluto. I've never figured out which would kill you first—cold or internal pressure. Would you freeze—or explode before you froze?

So Pluto is dark, airless, cold and smooth. Those are the externals only. You stand there and look at the sun and realize how far away you are. You know you are standing at the edge of the solar system, that just out there, a little way beyond, you'd be clear outside the system. Which doesn't really have to be true, of course. You know about the tenth planet. Even if it's theory, it's supposed to be out there. You know about the millions of circling comets that technically are a part of the solar system, although they're so far out no one ever thinks of them. You could say to yourself this really is not the edge—the hypothetical tenth planet and the comets still are out there. But this is intellectualization; you're telling yourself something that your mind says may be true, but your gut denies. For hundreds of years Pluto has been the last outpost and this, by God, is Pluto and you're farther away from home than man has ever been before and you feel it. You don't belong to anything any more. You're in the back alley, and the bright and happy streets are so far away that you know you'll never find them.

It isn't homesickness that you feel. It's more like never having had a home. Of never having belonged anywhere. You get over it, of course—or come to live with it.

So we came down out of the ship after we had landed and stood upon the surface. The first thing that struck us—other than the sense of lostness that at once grabbed all of us—was that the horizon was too near, much nearer than on the Moon. We felt at once that we stood on a small world. We noticed that horizon's nearness even before we noticed the buildings that the probe had photographed as dots and that we had dropped down to investigate. Perhaps buildings is not the right word—structures probably would be better. Buildings are enclosures and these were not enclosures. They were domes someone had set out to build and hadn't had time to finish. The basic underlying framework had been erected and then the work had stopped. Riblike arcs curved up from the surface and met overhead. Struts and braces held the frames solid, but that was as far as the construction had gone. There were three of them, one larger than the other two. The frames were not quite as simple as I may have made them seem. Tied into the ribs and struts and braces were a number of other structural units that seemed to have no purpose and make no sense at all.

We tried to make sense out of them and out of the scooped-out hollows that had been gouged out of the planetary surface within the confines of each construct—they had no floors and seemed fastened to the surface of the planet. The hollows were circular, some six feet across and three feet deep, and to me they looked like nothing quite as much as indentations made in a container of ice cream by a scoop.

About this time Tyler began to have some thoughts about the surface. Tyler is an engineer and should have had his thoughts immediately—and so should the rest of us—but the first hour or so outside the ship had been considerably confusing. We had worn our suits in training, of course, and had done some walking around in them, but Pluto seemed to have even less gravity than had been calculated and we had had to get used to it before we could be reasonably comfortable. Nor had anything else been exactly as we had anticipated.

"This surface," Tyler said to me. "There is something wrong with it."

"We knew it was smooth," said Orson. "The pictures showed that. Coming in, we could see it for ourselves."

"This smooth?" Tyler asked. "This even?" He turned to me. "It isn't geologically possible. Would you say it is?"

"I would think not," I said. "If there had been any upheaval at all this floor would be rugged. There can't have been any erosion—anything to level it down. Micrometeorite impacts, maybe, but not too many them. We're too far out for meteorites of any size. And while micrometeorites might pit the surface there would be no leveling process."

Tyler let himself down on his knees rather awkwardly. He brushed a hand across the surface. The seeing was not too good, but you could see that there was dust, a thin layer of dust, a powdering.

"Shine a light down here," said Tyler.

Orson aimed his light at the spot. Some of the gray dust still clung where Tyler had wiped his hand, but there were streaks where the darker surface showed through.

"Space dust," said Tyler.

Orson said, "There should be damn little of it."

"True," said Tyler. "But over four billion years or more, it would accumulate. It couldn't be erosion dust, could it?"

"Nothing to cause erosion," I said. "This must be as close to a dead planet as you ever get. Not enough gravity to hold any of the gases—if there ever were gases. At one time there must have been, but they've all gone—they went early. No atmosphere, no water. I doubt there ever was any accumulation. A molecule wouldn't hang around for long."

"But space dust would?"

"Maybe. Some sort of electrostatic attraction, maybe."

Tyler scrubbed the little patch of surface again with his gloved hand, removing more of the dust, with more of the darker surface showing through.

"Have we got a drill?" he asked. "A specimen drill."

"I have one in my kit," said Orson. He took it out and handed it to Tyler. Tyler positioned the bit against the surface, pressed the button. In the light of the torch you could see the bit spinning. Tyler put more weight on the drill.

"It's harder than a bitch," he said.

The bit began to bite. A small pile of fragments built up around the hold. The surface was hard, no doubt of that. The bit didn't go too deep and the pile of fragments was small.

Tyler gave up. He lifted out the bit and snubbed off the motor.

"Enough for analysis?" he asked.

"Should be," said Orson. He took the bit from Tyler and handed him a small specimen bag. Tyler laid the open mouth of the bag on the surface and brushed the fragments into it.

"Now we'll know," he said. "Now we will know something."

A couple of hours later, back in the ship, we knew.

"I have it," Orson said, "but I don't believe it."

"Metal?" asked Tyler.

"Sure, metal. But not the kind you have in mind. It's steel."

"Steel?" I said, horrified. "It can't be. Steel's no natural metal. It's manufactured."

"Iron," said Orson. "Nickel. Molybdenum, vanadium, chromium. That works out to steel. I don't know as much about steel as I should. But it's steel—a good steel. Corrosion resistant, tough, strong."

"Maybe just the platform for the structures," I said. "Maybe a pad of steel to support them. We took the specimen close to one of them."

"Let's find out," said Tyler.

We opened up the garage and ran down the ramp and got out the buggy. Before we left we turned off the television camera. By this time Moon Base would have seen all they needed to see and if they wanted more they could ask for it. We had given them a report on everything we had found—all except the steel surface and the three of us agreed that until we knew more about that we would not say anything. It would be a while in any case until we got an answer from them. The time lag on Earth was about sixty hours each way.

We went out ten miles and took a boring sample and came back, following the thin tracks the buggy made in the dust, taking samples every mile. We got the answer that I think all of us expected we would get, but couldn't bring ourselves to talk about. The samples all were steel.

It didn't seem possible, of course, and it took us a while to digest the fact, but finally we admitted that on the basis of best evidence Pluto was no planet, but a fabricated metal ball, small-plant size. But God-awful big for anyone to build.

Anyone?

That was the question that now haunted us. Who had built it? Perhaps more important—why had they built it? For some purpose, surely, but why, once that purpose had been fulfilled (if, in fact, it had been fulfilled) had Pluto been left out here at the solar system's rim?

"No one from the system," Tyler said. "There's no one but us. Mars has life, of course, but primitive life. It got a start there and hung on and that was all. Venus is too hot. Mercury is too close to the sun. The big gas planets? Maybe, but not the kind of life that would build a thing like this. It had to be something from outside."

"How about the fifth planet?" suggested Orson.

"There probably never was a fifth planet," I said. "The material for it may have been there, but the planet never formed. By all the rules of celestial mechanics there should have been a planet between Mars and Jupiter, but something went haywire."

"The tenth planet, then," said Orson.

"No one is really positive there is a tenth," said Tyler.

"Yeah, you're right," said Orson. "Even if there were it would be a poor bet for life, let alone intelligence."

"So that leaves us with outsiders," said Tyler.

"And a long time ago," said Orson.

"Why do you say that?"

"The dust. There isn't much dust in the universe."

"And no one knows what it is. There is the dirty ice theory."

"I see what you're getting at. But it needn't be ice. Nor graphite nor any of the other things that have been—"

"You mean it's that stuff out there."

"It could be. What do you think, Howard?"

"I can't be sure," I said. "The only thing I know is that it couldn't be erosive."

Before we went to sleep we tried to fix up a report to beam back to Moon Base, but anything we put together sounded too silly and unbelievable. So we gave up. We'd have to tell them sometime, but we could wait.

When we awoke we had a bite to eat, then got into our suits and went out to look over the structures. They still didn't make much sense, especially all the crazy contraptions that were fastened on the ribs and struts and braces. Nor did the scooped-out hollows.

"If they were only up on legs," said Orson, "they could be used as chairs."

"But not very comfortable," said Tyler.

"If you tilted them a bit," said Orson. But that didn't figure either. They would still be uncomfortable. I wondered why he thought of them as chairs. They didn't look like any chairs to me.

We pottered around a lot, not getting anywhere. We looked the structures over inch by inch, wondering all the while if there was something we had missed. But there didn't seem to be.

Now comes the funny part of it. I don't know why we did it—out of sheer desperation, maybe. But failing to find any clues, we got down on our hands and knees, dusting at the surface with our hands. What we hoped to find, I don't know. It was slow going and it was a dirty business, with the dust tending to stick to us.

"If we'd only brought some brooms along," said Orson.

But we had no brooms. Who in his right mind would have thought we would want to sweep a planet?

So there we were. We had what appeared to be a manufactured planet and we had some stupid structures for which we could deduce not a single reason. We had come a long ways and we had been expected to make some tremendous discovery once we landed. We had made a discovery, all right, but it didn't mean a thing.

We finally gave up with the sweeping business and stood there, scuffing our feet and wondering what to do next, when Tyler suddenly let out a yell and pointed at a place on the surface where his boots had kicked away the dust.

We all bent to look at what he had found. We saw three holes

in the surface, each an inch or so across and some three inches
deep, placed in a triangle and close together. Tyler got down on
his hands and knees and shone his light down into the holes, each
one of them in turn.

Finally he stood up. "I don't know," he said. "They could
maybe be a lock of some sort. Like a combination. There are little
notches on the sides, down at the bottom of them. If you moved
those notches just right something might happen."

"Might blow ourselves up, maybe," said Orson. "Do it wrong
and bang!"

"I don't think so," said Tyler. "I don't think it's anything like
that. I don't say it's a lock, either. But I don't think it's a bomb.
Why should they boobytrap a thing like this?"

"You can't tell what they might have done," I said. "We don't
know what kind of things they were or why they were here."

Tyler didn't answer. He got down again and began carefully
dusting the surface, shining his light on it while he dusted. We
didn't have anything else to do, so helped him.

It was Orson who found it this time—a hairline crack you had
to hold your face down close to the surface to see. Having found
it, we did some more dusting and worried it out. The hairline
described a circle and the three holes were set inside and to one
edge of it. The circle was three feet or so in diameter.

"Either of you guys good at picking locks?" asked Tyler.

Neither of us were.

"It's got to be a hatch of some sort," Orson said. "This metal
ball we're standing on has to be a hollow ball. If it weren't its
mass would be greater than it is."

"And no one," I said, "would be insane enough to build a solid
ball. It would take too much metal and too much energy to
move."

"You're sure that it was moved?" asked Orson.

"It had to be," I told him. "It wasn't built in this system. No
one here could have built it."

Tyler had pulled a screwdriver out of his toolkit and was poking
into the hole with it.

"Wait a minute," said Orson. "I just thought of something."

He nudged Tyler to one side, reached down and inserted three
fingers into the holes and pulled. The circular section rose smoothly
on its hinges.

Wedged into the area beneath the door were objects that

looked like the rolls of paper you buy to wrap up Christmas presents. Bigger than rolls of paper, though. Six inches or so.

I got hold of one of them and that first one was not easy to grip, for they were packed in tightly. But I managed with much puffing and grunting to pull it out. It was heavy and a good four feet in length.

Once we got one out, the other rolls were easier to lift. We pulled out three more and headed for the ship.

But before we left I held the remaining rolls over to one side, to keep them from tilting, while Orson shone his light down into the hole. We had half expected to find a screen or something under the rolls, with the hole extending on down into a cavity that might have been used as living quarters or a workroom. But the hole ended in machined metal. We could see the grooves left by the drill or die that had bored the hole. That hole had just one purpose, to store the rolls we had found inside it.

Back in the ship we had to wait a while for the rolls to pick up some heat before we could handle them. Now, seeing them in good light, we realized that they were made up of many sheets rolled up together. The sheets seemed to be made of some sort of extremely thin metal or tough plastic. They were stiff from the cold and we spread them out on our lone table and weighed them down to hold them flat.

On the first sheet were diagrams of some sort, drawings and what might have been specifications written into the diagrams and along the margins. The specifications, of course, meant nothing to us (although later some were puzzled out and mathematicians and chemists were able to figure out some of the formulas and equations).

"Blueprints," said Tyler. "This whole business was an engineering job."

"If that's the case," said Orson, "those strange things fastened to the structural frames could be mounts to hold engineering instruments."

"Could be," said Tyler.

"Maybe the instruments are stored in some other holes like the one where we found the blueprints," I suggested.

"I don't think so," said Tyler. "They would have taken the instruments with them when they left."

"Why didn't they take the blueprints, too?"

"The instruments would have been worthwhile to take. They could be used on another job. But the blueprints couldn't. And there may have been many sets of prints and spec sheets. These we have may be only one of many sets of duplicates. There would have been a set of master prints and those they might have taken with them when they left."

"What I don't understand," I said, "is what they could have been building out here. What kind of construction? And why here? I suppose we could think of Pluto as a massive construction shack, but why exactly here? With all the galaxy to pick from, why this particular spot?"

"You ask too many questions all at once," Orson told me.

"Let's look," said Tyler. "Maybe we'll find out."

He peeled the first sheet off the top and let it drop to the floor. It snapped back to the rolled-up position.

The second sheet told us nothing, nor did the third or fourth. Then came the fifth sheet.

"Now, here is something," said Tyler.

We leaned close to look.

"It's the solar system," Orson said.

I counted rapidly. "Nine planets."

"Where's the tenth?" asked Orson. "There should be a tenth."

"Something's wrong," said Tyler. "I don't know what it is."

I spotted it. "There's a planet between Mars and Jupiter."

"That means there is no Pluto shown," said Orson.

"Of course not," said Tyler. "Pluto never was a planet."

"Then this means there once actually was a planet between Mars and Jupiter," said Orson.

"Not necessarily," Tyler told him. "It may only mean there was supposed to be."

"What do you mean?"

"They bungled the job," said Tyler. "They did a sloppy piece of engineering."

"You're insane!" I shouted at him.

"Your blind spot is showing, Howard. According to what we think, perhaps it is insane. According to the theories our physicists have worked out. There is a cloud of dust and gas and the cloud contracts to form a protostar. Our scientists have invoked a pretty set of physical laws to calculate what happens. Physical laws that were automatic—since no one would be mad enough to postulate a gang of cosmic engineers who went about the universe building solar systems."

"But the tenth planet," persisted Orson. "There has to be a tenth planet. A big, massive—"

"They messed up the project fifth planet," Typer said. "God knows what else they messed up. Venus, maybe. Venus shouldn't be the kind of planet it is. It should be another Earth, perhaps a slightly warmer Earth, but not the hellhole it is. And Mars. They loused that up, too. Life started there, but it never had a chance. It hung on and that was all. And Jupiter, Jupiter is a monstrosity—"

"You think the only reason for a planet's existence is its capability of supporting life?"

"I don't know, of course. But it should be in the specs. Three planets that could have been lifebearing and of these only one was successful."

"Then," said Orson, "there could be a tenth planet. One that wasn't even planned."

Tyler wrapped his fist against the sheet. "With a gang of clowns like this anything could happen."

He jerked away the sheet and tossed it to the floor.

"There!" he cried. "Look here."

We crowded in and looked.

It was a cross section, or appeared to be a cross section, of a planet.

"A central core," said Tyler. "An atmosphere—"

"Earth?"

"Could be. Could be Mars or Venus."

The sheet was covered with what could have been space notations.

"It doesn't look quite right," I protested.

"It wouldn't if it were Mars or Venus. And how sure are you of Earth?"

"Not sure at all," I said.

He jerked away the sheet to reveal another one.

We puzzled over it.

"Atmospheric profile," I guessed half-heartedly.

"These are just general specs," said Tyler. "The details will be in some of the other rolls. We have a lot of them out there."

I tried to envision it. A construction shack set down in a cloud of dust and gas. Engineers who may have worked for millennia to put together star and planets, to key into them certain factors that still would be at work, billions of years later.

Tyler said they had bungled and perhaps they had. But maybe not with Venus. Maybe Venus had been built to different specifications. Maybe it had been designed to be the way it was. Perhaps, a billion years from now, when humanity might well be gone from Earth, a new life and a new intelligence would rise on Venus.

Maybe not with Venus, maybe with none of the others, either. We could not pretend to know.

Tyler was still going through the sheets.

"Look here," he was yelling. "Look here—the bunglers—"

# TIME DEER
## (DECEMBER 1974)
## CRAIG STRETE
## (B. 1950?)

*If* went out in a blaze of glory in its last issue with this story, which nearly won the Nebula Award and was honored by inclusion in the Harrison/Aldiss *Best Science Fiction of 1974*. Craig Strete (not his real name) is an extremely accomplished Native American writer who appears too infrequently in the science-fiction magazines and original anthologies.

## MEMOIR BY CRAIG KEE STRETE

Since I can easily lay claim to being the most invisible of those who are accused of writing science fiction (now that they unveiled Tiptree the he as a she), no doubt those who doubt I exist will find the following information just as mystifying.

This story, "Time Deer," which has come back to haunt me like the traditional morning after, was my first published short story. Well, sort of. Another story appeared the same month in *Galaxy*. Both stories were bought by my favorite Irish leprechaun, that dazzlingly handsome godlike editor named Jim Baen.

Jim Baen launched me as a writer, plucked me out of the slush pile, so to speak (I mailed myself in the envelope), and bravely thrust my first six stories into print. I say bravely because the fans burned overdue library books on his lawn in protest. *Galaxy* and *Worlds of If* (which Jim edited with much success) were having circulation problems and times were not exactly ripe for material that was not, shall we say, tried and true.

Be that as it may, Jim Baen is responsible for your seeing this particular story in print. This story, "Time Deer," has been continuously in print since December 1974. It made the final Nebula ballot in the short story category just as that other story which came out the same month made the final Nebula ballot in the novelette category. It seemed a rather curious beginning for a writer.

If I told you how many times "Time Deer" had been printed, grown professional writers would weep. It has been translated thirty-seven times. More than once in the same language. The sun never sets on this story. My only regret (aside from wanting to take back that statement about Jim Baen when I said: "When he dies and they make a movie of his life, Annette Funicello will play him in the movie") is that I did not take years writing it.

I was in my early twenties when I wrote "Time Deer," trying to recover from my first experience (a bad one) of having a film I was directing (a horror film of the *Night of the Living Dead* variety) for an independent producer go into bankruptcy. I had struggled for weeks trying to keep a hopelessly underfinanced production alive. I was directing, rewriting as I went along, lighting, frantically rehearsing actors who had never acted before (and some of them after the film could still make that claim), conning about forty people into donating free labor, equipment that once in a while worked, cars, props, and what have you. I think the worst of it was having to do all the stunts myself, which found me leaping off the front end of a car at forty miles an hour while shouting not too coherent stage directions to a cameraman in the car who was at least as scared as I was. Nobody got paid, least of all me. Not that I really minded. I had lied my way into the job in the first place, swearing up and down I had directed films in Europe (which I had not seen yet). I got used to working eighteen to twenty hours a day with almost no sleep in the hopes of keeping a production alive that I hoped would be a showcase for me, the first Cherokee John Ford, or something like that.

It was not to be.

In the aftermath, I found myself attuned to an eighteen-hour working day. I had little to occupy my time except (young ladies) attending a university full time in the hopes of finding a B.A. in film under my pillow (and young ladies).

So I got the less than intelligent idea that I would do (without benefit of clergy or money) a magazine of American Indian fiction. I had no intention of writing anything myself. I would edit and look noble and pained and wise beyond my years. I would pay nothing except a sneer and plenty of that. It was not to be.

There was a kink in my plans. I was forced to become a writer. I knew lots of Indians (myself included) but none of them wrote. I searched a lot of bars. Lots of Indians and lots of fiction but not much of it printable if you know what I mean.

I had already announced the first issue was forthcoming, so I sat down and wrote the first few issues myself. I had no definite idea in mind. I just sat down at the typewriter and began writing. "Time Deer" was first out of the chute and it took an hour. I wrote two short stories and one novelette the first day. Got up the next day and wrote three more short stories. I thought that was the way writers did it. In a week, despite occasional naps (and young ladies) I had about fifteen short stories. Enough to publish a magazine. What happened next, you ask?

This is where the mystery comes in. I actually can't tell you what happened next. I can tell you only what happened later. Somewhat later, after a number of wonderful writers like Tiptree and so on suggested that perhaps I ought to submit something, I mean to a magazine that actually pays, I did it. Those fifteen stories appeared in places like *Playboy, Orbit, New Dimensions,* and *Galaxy* exactly (almost without exception) as I wrote them. I didn't discover rewriting until it was too late to acquire the habit. It wasn't until my eleventh submission that I got one of those printed rejection slips. All writers can tell a similar tale about how easy it was to get started.

More than a hundred short stories, seventeen books, seven foreign film scripts, five television scripts, and twelve pen names later, I now trot as mysteriously before you as if I had never existed.

In America, I am little known. Nobody knows exactly what I have done or do. I have a large cult following in Europe and spend my summers there. I've done over four hundred newspaper, magazine, and television interviews in Europe and never one here in America. I note all this with wild glee. I am rarely seen at conventions, never wear a name badge if I go, and intensely dislike being photographed or identified. I have more than a dozen books in print in Europe and only four here in America (under my own name, which is not to say that there aren't more).

Writing has been awfully good to me. I live well if not too wisely. In the last year I traveled over 250,000 miles as if to prove that jet lag can be a way of life. Its an incredible way to live. I wouldn't do it if I didn't believe in the things I write. I have yet to do my best work. Therefore, the road goes ever on.

There are a number of people trying to track down my pen names and so on. I really wish they wouldn't. As I write this, I am lying on a beach in the South of France, working on a couple new books and hiding out. Rona Barrett and *People* magazine and other vermin are looking for me. You see, there's this rumor that Diane Keaton and I are in love and it looks serious, as serious as anything like this ever gets out here in Hollyweird. Don't believe rumors. Only facts. The fact is, Diane got a bad sunburn the first day and we're both drinking too much French wine.

# TIME DEER

The old man watched the boy. The boy watched the deer. The deer was watched by all, and the Great Being above.

The old man remembered when he was a young boy and his father showed him a motorcycle thing on a parking lot.

The young boy remembered his second life with some regret, not looking forward to the coming of his first wife.

Tuesday morning the Monday morning traffic jam was three days old. The old man sat on the hood of a stalled car and watched the boy. The boy watched the deer. The deer was watched by all and the Great Being above.

The young boy resisted when his son, at the insistence of his bitch of a white wife, had tried to put him in a rest home for the elderly. Now he watched a deer beside the highway. And was watched in turn.

The old man was on the way to somewhere. He was going someplace, someplace important, he forgot just where. But he knew he was going.

The deer had relatives waiting for her, grass waiting for her, seasons being patient on her account. As much as she wanted to please the boy by letting him look at her, she had to go. She apologized with a shake of her head.

The old man watched the deer going. He knew she had someplace to go, someplace important. He did not know where she was going but he knew why.

The old man was going to be late. He could have walked. He was only going across the road. He was going across the road to get to the other side. He was going to be late for his own funeral. The old man was going someplace. He couldn't remember where.

\*　　\*　　\*

"Did you make him wear the watch? If he's wearing the watch he should—"

"He's an old man, honey! His mind wanders," said Frank Strong Bull.

"Dr. Amber is waiting! Does he think we can afford to pay for every appointment he misses?" snarled Sheila, running her fingers through the tangled ends of her hair. "Doesn't he ever get anywhere on time?"

"He lives by Indian time. Being late is just something you must expect from—" he began, trying to explain.

She cut him off. "Indian this and Indian that! I'm so sick of your god damn excuses I could vomit!"

"But—"

"Let's just forget it. We don't have time to argue about it. We have to be at the doctor's office in twenty minutes. If we leave now we can just beat the rush hour traffic. I just hope your father's there when we arrive."

"Don't worry. He'll be there," said Frank, looking doubtful.

But the deer could not leave. She went a little distance and then turned and came back. And the old man was moved because he knew the deer had come back because the boy knew how to look at the deer.

And the boy was happy because the deer chose to favor him. And he saw the deer for what she was. Great and golden and quick in her beauty.

And the deer knew that the boy thought her beautiful. For it was the purpose of the deer in this world on that morning to be beautiful for a young boy to look at.

And the old man who was going someplace was grateful to the deer and almost envious of the boy. But he was one with the boy who was one with the deer and they were all one with the Great Being above. So there was no envy, just the great longing of age for youth.

"That son of a bitch!" growled Frank Strong Bull. "The bastard cut me off." He yanked the gear shift out of fourth and slammed it into third. The tach needle shot into the red and the Mustang backed off, just missing the foreign car that had swerved in front of it.

"Oh, Christ—we'll be late!" muttered Sheila, turning in the car seat to look out the back window. "Get into the express lane."

"Are you kidding? With this traffic?"

His hands gripped the wheel like a weapon. He lifted his right hand and slammed the gear shift. Gears ground, caught hold, and the Mustang shot ahead. Yanking the wheel to the left, he cut in front of a truck, which hit its brakes, missing the Mustang by inches. He buried the gas pedal and the car responded. He pulled up level with the sports car that had cut him off. He honked and made an obscene gesture as he passed. Sheila squealed with delight. "Go! Go!" she exclaimed.

The old man had taken liberties in his life. He'd had things to remember and things he wanted to forget. Twice he had married.

The first time. He hated the first time. He'd been blinded by her looks and his hands had got the better of him. He had not known his own heart and not knowing, he had let his body decide. It was something he would always regret.

That summer he was an eagle. Free. Mating in the air. Never touching down. Never looking back. That summer. His hands that touched her were wings. And he flew and the feathers covered the scars that grew where their bodies had touched.

He was of the air and she was of the earth. She muddied his dreams. She had woman's body but lacked woman's spirit. A star is a stone to the blind. She saw him through crippled eyes. She possessed. He shared. There was no life between them. He saw the stars and counted them one by one into her hand, that gift that all lovers share. She saw stones. And she turned away.

He was free because he needed. She was a prisoner because she wanted. One day she was gone. And he folded his wings and the earth came rushing at him and he was an old man with a small son. And he lived in a cage and was three years dead. And his son was a small hope that melted. He was his mother's son. He could see that in his son's eyes. It was something the old man would always regret.

But the deer, the young boy, these were things he would never regret.

Dr. Amber was hostile. "Damn it! Now look—I can't sign the commitment papers if I've never seen him."

Sheila tried to smile pleasantly. "He'll show up. His hotel room is just across the street. Frank will find him. Don't worry."

"I have other patients! I can't be held up by some doddering old man," snapped Dr. Amber.

"Just a few more minutes," Sheila pleaded.

"You'll have to pay for two visits. I can't run this place for free. Every minute I'm not working, I'm losing money."

"We'll pay," said Sheila grimly. "We'll pay."

The world was big and the deer had to take her beauty through the world. She had been beautiful in one place for one boy on one morning of this world. It was time to be someplace else. The deer turned and fled into the woods, pushing her beauty before her into the world.

The young boy jumped to his feet. His heart racing, his feet pounding, he ran after her with the abandon of youth that is caring. He chased beauty through the world and disappeared from the old man's sight in the depths of the forest.

And the old man began dreaming that—

Frank Strong Bull's hand closed on his shoulder and his son shook him, none too gently.

The old man looked into the face of his son and did not like what he saw. He allowed himself to be led to the doctor's office.

"Finally," said Shelia. "Where the hell was he?"

Dr. Amber came into the room with a phony smile. "Ah! The elusive one appears! And how are we today?"

"We are fine," said the old man, bitterly. He pushed the outstretched stethoscope away from his chest.

"Feisty isn't he," observed Dr. Amber.

"Let's just get this over with," said Sheila. "It's been drawn out long enough as it is."

"Not sick," said the old man. "You leave me alone." He made two fists and backed away from the doctor.

"How old is he?" asked Dr. Amber, looking at the old man's wrinkled face and white hair.

"Past eighty, at least," said his son. "The records aren't available and he can't remember himself."

"Over eighty, you say. Well, that's reason enough then," said Dr. Amber. "Let me give him a cursory examination, just a formality, and then I'll sign the papers."

The old man unclenched his fists. He looked at his son. His eyes burned. He felt neither betrayed nor wronged. He felt only sorrow. He allowed one tear, only one tear, to fall. It was for his son who could not meet his eyes.

And for the first time since his son had married her, his eyes fell upon his son's wife. She seemed to shrivel under his gaze, but she met his gaze and he read the dark things in her eyes.

They were insignificant, not truly a part of his life. He had seen the things of importance. He had watched the boy. The boy had watched the deer. And the deer had been watched by all and the Great Being above.

The old man backed away from them until his back was against a wall. He put his hand to his chest and smiled. He was dead before his body hit the floor.

"A massive coronary," said Dr. Amber to the ambulance attendant. "I just signed the death certificate."

"They the relatives?" asked the attendant, jerking a thumb at the couple sitting silently in chairs by the wall.

Dr. Amber nodded.

The attendant approached them.

"It's better this way," said Sheila. "An old man like that, no reason to live, no—"

"Where you want I should take the body?" asked the attendant.

"Vale's Funeral Home," said Sheila.

Frank Strong Bull stared straight ahead. He heard nothing. His eyes were empty of things, light and dark.

"Where is it?" asked the attendant.

"Where is what?" asked Dr. Amber.

"The body? Where's the body?"

"It's in the next room. On the table," said Dr. Amber coming around his desk. He took the attendant's arm and led him away from the couple.

"I'll help you put it on the stretcher."

The old man who watched the deer. He had dreamed his second wife in his dreams. He had dreamed that. But she had been real. She had come when emptiness and bitterness had possessed him. When the feathers of his youth had been torn from his wings. She filled him again with bright pieces of dreams. And for him, in that second half of his life, far from his son and that first one, he began again. Flying. Noticing the world. His eyes saw the green things, his lips tasted the sweet things and his old age was warm.

It was all bright and fast and moving, that second life of his and they were childless and godless and were themselves children and gods instead. And they grew old in their bodies but death seemed more like an old friend than an interruption. It was sleep. One night the fever took her. Peacefully. Took her while she slept and he neither wept nor followed. For she had made him young again and the young do not understand death.

"I'll help you put it on the stretcher."
They opened the door.

And the old man watched the boy and did not understand death. And the young boy watched the deer and understood beauty. And the deer was watched by all and the Great Being above. And the boy saw the deer for what she was. And like her, he became great and golden and quick. And the old man began dreaming that—

Frank Strong Bull's hand, his son's hand, closed on his shoulder and shook him, none too gently.

They opened the door. The body was gone.

The last time it was seen, the body was chasing a deer that pushed its beauty through the world, disappearing from an old man's sight into the depths of the forest.

# AFTERWORD: FLASH POINT, MIDDLE

So here I am in the cathedral, the service is over, the elegies are echoes, the mourners have been excused, and the coffin itself with all discretion has been trundled off stage left and consigned to the fire (bodies are buried, perhaps, but dead science-fiction magazines have their covers ripped away and go straight to the crematoria). The writers have spoken of their stories, their stories have been exposed once again, the three wise men—Budrys, Pohl, and Shaw—have gone beyond the amenities to explain what *Worlds of If* was and even what it might have been, and here I am alone amongst the eaves, still muttering around, the sounds of the night stirring beyond the walls. I should have been out of here meself, methinks, but the historian's task is not a happy one, and furthermore in the shadows there are the indications of a couple of forms in the pews, heads bobbing, voices muttering special evening prayers. I seem to however self-invitedly have been called upon; I will do my faltering best. There are not many science-fiction magazines left to die. There are, in fact, now only four of them left, three of them by any standard quite elderly, older than the deceased. One must not in the ruins of the last fifth of the twentieth century take any departure lightly. The great (or even the counterfeit) pulp era shall not come again.

My own contribution to *Worlds of If* can be taken as vanishingly minimal, granting me if little else a certain objectivity. Two stories: "By Right of Succession" in the 10/69 issue, "What Time Was That?" in that of 12/69. The first was offered to the Galaxy magazines in 1968; another one of my characteristic assassination stories of that period rejected by several magazines. The astonishment was that Fred Pohl bought it at all, which after asking for a slight revision he did, placing it in the lesser-pay magazine where, as I understood even at that time, all of the crazy stuff went where it could be buried amongst adventure stories. "What Time Was That?" was sold to Ejler Jakobsson in the first month of his tenure; it had already, a year earlier, been rejected by Fred Pohl, but cunningly (I got cunning early enough in this business although not at sufficient breath) I changed the title and managed to unload it; it was an energetic but unoriginal time paradox story and sixty-nine dollars for twenty-three hundred words seemed at the time a steal. My name never graced the contents page of *Worlds of If* again; in fact I sold only five stories to *Galaxy*, none of them longer than twenty-five hundred words. In the period 1969–1975 I was making something of a reputation for myself, selling stories in spree and welter to all of the original anthologies, to *Amazing/Fantastic* and to my best and most loyal editor, Ed Ferman of *Fantasy & Science Fiction*, but if my career had been judged in terms of how I was succeeding with the great traditional magazines which had carried the medium of science fiction through that time, it would have to have been judged disastrous. Five sales to *Galaxy*, two to *Worlds of If*, four short stories (again none of them longer than twenty-five hundred words) to *Analog*. I was the paradigm of the science-fiction market at that time, moving beyond the landscape of the field, finding new outlets, retreating from the traditional for the simple reason that I could not deal with it. For a long time most of those stories appearing in *Nova*, *Universe*, *Generation*, *Infinity*, the Roger Elwood anthologies were work that had first been submitted to the magazines.

Despite the fact that the true history of *World of If* can be compiled wholly without reference to me, however, the magazine had rather larger personal significance than even I might have thought at first, and the transfers of ownership were small shocks, each of them, superseded by the large and final shock of its demise, which to me took something out of the center of the science-fiction market. One could found a certain reading of modern science fiction upon the proposal that it really began to go to pot when *Worlds of If* folded, that in a strange and subtle way *If*'s collapse signaled the imminent failures of *Galaxy* and *Vertex* and brought home to writers at every level and a number of sophisticated readers the fact that science fiction had changed: dwindled, narrowed in an irreversible way. This was so, to me, because *Worlds of If* was the only successful magazine in the difficult history of this genre that (at least until its last year under Jim Baen when it became, along with *Galaxy*, according to Baen himself, a would-be tool of the scientific/military/industrial complex) had no defineable editorial bias. It printed stories that the various editors wanted to print (or for reasons of inventory pressure *had* to print) on their own merits and without regard to how they conformed to what on the sunnier days might be called "editorial philosophy."

To those not familiar with the field of science fiction—there might be two or three reading this book—this may seem an unremarkable statement: a magazine that accepted or rejected work simply on the basis of quality judgment arrived at by its editors. For science fiction as it was constituted from 1938–70 (and perhaps beyond) it was anything but unremarkable.

Science fiction was a magazine medium until the end of the sixties; its writers and its work moved within the context of these publications (ninety percent of the books were drawn from work and writers which had appeared in the magazines; the book market was a parasite and appendage until the magazines began to run down), and the important magazines were under the aegis of strong-willed, idiosyncratic editors who, in their various ways, perceived of their publications and contributors as extensions of their own vision. Much has been written elsewhere of the canon of Gold, Boucher, and Campbell; sufficient to say here that every established science-fiction writer knew of their editorial prejudices and slanted their work to conform to those prejudices (or at least not to run up against them) or was unable to sell those publications with any consistency. At the third rank were a slew of penny-a-word magazines through the fifties and early sixties where rejects could be sold to editors whose only prejudice was to accommodate publishable work, but there was, with the single exception of *Worlds of If*, no magazine at the *second rank* . . . one which paid a median wage, one which did not impose editorial vision upon the writers, was *Worlds of If*, and in its humble way it might have occupied a position in the history of science fiction far more important than we are prepared to glimpse, even at this late hour.

The other magazines did the best that they could within their budget and limitations and some excellent work was published within them, but the run of material in these publications was, to put it charitably, the slightly crippled, the glass-eyed, the halt, the lame, and the unfleet of foot.* Although excellences did appear in *Space Science Fiction, Science Fiction Adventures, Rocket Stories, Cosmos, Thrilling Wonder, Planet*

---

*In fairness, *Infinity*, edited by Larry Shaw, the short-lived *Worlds Beyond* of Damon Knight, and James Blish's one-issue *Vanguard* were filled with striking work written on low wages but mostly at direct commission for the editors at the top of the writers' form. These three magazines combined, however, did not publish twenty-five issues and were a small factor in the market.

Stories,* the excellences were overwhelmed by that which surrounded them; most shone later on if at all when they were
extracted for anthologies, author collections, or the basis of novels. *Worlds of If,* however, edited by a sequence of men who
(until the days of Baen) had nothing to prove and nothing to assay
other than what entertained them and their readers, imposed no
rigors upon the material which it published. This could only be
conceived of as entirely liberating.

Liberation was not what the latter-day *Astounding/Analog* writer
felt; what the *Galaxy* crew felt (reminiscences in the companion
volume to this book make clear) was the imprint of shackles and
the elegant and civilized *Fantasy & Science Fiction* of Boucher/
McComas was editing based upon an ignorance of science which
amounted to terror; technologically developed science fiction
was almost unpublishable in that magazine. *If,* on the other
hand—under Fairman, Shaw, Quinn, Knight (briefly), Pohl, and
Jakobsson sought and published work whose only criteria in the
editorial eye was quality. For that reason, *If* might have been
the only science-fiction magazine below the top three which
often enough saw manuscripts on first submissions (experienced
professionals knowing beforehand that they had written something which fell outside the range of all three major editors
and not wishing, perhaps, to prejudice those editors against
slanted work) and which was able to develop something of an
editorial identity.

The three essays in this book are worth consideration from that
point of view: Shaw, Budrys, and Pohl are diverse people, but in
their different way they seem to be saying almost the same thing
about the magazine. Larry Shaw was looking for good writing,
"controversial" work*, Fred Pohl was looking for "fun," Budrys
recalls "good, crisp tales swiftly told . . . better liked as distinguished from institutionalized than the Big Three." Campbell in
his way was seeking to change the world, Gold to wall it off like a
noxious disease, and Boucher and his successors in their amused
way to nullify it; less possessed, less inflamed by necessity, *If*'s
editors and its publisher who for a long enough period was also its

---

*Again in fairness, the large pulp magazines—*Planet, Startling, Thrilling
Wonder*—were looking for something entirely different than the digest
magazines and getting it so often for a demarcated audience that they might
for the purposes of this analysis be considered of another genre . . . trans-
planted science fiction; adventure stories.

editor simply wanted to get along. To get along was probably more signatory of the mood of the United States in the fifties than the attitudes of the others; one could follow things along from this perspective and identify *If* as the all-American science-fiction magazine, a Booster of pulp published by a genial and hardly insensitive Babbitt, emanating from a version of Zenith which probably would have fit neatly enough into Sinclair Lewis's perimeters. If George F. Babbitt had been a science-fiction editor/publisher he might well have turned out a *Worlds of If*, and this is to denigrate neither Babbitt nor the publication because George Follansbee—hopeless lover of women, ponderer upon mortality, friend of a tortured violinist, gentle and stricken soul in the dead center of technology's first awful deliverance—had far more quality and more to offer the world than is generally understood. Read now, *Babbitt*, is not satire but sullen celebration; its author was neither Booster nor Calvinist but Daniel in the lion's den.

This carries far enough from a modestly entitled, modestly budgeted digest-size magazine which did its best for nearly a quarter of a century and at the end died (unlike most magazines) not without a certain dignity, but it is worth some consideration; for Gold, Campbell, and Boucher science fiction was work at the flash point, written to dramatize intensely that intersection between the extant and the imaginary at which consequence begins; for James Quinn and his successors (even the restless Fred Pohl became genial within its pages) science fiction was work toward the middle; working out patiently and not without a certain honor the implications. In the true, unwritten history of science fiction *If* will not and does not deserve to take up the space that the other magazines will find, but if civilization, as we have been given to understand, moves not with the truly great but in the humble toilers who carry forth and pass on the world's business and issue, then *Worlds of If*, true servant and toiler in the fields, may be seen to be the paradise of this tortured and occasionally unlovely field. Eleven lean years gone as this anthology is published to that place in science fiction where all the lost magazines go, it is missed perhaps by more of us and more profoundly than genial Jim Quinn could have ever dared to imagine. A benedic-

---

*"Controversial" then as now was editorialese for writing of some obvious quality which was, at least to the editor, not immediately assimilable.

tion to this quiet and earnest man who asked for little, who gave in proportion to his desserts, and who no less than any of us other folks and brethren, keepers of the flame, cared for this field and brought to it measure. Science fiction in Kingston: citizen of the stars.

Barry N. Malzberg
18 February 1981: New Jersey

Rest in Peace, *Worlds of If*. We miss you.
—M.H.G.